L O U I S    T O S C A N O

# Mary Bloom

A Novel

ISBN: 0615747892
ISBN-13: 9780615747897

Library of Congress Control Number: 2012924343
Newstead Books, St. Louis, Missouri

Also By Louis Toscano

*Triple Cross: Israel, The Atomic Bomb and
The Man Who Spilled The Secrets*

For Jeanne-Marie

# *Prologue*

The passenger came aboard at Islamorada about midnight, smelling of Bengay and cigarettes and gripping a crinkled brown paper bag as if it held the family jewels. Ignoring the captain's outstretched hand, he marched into the dimly lit main cabin and settled in a leather club chair without uttering a single word. Morales followed him inside. Shrouded by shadow in the corner of the room, a slender brunette in a scanty bikini lay passed out on a chaise lounge. With an embarrassed grin, Morales moved to the woman and gently shook her shoulder. "Marta. Wake up." He lifted her hand and tugged her arm. "Come on now. Bedtime."

The woman moaned and jerked her hand free. Morales studied her for a moment. A centerfold's body and the most beautiful face her daddy's money could buy. She'd been drinking since four that afternoon. Not the girl he met and, truth be told, a pain in the ass these days. But the boss's daughter—she would tell him when it was over.

He glanced at the passenger, who fixed him with an unnerving stare, two icy blue eyes framed by thick black brows. Morales leaned over the woman and pulled her up. "Time for bed, Marta, yes? What do you say?"

A warm salty breeze rustled the cabin curtains. Marta opened one eye. "Shut the fuck up, Freddy," she said, and flopped back on the lounge, knocking a crystal tumbler full of vodka from its perch on the arm of the chair.

Morales picked up the glass and placed it on a bookshelf, rubbed the wet spot on the carpet with the toe of his shoe. Marta mumbled something unintelligible, and Morales grimaced. "The Stoli," he said, palms up. "She starts with the vodka, and all of a sudden she's speaking Russian."

The passenger tilted his head, considered Morales for a moment, then pointed at the door.

---

*La Vuelta* sailed south through the night, skirting the coast of Florida. Every hour or so, Morales came down from the third deck where he stood watch, slipped along the corridor, and peered into the darkened cabin. The picture never changed: Marta sprawled on the lounge, sleeping fitfully in the corner; the passenger sitting in the chair, paper bag in his lap. Nothing at all remarkable about him. His most striking feature was how ordinary he seemed. Dressed neatly, if from another era. A couple of inches shy of six feet, maybe 160 pounds, in good shape for a man of his age, which was itself a question mark—maybe seventy, maybe a hundred. He asked for nothing to eat or drink. He never stood to stretch his legs or use the bathroom. He ignored the pile of magazines strewn across the rattan table at his side. A half dozen cigarette butts in the ashtray, smoked down to the filter and meticulously stubbed out, were the only evidence he had even moved.

It was not until the yacht lay anchored off Key West that the passenger finally stirred. He rose, passed a palm over his salt-and-pepper buzz cut, and walked slowly out of the cabin to the stern, carrying his brown bag.

Morales lifted the binoculars draped around his neck and in a slow turn scanned the horizon, searching the darkness for pinpricks of light that would signal they were not alone. Nothing. All quiet in the Florida Straits. But they had to move quickly now. Coast Guard patrols would be crisscrossing these waters at first light. That much they were counting on.

The captain, sweat glistening on his bald head, dangled from the ladder off the stern and yanked the canvas from a battered twenty-foot launch tethered to the swim deck. As the cover came clear, it dragged off a large piece of the small boat's rusting metal rail, which fell harmlessly into the water. He scrambled back on deck and whistled softly. "*Las latas de la gasolina. Ahora.*"

Moments later the two Guatemalan crewmen burst into view with red five-gallon gas cans swinging freely from their hands. They dropped the cans into the launch, where they rattled around for a moment before coming to rest. The captain glanced at the sky, then turned to the passenger.

"*Somos listos,*" the captain said. He stood, waiting, hands on hips.

The passenger leaned over the railing and examined the boat: white with flaking black trim, powered by a single aging engine that would need work to qualify as failing. It was stripped—no radio, no life jackets, no navigational instruments, not even a map. A leaky ten-gallon water drum was jammed into one corner, and a bag of overripe plantains, picked up at the Publix market in Marathon the day before, sat near the wheel, next to several discarded skins. Tied up to *La Vuelta*, the launch looked like a child's toy, as if it belonged under a tarp on the third deck with the Sea-Doos and the kayaks.

The passenger turned back to the captain. "Get him," he said.

Footsteps in the corridor, and a young man appeared in the doorway, his eyes fixed on the floor. He was dressed in torn blue jeans, a faded yellow T-shirt, and stained sneakers of uncertain vintage. His face sported a three-day growth of beard, and his skin was an angry red, more like someone who had spent a long time on a boat without cover from the scorching sun, Morales thought, than a homeless kid who was living on the streets of Miami only a week ago.

The passenger rubbed his lips with the tip of his forefinger. "Make sure he has the papers."

"He does," the captain said.

"Ask him," the passenger ordered.

Frowning, the captain turned back to the young man. "*Usted tiene los papeles?*"

With an eager smile, he unbuckled the belt holding up his jeans and reached into his underwear to retrieve a roll of papers secured by a single thick red rubber band. He held the package out for inspection. "*Si, jefe,*" he said. "*Aqui.*"

The captain looked at the passenger, one eyebrow raised. "All right? We ready?"

The passenger said nothing, toyed with the crumpled edge of the paper bag. The captain made a show of looking at his watch, the Guatemalans crowding in behind him. Finally, the passenger nodded. "*Somos listos,*" he said. "*Vayamos.*"

One of the crewmen headed forward to start the engines. The other took the young man by the arm and led him to the swim deck, where he scampered down the ladder and onto the launch. The crewman slipped the line from the railing and tossed it in the water. The engines of the yacht suddenly rumbled to life. The young man looked up at the captain, who waved in the direction of Key West, a soft glow on the western horizon.

The passenger joined the captain at the rail, and they watched as the young man fiddled with the outboard for a moment, then pulled the cord to start it. The engine coughed, quickly died. He leaned over, played with the choke, then tried again. The engine lay silent in the water. He unscrewed the gas cap and peered inside.

As if on cue, the moon slipped from behind the clouds and the launch was bathed in an eerie white light. The captain reached under his shirt, drew a Glock 19 pistol from his belt, and held it at his side.

The young man picked up one of the gas cans, shook it, then unscrewed the lid and upended it. *Dry.* He looked up, arms spread helplessly.

"Do it," the passenger hissed. "Do it now."

Bracing himself against the rail, the captain raised the Glock and squeezed off one round. The bullet tore through the young man's right eye. His body sagged against the gunwale, bits of brain matter splattered along the deck. A rivulet of blood trickled down his T-shirt. The gunshot echoed in the night, then faded away, leaving only the growl of the yacht's engines as it began to knife through the sea.

Morales, his mouth agape, whirled around. "What are you doing?"

The passenger reached inside the paper bag, produced a black .45-caliber Colt automatic with a worn brown stock, and fired once, striking Morales in the forehead. The impact knocked him backward atop the railing. The passenger crossed to the body and shoved it into the ocean. Then he dropped the Colt in the bag and returned to the cabin.

Marta was awake now, stretching drowsily on the edge of the chaise, her tanned body straining against the skimpy bikini top. She watched as the passenger took his seat once more, reached into his paper sack, and pulled out a sandwich, which he unwrapped and slowly began to nibble.

"Where's Freddy?" she asked. The passenger ignored her and continued to eat. Marta slipped on her sandals and shuffled out on deck, craning her neck upward. "Freddy?" she called out. "You up there? Alfredo?" After a few moments, she walked back into the cabin and stood over the passenger.

"Where's Freddy?" she asked again, her voice tightening.

He finished chewing and swallowed. "Put some goddamn clothes on," he said.

Marta walked back outside. In the distance the launch was drifting slowly in the direction of the lights as *La Vuelta* moved off into the darkness.

---

Three hours later the crew of a US Coast Guard HH-65 Dolphin helicopter spotted a small launch bobbing in the water about three miles south of Key West, the body of what appeared to be a young man prostrate on the deck. The cutter *Lexington*, on routine patrol, arrived thirty minutes later, and a rigid inflatable boat was deployed, manned by a senior chief quartermaster named Hinkle and two boatswain's mates.

A boat in the ninety miles of open water between Florida and Cuba was nothing out of the ordinary. The Straits were regularly plied by *balseros* making the mad dash to freedom in El Norte, although this time of year, September, the tail end of the hurricane season, was a little unusual for that sort of thing.

The inflatable pulled alongside the launch, and the three crewmen stepped aboard. The body lay facedown in a sticky pool of dried blood blackened by the sun. Hinkle gingerly felt the neck for a pulse. Finding none, he rolled the body over with his left foot and stepped back. Insects were already playing in the bloody space where the man's right eye had once been.

"Oh, Jesus," Hinkle murmured, and turned away. Slowly he surveyed the placid waters. Not another vessel to be seen. "How 'bout that?" he said. "A sail-by shooting."

He leaned over and examined the victim. Unshaven, sun-blistered face, wearing rags. He'd been out here for a while. And the boat, a piece of shit, God only knows how it got this far. A gas can lay on its side near the outboard. He nudged it with his foot: empty. This was an old movie.

"Check him for weapons, drugs, whatever," Hinkle said, already bored with the exercise. One dead Cuban on a small boat that ran out of gas before he reached the promised land was not nearly enough to hold Hinkle's attention. And who shot him was someone else's problem.

One of the boatswain's mates searched the pockets of the man's jeans and found nothing. He felt a bulge just below the waistline. He reached inside the belt and found a roll of papers bound by a thick red rubber band. The top sheet bore the heading "*Ministerio de Defencia de la Republicca de Cuba*" and a black-and-white rendition of the Cuban flag. The mate flipped through the rest, all poor photocopies. Each page had been stamped with the same word, understandable in any language: "*Secreto.*" He returned to the first page and began to read, forming the words slowly as he tried to make sense of the document, until finally the point dawned, big and bright and alarming. He jumped to his feet, holding the papers aloft.

"Hey, Chief," he called out. "Chief Hinkle, look here."

# 1

Michael Savella leaned heavily against the Boardwalk railing and stared up the street at the gray-shingled house in the middle of the block.

A quick errand, Bobby had promised when he jumped out of the car and disappeared inside. Back in a flash. That was twenty minutes ago.

The wind shifted slightly, bringing with it a rancid stench. Savella wrinkled his nose in disgust. Rotten clams. Hundreds had washed ashore earlier in the week and lay in the sun for several days until city workers got around to burying them. But a few escaped the bulldozers, and now the stink returned whenever the breeze blew just right.

Savella pushed off the railing. The salt air, fetid or not, was at least a reminder that the Atlantic Ocean was still out there. You couldn't actually see the water, not from here, not over the giant looming sand dunes thrown up to hold back the tides. A losing proposition, Savella thought. You could wall yourself off from the world for only so long. The tide, relentless, always won. And meanwhile, the view was shot.

From somewhere on the other side came a burst of laughter and a playful scream, and a young boy in red swim trunks crested the dunes carrying a yellow water rifle. With a burst of spray, he scattered a flock of scavenging seagulls, then sprinted up the sands toward the distant casinos, their marquee lights just taking hold in the gathering dusk.

Savella watched him go. When the boy faded from sight, Savella sat down on a bench near the ramp leading to the street. He was tired, hadn't slept well for a week, maybe more. Nightmares, street noise, too much to drink—he couldn't say, but the insomnia would have to end. Getting out of bed this morning had been an ordeal. He wearily rubbed his face, his palm brushing the tiny scar above his left eye. Savella traced the bumpy ridge of the sutured skin with a fingertip. Maybe it would disappear one day; the doctor seemed to think so. So far, not so much. He glanced over his shoulder. No sign of Bobby. A half hour now. An *errand*. The breeze picked up, sending a discarded plastic water bottle cartwheeling past. Savella sniffed the air: the clams again. He got to his feet and started down the ramp to his car.

The screen door of the gray house suddenly flew open, and Bobby stomped onto the broad wooden porch. Hugging a large flat-screen television to his chest, he limped down the front steps and made a beeline for Savella's car, the power cord dragging behind him.

Savella fought the urge to laugh. The man was like an action movie hero, cinder block in a long, black, Italian leather coat. Shaved head, hard muscled, the battered nose of a man unafraid to raise his fists, and green eyes that narrowed to slits when he was suspicious, which was most of the time. An unstoppable force, even with the constant limp.

The porch door swung out again, slowly this time, and a small man in a New York Jets jersey stepped uncertainly onto the porch. Clinging to his legs was a young girl with long blonde hair, wiping tears from her cheek with her tiny fists.

Not good, Savella thought, no laughing now, and he broke into a run.

By the time he reached the Altima, Bobby was leaning the television against the engine hood. "Pop the trunk, huh?" he said.

"What for?" Savella asked.

Bobby looked down at the television, then back at Savella. "What *for?*"

"What are you doing with that? You said an errand."

"This is the errand."

The man in the Jets jersey was heading slowly toward them, his daughter now in full wail.

"Who's he?" Savella asked.

Bobby shrugged. "Guy owes money, he don't get to watch *SportsCenter.* C'mon, pop the trunk. This fucker's heavy."

The man shuffled to a halt several yards short of the car, tugged nervously at a diamond stud in his left ear. "Jackie said I could have more time," he said.

"Jackie likes to talk," said Bobby. "Pop the trunk."

"Who's Jackie?" Savella said.

The man inched a few steps closer, his arms spread wide. "C'mon. You guys don't need to do this."

"*I'm* not doing *anything,*" Savella said.

"One more day. C'mon. The kids watch it." The man looped a finger through his daughter's shirt collar. "A day, is all. I'll have it tomorrow. Swear."

"Pop the trunk," Bobby said.

They were attracting an audience: a woman in a brown caftan on the patio of the red brick bungalow, two men in flip-flops working on a Mercedes in the driveway of the faux Moorish palace. A teenage girl leaving the beach stood a few feet away, cell phone to her ear. Savella could almost hear the 911 calls: tall guy in jeans and sneakers and a two-day stubble, bigger guy in black leather, and a blue Nissan with Jersey tags.

He looked at Bobby and shook his head. "Forget it. You said an errand."

"Yeah? So?"

"This is not an errand. An errand is running to the market for a quart of milk. This is stealing a TV."

"Are you *serious?*" Bobby shifted the weight of the TV to his other arm. "No stealing. There's nobody stealing here. The guy owes money."

The man in the Jets jersey took a few steps toward Savella. "I'll have it tomorrow. You can believe it."

Savella held up a hand. A few more people leaving the beach had stopped to watch, and the teenage girl was scanning the scene with her cell phone camera. "Look at this, Bobby. You're going to be all over the Internet in a minute. Now, I'm leaving. You can either give him back his TV and come with me, or you can wait for the cops."

Bobby surveyed the street, jaw set, eyes narrowing. He could be stubborn, the kind of guy who wouldn't wear a coat on the coldest day of the year and would slow his pace to a crawl if someone asked if he was chilly. But this time, for once, he seemed to understand his dilemma. He started to speak, then slowly bent down and placed the TV on the curb, coiled the power cord, and tucked it under the base. He pointed at the man in the Jets jersey, who took an awkward step backward. "Tomorrow," Bobby said quietly. With a grunt he jerked open the car door and lowered himself into the passenger seat.

Savella slipped behind the wheel, started the engine, and pulled away from the curb. In the rearview mirror, he caught a glimpse of the father staggering back to the house with his Sony, his daughter running ahead. At the corner Savella turned into the stream of traffic heading uptown. "An errand," he said, shaking his head. "Jesus Christ, Bobby."

---

Ten minutes later the TV never happened, at least as far as Bobby was concerned. He spent six blocks apologizing ("Shouldna put you in that spot"), three blocks fiddling with the radio ("You mind? Need my tunes"), and finally threw in an offer of a couple of drinks at Max's as penance. Savella still seethed, but he knew he'd get over it. You took the good with the bad with Bobby Weiss. They had met one humid June afternoon nineteen years earlier, Savella's first day in Atlantic City, first day at the newspaper, the old *Post-Herald* building on Atlantic Avenue. After work he went across the street to the Copper Penny, a tapped-out lounge, for a burger. As he sipped his scotch, a fight broke out among three waitresses, who scratched and clawed at hair and blouses, rolling half-naked on the sticky wooden floor, until the front door flew open and in marched a man mountain. He held up a warning finger that silenced the boos of the customers and the shrieks of the girls as they tried to plead their cases.

"First thing we're gonna do, everybody gets dressed," he said in a no-nonsense rumble, and everyone listened. In short order the girls were paid off and gone and the peacekeeper was behind the bar. "I'm Bobby," he said as he refilled Savella's rocks glass with lots of ice and a hint of whiskey. "Never seen you in here before. You don't look like you match."

The lounge didn't last long; nothing ever did with Bobby. He went through a string of dead-end jobs in places that closed the day after summer, and wound up running a T-shirt factory in an alley behind the methadone clinic on Pacific Avenue. Not the life he wanted, but he didn't know how to get out of it either. Savella did, or so he thought, and Bobby was the first to cheer when he left town. And when he came back nine months ago and wandered into Max's, Bobby was standing at the bar.

"Almost," he said, and Savella was certain he saw a tear.

The late-afternoon traffic slowed around Providence, where a casino bus making a tight left had jammed the intersection. Savella drummed his fingers on the steering wheel. Bobby played with the radio again, all-news surviving the cut, if only for a moment, and Savella listened as the car filled with names and places that not so long ago had meant more to him. The bus completed its turn, and the traffic in the next lane resumed its uptown crawl. The dented gray Honda Civic just ahead didn't budge. Bobby peered through the windshield. "Who's driving that thing?"

He was right; there didn't appear to be anyone behind the wheel. Maybe a kid, Savella thought. The Civic began to move, but drifted across the center line, cars coming from the other direction swerving toward the curb to avoid a collision. Savella sounded his horn. The Civic moved back into its lane and resumed its slow journey before stopping for the red light at Georgia Avenue.

Savella pulled up next to the Honda. An older woman in a raincoat and a beige scarf sat behind the wheel, clutching it with both hands, even at a full stop. Her head bobbed up and down, as if she was forcing herself to stay awake. "Should I get out and check on her?" Savella asked. Bobby looked over at the driver and shrugged. "What, you're gonna drive her home and make her dinner? I'm thirsty."

Four more blocks, and another red light. They had been talking for thirty years about synchronizing the signals, never seemed to get around to it. Savella sat back in his seat. He knew this neighborhood, or at least he once did. The first time, this had been his playground: a White Castle on that corner, Hamilton's bar over there, next to a hole-in-the-wall Italian joint with a small rear garden where he would sit for hours and listen to stories, some of them true, about old men with schoolboy names. Now the White Castle was La Senora beauty salon, Hamilton's was a Vietnamese restaurant with an unpronounceable name, and his magic garden was a garbage-strewn vacant lot behind a boarded-up building with a sagging roof. He had come back to town nine months ago looking for the old familiar, and the new world had followed him back. See how well that worked.

Savella glanced up at the traffic signal. A long light—

A crunching sound, the tinkle of broken glass, and the Altima lurched into the intersection and stalled out. Savella's head jerked forward, the seat belt saving him from the windshield. Bobby managed to brace himself with his hands as he lurched into the dashboard. Savella yanked the emergency brake and the two men climbed out of the car. The gray Civic was mashed against the rear of the Altima, hood sprung open, the woman behind the wheel slumped in her seat.

"She ran into us," Bobby said, slowly rubbing his wrists.

Savella held out his cell phone. "Call nine-one-one." He reached through the open window of the Civic and switched off the ignition. "Are you OK?"

The woman slipped farther down in the seat, shivering slightly, tangled in her seat belt. In the collision a bag of groceries had been knocked off the passenger seat; two boxes of Wheat Thins lay on the floor at her feet. The woman looked down at her hands. "My finger is bleeding," she said thickly. "I hurt my finger. My finger is bleeding."

Savella gently took her hand. A thin stream of blood trickled from under the nail and ran down the side of her index finger. He took out his handkerchief and wiped the wound, then wrapped the cloth around her finger. "Keep that on there until the ambulance gets here, OK?"

He glanced across the street where three women, curlers in their hair and draped in plastic, stood outside the beauty salon, smoking cigarettes. "Hey, ladies, we could use some towels over here," he called out. "She's bleeding a little."

Savella slipped off his windbreaker and laid it over the woman's chest to warm her. She began to hum, first an incomprehensible drone, then a tune, off key but vaguely familiar. After several bars she suddenly grabbed his sleeve with her uninjured hand and pulled him close to her face.

"Listen to me," she said in a faint voice. "*Listen to me.*"

He patted her hand reassuringly. "They're almost here," he said.

Her body tensed. She sat upright, eyes wide open but seeing nothing, a few beads of spit on her lips. Her grip on his shirt tightened, then relaxed, and she fell forward on the steering wheel. The car horn blared briefly until Savella pushed her back against the seat. In the distance a siren wailed, coming closer, closer, until it crescendoed, then abruptly fell silent as the ambulance lurched to a stop in the intersection. Moments later Savella was pulled away from the car by an emergency services worker. He walked to the curb, where Bobby was sipping a paper cup of coffee.

"She dead?" he asked.

"Doesn't look good. Heart attack, stroke, who the hell knows," Savella said. "I'm going to try and move my car."

---

An accident investigator needed some information, and Savella left nothing out, from the moment he first spotted the Honda weaving down the avenue to the woman's last words, talking even after the patrolman closed his memo book. Attention to detail—old habits die hard. By the time he finished, the frenetic pace of the rescuers had slackened, the clipped commands replaced by snatches of small talk. Finally, the emergency workers wrestled the woman from the car, placed her on a gurney, and rolled it to the ambulance, which sat in the intersection for ten minutes before it eased down the street. She was dead, Savella knew. Always a bad sign when the ambulance stayed put so long. Even worse when it drove off stopping for red lights.

Bobby was leaning against the Altima, devouring the last of a Vietnamese spring roll.

"She didn't make it, huh?" he asked.

Savella shook his head.

"Hey, little old ladies," Bobby said, slapping the crumbs off his hands. "Whaddya gonna do?"

# 2

The giant maple table in the dining room was cluttered with duck decoys—a drake mallard, a brace of elegant pintails, three canvasbacks, a flying green-winged teal—the best of the best of the nationally renowned collection of the late Marvin Belding, who had dropped dead of a heart attack in the middle of the fourteenth fairway at Green Tree two weeks earlier. His daughter, Mavis, an elegant pintail in her own right, wearing a string of pearls and proper pumps even in the comfort of her own home at high noon, moved around the table from decoy to decoy, holding them up to let their delicate colors catch the light streaming through the bay window.

Sunk low in Mr. Belding's favorite easy chair, Savella sipped the cold dregs of his coffee and tried to focus. In another room someone was talking on the telephone. Outside he could hear the *beep-beep* of a truck backing up.

"He liked to say he did it for the art," Mavis said. "Folk art, that's what he called it. And they are very beautiful. But secretly I wonder whether he just liked the game. You know, the idea that you could fool a duck with a well-carved, nicely painted piece of wood. With good ones it's hard to tell the difference."

"Mmm," said Savella, balancing the notebook in his lap as he nibbled on a brownie.

"History too," Mavis said. "Dad said it brought him back to his ancestors. Who actually used the decoys." She picked up a Canada goose, its head nestled in its feathers, and pointed to indentations in the wood. "You see these? Shotgun pellets."

"Really," Savella murmured.

"He never did it, of course. Hunting. Just a collector."

Mavis placed the goose on the table and gazed out the window, hands clasped at her waist. "It's so nice that you decided to write about Dad." She touched a finger to her cheek. "Perhaps I should get his scrapbook."

Savella cleared his throat. "Actually, I think we're almost done here."

"Oh yes?" She walked around the table. "May I ask, when do you think your article will be in the paper?"

"Not up to me," Savella said with a smile. "I've got editors. They make those decisions."

Mavis considered his response for a moment. Her face brightened. "You know, that scrapbook. A lot of pictures from last year's national convention. Can I warm your coffee?"

Almost two hours, the display cases in the basement, the duck pictures in the hallway. No scrapbook. No more coffee.

"Thanks, really, but I think—" Savella made a show of examining his notebook, which was empty. "I think I've got what I need."

---

A white Audi was in his parking space. As Savella scanned the lot for another spot, a security guard sprinted over. He read the license plate on the Altima, then shuffled through the pages on his clipboard until he found a match. "Mr. *Savella*," he said. "Didn't think you'd be using it. I'll get him out of there."

Savella raised a hand. "No need. I'll find something else." He drove slowly down the aisle until he reached the end, slipped into an empty space, and switched off the ignition. He sat quietly behind the wheel, listening to the engine click and rattle as it cooled down. Across the bay the city skyline shimmered in the brilliant afternoon sun. He sank lower in the seat and soaked in the view. These were the days when he loved Atlantic City, when the salt air masked the exhaust fumes, when the hustlers in the bars were actually charming, when the blonde in the sunglasses in the Lexus at the light could be the woman of your dreams or your best friend's wife. The land of make-believe, a do-over every day if you wanted. The drug dealer became a plumber, the stripper a soccer mom, and it was all right. No one had time for the past. Today was all that mattered. You decided the truth.

There was once a local radio disc jockey stuck in the overnight slot, spinning tunes for no one. His boss gave him two weeks to find an audience or another job. One night the disc jockey came up with a gimmick. Radio Blackjack, he called it, him against his listeners, one caller at a time. The first person to beat him got a new car. In a few days, the station's switchboard was jammed with callers between two and six, every last one of them eager for a chance at the Chrysler. On the hour the disc jockey would announce a new deal, and the girl on the phones would put someone on the air. The disc jockey would slowly shuffle a deck of cards close to the microphone, then deal out a hand, slapping each card hard on the console.

"You have a six. Dealer draws a nine. A seven for you. Dealer's is facedown. Would you like another card? You sure?" A beat and a slap. "Ohhh, a king. Busted. Too bad." When the FCC finally shut down the game, there were protests outside the station for a week. That was Atlantic City, Savella decided. The town made sense only if you didn't stop to think about it.

A delivery truck rumbled through the parking lot, braking noisily at the entrance. No escaping it, Savella thought glumly. He got out of the car and trudged toward the three-story glass-and-chrome building at the other end of the asphalt.

---

The *Atlantic City Post-Herald* was a peculiarly uninspired newspaper. A decade earlier it had been purchased by an investment banker in Tampa who had spent the years since squeezing the life out of its shrinking pages. His publisher was an accountant for whom the news business meant party invitations and show tickets. The editor was an English major hired right out of Rutgers who decided the day he started that he had gone as far as his talent would take him. He presided over an ever-changing cast of recent graduates who filled the *Post-Herald* with unremarkable stories and climbed over one another to find better jobs.

Maybe he was just an old guy on a park bench feeding the squirrels, Savella thought, but he remembered a very different paper when he arrived nineteen years earlier. The owner then was also its editor-in-chief, a veteran journalist who knew his way around a news story and was eager to pass along his knowledge. He stocked his newsroom with curious people, deeply skeptical, always questioning, and unleashed them on the city, reveling in their achievements, commiserating when the big fish got away. The paper's office was a dark place downtown, the air thick with smoke and the smell of stale coffee. Amid the constant jangle of telephones, editors and reporters, their desks jammed together in the squalor, argued every day about the news, the way it was covered, what it meant. City officials and average citizens wandered in to press a point or exchange gossip. Nothing was ever settled, and the arguments often spilled over into long boozy nights. And what was wrong with all of that, Savella thought as he navigated the last few yards to the entrance. What was wrong with dying to know?

In the mailroom, his box was stuffed to overflowing: office memos, a stack of press releases, direct-deposit receipts for his last several paychecks. He grabbed a copy of the morning paper from a pile in the corner and headed into the newsroom.

Savella often felt he should take off his shoes and wash his hands before he wandered inside the new *Post-Herald.* It was a thoroughly antiseptic space, Hollywood fresh, rows of work cubicles, potted plants and trees at regular intervals, soft lighting, a hint of lemon in the air. Nothing was out of place. Rules about wall hangings, food at the desk, and garbage disposal were strictly enforced; smokers were exiled to the loading dock. And no noise in the newsroom, just the murmur of hushed conversations and the incessant clicking of computer keyboards. Laughter or a raised voice brought heads popping up in cubicles in search of the culprit.

His cubicle hadn't seen much use. The canvas walls were bare, save for a memo from Human Resources welcoming him back. A Dell computer with the packing slip still taped to the monitor sat atop the desk. As he sat down, his sleek black telephone purred. Savella hesitated for a moment, then lifted the receiver. "Yes?"

"Michael." Cynthia, the editor's secretary and office spy. "You're *here*."

"What do you need, Cynthia?"

"Not me, actually. It's Janice. She'd like a word, if you've got a minute."

"All right. Put her on."

"No, no, no. Not *now*. She wonders if you can be in her office in, say, twenty minutes?"

"OK," he said.

"You're not going out again?"

"Not right now, Cynthia."

"Because if you've got something..."

"Cynthia. I said I'll be here."

"That's great. I'll call you when she's ready." The line went dead.

Savella replaced the receiver, looked down at his clothes: old blue blazer, faded jeans, beat-up deck shoes. Good thing he'd dressed for the occasion. Forty-eight tomorrow and he dressed like he was back in college. Isabella had tried to spruce him up—"You're a good-looking guy, Michael, you could just use a little... *updating*"—and gave up only when he even balked at a new jacket for his jeans. What was the point, he thought. Good-looking, OK, if she said so, but in a played-out sort of way. Slumped shoulders whittling his six-foot frame, gray flecking a shag of black hair that wanted a trim, crow's feet framing weary brown eyes that belied his crooked smile. A worn coat, he decided, colors faded, edges frayed, flaws exposed, like the scar on his forehead, a constant reminder of what came before. *Updating.* He loved her for trying, anyway. She was in Illinois, a riverboat gig. But she'd be back for his birthday, dinner at Max's, and the thought made him smile.

Savella flipped through the morning paper. The accident had made page six of the region section. Someone had grabbed a copy of the police report and churned out a serviceable news brief, names spelled correctly, Savella identified as a *Post-Herald* employee. But somewhere along the line, Savella's car had wound up rear-ending the dead woman's vehicle.

There was also an obituary, such as it was:

BLOOM, MARY, 65—*of Atlantic City, passed away at Atlantic City Medical Center. She was an area resident for many years. There are no immediate survivors. A Mass of Christian Burial on Friday at 10:00 a.m. at Our Lady of Assumption in Atlantic City. Arrangements are by Hershberger Funeral Home.*

Not much to speak of for sixty-five years, Savella thought, as he drew a circle in red ink around the death notice.

"Hey, Michael?"

He didn't have to look up to place the voice: Scott Williams, a lanky blond-haired feature writer, a newsroom star, one of Janice's babies, as she liked to call them. "Scott Williams," he said, his hand snaking over the cubicle wall. "Nice to make your acquaintance."

Savella forced a pained smile, but said nothing. Williams made a point of introducing himself whenever Savella turned up. An annoying little play, with a script that never varied. "If you need any help finding things," Williams said, "I'm right over there."

And Savella, on cue: "Nice to see you, Scott." Same thing, every time.

Williams wasn't alone in noting Savella's absences. Savella felt the buzz, heard the whispers whenever he wandered in. Nine months earlier he had been a genuine curiosity. *Why had he left the first time? What brought him back?* Savella kept his distance, reluctant to come out from behind the curtain, but in the end, it didn't matter. One day the Man of Mystery became just another broken-down hack, a cautionary tale to all the bright young things tripping through the *Post-Herald* newsroom, Boo Radley lurking in the basement, nibbling at the edges of the imagination just enough to scare Scout and Jem and Dill whenever they needed the rush.

He heard titters as Williams walked off. Savella wanted to smack him, but he understood. He had been Scott Williams once.

The first time around, truly a star: a series of corruption investigations, the flotsam of a government run by renegades. A city councilman brought low by a hooker with a videotape. A zoning commissioner with a vacation house in Arizona built on yes votes. And the Big One, Savella's ticket out, a mayor and a police chief with a trunk full of cocaine and three dead bodies in a woodsy grave. Job offers followed and one day Savella packed his worldly possessions in the backseat of his Datsun and headed for Washington. A few years later, he was working overseas.

For fifteen years, he was a journalistic nomad, darting from one crisis to the next. But with it came a gnawing sense that he was off his moorings, adrift in a sea of misfortune. Somewhere along the line, it stopped being an adventure, started feeling more like the cheapest kind of voyeurism.

The string ran out on a sweltering July morning in Jerusalem, so hot the packs of wild dogs that roamed the hills had abandoned their search for food and lay in the shade, panting in the dust. Savella was at an army checkpoint north of the city waiting for his Arab translator. Gradually he became aware of loud voices off to his right. He got out of the car, shading his eyes from the intense sun.

In the distance a boy with a knapsack on his back stood in the middle of a field, a few dozen Israeli soldiers falling back from him, even as they shouted for him to stay still. Maybe ten, Savella thought, and something about him seemed familiar. Black hair, dark complexion, large almond eyes—that was it: Savella at that age. The boy was sobbing and holding his arms out in a plaintive appeal for help, and all of a sudden Savella knew: the knapsack contained a remote-controlled explosive. The boy, whether he knew it or not, was a courier of death.

Suddenly the faint warble of a cell phone. The soldiers ducked their heads. Savella dropped behind a concrete blast barrier.

One ring, two rings, three rings, and...nothing. No boom, no shower of murderous metal rain, no death. Savella poked his head above the barrier. Through his tears the boy was begging in Arabic, then Hebrew—"Please! I want to live!"

Out of the crowd moved a young Israeli soldier, a woman, a girl, actually. She could have been the boy's older sister, eighteen or nineteen, same dark hair, same olive complexion. Ignoring her comrades' shouted warnings, she slowly made her way to the center of the field. It seemed an eternity before she reached the boy, but then there she was, one hand on the bag, the other stroking his face, telling him not to be afraid.

And then the knapsack rang again.

The soldier froze.

The boy looked up at her for reassurance.

In a flash of orange, they disappeared.

A small bomb, and poorly made. The two dead, another soldier who would soon join them, and a dozen wounded, showered with tiny pieces of shrapnel that fell from the sky like black stinging rain. But it was a plastic doll that ended it for Savella. As he walked the perimeter of the bomb site, he noticed a streak of red in a pile of rubble. A soldier in the search party pushed aside the debris to uncover what was left of the boy's Spiderman, a child's toy sharing space in a school bag with a nail bomb.

Savella filed his story, went home, and packed a bag. At Ben-Gurion airport, he telephoned Washington and resigned, and boarded the next El Al flight to New York. It was best, he decided. The good ones could feel the pain, but turn it off at some point, write their stories, and move on. He couldn't do that anymore. It was enough.

For a few months, he drifted, moving between friends' apartments, living off his dwindling savings. One night, at a birthday dinner at a Thai restaurant on the West Side, he ran into Janice Garabedian, a former *Post-Herald* colleague. She was the managing editor now, and they chatted over cocktails, catching up on the years. Somewhere between the prawns with glass noodles and the iced coffee, they slipped out and started walking downtown, nowhere in particular in mind. It began to rain, and they found a cab and headed for a bar on Lafayette Street, a dark, crowded room with loud voices and louder music, where they holed up until last call, floating on a river of scotch and cosmopolitans. As the music raged, Janice grabbed him by his arm.

"Come back, Michael," she shouted over the din. "It's where you belong."

Well, maybe. The truth of the matter was, he had nowhere else to hide. And one day he was sitting in the *Post-Herald* newsroom, in his own tiny cubicle, with his own parking space in the sprawling lot, with his own very nice paycheck. And there was no past, no history, just a much-thumbed passport in a white envelope. A life stashed in an envelope and tossed in the back of a drawer in a desk in a newsroom filled with artificial plants—a life that, like the plants, didn't need the light of day anymore.

But Janice hadn't thought it through, or maybe she never figured he'd say yes. Here was Savella and there didn't seem to be a place for him. They sent him to cover courts. They sent him to cover transportation. They sent him to write about the casinos. But Savella kept returning with stories they didn't want. Disparities in sentences for minority defendants. The traffic impact of another shopping mall. Accounting tricks the casinos used to reduce their taxes. Stories that would have landed him on the front page in the old days. This time impatient sighs and exasperated glares from the editors, who cut them to shreds and crammed them deep inside, if they ran at all.

When he began to dig into rumors that the new mayor had paid an ex-convict to produce the absentee ballots that won him the election, Janice took him to lunch.

"We're looking for a lighter touch, Michael," she said, tearing into a Caesar salad. "The game's changed since you've been gone. We're just not that kind of newspaper anymore."

"Maybe I'm still that kind of reporter."

She picked a piece of lettuce off her lower lip and dabbed it on the paper napkin. "Maybe you should have thought of that before you got on the plane in Tel Aviv."

Janice had an idea, or claimed to—it was probably the publisher's: a weekly feature chronicling the lives and deaths of ordinary people. *Ordinary Lives*, the column would be called, just in case someone missed the point.

"Obituaries," Savella said, twirling a coffee stirrer between his fingers. "You want me to write obits."

"Not obits, Michael. We already do that."

"Let's see. Stories about the lives of dead people. What would you call it?"

"OK, OK. But we want something a little...different. Look, nobody's reading newspapers anymore. We've got to find another way."

"How about news? Maybe hire some smart people, call them reporters, send them out to ask questions, find stuff out. Then put it in the paper. How about that?"

Janice laughed. "The last of the romantics. Anyway, people like to read about their neighbors, Michael. Especially after they're dead."

It's all in the writing, she told him, and that's where you can shine. "And let's face it"—her voice dropped as she leaned over the table, two kindred spirits conspiring—"it's not like anyone's banging on your door. You don't think everyone's heard by now how you walked away from the job?"

She had a point. And he could knock these out in his sleep.

Janice handed Savella the subjects to get him started. A high school history teacher in Millville who dragooned his students into helping him build a replica of Mount Rushmore in his backyard. A Cape May spinster who collected 14,095 postcards from places she'd never visited. A railroad conductor in Buena who joined the Boy Scouts on his ninety-second birthday. It quickly became apparent that the very last thing Janice wanted was a column about an ordinary person. She wasn't interested in chronicles of the lives of people who got married, raised families, worked twenty or thirty years at humdrum jobs, and spent the twilight in the company of their grandchildren. To be worthy of attention, *Ordinary Lives* had to feature the very un-ordinary—he played Santa Claus for forty-seven Christmas Eves, she learned to read at seventy-six, he had a stamp collection, she worked with the blind. Twenty years ago Savella might have relished the challenge. But now he couldn't muster the strength. Which was why he was sitting at his desk reading the obituary of a woman who seemed to have barely existed, waiting for an editor who was probably beginning to think he didn't either.

His phone rang. "She wonders if you've got a minute," Cynthia said sweetly.

Savella stuffed the newspaper in his jacket pocket and padded across the carpeted newsroom.

# 3

Janice was hunched over her computer, typing furiously. "One second," she said without looking up, and waved him to a chair. He watched her pound the keyboard. Janice had been a comer since she first arrived in the newsroom, a few months after Savella, a mousy blonde dressed somewhere between Kmart and Macy's. While the rest of her colleagues jockeyed for the best assignments, Janice made it quickly known that the hurlyburly of the streets was not for her. But the big desk up front, where the man who made the decisions sat—that would do just fine. Now she had the chair, and the transformation was complete: the blonde mouse banished, shoved aside by a confident brunette draped in loot brought back from her monthly hunting expeditions through the trendy salons of Soho. And a pretty good editor, Savella thought, when she bothered to read the copy. She could spot wasted words at a hundred paces and was quick to ditch failed efforts with a ruthless efficiency.

Janice finished with a furious clatter and swiveled around to face him.

"OK, sorry." She flashed a toothy smile. "That time of year again."

Savella's eyes narrowed in puzzlement.

"The pageant," she said helpfully. "The American Beauty pageant."

"Ah, yes. Your skin game."

"Well, they're not all gonna be Einstein." Janice leaned back in her chair. "Henry wants it on the front page every day."

"And you, of course, have no problem with that."

"What can I tell you? The man's right. Pretty girls sell papers."

Savella had always been bemused by the city's fascination with pageants. In the beginning it had been Miss America, which reigned supreme for decades. It was a story he'd been forced to cover during his first tour at the paper, two nightmarish descents into a world of Vaseline smiles, duct-taped cleavage, and social causes carefully designed to offend no one. Miss America was gone now. The country stopped believing in virgins, and when the television ratings slipped beneath the waves, the pageant fled town in search of a second act. Up stepped Henry Kipp, the *Post-Herald*'s publisher, who saw a chance to make a name for himself by filling the void. He persuaded the casinos to pony up big bucks for a new pageant, this one much less concerned with good taste and far more willing to do whatever it took to keep eyeballs trained on the screen. No more naming the president of Afghanistan or offering a plan to save the rain forests. Just sex and sizzle. The first few years had been modest successes, but Henry knew he was one bad Nielsen rating from the D-list.

"Anyway," Janice said. "How are you? You weren't hurt?"

Savella, confused again.

"Your accident," Janice said patiently.

"Oh. Right."

"What happened? She stop short?"

Savella shook his head. "She ran into me. Someone got the story wrong."

"Really? You tell anybody?" Janice scribbled a note on the pad in front of her. "Well, I'm glad you're OK. That's the important thing. So did you see Belding's daughter?"

So much for the pregame festivities, Savella thought.

"Yeah," he said. "Saw her this morning."

"And?"

"Duck decoys? Come on."

Janice rolled her eyes. "We're not going to do this dance again, are we?" She pointed toward the newsroom. "Might be good if you showed up in the office more often. Maybe you'd notice all those empty desks in there. The business is changing, Michael. We either change with it or we're gone." She fondled the diamond bracelet on her wrist. "And you had better believe that I am not going anywhere."

He couldn't argue the numbers with her. The *Post-Herald*, like every other paper in the country, was hemorrhaging readers.

Janice lightly tapped the desktop with her long fingernails. "So, listen. We've got a problem."

"What's that?"

"Your column."

"*My* column. You remember the part where I wasn't sure it was such a great idea?"

"Look, Michael," she said, her voice suddenly edgy. "I went out on a limb to get you this assignment. I told Henry you were the guy to handle it for us. And he agreed, and away we went. But you haven't kept your end of the deal. I have to drag the pieces out of you.

And frankly, they haven't been all that great. Not what I promised. Not what I expected."

Janice shuffled through some papers on her desk and pulled out a computer printout, holding it like a piece of spoiled fish. "And this latest one"—she shook her head and let the paper drop to the desk—"this is a piece of crap."

The doctor with the bad leg who made house calls until the morning he keeled over in a convenience store. Savella shifted uneasily in his seat.

"Wait a minute," he said. "I didn't come up with that guy. That was Henry. I don't care how long they were friends; what did you want me to do, turn him into Jonas Salk?"

"That was the whole point, Michael. That's how I sold you. You could make something out of nothing."

She picked up the printout and let it fall again on her desk.

"It won't run. I'll stall Henry. But you gotta get it going."

Cynthia poked her head in the door and pointed at the telephone. A red light was blinking, but Janice ignored it. When she spoke again, the edge was gone, replaced by a more sympathetic tone.

"I'm not trying to make things tough for you, Michael, I'm really not. But we took a chance on you— *I* took a chance on you, bringing you in here. You're, well, *older*. You were a good reporter, Michael. You *are* good. I know it. You know it." She pointed again toward the newsroom. "Everybody out there knows it. But you're not showing us much."

He wanted to tell her she was wrong. But he couldn't.

"OK, maybe—"

She held up a hand to silence him.

"Look, we could go round and round on this. But the truth of the matter is—" She stopped, rubbed her eyes with the heels of her palms, and groaned. "The truth of the matter is you've got to get it together. Fast. So where do we go from here?"

Savella sat quietly for a moment. A bone, he thought. He needed to throw her something. He plucked the paper from his blazer pocket, tapped the Mary Bloom obituary with his forefinger, and handed it to Janice, who scanned it quickly, then looked up at him.

"So what's this?"

"My accident."

"Oh, this is the woman."

"Yeah. The woman."

"So?"

"So I think it's a column."

"Because you ran into her?"

Savella looked at the ceiling. "First of all, she ran into me."

"Whatever. And?"

"Look at her obit."

Janice read it again. "What am I missing?"

"Exactly. That's exactly the point."

"*What's* the point? That there's nothing there?"

Savella stood up and began to pace slowly around the office as he fashioned an argument fueled by desperation. "I mean, an older woman, sixty-five. And that's her obit. No family, no friends, no life history. Isn't that something?"

Janice rested her head in her hands, her gaze fixed on the desktop. "I don't think this is what we had in mind, Michael," she said slowly.

"It's *precisely* what you had in mind, Janice," he said, warming to the task. "Ordinary lives. No headlines, no drama, no nothing. Just life. Lived."

"The point is—look, the point is we're getting off the point. You want to try and fill in the blanks in the life of a sixty-eight-year-old woman—"

"Sixty-five."

"Sixty-five." She glared at Savella, daring him to correct her again. "Do you understand the situation here, at the paper?" Janice looked at her watch. "I have another meeting. But you understand where we are?"

"I got it." Relieved to escape, Savella moved to the door.

"And oh, hey, wait a minute. Happy birthday."

Savella slapped his forehead in mock surprise. "And they said she wouldn't remember."

Janice smiled. She stood and walked him out, her arms windmilling toward the newsroom. "Go. Bring me the stories of the ordinary." She burst through the door and cried out, "Let's see how my babies are this afternoon." Two dozen fresh faces glanced up, all anxious smiles, eager to be noticed. In the commotion Savella slipped away.

Outside he squinted through the glare at the skyline. These were the days he hated this city, when the still air reeked from the fumes of a thousand cars, when the hustlers in the bars flashed phony smiles and didn't bother to hide it, when the polished brunette behind the big desk would pour herself a Perrier and talk about you after you'd gone. These were the days when Atlantic City was the last place in the world he wanted to be.

Because Janice Garabedian wouldn't remember her own *mother's* birthday on a bet. She must have been looking at his personnel file, and that couldn't be good.

# 4

The man with the finely trimmed mustache standing outside the theater on West Forty-Fourth Street was Julio Gonzalez once, his picture in a Chilean passport in 1969. He was Geraldo Stanley of Nicaragua twice, in Caracas in 1975 and in San Salvador three years later. In Panama in 1981, he was Jack Russo, an American, and in Tegucigalpa six months later, he was Nestor Ochoa of Medellin, Colombia.

There were others, but Ochoa was the last of them. Late at night he could still hear the doctors calling out the name as they bent over the gurney in the emergency room, frantically trying to stop the bleeding from the bullets that had ravaged his body. And he could still feel Pilar's fury as she issued the nonnegotiable demand: no more lies.

She had been right. It was a relief to reclaim his birth name: Abel Garcia. After so many years, Abel Garcia of Englewood, New Jersey, with a driver's license, a passport, credit cards. He had been Abel Garcia at the beginning, when he thought he would make a difference, and now, at the end, he was Abel Garcia again.

He lifted his arm, wiggled the band on his watch until it slipped on top of his thin wrist, and tilted the face toward the marquee lights. Intermission would be around nine thirty. Ten more minutes. Miller would be among the first through the door, Garcia was sure of it. Richard Miller was a very weak man.

It wouldn't take long, this meeting. Garcia's instructions were simple: *Miller's gonna be in New York, taking his wife to a show. Go see him. Make sure he knows we know. Make sure he knows we're running out of patience.*

"We're not gonna spend the rest of our lives waiting for somebody who has a friend who has a fraternity brother who might be able to get the job done a week from next January," the son had growled. Whatever that meant. It wasn't until later, when Garcia was home in bed, watching the shadows dance on the ceiling, that he managed to decipher it: no more third chances.

The pain came again. He arched his back and stretched in a vain attempt to defend against the assault. Pilar, a doctor's daughter, had noticed first: the weight loss, stomach pains, no appetite, sleepless nights. Garcia waved off her concerns—*the flu, indigestion*—but as the symptoms grew more intense, she insisted on a checkup. The test results were final; while he had swilled Pepto-Bismol, a cancer had grown in his pancreas. Nothing to be done, the doctors said; six months, a year if he were lucky. Garcia demanded their silence. He would tell his wife, but in his own time, in his own way. So they loaded him up with the pills and sent him home. An ulcer, he told Pilar. No more sweets, she said.

The pills were in his pocket—Tylenol with codeine, as many as you need, the doctor had said—but Garcia wouldn't take them, not if he could help it. They made his brain misty. Pilar said what was the difference, did he like the pain? No, he didn't like the pain. But he was an old man. As it was, he had trouble with simple words, routine thoughts. The pills only made it worse.

He leaned against a building, his breathing short and labored as he willed the pain to disappear. The hour was late for him these days. Not like old times, when sleep seemed an admission of failure. Now he turned in by nine most nights. And no more fieldwork; he had promised Pilar. But he had also made a promise to the man in Miami. Some debts you never repaid, some allegiances never faded. Don Arturo would never know if Garcia reneged. The second stroke had left him slumped in a wheelchair, his eyes vacant to the world. But Garcia had given his word; no matter what, he would help the son.

Intermission, finally, and a crowd spilled through the doors. Garcia quickly spotted Miller, a short, stocky man with a thick thatch of hair the color of milk chocolate, a cigarette between his lips before he'd even cleared the doors. A tall woman with uneven looks and a severe mouth kept a firm grip on the sleeve of his rumpled navy-blue suit: the wife, Garcia figured, Lidia, the general's daughter, who had dragged Miller out of academia and thrust him into the Washington spotlight, undersecretary of state for arms control and international security and chairman of the Imminent Threat Task Force. Garcia pushed his way through the crowd until he found a clearing directly in front of Miller. He stopped, straightened his shoulders, and waited to be noticed.

Miller looked through him at first, leaned in to speak with his wife, then suddenly turned back to Garcia, trying to make sense of what he saw: a frail old man, thick silver hair that ran in wavy rows like the tide rolling out, a nose like an eagle's beak above that perfectly tended mustache. Maybe the State Department…no, the university…no, that's not it…*Abel Garcia.*

Miller whispered something to his wife and a cross look clouded her face. He dropped his cigarette on the pavement and walked quickly over to Garcia.

"Abel!" A big smile, arms outstretched. "What a pleasant surprise. How long has it been? How have you been? Are you inside?"

Garcia shook his head.

"Too bad. It's quite an entertaining show. Lidia prefers the new hits, but revivals like this remind me of better times, yes? Lidia, of course, never saw it when it first played."

Of course not, Garcia thought. When it first played, she was a little girl living in a palace in Asuncion, taking riding lessons and learning French while Daddy terrorized the countryside.

Miller stared intently at Garcia for a few moments, then reached into his pocket for his cigarettes. "But I don't suppose you're here for theater criticism."

Garcia took Miller by the elbow and steered him to the street, a narrow space between two idling limousines. "Have you seen them yet?" he asked quietly.

Miller fumbled for his lighter. "Have I"—he paused to light a cigarette—"have I seen what?"

Garcia cocked his head but said nothing. Miller glanced over his shoulder. His wife had taken up a position several yards away and was thumbing aimlessly through her program as she watched the two men. Miller scratched his cheek and frowned. "I thought you were out of this business, Abel. After Honduras."

"The papers, Richard."

Miller nodded. "Yes, of course I've seen them."

The document discovered in the Florida Straits was on his desk a few hours after it arrived in Washington. Miller had read through it once, then again to make sure he hadn't imagined it. Mind-boggling stuff: an attack on America. The Cubans had slipped dozens of agents armed with deadly biochemical weapons into the United States. Their targets were outlined in remarkable detail: schematic drawings of federal buildings in Washington; descriptions of entertainment venues in New York, Chicago, Las Vegas, and Los Angeles; locations of hospitals, city halls, police headquarters in a number of smaller cities, and airports and train stations on the East and West Coasts. Thousands of casualties, billions in damages. And a devastating aftermath: Americans afraid to leave their homes—a shock to the social order that would cripple the nation.

Garcia put a hand on Miller's shoulder and drew him close. "So what is to be done?"

"We're discussing it, Abel. I can't go into details, but you know how this works."

"Yes, I do. Unfortunately."

Miller shrugged. "It is what it is."

"This is important, Richard. The threat is already here, on our shores. There isn't time to be wasted."

Miller twisted around and waved to his wife, held up one finger. She squeezed her program into a tight tube.

"Help me out here, Abel," Miller said. "I'm a little puzzled."

"Why? We have our sources."

"No, no, no," said Miller. "That's not what I meant. Did you have anything to do with this? Getting this out?"

"If we did, do you think the courier would be dead?"

A stupid mistake, he knew it instantly. The pain, the pills, a misty brain. *La lucha*, the struggle—a young man's game.

Miller was quick off the mark. "How could you know that, I wonder."

"What do you mean? Wasn't the courier killed?"

"Yes. Yes, he was. But only a few people in Washington know it."

"That's Washington," Garcia countered, trying to repair the damage. "In Cuba the courier's fate is well known."

Miller kept his eyes on Garcia while he considered the explanation. Finally, he nodded. "Yes, I see. All right."

"*Richard.*" Lidia was losing patience.

"And these documents—they're authentic?"

"Why would you ask that?" Garcia said.

Lidia, again: "You'll make us late, Richard."

Miller turned around and smiled an apology. When he turned back, Garcia was gone, swallowed up by the night. Vintage Abel, Miller thought, always a flair for the dramatic. On the other hand, Miller thought as he tossed his cigarette in the gutter, the man never answered the question.

# 5

The sun woke Savella, but not until the day had slipped away from him. For a few minutes he lay in bed, watching dust motes playing in the rays of light stabbing through the curtains. When he could no longer avoid it, he sat up and reached for the alarm clock on the bed table: *one fifteen*. Savella groaned softly. There had been work to do.

He fell back on the pillows and stared up at the ceiling. A long, narrow crack had appeared overnight in the plaster; beads of water were collecting in the space. As he watched, three fat drops fell to the hardwood in quick succession. *The storm*. A hazy memory: roaring wind rattling the salt-eaten window frames in the middle of the night, pounding rain drumming on the roof and pouring down the copper gutters.

Savella got out of bed, moved a plastic trash can to catch the water, then retrieved a flashlight from the kitchen and slowly climbed the stairs to the second floor.

A door in the upstairs hallway led to a storage space under the roof; the landlord had left the key in the lock, but Savella had never had reason to open it. The lock turned, but the door would not budge until he yanked hard on the knob. Savella slowly panned the flashlight around the eaves. A dress mannequin sat in one corner, next to several empty picture frames, and a mauve suitcase with a gash in one of its side panels. A pair of French doors, the panes broken, the wood warped and chipped, lay between the floorboards. In the middle of the space, a child's hobbyhorse, one of its runners missing, sat atop a jumble of old shoes, women's mules mostly, and a man's work boot. Savella edged his way along the wall, shards of glass crunching under his weight, and played the torch against the underside of the roof. Rainwater was seeping through an opening between two rafters and falling through a gap in the insulation to his bedroom ceiling. He eased back out to the hallway and went downstairs to call the landlord.

---

Savella had never been much for home life, but he liked this house the moment he saw it. Shrouded by three tall pines, the bungalow was tucked into a tiny corner lot at the end of a small street two blocks from the ocean. The haunted house, the neighborhood kids called it, and Savella could see why. The wrought-iron fence around the property wanted paint; the railings on the front steps were rusted and wobbly. A cracking stone porch ran the length of the house; dead herbs filled the flower boxes. The mortar between the bricks was crumbling.

The previous tenant had been a divorced man who reconciled with his wife; neither of them wanted any reminders of the difficult years. So the place came furnished, after a fashion: a sofa, a few chairs, a closet filled with fishing gear, silverware in a kitchen drawer, a collection of battered pots and pans hanging from an iron ring over the sink, bed linens and towels stacked neatly in the bathroom closet. The small kitchen hadn't been remodeled since Julia Child learned to cook. Children's growth marks scratched in pencil ran up the doorjamb by the refrigerator. The kitchen table, missing a leg, was propped up by a tall stack of *Field and Stream* magazines; a liquor store calendar was tacked to the wall. The rest of the house shared the slapdash quality. Built-in bookshelves lined one wall of the living room; a framed Cezanne print hung alone, slightly off-center, across the room. In the dining room, a glass chandelier loomed over a paint-splattered wooden cable spool that served as a dinner table. The bathroom wallpaper bulged in the corners, and the tub needed grouting.

"Needs some work," the agent had sniffed.

"It'll do," Savella said. He bought a mattress, unpacked his suitcase, and settled in, taking the bedroom off the kitchen.

More than he wanted, but in the end probably just what he needed. On nice evenings he would sit outside in a deck chair, sheltered behind a green wall of overgrown bushes, and watch his street as if it were an open-air theater. He had come to see his neighbors as cast members in a long-running drama—Mrs. DiLorenzo, who lived by herself next door, racing onto her porch, cigarette in one hand, glass of something in the other, to rail against "the Spanish" whenever the Latin kids dawdled outside; the screechy little Pakistani boy in number twelve running up and down the sidewalk with a toy M-16 while his sister sat on the front steps combing her doll's hair; the two middle-aged gay men in number twenty-eight taking a nightcap under the stars before settling in to watch a movie; the loud family in number thirty, a retired dock worker from Philadelphia and his cowering wife and a revolving cast of relatives, arguing over every little thing in angry voices that carried the block. Young Irish casino workers passing silently in the night as they took turns sleeping in the basement apartment of number thirty-two; upstairs, waves of newly arrived Latin Americans—Hondurans, Guatemalans, Mexicans—filtered through, anxious not to draw the slightest attention to themselves.

Savella liked them, his neighbors, this disparate bunch. Aside from a shy smile or tentative wave when it absolutely could not be avoided, they mostly kept to themselves, and in the months since he moved in, Savella had relished the anonymity and the solitude. His was a rough-hewn sanctuary, a place to hide—from what, he wasn't sure. But within his four walls, he felt safer than he had in years. Not a home, really—certainly not his home, not his kids who climbed the doorjamb, not his Japanese wallpaper, not his French doors or his lame hobbyhorse. But it would do for now, and the herbs, when finally they revived, were a very nice touch.

———

A roofer turned up an hour later, an elfin black man with dreadlocks and a curly white beard. Savella showed him the leaky ceiling, took him upstairs under the eaves. Back outside, the roofer threw a ladder against the side of the house and went to work.

"Still pretty wet. You sure it's safe?" Savella called up to him, and received an indecipherable grunt in response.

Savella went into the kitchen and made some coffee. As he spooned out the grounds, he noticed for the first time a smudge of dried blood at the base of his right thumb. Where had it come from? With a moistened forefinger, he rubbed it away and sat down at the three-legged table, which wobbled precariously as he rested his elbows. He remembered a taxi, and a giant Ethiopian driver who talked loudly on his cell phone. Savella glanced outside. His car wasn't in the driveway. At least he had the good sense not to drive. Now, the rest of the evening slipped into focus: a stumble as he got out of the cab, scraping his palm on the pavement, the driver asking, "Mister, you all right?"

He sipped his coffee and allowed the reel to continue spooling backward: Bobby, a bar on Atlantic Avenue, a bachelor party at the eight-top in the back, somebody, after midnight, insisting on buying him a birthday drink—

*Shit. Forty-eight.*

From the roof came pounding. Savella glanced around the kitchen, at the garish red-and-yellow cabinets, two of them missing doors, at the linoleum impervious to cleansers, the pile of fishing magazines. And the rest of it: his car—missing if he was lucky, stolen if he wasn't. A job he hated but couldn't afford to lose. And a man crawling over a slick rooftop, trying to keep the rain from coming in.

Happy fucking birthday.

The roofer was down twenty minutes later, standing in the doorway as he slowly completed the work order. "Shingles blew off," he said. "That's your protection. Without them, world's coming right down on you."

"Old house, old roof. Won't be the last time."

# 6

Seven at Max's, Isabella had said, but Savella knew she'd be late. She would turn up with a rueful smile, not asking forgiveness, exactly, but understanding. And the story of what delayed her—the Bosnian cleaning lady looking for a dress at the Salvation Army, a cup of coffee with a sax player who toured with Basie—would always trump her tardiness.

The overnight storm had puddled the street and the bay was up, its waters lapping under the dented guardrail along West End Avenue. A steady stream of cars headed to the baseball game at Dunes Stadium, the drivers glancing anxiously at the rolling bank of wispy clouds that masked the evening sunset. Savella pulled into Max's lot just before seven, parked the car, and headed into the restaurant.

Max's was an eccentric neighborhood bistro: low ceiling, wicker tables draped in white, wide picture windows affording a view of the bay just across the street, an eclectic collection of paintings, prints, and photographs framed on the peach-colored walls. Max Zobrist, a tall man with a pinched face who favored golf shirts in light pastel colors, ran the restaurant on whims. Waiters were sent packing over squeaky shoes, popular dishes lost menu position with a change in the weather. Savella was in the house one night when a party of six was shown the door in the middle of their appetizers for complaining about the music.

Max was behind the bar in the lounge, counting the cash in the till and doing his best to ignore the only customer, a woman in a loose red Hawaiian beach dress, nursing a beer.

"Well, he's eighty-five," the woman was saying. "Never thought he'd live this long, be honest with you. He loves it down there."

Savella slid onto a bar stool in the corner. Max held up a bottle of Johnny Walker Black and waited for Savella's nod before reaching for a glass.

"Left everything here, the house, the business," the woman said. "Everything he'd worked his whole life for, all of it. Told Betty, I gotta get outta here. And that was it, you know?"

Max moved down the bar to Savella, dropped a cocktail napkin, and placed the drink on it. "Here you go, killer," he said.

Savella grimaced. "You don't even *read* the paper."

"It was on the news." Max jerked a thumb at the television.

"A fender bender? Jesus. Listen, I'm gonna need a table for two a little later. Something inside. By the window."

"Isabella?"

"Yeah." Savella hesitated. "My birthday."

"No kidding? Then that's on us," Max said, pointing at the scotch. The woman tapped her beer bottle on the bar. "Let me get back to tales from the crypt. Maybe you want to take *her* for a ride."

Savella swirled the ice in his glass with his finger. The television over the cigarette machine was tuned to a Yankees game, the volume muted. Tierney Sutton filtered out of the speakers in the corners. Forty-eight, OK. But not so bad. He sipped his drink and felt the burn of the scotch warm his body.

---

A retirement party swamped the room a half hour later. Savella rested his elbows on the smooth mahogany of the bar and drank in the chatter around him. *That's my sister and ain't nobody gonna hit my sister if they ain't married to her...still smoking, thinks those faggot cigarettes, the Slims things, are gonna save him...big boned, not fat, big boned...got engaged underwater, dolphin delivered the ring, a year later, they're divorced...I said one more, OK, then we eat...*
"It's getting busy." Max was refilling his glass.
"She'll be here."
Late, sure, but she always turned up.

---

Even in the packed room, Savella could tell when Isabella arrived. The din of conversation died down for just a moment as she made her entrance, sweeping through the front door in a loose white blouse, khakis, and sandals, a speckled leather bag slung over her shoulder. Two waitresses at the service bar shouted her name and waved. Isabella spotted him, smiled broadly, and pointed toward the waitresses, eyebrows arched—*do you mind?*—then headed over to say hello to the girls.

A mere glimpse of Isabella Logan was always enough to give him pause. Long raven hair that fell carelessly about her face when she looked down. Wide blue eyes that crinkled into shimmering pools when she smiled. A tall, languid body that moved effortlessly, almost without notice when she wanted to. She wasn't classically beautiful, or pinup perfect, not young, not ripe, not dewy morning fresh. Her most striking feature, in fact, was a nose ever-so-slightly off-center. Not enough to fix, and anyway, a conversation piece, she once told him with a laugh. Such a great laugh too, a throaty, rumbling guffaw, and whether she meant it was never in question.

Isabella devoured life, relished contradiction. Fine dining could be a three-star French restaurant with the rarest of wines, or a picnic table piled high with crabs just pulled from the bay and washed down with pitchers of cold beer. She loved crowds, cherished her solitude. She'd lived enough to form opinions, and was eager to share them—never overbearing, only occasionally critical, but you always knew where she stood. And she would never stop growing. On most days, she went for a run, a chance to explore herself, she explained once when Savella wondered why.

Isabella was a refugee, a jazz singer who washed up in town from somewhere out West, the daughter of an Irish printer and an Italian pastry chef who gave her a pretty name, a glorious voice, and not much else, then receded into the mist. She was married at twenty-five, to a pediatric surgeon who liked the idea of show biz when they were dating but wanted her on his arm after the vows were exchanged. She gave it her best, traded the nightlife for a luxurious cage, singing at the piano in someone else's living room whenever the good doctor gave her the nod. In the end, it didn't work, and a thin scar on her left forearm was evidence the breakup hadn't been smooth. She moped for a couple of months, drank too much and slept too little, trying hard to figure out just where she had lost the trail. Then one night the phone rang: her old agent, Harold Cobb, a former horn player who found another way to stay in the game after the session gigs dried up.

"How's it going?" he said.

"What do you think?" she said.

"Well, this should cheer you up, hon," he said. "I got somebody wants you to sing."

So she fixed her hair and lost some weight and headed back out on the road. It was different, of course. She was older, the crowds were younger, and she was years behind. But the work made her whole again.

Isabella was appearing nightly at the Tropicana when Savella returned to town: The Clouds, a rooftop lounge with overpriced drinks. Three other customers were in the place the night Savella stumbled in and took a seat on a tiny stool at the low-slung bar. Isabella was slowly working her way through "New York State of Mind" to the evident boredom of her piano player, a runty man with bad skin. When she finished the song, he rolled into a self-indulgent little riff, designed to show he could do more than back up girl singers. Isabella listened patiently and when he had finished, she turned to the room and asked, "You guys want to hear anything in particular?"

The other customers and the yawning waiters aching for the night to end ignored her. Her gaze settled on Savella. "How about you? Anything?" He would forever remember the moment: hands on her hips, head slightly tilted, and a smile that screamed I dare you not to.

"You're on the right track," Savella said, and when she laughed, he was sucked under.

He was back every night. He would wait for her show to end, then the two of them would fill the hours until dawn talking and drinking and laughing. She couldn't understand why he was there, but she was glad all the same. And he felt himself falling, in a way that he could never remember, if he ever had. At the end of the night, as the sun forced its way into the eastern sky like some uninvited guest, he would drive her home, a warren of rooms on the second floor of a restored carriage house hidden from the street a block from the ocean, and they would sit for a few minutes more in her tiny yard, next to a koi pond, her pride and joy—"my little oasis," she called it. They would watch the huge golden fish lying motionless in the shallow water, and then she would kiss him softly on the cheek, and walk inside. He would wait until the lights went off, and then head home. Never physical, not until one dawn when she led him out of the car, past the pond and the grand fish standing guard, and up the stairs, silently. And the next morning his sanctuary didn't look quite the same.

---

She was finished with the girls now, moving through the crowd to his side. A lingering kiss and a tight embrace, and he breathed in the heady aroma of salt and lemon. "You were on the beach," he said.

"All afternoon. Did I get any color?"

Savella gently pushed her back and squinted. "Charred. You look charred."

"Funny man."

"Good trip?" he asked.

"Tired. Is this mine?" she said, picking up the Campari and soda that Max had just put down. "But yeah, it was worth it. They're talking about a six-city tour. Mostly small clubs."

"Terrific." He pointed toward the rear. "Let's grab the table before they give it away."

In the dining room, Max's hostess, Donna, an older woman with short blonde hair and freckles, guided them to a corner table with a view of the bay. As Savella settled in his wicker chair, Donna massaged his shoulders, then leaned down and kissed him on the cheek. Isabella grinned as she watched her go. "So you managed to keep busy while I was gone, huh?"

"Are you kidding?" He looked around the room. "They would never let me cheat on you."

Isabella deliberately draped her napkin across her lap. "Oh, I think they would. They'd be disappointed in you, think less of you, some of them, anyway, but they wouldn't rat you out."

"What is this, *The Godfather?*"

"They'd never turn you away. And that"—she lifted her water glass and took a sip—"is why you like it here so much."

The sunset broke through the wood-slatted Venetian blinds, bathing Isabella's face in a reddish orange glow. Suddenly Max was beside them, fumbling with the cords.

"You want me to close them?" he asked.

"No, she's OK," said Savella. "She looks great in that light."

"I meant, is it in her eyes?"

Isabella raised a hand. "Hey, guys? I'm right here. And I'm fine."

"But you can't see," Max said.

"Never," Isabella said.

"All right," Max said. "Be nighttime before you know it, anyway. So enjoy your dinner. But you, Michael, wash the blood off your hands before you eat."

Savella sighed heavily. "*She* hit *me*."

Isabella offered an uncertain smile as Max retreated. "What was that all about?"

Savella described the accident.

"Oh, that's terrible," she said. "The poor woman."

"Wait, it gets worse."

"Not for Mary Bloom," she said glumly.

Savella told her about his meeting with Janice Garabedian. When he finished, he sat back and rattled the ice in his glass. Isabella was quiet for a moment, then asked, "You really think Janice is upset enough to fire you?"

Savella shrugged. "I don't know. And here's the problem—I'm not sure I really care all that much. Right now, I've got the urge to say, 'Enough.'"

"But you're going to try the woman first. That sounds like a perfectly reasonable idea to me."

Savella took a deep breath and exhaled slowly. "I'm going to try Mary Bloom first. Because I said I would. But I'm not holding out much hope. I mean, come on—'she was an area resident for many years.' Probably nothing there to find."

Isabella faked a shudder. "Boy, I don't get you sometimes. You come back here and OK, it's a crappy little column at a crappy little newspaper. But it's a chance to start over. And all you see are dead ends." She stretched across the table, took his hand and smiled. "Give it a chance, huh? Come on. See where the ride takes you."

That smile, Savella thought. Who the hell could resist?

"Excuse me, guys." Donna was at the table again, setting down a bottle of wine and two glasses. "This is from Bobby." Savella craned his neck and scanned the room.

Bobby stood in the entrance to the dining room, shifting uncomfortably from foot to foot.

"I think he wants to join us," Savella said.

"Why didn't he bring it over himself?"

"I guess he wanted to make sure he wasn't intruding."

Isabella ducked her head, gently rubbed her temples, then laughed in spite of herself. "Oh, what the heck," she said, and waved him over.

"Hey, Isabella," Bobby said. "Just wanted to say happy birthday, Michael."

"You want to join us?"

"Nah, not right now."

Savella gestured toward the wine. "It wasn't necessary, but thanks."

"Well, it's not just your birthday. The other day—sorry I jammed you up."

Savella avoided Isabella's curious gaze. Bobby glanced from one to the other, then realized his time was up. "Anyway, I gotta run. Enjoy the wine, guys. Maybe I'll see you at the bar later."

When he was gone, Isabella picked up the wine bottle and examined the label. "OK, now what was *that* all about? He jammed you up?"

"You don't even want to know."

"You're probably right." She placed the bottle on the table and picked up her menu. "Strange choice of pals, Michael."

Maybe, Savella thought. An odd couple, certainly, right from the jump—the rising star with the front-page reputation and the shadow man who ran other people's errands. Bobby wouldn't speak of himself; he shut off questions with an economical laugh, a single terse "Ha!" followed by an enigmatic smile, and if that didn't work, he would simply lie, whatever it took to end the interrogation. But Savella was a digger, wouldn't give up, would go to China if he had to. The answers were closer to home: a single-mom kid who grew up in the streets of Camden until a high school football coach tapped the rage; headed for Delaware on a scholarship when he tore up his knee in the big game with Gloucester Catholic; a botched surgery that left him with the gimpy leg. The school honored the scholarship, but it had never been about the degree, and Bobby was gone three weeks into his freshman year. He drifted down to Atlantic City and bounced from job to job, but always avoiding the casinos. Too confining, he explained, but Savella was sure it had more to do with the need for a state license, which would have ruled out errands. Strange choice of pals? Maybe. But they understood each other.

---

Savella ordered the raspberry filet; Isabella chose the Creole shrimp, and they ate with gusto. Isabella did the talking, stories from the road, and Savella was content to sit back and listen. The sun was soon gone; beams of light from the cars along West End poked through the drawn blinds and strafed the walls of the dining room. After dinner a group of waiters came out with two pieces of chocolate banana cake topped with lighted candles. Isabella jumped to her feet and shanghaied the rest of the diners into joining her in singing "Happy Birthday," complete with her own little scat at the end.

Around ten, distant thuds signaled the start of the postgame fireworks show at the baseball stadium, and they opened the blinds and watched showers of gold, green, and yellow arc across the sky, teardrops of light that hung in the air for a few seconds before falling slowly to the ground. As the grand finale filled the horizon with rainbows, Savella glanced at Isabella. She was pressed up against the window, like a kid in love with a puppy.

Later, over coffee and Nocello, she leaned across the table and took his hand. "You know, I see you and Bobby together, and I gotta wonder. What are you doing here, Michael? Really. I want to know. What are you even doing here?"

He sipped the last of the liqueur, then rubbed the tablecloth with the tips of his fingers. "It seemed like the place to be at the time. But now, I don't know. I feel lost." He offered a wan smile. "Maybe you're making a mistake."

She looked at him for a few moments, long enough that he began to worry about her answer. Then she smiled and dabbed her lips with her napkin.

"Oh heck, Michael, that's what it's all about, though, right?" she said. "Making the right move at the wrong time." She lifted her glass. "Happy birthday, baby."

---

Bobby and Max were deep in conversation at the bar as they left. Max plucked a white rose from the vase next to the mirror and offered it to Isabella. "You guys want a nightcap?"

Isabella played with her flower. "You know what, I don't think so." She turned to Savella. "The beach did me in. Let's just go home, huh?"

Yeah, that would be the thing, Savella thought as they walked out into the cool evening air. That would be tonight.

# 7

Mary Bloom had picked the time and place for her funeral. Inside her purse the police found a badly creased white envelope with the instruction "To Be Opened If I Die" scrawled in pencil across the front in a spidery hand. Inside was a single sheet of lined notebook paper laying out the directions for her send-off: the Hershberger Funeral Home, her own bare-bones death announcement, a simple morning service at Our Lady of Assumption, Father N'gala Shmongo presiding, and afterward a cremation. No flowers, no Communion, and no music. Especially no music. "Father Shmongo is not to sing," she wrote, and the sentence was underlined in case anyone doubted her intent. A check for five thousand, dated eighteen months earlier, was included to cover expenses and a donation to the church.

*To Be Opened If I Die.* So we know something, Savella thought. Organized. No frills, no nonsense. And an optimist.

A long black hearse was idling outside the church when Savella arrived. Four pallbearers in black suits and ties, hands buried in their pockets, shuffled their feet on the sidewalk. Inside he stood for a moment until his eyes adjusted to the gloom. A condolence book lay atop an aluminum pedestal, its pages blank. Savella sniffed the incense hanging in the air and opened the glass door to the sanctuary.

A stained wood coffin, plain and closed, sat at the altar, flanked on either side by two modest bouquets of flowers. Propped on an easel beside the coffin was an eight-by-ten photograph of a woman, framed in red crepe paper. Savella glanced around the church. The pews were empty, save for three women sitting by themselves in the first few rows and a man in a stained maroon sweater reading a book by the confessionals. Savella walked up the aisle and stood for a moment to pay his respects, then made a sign of the cross and studied the photograph. Mary Bloom at forty-something, he guessed. A waitress, maybe, or a hostess, in a black vest and bow tie, a red rose pinned to her lapel, her long brown hair pulled back from her face and tied loosely with a strand of white lace. She stood in front of a bank of coffee machines. A defiant pose, Savella decided: back arched, chin raised, fingertips bridged on the counter, a slight smile overwhelmed by distrustful eyes.

Her choice, the photo, Savella thought. Strange.

The woman in the first pew was furiously working her rosary beads, her lips moving in silent prayer. Savella walked over and touched her shoulder.

"Thank you for coming," he said softly. "How did you know Mary?"

She furrowed her brow, then glanced at the coffin and shook her head. "Didn't," she said, her eyes riveted again on her fingers as they ran across the beads. "It's my regular time."

He made the rounds, but the answer was the same. The woman in the fifth pew was a widow observing the anniversary. "Was she your sister, hon?" she asked sorrowfully. The woman in pew eight reeked of the street and vigorously waved him away. The man in the sweater put down his novel and smiled when Savella approached.

"I'm waiting for Father," he said cheerfully, nodding at the confessional. "Was she family?"

"No, just a—just a friend, I guess you could say."

"Well, sorry all the same," he said, and picked up his book.

Savella walked to the back, the sound of his footsteps echoing off the bare stone floor, and slid into a pew three rows from the door. An empty church. No one to fill his notebook with the story of a life. Just a coffin, plain and closed, some flowers and a photograph of a dead woman.

A rough hand cupped his shoulder. "Guess you must've known someone to get in today, huh?" Savella started at the voice and looked up. Bobby Weiss loomed over him, blocking the weak light that pierced the stained-glass windows.

"What are you doing here?"

"Thought you could use the company." Savella shot him a skeptical look. "OK, I was there when she *died*, so..." Bobby slipped into the pew, sat down next to Savella, and nudged him in the ribs. "So we're it? Me and you and those three up there? And the ugly sweater?"

"Three regulars and a homeless woman. None of them knew her."

"No friends? Neighbors?"

Savella shook his head. "Maybe no one knows she's dead."

"Uh-uh. At that age they can smell it miles away. And if one finds out, they all do. It's like Indians with those drums."

"Well, I was counting on the friends to fill in the blanks." Savella jerked his head toward the door. "Maybe the pallbearers."

"Nope. I know the little guy." Bobby rubbed his forefinger against his thumb. "They come with the hearse."

They could hear a voice from behind the altar, loud and deep, rising and falling, a trace of an accent. "No, not tomorrow, not tomorrow. I shall be here all day, I'm afraid…Dinner, perhaps…Eight would be lovely…Yes, good-bye, then." A tall black priest in a white vestment, a cell phone to his ear and a lapel microphone clipped to his stiff white collar, stepped through a side curtain and stopped short, trailed by a yawning altar boy. The priest scanned the nearly empty church, then adjusted his horn-rimmed glasses. "No one here," he muttered, his words amplified throughout the church. He slipped the phone under his robes, then mounted the altar and busied himself with the Bible. Then he cleared his throat and clasped his hands in prayer.

---

The budget package, Bobby called it later, Father Shmongo's rapid-fire Mass for Mary Bloom. In truth, the priest admitted, there wasn't much he could say about the deceased. "I did not know"—he plucked a paper from the pulpit and glanced down at it—"Mary Bloom. So far as I know, she never attended services here."

"Perfect," Savella muttered.

"But there was a reason she chose this church. And she was God's child. So let us join together to send her home."

He raced through the readings in a drone, battling static on the wireless mic, the words spilling over each other in an often-unintelligible tangle. At times the clamor of traffic on Atlantic Avenue crashed inside, drowning out his voice. As he consecrated the host for Communion—so much for Mary's wishes, Savella thought—two men on the street argued loudly in Spanish, and a bus pulled to a stop, its brakes whining. A gust of wind through the open window at the side of the altar extinguished one of the two candles.

"Jesus," Bobby murmured, "this is fucking depressing."

Father Shmongo prepared Communion, then mounted the pulpit again.

"In her instructions, Mary asked that two Bible readings be delivered here. And so." He opened his Bible. "The first is Romans twelve, seventeen twenty-one." He turned to a page marked by a red ribbon and began to slowly read.

"Do not repay anyone evil for evil. Be careful to do what is right in the eyes of everybody. If it is possible, as far as it depends on you, live at peace with everyone. Do not take revenge, my friends, but leave room for God's wrath, for it is written: 'It is mine to avenge; I will repay,' says the Lord. On the contrary: 'If your enemy is hungry, feed him; if he is thirsty, give him something to drink. In doing this, you will heap burning coals on his head.' Do not be overcome by evil, but overcome evil with good.'"

The priest paused to drink some water, then flipped the pages again. "The second is Ezekiel eighteen twenty. 'The soul who sins is the one who will die. The son will not share the guilt of the father, nor will the father share the guilt of the son. The righteousness of the righteous man will be credited to him, and the wickedness of the wicked will be charged against him.'"

Bobby and Savella exchanged glances. "Lotta fun at a party, this one was," Bobby whispered.

The priest took Communion with the altar boy and offered it to the three women and the man in the sweater. Savella and Bobby remained seated. And finally, mercifully, it was over.

Father Shmongo looked to the rear of the church and nodded once. The pallbearers filed silently up the aisle and took positions around the coffin as he delivered a last blessing.

"Go in peace, Mary," the priest said finally, and the four men lifted the coffin and carried it out the front door. Father Shmongo and the altar boy headed back through the curtain. By the time Savella and Bobby reached the sidewalk, the hearse was edging into traffic.

Bobby lit a cigarette as Savella considered his next move. The funeral had been a bust. The cops had closed the case. He had cajoled a friend in the department into reading him the accident report: nothing in the car, nothing in her pockets, nothing in her purse except the funeral instructions, some makeup, her apartment keys, a wad of tissues, and a wallet with seventeen dollars in crumpled bills. The woman was a cipher. He had an eight-hundred-word hole to fill, and all he could say for certain was that she believed in planning ahead.

But the funeral, if anything, had made the mystery even more intriguing. How the hell could one woman live so long in one place and have nobody turn up to bury her?

"You know, I don't even have a picture," he said.

Bobby looked at him. "Hang on."

He ducked back into the church and emerged a few minutes later with the photograph from the easel. "Now you do," he said, handing it over.

Savella shook his head. "Stealing from a church."

"You want me to put it back?" Savella was silent. "I didn't think so."

A man in a worn brown corduroy blazer turned into the path leading to the church entrance. Glancing at his wristwatch, he scurried along the paving stones until he noticed Savella and Bobby standing outside the doors.

"The funeral?" he asked in heavily accented English. "Please. Is over?"

"Just ended," Savella said.

The man frowned. "So soon?"

Savella slipped down the steps. "You here for Mary Bloom?"

"She lives in my building," he said, and turned to leave.

*Someone who knew her.*

"Wait, wait a minute." Savella reached out and took hold of the man's shoulder. "I need to talk with you a minute." The man tried to pull away, but Savella slowly tightened his grip. "It's nothing bad. I'm a reporter. I'm writing a story for the newspaper about Mary. My name's Michael. Michael Savella."

The man wriggled out of Savella's grasp. "Journalist?"

"Yes, journalist." Savella pulled his wallet from his hip pocket and drew out a business card. "The *Post-Herald?*" he said, holding out the card. "You know?"

The man took the card and slowly read it.

"Can I ask your name?"

"Marek," the man said, pocketing the card.

"Great, Marek. And you live in the building?"

The man nodded. "I manage it."

*The building superintendent.* Savella wanted to hug him.

"That's great. So how long did she live there, in your building?"

"Many years. Many years. Since before I come."

"Can you tell me anything about her?

Marek shrugged. "She died in car crash."

Bobby laughed, took a last drag on his cigarette, and flicked it on the lawn.

"But what kind of woman was she?" Savella said. "Nice? Was she nice?"

"She was nice lady."

"Visitors? Did she have a lot of visitors? Family?"

The super shook his head firmly.

"No visitors. Nice lady. Is all."

"She wasn't married? No children came to visit her? How about friends in the building? Other ladies? Did they go to the casinos together, anything like that, Marek?"

"No friends. No visitors. Nice lady. Is all."

Savella grimaced. "Listen, this is kind of important. What I do is write about people, about their lives." He wasn't sure Marek even understood him, but he plowed ahead. "This is going to be a good story about Miss Bloom. About how she was a nice lady, right?"

Marek looked confused.

"Nothing bad. It's all good. Think for a minute. Anything else you know about her? Did she work?"

"No work, nothing." Marek was tired of the questions. He chopped the air with his right hand to signal the end of the conversation, then backed away.

"You think he understood a word I said?" Savella asked.

"Oh, man," Bobby said. "You got a problem, pal."

Marek trudged slowly down the path to the street. The one link to Mary Bloom, and he was disappearing. Savella couldn't let it happen.

"Marek," he called out, "you think you could show me where she lived?"

The super took a few more steps, than stopped and spun around. "You drive me home," he said, "you see apartment."

---

The building was a small brick affair, just steps from the sand. A hotel once, Savella guessed, but somewhere along the line, a desperate owner had knocked down walls to create two-room budget apartments. A coat of white paint was slapped on the faded brick, and an awning hung over the front door in a halfhearted attempt to spruce things up.

Marek, Savella, and Bobby squeezed into the narrow elevator cage, and the super closed the gate and pressed the button. The car shuddered, and they rose slowly, the creaking elevator straining against its cables. When it jerked to a halt on four, Marek threw open the gate and led them to a peeling door directly across the dimly lit corridor. He unlocked it, then glanced up and down the hall before waving them inside.

"A few minutes," he said quietly.

Mary Bloom had done her best to fashion a home out of her two rooms. Flowing white silk curtains framed large windows that looked out on the Atlantic. A few seascapes, motel art, hung on the walls, along with a picture of Jesus Christ, a brittle palm taped to its borders.

In one corner was a calendar featuring snapshots of cats.

An antique sofa covered in red stretched along one wall of the small living room. Against the other wall stood a small metal dining table draped in white linen and set for one with fine china and a cloth napkin. Dried flowers sat atop a mahogany coffee table. Wedged in the corner was a small bookshelf holding a handful of mystery novels, a dozen snow globes, and an old boxy gray-and-silver camera—a relic from the fifties, Savella thought as he turned it in his hands.

In the galley kitchen, a few plates and glasses were stacked neatly on the drainboard. A teakettle sat on the gleaming stove. Savella opened the small refrigerator and found a quart of milk, half a banana, a jar of pickles, and a plastic bag filled with fast-food packets of mustard and ketchup. In the freezer were two steaks, a bag of chicken breasts, and an empty ice tray.

A double bed took up most of the floor space in the second room. Three throw pillows, little-girl frilly, lay atop patterned sheets. A large armoire and a wooden dressing table, its surface covered with makeup jars and a family-sized box of tissues, took up the rest of the space. Perched in the corner was a twenty-inch television set; the remote control and a copy of *TV Guide* rested on the bed table next to an old rotary telephone.

In the bathroom a robe hung from the back of the door, and two towels were thrown over the shower rod. A toothbrush sat in a glass by the sink. The medicine cabinet was filled with aspirin and stomach medicines and an assortment of prescription drugs, none of which Savella recognized.

He walked back through the two rooms again, looking for something he might have missed. On the dining table, tucked neatly between the salt and pepper shakers, were several utility bills. Savella quickly scanned them: basic cable service, no long-distance charges on the Verizon statement, the gas bill on a monthly installment plan.

"Not much here," he muttered.

"You seen enough?" Bobby asked.

Savella glanced back at the door. Marek was standing in the hall, watching for neighbors. "Keep an eye on him, huh? I want to take a quick look in the drawers."

Bobby moved to the door. "So, Marek, you from Poland or what?"

Savella returned to the bedroom and opened the armoire. Mary Bloom's modest wardrobe was hanging neatly inside, good-quality blouses and dresses, carefully mended in places. One drawer was filled with bras and cotton panties, all white. Another held several sweaters in muted colors, folded perfectly, as if someone was expecting a surprise inspection. Under the sweaters, wrapped in tissue paper, lay an old beige jumper with a faded grass stain on the front and a white cotton blouse with a Peter Pan collar—a teenage girl's clothes. In a third drawer, Savella found modest scarves and discreet jewelry. The wardrobe of a woman who shunned attention. Savella felt a twinge of embarrassment at invading a dead woman's privacy, but he pressed on, looking for something, anything, that would help him find Mary Bloom.

The dressing table was next: a drawer on the left filled with more makeup and an assortment of combs and brushes, the drawer on the right crammed with old magazines, a book of crossword puzzles and some pencils, two ripped file folders stuffed with yellowing newspaper clippings of movie-star obituaries—Orson

Welles, Simone Signoret, Rock Hudson, Lloyd Nolan. As he rifled through the stack, his hand brushed against metal. Lifting out the folders, he found a battered tin box. Once it had been adorned with a brightly colored parrot, but the paint had long since chipped and faded. Savella took the box from the drawer and raised the lid. A tattered black leather address book. Four black-and-white photographs. A color snapshot. A gold high school class ring.

Savella quickly examined his discovery. The address book contained dozens of listings, some crossed out, a few with new telephone numbers or street addresses penciled in. The ring was a typical senior class memento, a scarlet stone circled by the words "Western High School." He turned to the photographs. The first showed three young women, a young man, and an older man dressed in evening clothes and sitting in a horse-shoe-shaped restaurant banquette. The second was of a grinning boy standing under the propeller of a small airplane, holding his arms in the air in what appeared to be a gesture of triumph. In the third, a soldier in military camouflage posed uncomfortably under a palm tree, squinting in bright sun. The fourth was of a middle-aged woman with tousled hair and a crooked grin wearing a sweatshirt with the word "Leathernecks" blazoned across the front. The color image was of a younger woman in a white raincoat, her head covered with a scarf, standing next to a car, a confident smile crossing her face.

Savella flipped over each of the pictures: nothing to identify any of them, no names, no dates, no locations.

From the corridor came the whine of the elevator, and Bobby stuck his head in the bedroom. "He went downstairs for something. You're done when he comes back up."

Savella handed him the photographs.

"You think one of these is her?" Bobby asked.

"I don't know. The only time I met her, she was white as a sheet and a step away from dying. And it doesn't look much like the picture from the church." He looked around the bedroom. Then, taking the pictures back from Bobby, he moved into the living room, slowly scanning the walls and the bookshelves. "You see something strange here?"

The elevator motor clicked on again, and the drone of the approaching car drifted in from the hall.

"What strange? It's like my grandmother's place." Bobby sniffed the air. "Brussel sprouts."

Savella nodded. "Exactly. That's my point. Your grandmother's place. But look at the walls, the shelves, the tables. What do you see?"

Bobby shrugged. "Nothing."

"An old woman's apartment," Savella said. "And there's not a picture of the kids or the grandchildren. Not a picture of a husband, or her parents, or her brother and sister. Not one shot of a family picnic at the lake or her best friend Betsy in front of the Eiffel Tower. Nothing."

The elevator gate screeched open. Savella held up the photographs. "And she's got these, stuck in a box in the drawer of her dressing table."

"So?"

"So why are the only pictures she has of people hidden away?"

Marek's footsteps grew louder. Savella quickly dropped the ring in his pocket, placed the photos and the address book back in the box, and slipped it under his shirt, buttoning his jacket to cover the bulge.

"No fucking idea," Bobby said impatiently as the super bounded back into the apartment. "You get what you need?"

———————————

Marek stood in the hallway and listened to the elevator make its labored descent. The journalist had taken the box from the bedroom, the painted box with the book and the photographs, stuffed it under his coat. Marek should have challenged him, *would* have challenged him, if it hadn't been for the money he'd taken out of the same box a day earlier. Almost two hundred dollars. She wouldn't be needing it, and would probably have wanted him to have it, that's how she was. But robbing the *dead*. Was there anything lower?

A good woman, Miss Bloom, the only one in the building who didn't treat him like an animal. Miss Bloom, who applauded when he came home from English classes and proudly called a sofa a sofa, and who gently corrected him when he called a lamp a table. Miss Bloom, who invited Marek and his wife upstairs every Christmas for a holiday toast, good Polish vodka, and some reassuring words about their new world.

"We all come from someplace else," she told them once, "and we all had excellent reasons for leaving."

A good woman. And he had stolen from her. Marek winced in shame.

# 8

Isabella ordered takeout, Vietnamese, and set a small table outside, at the edge of the koi pond. She pulled the last of the Jersey tomatoes from their scraggly vines and made a salad with herbs from her little garden. They pulled on sweaters against the September chill and drank a nice Riesling as darkness fell, and the crystalline water gurgled over the rockfall at one end of the pond. The conversation was light, the comfortable kind that two people fall into if they spend enough time together; not a word about bad jobs or murky futures, and that alone, in Savella's view, made the night a treasure. There was coffee afterward, thick, strong, the way she liked it, and Savella knew that meant he'd never sleep, but he drank it just the same, three cups when all was said and done, so anxious was he to preserve the moment.

They carried the dishes upstairs, and he washed them and put away the leftovers. When the chores were done, Isabella was stifling yawns, desperate for her pillow; her day off, and she'd run errands, puttered around the garden, and now the Riesling had finished the job.

Upstairs, no lights, odd for Isabella, but not invisible in the soft moonglow. Leaning awkwardly against the headboard, he consumed her as she kicked off her sneakers, slipped her sweater over her head, unhooked her bra, and let it fall to the floor. She wriggled out of her jeans and panties, then lingered for a moment, examining a blemish on the inside of her left elbow. Savella never tired of the sight: the tangled tresses of raven hair shrouding her shoulders, the sweep of her olive skin, rushing past the supple breasts, then narrowing to a doll's waist that gave way to broad hips, a thicket of matted curls, and, finally, long, smooth runner's legs. She was attractive that first night in the Clouds, and a few weeks later, when she took off her clothes for the first time, he couldn't breathe. But it was the second night he would never forget, not the first rushed, awkward, get-acquainted session, but after that. He had never known a woman like her, who relished, devoured sex in all its simple glory. In the first weeks, they made love everywhere, always in the end falling asleep entwined in a sweaty jumble of arms and legs, inhaling the sweet earthy fragrance of intimacy.

The memories aroused him, and when Isabella slipped between the sheets and tugged the blanket to her chin, he shifted slightly to face her, searching for a sign that sleep could wait after all. But she rolled onto her left shoulder and scrunched the pillow under her head until she sank comfortably into a downy crevice. "God, I'm tired," Isabella murmured, and in seconds she was asleep.

From outside came the sound of a mother's voice as she tried to soothe a wailing baby. Someone scraped the lid off a metal trash can, and a dog growled, low and menacing. Savella lay back in bed. The coffee was working its black magic; he would never sleep tonight.

He liked this place, felt comfortable here. His house was somebody else's home, streaked with traces of others' lives. Some exiles were like that: nothing much more than the clothing on their backs. No books, no pictures, no letters, no music. Memories were dangerous, he had long ago decided. The more you accumulate, the closer you are to the end. Isabella was an exile too, but she was different. Her house was a home, brimming with artifacts. She had saved all of it, carted it across America until she ran out of country. Her baby shoes, bronzed. A paw print of Barney, her first dog. A three-shot photo strip taken at an Instapix booth of a mugging Isabella and her pal Claire, who joined the navy. In a way Savella envied her, he who had nothing. When she went to the store, or lingered in the bath, he would roam the small apartment, studying knickknacks, examining photos. He knew their stories by now: the Route 66 coasters picked up at a truck stop on the way to a gig in Joliet; a ceramic bottle discovered on a folding table on a street corner in Old San Juan; a plastic jar of dried elephant dung from South Africa, a gag gift from a headliner to his band after two weeks in Sun City; a jar filled with swizzle sticks, souvenirs of a singer's life on the road. And on a sagging sewing table, isolated as if to keep them from infecting the happier memories, three pictures of Isabella and her ex. "You can't just take scissors, cut him out, and pretend none of that happened," she explained one night. "Life isn't all neat like that, is it?"

Her past, not his. Yes, they were exiles, but different in so many ways. He had grown up in turmoil, escaped a house in uproar, and never stopped moving, packing a bag and leaving when things or people went bad. Always the easy way out, his weakness, and so years of old apartments that smelled of dying hopes, and balky fans on hot, humid nights, and cars with shot mufflers and no chance of making it over the next rise. Until he went to ground on this island. Until he knocked on a door and somebody wanted to open it. Until Isabella. She had been through the storm and survived, eager to reach out to the world again, to see the best and hope for more.

A few weeks after they met, she sat outside his house on Halloween with a huge white ceramic bowl filled with candy, sipping wine, and waiting for kids. And when they didn't find their way down his dark street, she ran to the corner, waving her hands above her head and calling out, "Hey, hey. Candy! Over here. Watch the cars." She led them to his porch, an enchanting Pied Piper, critiquing their costumes—Superman was a good choice, a maid wasn't so scary. But everyone got candy, and when the first group ran off, she was at the corner again, dragooning a new bunch, and another, and one more, until the bowl was empty.

About Isabella he could write a dozen columns, but, Janice's rules, she'd have to die first and that wouldn't do at all. Isabella was his link to the world and after the storm, when the seas and the winds had calmed, she would bring him home.

She awoke suddenly and rolled over to look at him, her eyes still veiled with sleep. "Michael?"

"Sssh."

"What are you doing?"

"Just thinking. Go back to sleep."

"What time is it, anyway?"

"I don't know. After twelve. Go back to sleep."

She reached up and brushed his face with two fingers, then took his chin in her hand and held it, her look vague, wistful. Then she slowly shook her head and pulled him closer, and they kissed, a long, unbroken, tender exploration. His hands caressed her body, until finally, with a sigh, she wriggled beneath him, and he was inside her, her arms around him. A bit reserved, he thought, none of her feral abandon, but then she had been sleeping, and he quickly forgot it as they began to move together, slowly at first, then with more urgency, and finally in a fury until all too quickly it was over, and they collapsed in each other's arms, broken. Isabella stroked his face with her right hand, then let it fall away as she turned back to her pillow without a word. Before long she was asleep again.

He propped himself on one elbow and stared at her: a hand folded awkwardly against her cheek, mouth slightly agape. He loved her, that much he knew. And Isabella had made up her mind about him, Savella was sure of it, even if he didn't yet know the decision. There was nothing to be done. Still, it was a start. He could live with it, until life sorted itself out, anyway.

And Isabella would see him back to shore. When he was ready.

---

A small red bulldozer sat on the sidewalk, and a dump truck caked with mud was parked in front of his house when Savella returned home in the morning. A gaunt man with a turquoise earring was giving instructions in halting Spanish to a work crew. The landlord, it seemed, had made a decision about the landscaping.

"It's all dead," the gardener said. "He wants it all out."

"Are you sure?" Savella asked. He turned a slow circle as he examined the foliage that shrouded the house. "Everything looks so green."

The gardener shook his head and waved at the drooping trees and overgrown bushes. "Dead, dead, dying, never really grew," he said curtly, his finger dancing down the line. "They're gone." He jostled a pine bough and a shower of needles blanketed the ground. "It's all coming out."

Savella glanced at the living room window. "Leaves me kinda..."

"Exposed?"

"Yeah, exposed."

"Yeah, it does."

The gardener barked an order in Spanish. His crew filed over to the truck and began pulling out hoes and shears. The exile's life, Savella thought as he went inside. Always living in someone else's house.

He showered, threw on a pair of blue jeans and a gray T-shirt, and put on a pot of coffee. As the coffee brewed, Savella laid the tin box he had found in the Bloom apartment on his kitchen table and spread the contents in front of him. One by one, he studied the photographs, searching for a clue he might have missed the first few times through. He picked up the class ring and carefully inspected it. Finally, he turned to the address book.

Mary Bloom had evidently used it a very long time. The black leather cover was cracked and dry, the spine mended with tape. The edges of the pages were yellowing, and several of the alphabet tabs were missing. The slender red ribbon she used to mark her place was frayed and had been cut in half. Savella slowly thumbed through the pages. Seventy-one phone numbers, some entered so long ago that they carried letter exchanges. The older entries had been made using a fountain pen. Mary had a nice hand, he thought, left over from the days when penmanship counted. But in the newer entries, made with a ballpoint or even a pencil, the writing lost its grace and authority.

Savella got up and poured himself a cup of coffee and leaned against the counter. He picked up the address book and moved to the Bs, running his finger down the pages in search of a relative, but there were no other Blooms. Next, he went through the book page by page, looking for a listing that mentioned an uncle or aunt, but again he came up empty. He dropped the book on the table. All that was left was to start calling the numbers, one at a time, in search of someone who could help him. It was work he hated. He flashed on his first job in the business, covering cops, the city desk calling every few hours with lists of names wheedled out of the medical examiner's office, expecting Savella to figure out whether the circumstances of the deaths were grisly or poignant enough to be newsworthy, or whether any of the dead were sufficiently well known to merit a few lines. Most of the time, the cops could help him, and sometimes he could track down neighbors or coworkers. But if none of that worked, there was nothing to be done but to call the mothers and fathers, brothers and sisters, aunts and uncles. Some resented the intrusion and hung up. But for others, the call gave meaning to the deaths of their loved ones, and they would stay on the telephone long after Savella had determined there was no story. He could never bring himself to say good-bye.

Until one awful autumn afternoon, when an eight-year-old boy named Shawon Elliot darted into the middle of the street and was run over by a delivery truck. The boy's age made him a candidate for poignant. Savella found a number for the Elliot home and dialed it. A woman answered. Savella identified himself and asked whether she was Shawon's mother.

"What he do now?" the woman asked.

Savella felt his stomach churn.

"Well, have the police been in touch with you, Mrs. Elliot?" he asked.

"Police? I been out all day. Where Shawon at?"

He could hear her screaming as he hung up.

---

He began with the As. Some of the numbers were no longer in service; others weren't answered in the middle of the day. At Carnes he found a woman who thought she once knew a Mary Bloom, but couldn't remember. Juniper was a man who sold her some furniture, "but that was a long time ago." Four people told him they already got the paper.

His luck changed at Vicki Luzinski, who had worked as a waitress at Hafner's on the Boardwalk, where Mary was a hostess. Mary had heart problems, Luzinski remembered, and left the job on disability shortly before the owners shut the doors about fifteen years ago. Luzinski didn't know much about her.

"She had her own way of doing things. The help loved her, the busboys, the guys in the kitchen. And she liked music, I remember that, the oldies. We went to lunch a few times, but she kept to herself. We weren't really friends. I can't imagine why she had my number."

George Norwood knew Mary Bloom too. He was a plumber who had tried without much success to date the pretty hostess. A few dinners and a casino show and Mass one Christmas, but the relationship never got off the ground.

"She didn't talk much about herself," he said. "She wasn't from around here, I don't think. She didn't talk like us, her accent. You know, she never seemed to be having a good time. Very quiet. Even when we were out.

Especially when we were out." He laughed. "Maybe it was me. Anyway..." His voice trailed off. "Sorry to hear she's gone, though."

The next few calls were dead ends, and Savella was thinking about taking a break when the Rs caught his attention. Midway down one page were listings for a Brenda Radcliffe and another for a Betty Rincon. Both were done in early Bloom, a confident, flowing cursive written with a fountain pen, and both had faded with time. The telephone numbers carried letter exchanges. In the space between them was a Joseph Remsen with six numbers, five of them crossed out, and one apparently fresh entry—modern, seven digits, with a 309 area code entered in pencil in the wispy handwriting of an older woman. Worth a shot, Savella decided. Maybe he knew her in the last few years.

He grabbed the telephone directory off the top of the refrigerator and found the 309 area code: west central Illinois. That was odd; it was the first listing he'd found outside New Jersey. He picked up his cell phone and dialed the number. After four rings a man with a slight Hispanic accent answered.

"New Beginnings, may I help you?"

"Good morning. I hope so. I'm looking for Joseph Remsen," he began.

"Father Remsen's in a meeting. Would you like his voice mail?"

*Father* Remsen? "Fine, thanks."

A series of clicks, then an automated announcement and a beep, his cue to leave a message. Savella identified himself as a reporter trying to track down the family or friends of a woman who had recently died. A listing for Joseph Remsen appeared in her address book, and he would appreciate a call back. Then he hung up and stared out the window. Mary Bloom had heart problems. She liked old music. She wasn't much of a date. And she knew a priest in Illinois.

Outside a chain saw started up. Savella walked to the front door and stepped out on the porch. One of the workers was perched on a ladder, lopping off the branches of the first tree.

The chirping of his cell phone drew him back inside. Savella glanced at the caller ID. Father Joseph Remsen was returning his call.

The priest was friendly, sounded eager to help. He was the executive director of New Beginnings, a residential drug treatment facility in rural Illinois, a working farm where about two hundred clients were struggling to overcome their addictions and get their lives in order. "But you're not calling about that, I gather," he said. "How can I help?"

Savella outlined his effort again, then told the priest about the skeletal obituary and the empty church.

"I suppose this happens frequently enough, but it just struck me that here is a woman who led a life and when she dies, it's as if no one ever knew she existed. I thought it might be worth filling in the blanks. So far, I'm not having much luck. I found a few people in her phone book who knew her, more or less in passing. But your listing has six numbers. Five of them are crossed out, old ones, I guess, with letter exchanges or just five digits. And this new one, where I found you."

"Mary Bloom...Mary Bloom," Remsen said slowly, turning the name over as he tried to make a connection. "I'm sorry, but I don't recognize it."

"Kind of strange, don't you think? Your numbers in her phone book?"

"Did she ever live out here?" Remsen asked. "Maybe I met her through the church, at some function."

"She's been in New Jersey for at least fifteen years," Savella said.

"I've been out here for twenty. Perhaps she was a patient. Or a relative of a patient. That's possible. Obviously, I couldn't tell you. Patient confidentiality and all."

"Well, she's dead, Father, so I'm not sure—"

"I'm just saying—"

"Anyway, I don't think that's how you wound up in the book. I'm looking at this now, and the listings are under Joseph Remsen, not *Father* Joseph Remsen. If the church was the connection, you'd think she'd have you down as Father."

"Well, I don't know. That's true, I guess."

"And the way the last one's written, it's like she entered it recently. It's hard to explain without showing you, but I think she put it in the book not all that long ago. Maybe the last few years. So it's not too likely it's just a weird coincidence."

"Maybe," Remsen said. "Maybe. But I'm just saying I don't think I know the woman. Or knew her."

Savella examined the listing. There was something here, but it wasn't coming to him. Keep the priest talking, he told himself. Maybe it will tumble out.

"Can I read you the numbers? One of them might jog your memory."

A television droned in the background, the sports news, and Savella could make out the voices of men talking somewhere near the priest.

"Sure," Remsen said, "go ahead."

Let's start with the most recent, Savella suggested, and the priest recognized the first number immediately—"The diocesan office in Peoria. I was there for, oh, a year before coming down here." The second and third also came quickly: Christ the King in Galesburg, his last parish, nine years as pastor, and St. Barnabas in Chicago before that, a seven-year stint. Remsen sounded almost gleeful when he matched the numbers to his memory, as if he were on a game show, winning prizes.

The fourth was a struggle; Remsen thought for a few minutes before triumphantly announcing the answer: Holy Redeemer, Northbrook, Illinois, a history teacher in the parochial school for two years.

"Boy, that's a lot of years right there," he said.

"Almost like you had a stalker," Savella said.

Remsen laughed. "Oh no. Lord, no. I'm just some broken-down old Bible-thumper here. No one stalking me."

The game show ended with the fifth number.

Savella read it once, slowly, and Remsen asked him to repeat it. The priest was silent for a few moments.

"I'm sorry," he said finally, and his playful tone had vanished. "I do remember this one. The seminary. In Mundelein. Near Chicago."

"We're going way back now," Savella said.

"We are, yes."

"And you still can't place the name?"

"No."

"Because she sure has followed you around a while."

Remsen said nothing.

"One more number, Father. Five three six nine zero. No exchange or anything. Just five three six nine zero."

On the other end of the line, Savella heard what sounded like fingers snapping, then the voices in the background faded away and the television was muted.

"Father? Are you still there?"

"How old, how old did you say she was?" Remsen said quietly, how-can-I-help suddenly replaced by beware-of-strangers.

"Sixty-five."

The priest coughed once. "No. Sorry."

He had to go. Savella wanted him to hear some of the other names in the book, but Remsen was late for a meeting with the medical staff. Later, there were chores, and the boys needed supervision. The priest promised to call if he remembered anything about a Mary Bloom, and hung up.

Savella put the phone down. He wasn't sure what to make of the conversation. It was inconceivable that Remsen didn't know Mary Bloom, a woman who had squeezed a record of the priest's life work into a tiny box between Radcliffe and Rincon. The last two numbers in particular seemed to have shaken him. Had they stoked memories he'd prefer to bury? If that were so, perhaps he only needed a little more time before he could bring himself to remember Mary Bloom.

Through the kitchen window, Savella could see one of the pine trees stripped of its branches, a workman with the chain saw poised at the top of the ladder, preparing to attack the trunk. Savella turned back to the telephone. He would make a few more calls, but he wasn't expecting much.

---

A few minutes after the doctors left, Jaime Figueroa heard the door to the study close with a click. He knew what it meant: no calls, no visitors. Father would come out when he was ready.

An hour went by, then two, but Jaime wasn't worried. He had seen this before, the last time just a few days ago. The pack of wild dogs that had been terrorizing the chickens returned with a snarling vengeance, hurling themselves against the coop wire in their blood frenzy. Father had emerged from the farmhouse carrying the old rifle he kept locked in his closet. He stood on the porch, took aim on the pack a football field away, and pulled the trigger once, twice, three times. Three dogs yelped and fell to the ground, dead; the rest quickly scattered. The boys broke into relieved applause. Father's face was ashen.

"Jaime, please bury them," he said softly. Then he tucked the rifle under his arm and walked back into the house. Jaime had gently cracked the office door a few hours later and peered inside. Father Remsen was sitting on a hard wooden chair in the middle of the room, staring out the great bay window at the long rows of corn that ran to the horizon as if he expected someone to suddenly emerge from the fields and wave hello. Just like the other times. Jaime quietly shut the door and returned to his desk to wait.

Nothing to worry about—Father always came out of it. Always came back for his boys. He would this time too, by dinner, probably.

But the dinner hour came and went, and still Father sat in his study. Jaime thought briefly about interrupting, asking whether everything was all right, but decided against it. Perhaps Father needed some time alone, but you could count on him. No one knew that better than Jaime Figueroa. After his last conviction, a sympathetic judge had spared him a stretch in juvenile detention and sent him instead to New Directions. He stumbled off the bus a resentful teenager bridling at the rules—no phone calls, no gym, no television, up before dawn, lights out at nine. It was Father who had made the slow, laborious effort to win his trust. It was Father who finally convinced him to embrace the church and confess his sins, the robberies, the assaults, even the time he spied on Veronica in the bath when he was six. Prior bad acts, Father called them. People hold them against you. But God knows everybody's done something. All he wants is that we try to make up for it. And that starts with confession. What you tell me goes no further, the priest told the skeptical street kid. Just you and me and God.

He was always there for the boys. Maybe tonight he needed time for himself.

Just before nine Jaime switched the telephones to voice mail, put a cover on his computer keyboard, and turned out the lights. Father would be back by morning prayers, standing on the porch in his faded Cubs cap, a sloppy grin on his sun-reddened, double-chinned face. No doubt about it—Father always came back for his boys.

———

Remsen heard his assistant bustling around the outer office. A good boy, Jaime, knew when to poke his head up and when to stay away. The courts had sent him five years ago, a bitter fifteen-year-old with a nasty crack habit. He had been clean and free to go for three years now, but Jaime wanted no part of East St. Louis anymore. He liked the country, clung to it like a shipwrecked sailor with a piece of driftwood, and Remsen was glad to have him. Jaime was clever at his job; more importantly, he was a constant and desperately necessary reminder that good things did happen. And Remsen badly needed that today.

The phone call from the reporter had triggered an avalanche of emotions. For most of the afternoon, he had been lost in the weeds, trying to find the trail that would lead him away from the agony before it engulfed him again. He had no illusions. In the end it was a hopeless journey. He could try, and he would, again and again and one more time, but he could never escape.

A lifetime, and yet not really. Too much unfinished business for that. A life interrupted was more like it. And he was to blame—of that much he was certain.

All afternoon Remsen had remained in the hard chair, his penance chair, his seat of choice when the guilt dug too deeply, as it had this day. Oh Lord, Mary, was it you? *Five three six nine zero.* Was it really you? *Five three six nine zero.* It had to be.

He could see her face as if it were yesterday, would never forget it, the flash of horror that erased the innocence forever. A last look, then into the shadows, and she was gone. And I never went back for her. I never fixed it.

And the phone numbers. My God, she had followed him from the seminary, and when he lost the edge for the pulpit, when he couldn't speak the words anymore, she had tracked him to the corn. But she never called. So why had she followed?

*The phone.* He had no choice. Remsen rose slowly and struggled to his desk. A little after nine. An hour later down there, but he would be up. Remsen closed his eyes and pictured the colonel as he had seen him last, just before the surgery, sitting on his terrace high in the hills, sipping beer, and staring out at the distant lights on Tortola.

He picked up the phone and punched in the number. Four rings before a curt hello.

"It's Joey. How are you?"

"Why are you calling?"

As if he needed a reason. Remsen dug a fingernail into the soft skin of his thumb. This was hard enough.

"I have news."

There was no response.

"Mary's turned up."

Neither man spoke for several minutes. Faint voices and easy laughter floated in from the nightly staff volleyball game. In the eaves, a nightingale cooed. A slight breeze rippled the curtains, welcome relief after the heat of the day. All this peace—shattered.

"Where?"

"New Jersey. Atlantic City. She's dead. A reporter named Savella called me earlier. He found her address book and was trying to figure out who she was. Apparently she died in the last few days. Alone. Paid for her own funeral, if you can believe that."

"What did he know, the reporter?"

Not how did she die, not what had she been doing, not what was her life like. *What did he know, the reporter?*

"Nothing, as far as I can tell."

"And what did you tell him?"

"Nothing."

"You didn't say you knew her?" The colonel sounded skeptical.

"No. No, I lied. Again."

The colonel sighed deeply. "Don't start that shit, please."

Remsen could hear the shuffle of his sandals against the veranda stone, then the sound of a bottle being opened.

"You have to go talk to this reporter, find out what he knows. And get her things," the colonel said. "Collect her things."

"How can I do that?" Remsen protested. "I told him I didn't know her."

"Make something up. You suddenly remembered she was one of your junkies. Whatever. No one's going to care. But you have to get her things. You understand?"

"All right. I'll try."

"You can't *try*," the colonel said, his voice rising. "We have to know. There's another project. We can't let her fuck things up. Do you understand me?"

"Yes."

"Good." The colonel was quiet for a moment. "I have to go. I have calls to make."

"Yes," Remsen said, "yes, I'm sure you do."

The connection was severed. Remsen suddenly felt very tired. He dropped the receiver, and it bounced off the desk and dangled by its cord a few inches from the floor. With great difficulty he pulled himself to his feet and shuffled across the floor to his sofa. His back ached from the long afternoon in the chair. He wanted to fall asleep and wake up with all of it behind him. Nothing good could come of this. Nothing ever had.

His eyes grew heavier.

Mary, after all this time…

# 9

Abel Garcia's bodega was a hole in the wall, really, a long narrow room that ran from sidewalk to alley, just enough space for a chipped red counter and an aging Coca-Cola cooler chilling a few six-packs of beer. The sagging metal shelving on the brown walls was mostly bare these days: loose candy, a few dusty Goya cans, an assortment of soaps, and cartons of bootleg cigarettes up from the Carolinas. Garcia had an office of sorts in the rear, hidden behind an orange curtain drooping from a bent white rod, but he spent his days in the front, sitting in the lone window, perched on a high stool behind the cash register under a picture of Pope Paul VI tacked to the wall. A Lotto machine, a rack of phone cards, and that was it. In the years he had sat there, nothing had changed. And nothing ever would, not if Pilar's nephews could help it.

They had bought up the block and were busy running out the tenants, mostly old Hispanics, so they could flip the property to the rich young people hunting for the next hot Brooklyn neighborhood. Nothing, the nephews decreed, could be allowed to interfere with the mission. Last month they'd called a halt to the dominoes on the sidewalk outside, the old guys huddled around a piece of plywood laid atop a bank of milk crates. It was too much, they told him, bad for business, the click-clack of the *fichas* slapping the table, the heated arguments in Spanish, the cigarettes and cigar butts littering the sidewalk, a bunch of Cubans loitering on the curb until it was too dark to see. *The new people don't want that, Tio Abel. You understand, right?* So he would punch out the Lotto, sell the phone cards, whatever they wanted, but the store was history the minute they found a buyer. The sooner the better, he told his wife. He was no shopkeeper.

Late afternoon, a sizzler, the unending stream of cars and taxis and trucks edging up the avenue, stoking the furnace. Garcia stood in the doorway in an immaculate cream-colored suit that didn't fit him so well anymore, sipping a small cup of the strong Cuban coffee that Jorge retrieved from Francisco's place down the street. Francisco, who had seen the English writing on the wall and surrendered, started selling lattes. Frank, he was now, and who really cared. Well, Garcia, but that battle was lost. Once he had insisted on Spanish, at home, at work, in the shops, on the street. That was fine in South Florida, a colony of outcasts awaiting *La Vuelta*—The Return—but now, here, there was no longer any point in fighting. And the flood of English that swamped him when he stepped outside was a daily humiliation, forcing him to concede, as if he needed a push, that he was a long way from home and unlikely to ever get back.

He drained the last dregs of Francisco's coffee as the tongue of exile babbled around him: a mother on the march chastising her young son for straggling; a jogger in sweats chortling into a cell phone; the gas man shouting upstairs to let 2-F know the buzzer was broken. It was evidence of his agony that Garcia found solace in the noise of the traffic rumbling down the avenue, bleating horns, shrill sirens, thumping music, whatever it took to drown out the words.

Garcia checked his watch. Enough suffering. Don Arturo's son would be here soon.

----

A few days earlier, the colonel on the phone. He had been drinking, enough to make a difference. *You need to know this. It's Mary.*

The girl. Garcia could barely remember what she looked like. But the attitude, the way she toyed with her shrimp cocktail and froze the table with just one sentence that night so long ago—he would never forget that.

She was dead, which should have been good news, but the colonel was in a panic. A reporter had her phone book, had called Joey, asking questions. The colonel needed to know: What else did she leave behind? What had she been doing all these years? *And did she tell anybody?* Garcia tried to calm him, but the colonel was having none of it. He raged for ten minutes before finally lapsing into silence. A few minutes later, the receiver fell to the floor with a dull thud. He would sleep it off.

Garcia had heard the colonel like this before, in the winter of their disillusion, during long nights in seedy bars with the Crown Royal fueling their hatred of the traitors who sold them out. Once upon a time, the colonel seemed the source of all wisdom. Garcia was young then, and the colonel wasn't much older, but he had already lived a lifetime, and Garcia soaked in his version of history. Now he knew better. "*Nosotros estan bueno amigos,*" the colonel would tell Garcia in a tortured Spanish made worse by the whiskey. *Amigos.* Friends was too strong a word, Garcia thought. Allies would do. And, with their bloody history, doomed to stay that way.

In the morning he put in a call to Don Arturo's boy, let him know about Mary. It was the least he could do. Not for the son, but for the father.

———————

The night before Castro took the capitol, Abel Garcia, who knew what was coming out of the mountains, slipped aboard one of the last National Airlines flights out of Havana. Crouching in the aisle without a ticket, he found himself at the knees of Arturo Pena, one of Cuba's wealthiest men, owner of the legendary Havana casino, El Miramar. Impressed by his audacity, Don Arturo let him stay, and by the time the DC-9 set down in Miami, Garcia had a job.

Before the revolution, Arturo Pena had the foresight to stash huge sums of money in American banks, and now he used his fortune to build a new empire—parking lots in Miami, a few motels, a restaurant, and on the other side of his adopted country, a new Miramar in downtown Las Vegas. Garcia was by his side every step of the way, and when he fell in love and married Pilar Alcazar, Pena took great pleasure in helping the young couple settle into a stylish home on Key Biscayne.

But even with all his success, Pena still lusted for revenge. From a dark-paneled office on his sprawling estate on Biscayne Bay, he plotted and schemed, bought politicians and journalists and diplomats at a furious pace, all with a single, unwavering purpose in mind: a return to Cuba to reclaim the life Fidel Castro had stolen from him. His trusted aide would help with that as well. Pilar, a doctor's daughter who was happily ignorant of politics, knew nothing of her husband's shadow life in the company of hard young men, anti-Castristas who knew him only as the Bomber. Garcia crisscrossed the Caribbean and Latin America, different names, different nationalities, the same goals—hunting Castro and those who stood with him. To Garcia and his men, any act of terror was permissible if, by even the most tortured logic, it advanced *la lucha*.

He was a marked man, from Castro's agents, surely, but as the movement splintered, from rival factions as well. His body bore the scars: a gash under his collarbone where a bullet had narrowly missed his heart, bullet holes up and down his right arm and left leg, a slug that lodged in the soft tissue of his right buttock—a wound of shame, Garcia called it. The end came as he walked out of a hotel in Honduras. A bullet slammed into his left shoulder and spun him to the ground, where he lay bleeding in the gutter for what seemed an eternity until the bellman decided it was safe enough to come out and drag him inside.

Pilar, who had quietly puzzled over her husband's extended absences and ravaged body, was finished with silence by the time she arrived at the hospital. "Who wants to kill you?" she demanded. "What have you done?" Garcia refused to answer, but she would not relent, and so he swung his legs over the side of the bed and struggled into the plastic chair by the window and told her. Her eyes began to glisten around the bazooka attack on the embassy in Caracas. She was weeping by the bombing of the hotel restaurant in San Salvador, and fighting sobs when he told her of the downing of the jetliner over Bermuda. Once a nurse came in to see if everything was all right, but they sent her away and Abel pulled his beloved wife close and told her of the grotesque mistake that ran out the string, the attack on the convoy in Guatemala: a busload of school children, not envoys of the dictator. But as horrific as it was, in the end he couldn't tell her everything. He could not let the woman he loved live with that monstrous burden.

It took him three months to recover, and by the time he healed, it was over. He had promised Pilar. They sold the place in Miami and moved north to be with her family in New Jersey. Safer, she said, keep you out of trouble. "We're Americans now. Forget him," his wife would crossly demand when Garcia fumed about Castro.

And she didn't leave it there. A call to her nephews, and of course the boys had something—a job managing their little store. So he got up every morning and went across two rivers to Brooklyn, and slowly he slipped away from the conspiracy and paranoia, from the unwavering focus on the past that helped *los exilios* relive every excruciating detail of their wrenching loss, from the single-minded sorrow and fury that could make a cobwebbed political killing in Camaguey in 1962 seem as fresh as last night. It became too much even for Garcia. Nights out with friends went first, then golf, the movies, and finally quiet evenings with family—no more, he vowed as he walled himself off from his memories. Instead, he sat in the living room, picking at the dinner on the tray in front of him and growing old watching Pilar's *telenovelas*.

Then last year the phone rang: Help my son, please. And Abel Garcia gave his word. But two strokes, a minor one that froze Don Arturo's left arm, then a massive attack that left him sitting dull-eyed in a wheelchair in a Miami rehabilitation center, and Garcia put the promise out of his mind. Arturo Pena would be dead before he saw Cuba again.

The son had other ideas.

---

Arturo Pena liked to say Enrique was his first accomplishment in America. An only child, he wanted for nothing—speed boats, fast cars, a recording studio the year he took up the guitar, a Davis Cup coach to teach him tennis. Arturo's money found Enrique a place at Harvard and kept him there after he was discovered to have plagiarized a European history paper. After graduation, the son moved into the executive suite, working at his father's side for twenty years until the old man, extracting a promise that one day the Pena name would again headline in Havana, bowed to time and handed Enrique the keys.

The company had grown—two Midwest riverboats, an Indian casino in California, a racetrack slot parlor in Pennsylvania. But the big breakthroughs eluded Pena: no fabled entertainment complex on the Vegas Strip, no glamorous casino-hotel on the Atlantic City Boardwalk. Worst of all, El Miramar in Havana remained a dream, and in time this came to consume Enrique Pena. Cuba rarely left his mind; the overthrow of Castro became his grail. It would be his way of proving to the old man, once and for all, that he was his son.

One last mission, he told Garcia over dinner a few weeks after the second stroke, one final effort to send his father home to die. What was the point, Garcia wondered. Would Don Arturo even know? Enrique's eyes narrowed slightly as he reminded Garcia of the promise he had made, and the older man sat back and listened. But as Pena laid out his plan, Garcia had to fight the urge to laugh: a boat in the Florida Keys, a dead man with forged papers that promised war. Who did he think he was kidding? This was a comic book. But the son was used to having his way. A hint of the brute about him. Pretty women, priceless art, a bloody steak—he got what he wanted. And what he wanted now was a war.

---

A black Lincoln Town Car slipped out of the traffic and rolled to a stop in front of the bodega. Oscar the bodyguard was out first, the bloody-fanged viper tattooed on his right arm on display in his short-sleeved shirt, and not until he was sure the coast was clear did the boy prince emerge. He looked the part, Garcia had to admit: tall and slim, a perfect suit draping his chiseled body, a dazzling Chiclet smile beaming from his bronzed face.

Pena nodded at Garcia as he buttoned his jacket, then reached back inside the car and drew out his daughter, Marta, a jewel in the Pena crown, sexy-elegant in a white linen jacket and a red silk tank top, a teardrop-shaped diamond pendant dangling between her breasts. Pena had raised Marta by himself. The wife was a pleasant thing who did as she was told, but Marta's was a difficult childbirth, and when Pena discovered there would be no son, the wife was gone. Money, lots of it, and a lavish condo above Biscayne Boulevard, but gone for good. The way of Pena: No dead weight.

The father said something to his daughter, then hugged her tightly, his hands sliding slowly down the curve of her body, holding her for so long that Garcia finally had to look away. When he turned back, Pena was striding briskly toward the store.

"Marta wants a sandwich, Oscar," Pena said as he walked up. "Then wait with her in the car. Abel, how are you?"

"I'm fine. I called you—"

Pena raised his hand. "Not here. Inside."

They walked back to the office, Garcia leading the way, Pena's soft brown Italian loafers slapping a cadence on the linoleum.

The office wasn't much: a tiny space crowded with a small wooden desk, a decrepit fake leather recliner, two metal folding chairs, and a twelve-inch black-and-white television set that received only an audio signal. The ceiling was splotched with sickly yellow water stains. Nailed to the wall was a map of Cuba circa 1959—the old country, frozen in time—that Garcia had rescued from the trash after Pilar banished it from her living room.

Pena gingerly moved a folding chair to the desk and sat down. He studied Garcia for a moment. "You're looking well, Abel. Lost some weight?"

"Have I?" Garcia dropped into the recliner. "Must be exercise."

"You? Working out?"

Garcia shrugged and shook his head.

"OK. What was so important that I had to drive to Brooklyn?"

"The girl," he said. "The girl from before. She's been found."

Pena flinched ever so slightly. "Where is she?"

"She's dead."

"She's dead?" Pena tilted his head. "How long?"

"A few days, a week. I'm not sure."

"Where?"

"In Atlantic City."

"Why is this a problem?"

Garcia described his conversation with the colonel: an address book, a call to Joey from a reporter named Savella, the colonel's panic.

"So how much does this reporter know?" Pena asked.

"We don't know."

"We *need* to know."

"Joey's going to find out."

"The priest?" Pena shook his head. "Not a priest's work."

"Well, but we don't want anyone else—"

"I've got a guy."

Garcia rubbed his chin nervously. "Not Deets."

Pena looked at him closely: *What of it?* Garcia frowned and slumped in the recliner. "If you think."

"I think," Pena said.

Over the years, through the birthdays and the weddings and the christenings, Garcia had grown to dislike Enrique, and he was reminded of that now as they huddled in the back of the store, the smell of the garbage in the alley seeping through the cardboard-thin walls. He reached into his pocket for his small pillbox and withdrew two tablets.

"You're sick?" Pena asked.

"It's nothing. A headache." Garcia gulped down the pills.

"Now, tell me about Miller. You saw him, as I asked?"

"Yes, yes. Outside the theater. He didn't have much to say. They're discussing their next step." Garcia hesitated. "He asked whether the papers were genuine."

"Why would he ask that?"

Careful now, Garcia told himself. A comic book, yes, but the son thought it was genius. And Garcia, truth be told, was proud of his handiwork. Pena had ordered a world-class forgery and Garcia had delivered the goods. In a lifetime of deceit, the Key West documents were one of his finest creations. No easy task, this sort of fake. Can't be too good—that invites suspicion. So pencil in flaws, make every page look well-lived. A name misspelled, a decimal point misplaced. Spill coffee on a couple of pages, run it all through the Xerox three or four times until it's blurred and crooked. And when it's done, don't force the issue. Let it float to the surface on its own. But even with all that, there would be questions.

"You can see how some might wonder," Garcia said. "And some could ask who in Havana would really want to launch an attack on the United States. With Fidel gone."

Pena studied Garcia for a moment. Then he smiled and got to his feet. "Yes, I forgot. It's Raul now. Raul the *reformer.* Raul, who has seen the light his brother missed, who will take the *Yanqui* hand his brother spurned, who will lead Cuba into, well, the *twentieth* century would be a start, wouldn't it?"

Garcia cleared his throat. "I didn't say I believed—"

"No, no. I understand, Abel. Not you. I can count on you, can't I? You know the Raul I know, right? The Raul whose army protected the dictator all those years, whose spies snuffed out any opposition. And they say, oh, but he's an old man. He'll be gone soon. And then what? Does he have a son or a nephew or a cousin? Or maybe he'll leave the country to some general who stayed up nights playing cards with him." Pena wiped his lips with the back of his hand. "But I can count on you, can't I?"

The smile was gone. Enrique was used to getting his way.

The bell over the front door tinkled. Garcia slowly stood. "I have a customer," he said, and walked unsteadily to the front.

A woman with her three kids, looking for Mega Millions and a pack of Marlboros. What does Pena expect? Garcia thought as he punched out the ticket. What was the point? Garcia was long past caring. Fidel or the brother or whoever came next—he had lost his taste for it. Killing Fidel—he would never regret trying. But the struggle had changed. The armies of the past had melted away. The old men couldn't lift a rifle anymore; the young ones didn't want to. To them, Cuba was a curiosity, not a dream; a vacation destination, not a homeland. And for the diehards, now it wasn't about freedom; it was about keeping families apart, starving millions to prove a point. He handed the woman her ticket and change, and watched her shepherd her family out the door. Now it was about indulging the fantasies of careless young men.

Pena was studying the map when Garcia returned, leaning in to make out the names of cities and villages he had never seen. He turned from the wall and wagged a finger at Garcia.

"When the Iraqis wanted to go home, the world went to war. Panama—Noriega is in prison and his exiles are home. In Nicaragua the Contras are in Managua today. But what do we get? Fifty years of empty promises."

He began to pace back and forth, a short route in the small room, like a prisoner in maximum security, Garcia thought, determined to take advantage of his hour of exercise before he was taken back to his cell.

"In the meantime, everyone else is getting in. *Everyone.* The Europeans. The Chinese." Pena was agitated now, the frustration spilling over, and his mood darkening. "Someone I know was down there last month. Tourists everywhere. He met some Israelis running a bunch of orange groves. British Petroleum had a cocktail party on the roof of his hotel. The Arabs are building a five-star resort on the beach. You get the picture? The competition is already there. They're already in the ground. Building hotels. Condos. Even the Canadians. *The Canadians.*"

The pacing stopped. Pena stood in front of Garcia, leaned down, his face so close that Garcia could smell the coffee on his breath. "I don't want to be last dog in, Abel. Last dog in gets to pick at the bones."

Strange, Garcia thought. No mention of vengeance for Arturo Pena. And not a word about El Miramar.

"How's the headache, Abel?" Pena asked, but he didn't wait for an answer. He raised his head and sniffed the air. *The garbage in the alley.* "It stinks in here. Walk me out."

They retraced their steps, the *slap-slap* of Pena's expensive shoes marking their progress, past the empty shelves, past the Lotto machine and the picture of the pope. On the sidewalk Pena stopped, put an arm around Abel's shoulders.

"Let me worry about the girl, all right? Let me handle that. You need to help me with the rest of it. See what they do in Washington. Keep in touch with Miller." He shook his head. "Do you have any idea how much I've raised for that guy in the White House, him and his party? A million and a half. And for that I get to pick up the paper and read about let's sell them grain, let's build bridges. And elections. *Elections.* What are they going to do if the Cubans vote to keep the system they've got? No. *Fuck* the politics. All I want is when the bastards are dead, I'm first in line. You understand? First in line. That's what I want."

He released Garcia, nodded at the car. Oscar got out and opened the rear door.

"So we wait and see what happens with the papers, And if that doesn't work, we'll think of something else. That's where I need you, Abel, where *we* need you, my father and I. We gotta give them something to rally around. You know? A remember-the-*Maine* kind of thing."

Garcia offered a weak smile. "Remember the Miramar."

"That's right. There you go." Pena slapped him on the back.

"It doesn't have quite the same ring to it."

Pena caught Garcia with a dead-eyed stare. "That depends on where you're standing, doesn't it?" he said. "Where are you standing, Abel?"

A promise made. Garcia nodded slightly and fumbled for his handkerchief. A race against time, he knew. What would kill him first.

# 10

You are looking for signs of life. They are very hard to find.

Two days in the newsroom, squirming in the soft light, gagging on the lemon scent, using every trick you ever learned in the business, and all you have to show for it is a lot of nevers.

Mary Bloom never voted. Never received a traffic ticket or applied for a passport. Never arrested, never married, never owned a house. Never held a credit card, paid cash for everything—her rent, her heart medicine, the Honda she died in. When all was said and done, Mary Bloom left this world with a library card she never used, a grand total of $4,179.21 in a savings account at the Sun bank, and five old photographs that meant so much to her she couldn't bear to see them. No friends, no family, no past, and no present. A woman who barely existed.

What you don't know about Mary Bloom would make a great column. But you can't write a thing about a lot of nevers.

So Janice Garabedian gets eight hundred words on an elderly school crossing guard who had worked the same intersection since the Depression and was about to hang up her orange safety vest. Never mind that she was alive and well, except for the diabetes. A nice story, you think. No kids of her own, but mom and Mom-Mom and great-grandmother to three generations of children, taking them in hand and promising safe passage across the wide unknown. As you're punching in the last sentence, Janice pauses at your desk and leans over, so close you can smell the Chanel and see the greenish glow in her eyes from the overhead light glinting off her contact lenses as she scans the screen. After a minute, she straightens up.

"This quote," she says, smudging it with her forefinger. "It's from the *guard?*"

"Uh-huh."

"She's not even *dead.*"

"I'll let her know."

She bends down, quickly finishes reading the column, then shakes her head.

"Jesus, Michael," she says. "What else you got?"

And before you can react, she's gone, bounding down the carpeted corridor. Later, you spot her across the newsroom, standing behind her glass wall, and when you catch her eye, a look of concern, or is it pity, crosses her face before she turns back to her desk. Because a mistake is only a mistake if you keep repeating it.

But you appreciate the chance she took, so you volunteer to help out on something else. Janice, pleasantly surprised, puts you on team coverage of the annual air show. You spend an hour on the Boardwalk, watching black warplanes arc through the sky and rush toward the ocean in a roar, and before long you're huddled in a corner of a hovel in a Gaza refugee camp, the Israeli Air Force sending a message from above. And all too soon the memories stray to a dusty West Bank checkpoint, and before that gets out of hand, you retreat to the comfort of a dark bar, where you cobble together the random observations of a couple of drinkers who wandered in after the planes had flown off. Your effort, if you want to call it that, covers two grafs at the bottom of a sidebar buried on B-14.

*Jesus, Michael. What else you got?*

Signs of life. Very hard to find.

———————

Isabella, on the other hand, was a hit. Midway through her latest gig at the Clouds, on most nights even arriving two hours early won't guarantee a table. The casino wanted to showcase her before a longer engagement next month. Tonight she would sing the national anthem before a minor-league baseball game at Dunes Stadium, then mingle at a high-rollers' party in one of the luxury suites.

She could live with the mingling; the anthem was another matter entirely. "It's not my thing, you know?" she said as they lay in bed the night before, drinking wine and looking for a good movie on television.

"Is it the music?" Savella asked, thumbing through the channels. "Because some of the best singers—"

"Forget the *music*. I can *hum* the music. They don't care about the *music*. No sports." Savella had paused on *Baseball Tonight*. Isabella tugged the remote control from his fingers. "It's the *words*. After 'by the dawn's early light,' I'm done. But I'm gonna tell them *that?*" She reached for the wine bottle. "It's part of the deal, these appearances. But I don't know, it really burns my toast."

His glass halfway to his mouth, Savella stopped. "It *what?*"

"You know. Makes me mad."

His eyes widened. "It burns your toast?"

"You never heard that?"

"Not since *Little House on the Prairie* went off the air."

Isabella grinned and slowly refilled her glass. "Little *what?*

"Very funny," Savella said. "You gonna leave me any of that?"

She handed him the bottle. "Drink up, sweetie," she said, and clicked off the television. "And let's see if we can think of something else to do."

---

Savella found a seat a few rows behind home plate. Along the third base line, two infielders were lazily playing catch, and Savella quickly fell into the rhythm of ball striking leather. He drew a deep breath, then slowly exhaled. The ballpark was a last redoubt, a perfect refuge. The team was all about dreams and memories, part of an independent league that lurked on the fringes of the national pastime. The players were a collection of youngsters unwilling to accept the conventional wisdom that they weren't good enough for the big leagues, and older men who once had a whiff of the majors and longed for another shot. The odds against them were staggering, but every year one or two were plucked from obscurity and catapulted to Houston or San Diego or Cleveland or Tampa or some other major-league Valhalla to commune with the baseball gods. Inevitably they fell back to earth, unpacking their duffel bags in the dimly lit locker room as the rest of the team craned their necks to see the gear, T-shirts, and caps, the odd glove or pair of shoes, talismans from another world that sparked new hope, if only for a little while.

Savella envied their faith, and marveled at their refusal to surrender. On some nights he would follow the players across the street to the Double Play Saloon, where they sucked down beers and flirted with the local girls. Their postgame chatter, so full of life and so sure of tomorrow, fascinated him. For them the horizon ended at the outfield wall; inside the stadium there was nothing they could not handle. And when it all went wrong, when the fastball caught the outside corner, when the line drive fell just beyond the outstretched glove, when the ground ball sneaked through the infield, there was always another game, a chance to fix things, to make the world work out right.

The infielders finished their catch and strolled back to the dugout, two young men weighed down by nothing more than a game ahead of them. How many times would they have to be bludgeoned before they finally fell? And then would it really be enough to simply know they tried? Would that explain the lost years and head off the second thoughts that were sure to engulf them on the other side of the stadium walls? Savella doubted it. But he would forever hope he was wrong.

A sudden flurry of activity on the field, stadium workers darting back and forth, and Isabella emerged from the corner of the home dugout. She took several steps, then stopped and said something to the small posse of men who had followed her onto the field. One of them pointed in the direction of the pitcher's mound, and Savella watched her amble across the well-groomed grass. She was dressed casually tonight, a soft white linen blazer over a light-blue silk shirt and flowing white linen slacks that fell around straw-colored sandals, her hair pulled back in a loose ponytail. The spectators in the field-level boxes nudged one another and nodded toward the diamond as she made her way to the mound, and a few of the players stood on the top step of the dugout. Isabella always captured a crowd.

The stadium public address announcer asked the crowd to rise for the national anthem, and someone pressed a microphone in Isabella's hand. She tapped it twice to make sure it was on, then brushed her hair back off her face, smiled broadly, and began to sing. She had managed to memorize most of the lyrics, but Savella knew two particularly vexing lines were written on the inside of her palms. For all her jitters, though, the performance was flawless. Isabella hit every note, remembered every word. As she finished, the crowd gave her a warm round of applause and Isabella waved her thanks. Savella left his seat and was standing behind the dugout when she came off the field.

"What'd you think?" she asked.

Savella leaned down and kissed her lightly on the lips. "You didn't miss a word."

"And a very good thing too." She held up her palms. The ink was badly smudged. "I forgot about sweat." Savella laughed and handed her his handkerchief. "You're coming upstairs to the party for a while, right?" she said as she scrubbed away at the ink.

It would be like a visit to the dentist. But Isabella didn't ask for much.

---

The door to the suite was open, and a steady buzz of conversation and laughter spilled into the hallway. About fifty people were crammed inside the room. Steam trays of hotdogs sat on a cabinet along one wall. A platter of cold cuts, chips, and pickles teetered on a coffee table. A bar laden with plastic cups and an ice bucket stood in a corner next to sliding glass doors that led to a set of seats overlooking the stadium.

Isabella was the center of attention in seconds, standing in the middle of a circle of admirers, displaying her inky palms as she told the story of how she prepared for her performance. Savella poured himself a scotch and slipped through the sliding doors. He was alone outside, save for an old man in the next box peering intently at the morning paper through a pocket-sized magnifying glass. Savella stole a glance over his shoulder: the legal advertisements, the fine print that hardly anyone ever examined but which offered an occasional nugget of news to anyone willing to slog through them. No way to spend an evening at the ballpark, he thought.

The stadium lights were taking effect, highlighting the lush green of the baseball diamond, gleaming off the players' uniforms as they took the field. Savella watched Phil Sheridan, the twenty-nine-year-old third baseman, smooth the dirt around the bag. Sheridan had been one of the chosen few last year, signed by the Seattle Mariners in late August. His run was over by the end of the season, but he made it count: one hit in twenty-five at-bats, and it was a home run. How must that have felt, Savella wondered. As he jogged around the bases, was he thinking he was up to stay? Or was it part of the deal, written in the fine print, the part no one ever reads—you get a taste, but then it's over.

"Is this any way for grown men to make a living?" Harold Cobb, Isabella's agent, stood in the aisle, holding a plastic cup filled with milk. A heavy-set black man in his sixties with a shock of white hair and a nose streaked red from years of alcohol that he could no longer touch, Cobb was a cheerful man with no good reason to be. In his youth he had enjoyed modest success as a trumpet player. Now he scratched out a living representing young singers who left him once the paydays got bigger. Isabella loved Cobb, but they both knew how it would end.

"A national treasure, Harold, that's what this is."

"It's baseball. Kids play it." Cobb stepped down to the front of the box and stood at the railing. "Well, what the hell, I couldn't take that crowd inside either." He sipped the milk as he inspected the crowd in the suite. "Look at them in there."

"Isabella's always telling me to give people a chance," Savella said. "She thinks everybody's a little better than they might seem."

"My experience says just the opposite." Cobb pointed at the party. "And she might change her mind after this guy."

Isabella was posing for a photograph with a man wearing a ropy gold chain. Her smile, her professional one, grew tighter as he draped his arm around her shoulders, and when the photographer was finished, she quickly pulled away to avoid the customer's lunging kiss. Savella slumped back in his seat. And all that effort for what? To show the guys back home that he went to Atlantic City and got close to a beautiful woman? What story would he make up to fill in the blanks? And the picture—where would that end up? At the bottom of a cardboard box in the back of a dusty closet, to be pulled from the shelf years from now and combed for clues to its provenance. Who was the woman? Where was this taken? Look at the size of that gold chain. Where—

Savella suddenly sat up. *The fine print that hardly anyone ever examined.* He reached inside his jacket and pulled out the envelope containing Mary Bloom's photographs. By now he was so familiar with the images that he thought of them in shorthand: Night Out, Airplane, GI Joe, Scarf, and Sweatshirt. No matter how often he'd pored over them, how hard he willed them to speak, the photos hadn't offered up a thing. But maybe he hadn't been looking in the right places.

He glanced across to the next box. The old man with the legal notices was still there, munching on a hotdog, the magnifying glass lying on the seat next to him.

"Excuse me," Savella called out, and when the man looked up, he held aloft his photos and pointed at the glass. "You think I could borrow it for a few minutes?" The man picked up the glass and stretched across the low cement dividing wall to hand it to Savella.

"Was it something I said?" Cobb asked.

"No, sorry, Harold. Something just occurred to me."

"OK. Gotta go to work." Cobb placed one foot on the bottom stair. "Guess you're not coming in."

"I'll watch the game for a little while, I think."

"Nice. Leave me to the mob." He leaned over and patted Savella on the shoulder, then slowly climbed the stairs.

Savella spread the pictures on his lap. He held the glass over GI Joe and squinted into the lens. The soldier's uniform was bereft of insignia or rank. He stood before a clump of palm trees, but otherwise there was nothing. He moved the lens to Airplane. Nothing unique about the boy, no numbers or identifying marks on the portions of the fuselage visible in the picture. The snapshot of the woman in the sweatshirt and the young girl in the raincoat and scarf were more of the same.

He picked up Night Out. The three women and two men were squeezed into a banquette. The women wore evening clothes and flashed hesitant smiles. The blonde with her hair bobbed in a sort of Doris Day style, a fur draped over her shoulders, had been captured with a glass raised to her face. Next to her sat a younger woman with long dark hair, her hands clasped in front of her, perched awkwardly in her seat, her expression sullen, as if she had been forced into playing grownup and was none too happy about it. He held the restaurant photo next to Scarf and examined them both through the glass. The dark-haired woman in the banquette bore a striking resemblance to the young woman in the scarf. The third woman at the table was dark-haired with a distinctive complexion—bone china turning fleshy. Her wardrobe seemed much more modest than the others.

Savella moved to the men. One was young, dark, with a head of luxuriant hair and a full mustache. The other was much older than his tablemates, his short dark hair slicked back from a widow's peak. He wore a dark suit, a light-colored shirt, and a tie that blended into oblivion. His hands were folded on the table, exposing a watch on his right wrist.

On the left edge of the picture was a man's arm, a ring inlaid with a large black stone on the finger of his cuffed hand. On the right, a trouser leg, finely creased, was barely visible.

The banquette table was strewn with coasters topped with glasses, one with a napkin balled up in the bottom. A small candle burned in the center of the table. A lighter lay on the table, and two cigarettes smoldered on the lip of a large ashtray. And finally, a break: with the help of the magnifying glass, Savella could just make out some printed letters on the side of the ashtray: Hotel Adolphus. *The fine print that hardly anyone ever examined.*

He slid the pictures back in the envelope and stood up. He'd never heard of the Adolphus, long since knocked down, he guessed, maybe a victim of one of the city's frenzied attempts to reinvent itself. The newspaper library might help. Or some of the old-timers. Maybe even Harold. Savella leaned across the wall and returned the magnifying glass, then ran up the stairs to the suite.

Cobb was standing by himself in a corner near the door. He brightened as Savella approached. "You come to rescue me?"

"I have a question. Where was the Adolphus?"

"The what?"

"The Hotel Adolphus. When did it come down?"

Harold scratched his chin. "Don't know what you're talking about."

"You never heard of it?"

"Michael, I'm older than dirt and I've been in and out of here forever. And I don't remember any Adolphus."

A slender arm sheathed in white linen wrapped around Savella's waist. "Hey, sailor, you looking for a good time?" Isabella moved around to face him with a broad grin.

"If I was, this would be the last place I'd come," he said.

"And it looks like it's going to be a little longer." She offered a playful frown. "I'm sorry, baby. But gotta work."

Savella waved off the apology. "Not a problem. But I'm going to take off. Call me later?"

"Sure, but—"

"It's nothing. Just something I want to take a look at."

They kissed quickly, she turned back to the room with Harold in tow, and Savella fled.

---

The research assistant who answered the telephone at the *Post-Herald* library had never heard of the Hotel Adolphus, and when he found out it was Savella who was asking, was even less interested in the subject.

"I'm off twenty minutes ago," he snapped. "Try calling when we're open."

Savella hung up and poured himself a drink. Try calling when there's someone here who gives a shit— that's what he meant. But Savella could do some of it himself. He carried his drink to his desk, switched on his computer monitor, and brought up Google. He typed in "Hotel Adolphus" and hit the Enter button. In seconds a website for the hotel, the first of almost 2,500 items, appeared on his screen.

The Hotel Adolphus was apparently a landmark in Dallas, Texas. Regarded as "the most beautiful building west of Venice" when it was opened on Commerce Street in 1912 by the beer magnate Adolphus Busch, the hotel had through the years maintained a reputation for luxury. Rooms went for as much as five hundred dollars a night. Its walls were adorned with museum-quality art. Queen Elizabeth stayed at the Adolphus when she visited Texas in 1991, and the names of the rich and famous of the twentieth century filled its guest book: Irving Berlin, George Burns, Amelia Earhart, B.B. King, Yo-Yo Ma, Mickey Mantle. For years its signature dining room, the Century Room, where men wore coats and ties and women carried furs, had offered the finest cuisine in the city.

Savella rubbed his cheek. What was Mary Bloom doing with a photo taken at a hotel in Dallas? Had she lived there? Was she a guest? Was she one of the women in the picture? He narrowed the search, typing in her name, but there were no matches. A dead end, unless he wanted to cull through 2,500 listings. One click and you get it all. Everything but what you need.

He glanced at his watch. A few minutes before nine. He was in for the night. What else did he have to do?

For the next hour, he drifted through the search results, an enervating collection of city guides and restaurant listings. The name of the Adolphus surfaced in every imaginable hotel guide, from architectural tours to Southern historical sites to gay romantic weekend getaways. Chef William Koval's recipes for roasted red pepper chutney, quick tomato sauce and kid's meatballs, and his pear tart with cardamom Anglais were included. The hotel was the site of the Annual Meeting and Scientific Session of the North American Society for Cardiac Imaging, September 13–16. But it wasn't until just past ten, not until he stumbled across one last crumb, that Savella finally woke up.

"The Hidden History of Dallas," the file was called, a *Dallas Morning News* website. The reference to the Adolphus was in the third paragraph, highlighted in blue, but Savella didn't see it right away. It was another name that grabbed his attention.

Jack Ruby.

The Dallas strip club owner who killed Lee Harvey Oswald, the bitter ex-Marine who assassinated John F. Kennedy, the president of the United States. Ruby's sordid slice of Dallas history, the Carousel Club, was across the street from the hotel.

Savella scrolled down: more detail about the Carousel and Ruby's place in the city's netherworld of strippers and mobsters and cops. And at the very end, a picture. A small fuzzy black-and-white snap that brought Savella to his feet: Jack Ruby and two of his girls, standing outside the Carousel under a marquee announcing the appearance of a stripper named Kathy Kay. The girls were smiling at the boss, who looked impassively at the camera. He was wearing a dark suit, a light-colored shirt, and a tie that blended into oblivion.

"It can't be," Savella said aloud. "Not possible."

He raced across the room for his sports coat, yanked the Mary Bloom photos from the inside pocket, and plucked Night Out from the envelope. Moving back to the monitor, he held the picture up to the screen.

There was no doubt. The man in the Night Out picture was Jack Ruby. And the blonde with the fur across her shoulders and the glass at her lips was one of the girls standing outside the Carousel with a glowing smile for the man who paid her to take off her clothes.

---

A light rain had fallen earlier, and the tires of the cars passing down the street hissed on the wet pavement. Savella went outside and sat under the deck umbrella. The landscaper was midway through his ravaging. The pines were down; the bushes had been ripped from the ground and carted away. In a few days, new topsoil would be spread. When it was ready, there would be flowers and plants and a half dozen saplings. But it would be a long time before they provided protection from the street.

It was quiet, for once. The immigrants who rented rooms and apartments in the houses across the street were at work in the casinos or sound asleep, their homes dark and silent. Nothing in the air but a dog's single bark and the tinkle of wind chimes somewhere down the block.

An old man in baggy shorts and a baseball cap came out on the porch of number thirty. He stood for a minute, smoking a cigarette, then adjusted the bricks that held an American flag to the balustrade, and receded into the shadows, with only the glowing ember of his cigarette to mark him.

Savella sipped his scotch, mostly water by now, after the ice melt.

Kennedy. Oswald. Ruby.

He remembered the first time he heard the names: sitting in the living room with his father watching a television special, an anniversary of the assassination, maybe the tenth, maybe later, the screen filling with mystifying images: a man in the back of a big car, his head recoiling, as a woman in pink reached across the seat; a man in a hat coming out of the crowd in a dingy garage and a firecracker going off and a man in a sweater making a face and falling backward. Later that night, he had crouched in the darkness at the top of the stairs, listening to the sounds of sorrow rising from the guests around his parents' dinner table, quiet talk of a country losing its moorings, adrift at sea, searching for solid ground. Then the music, his father's attempt to lighten the mood, and the party turned raucous, but not nearly loud enough, when he crept downstairs for a glass of milk, to mask his mother weeping in the kitchen.

No safe harbor. And now here was Jack Ruby in Mary Bloom's dressing-table drawer.

# 11

Every afternoon, after the trash was put out, the floors mopped, the leaks repaired, Marek Ravic would return to his basement apartment and work on his English.

He would sit on the sofa, weak sunlight streaking the cushions, and play the tapes over and over again, the strange new language dropping awkwardly from his mouth. The English was everything, if he wanted to succeed in this new land. And he would let nothing get in his way.

Which was why the knock at the door on this quiet afternoon was so annoying. He started at the noise and quickly muted the tape player. There was silence for a moment, then a short series of insistent raps. "Mr. Ravic? Are you in there?" A woman's voice, and he would recognize it anywhere: *Mrs. Lancaster. The building pest.*

"Will you answer?" asked Agnieszka, peeling potatoes at the kitchen counter.

"Quiet. She'll go away."

"Mr. Ravic?" He could hear the locked doorknob slowly turning, first one way, then the other. "Mr. Ravic? I need you." The voice an imperious whine. Another pause, then the door shook from the force of three heavier blows, metal striking wood. "*Spierdalaj,*" he muttered, and then caught himself: "Fuck off." English first, always.

"All right, Mr. Ravic. I'll just wait here until you're through."

It was no use. Marek rose and marched to the door, and yanked it open. Standing in the hallway, an aluminum cane raised in her right hand, was Mrs. Lancaster, a frail woman in purple slippers. She lowered the cane and made a halfhearted attempt to straighten her disheveled gray hair.

"I'm very sorry," she said.

"Yes, yes," he said dismissively. "What, then?"

"It's Miss Bloom's apartment." The woman hesitated. "I think there's someone in there."

Marek frowned.

"No one is there, Mrs. Lancaster. No one. Miss Bloom is *dead*. You see? No one there."

The woman slowly shook her head. "Yes, there is, I'm afraid. I stood at the door and listened. And someone was in Miss Bloom's apartment. There were thumps."

Marek reached into his pants pocket, pulled out a thick jumble of keys, and shook them in Mrs. Lancaster's face.

"You see here? It is keys to apartments. All. No one in Miss Bloom's apartment without a key. And I have. OK?"

Mrs. Lancaster tapped the floor twice with the tip of her cane. "I know what I heard, Mr. Ravic. I heard someone in Miss Bloom's apartment. Just now."

She would not give up until she got her way, Marek glumly realized. "OK, we check. We see." He glanced over his shoulder and shouted, "To 4-C a minute. Mrs. Lancaster hears noises in a dead woman's apartment." He slammed the door, stalked to the elevator, and stood in the cage, glaring, until Mrs. Lancaster finally joined him.

They rode in silence to the fourth floor. Marek threw open the gate and impatiently waited for Mrs. Lancaster to hobble out of the car, then crossed to the Bloom apartment and stood outside the door, fumbling through his key ring.

Inside, something scraped across the floor. Startled, Marek looked up at the number on the door to see if he was at the right apartment. Mrs. Lancaster poked him with a bony finger. "You see?" she whispered.

Marek reached for the doorknob. It was unlocked. He opened the door and poked his head inside the apartment. The smell of cheap cologne filled his nostrils.

"Yes?" he called out. "Who is there?"

The door suddenly flew open. Marek stumbled backward, nearly toppling Mrs. Lancaster. An enormous man wearing black leather gloves appeared in the doorway, ducking to avoid hitting his head on the archway. From a few feet away, he almost appeared to be melting. Tiny streams of perspiration rolled from his wavy black hair, slick with styling gel, and dripped down his pudgy red cheeks. The jacket of his jet-black suit sagged like a garment bag around his shoulders, and the cuffs of his trouser legs drooped dangerously close to the heels of his wingtips. He adjusted his tinted aviator glasses and gazed quizzically at Marek, then Mrs. Lancaster.

"Yes?" he asked, his thick black eyebrows raised in question.

Marek looked up at the man in amazement.

"Yes? What do you mean?" he said. "I am super. Who are you?"

The man smiled and reached for his wallet. "It's OK. I'm a policeman," he said, flashing a badge. "We're investigating a death. I looked for you, but no one was around, so I let myself in."

His smile widened as he turned his attention to Mrs. Lancaster. "Hope I didn't startle you, sweetheart."

Marek was confused. No one had rung his buzzer or knocked on his door until Mrs. Lancaster disturbed his peace. "Miss Bloom died in car accident," he said uncertainly.

"But there were questions. Maybe you can help me. You got a minute?"

Marek hesitated. The police—never good to see them. But to say no, to refuse to help, was worse. "You go home now," he said to Mrs. Lancaster. "I lock up after."

The woman opened her mouth to object, but a glance at Marek's stony face seemed to dissuade her. Leaning on her cane, she plodded down the hallway.

"Always everybody's business," Marek muttered as she unlocked her door and disappeared. With a short laugh, the policeman stepped back and ushered Marek inside.

Mary Bloom's simple world, the two tidy rooms where Marek and Agnieszka had toasted the holidays every winter, seemed in order. Only an open drawer in the kitchen and a small pile of books stacked on the coffee table offered any evidence that anything was out of place. But the air in the apartment, sealed since she left to go shopping and never returned, was hot and stale.

"Let's have a seat and talk for a minute, huh?" said the policeman, waving Marek to the sofa. "What can you tell me about Mary? Friends? Family?"

That question again. Marek groaned softly and sat down. "What?" the policeman said. "Did I say something wrong?" He lifted two snow globes off the top of the bookshelf, shook them, and watched the landscapes turn white.

"She died in car accident," Marek said. "There was funeral, OK? Nobody there. So why now does everybody ask for family, the friends?"

The policeman carefully replaced the snow globes. "Who else?"

Too late, Marek realized he had gone too far. Eyes riveted on the floor, Marek told the story of the funeral, the two men from the newspaper who approached him outside the church, *accosted* him, and asked, *demanded*, to see where Mary Bloom had lived. "I was afraid, so I let them," Marek said. "But that is all. That is all. They look. Nothing more."

The policeman turned back to the souvenirs. "Mary sure got around. The Philadelphia zoo, the aquarium in Baltimore, the Poconos," he said. "So what was it they took?"

Marek glanced nervously at the front door. "What they took?" he said. "Who?"

The policeman walked to the sofa and hovered over him, the smell of his cologne engulfing Marek until he felt faintly nauseous.

"What was it they took?" the policeman said, his tone hardening.

"She died in car accident."

"I asked you a question."

Marek shook his head. The policeman's arms dangled in front of him, sweat drizzling through the cuffs and beading on the black leather gloves. Why would he wear gloves in such warm weather? And leather. On the television they were plastic.

"You are police?" Marek asked.

"I asked you a question."

Marek's stomach churned. What had he done? He should never have allowed the journalists inside, that much was certain, not even for a ride home. And he should never have stood by while they robbed. Did the police know this already? And worse, did they know about the money that he took the day before? Yes, she was dead, but it was not his. He needed time to think.

"Let me please see badge again," he said, straining for bluster. "Your badge."

The policeman walked to the kitchen, drew several steak knives from a wooden block on the counter, and quickly flicked each of them against his thumb before settling on one and dropping the others in the sink. He returned to the sofa and knelt down. Marek wanted to jump up and run, flee to the safety of the basement, but this man—so large, only inches from his face.

"Now, I want an answer." Pressing down firmly with the tip of the knife, the policeman slowly traced a line along Marek's left arm. Tiny red dots appeared from the elbow to the wrist. "What was it they took?"

Marek brushed a finger through the blood. "A box. They took a box. Is all."

"What kind of box?"

Marek's mouth dropped open, but he could not speak. The tip of the knife dug into his skin, deeper this time, and the policeman drew a new line in his arm. "What kind of box?"

"Metal. It was metal." Marek was almost shouting. "With picture of bird. Please. No more."

The policeman smiled, then reached up and rubbed Marek's left shoulder. "It's OK. You don't need to yell. We're gonna be all right here. You just got to help me, is all. Right?"

Marek nodded and fought the urge to cry.

"Good. Good. Now these reporters. Was one of them a guy name of Savella?"

*He knew.* Marek closed his eyes. *The policeman knew all along.* "Savella, yes. And his friend. I did not have his name."

The policeman scraped the nail of his forefinger against the knife blade. "Savella and his friend."

"Yes."

"No one else."

"No."

"And they took a box."

"Yes. The box."

Marek glanced down at the rivulets of blood on his arm. He needed a bandage for the cuts. He needed something for his stomach. He needed for this to be over. But the policeman was speaking again. Marek forced himself to pay attention.

"And you know what was in it, right? The box? Because you went through here first, didn't you? You tossed the place yourself. Sure, you did. That's what supers do."

*He knows about the money.*

"No, no, no," Marek moaned. "I took nothing. Please."

With a deft stroke, the policeman jabbed the tip of the knife into Marek's left cheek, then slapped a meaty palm over his mouth to stifle the scream. He pushed him into the sofa cushions, then sat down and leaned over, so close his lips grazed Marek's ear.

"When I take my hand away, you're gonna tell me," the policeman whispered. "You're gonna tell me what was in the box. Understand?"

Marek nodded. The policeman slowly withdrew his hand.

"A book," Marek gasped. "Black book. Telephone numbers. And photographs. Four, five. And a ring."

"All right. All right." The policeman sat back with a satisfied smile. "Now we're getting somewhere. And you—what did you take?"

"Money. Just...money." Stealing from a friend. It could never come to any good.

"How much?"

"Maybe two hundred. I don't know."

"Dollars?"

"Yes, dollars. Yes. It was wrong."

"Nothing else."

"Nothing." He felt the blade again, a slow probe. "*Nothing.*"

"Only money."

"Only money. Please."

The policeman regarded Marek for a moment, then patted his knee.

"You know something? I believe you. I do. Just the money."

Relief washed over Marek. Maybe it was over.

"But now you're gonna tell me about those photos."

The terror returned. "Just people. Men and women. And a soldier."

"A soldier. What else?"

"I don't know anymore."

"What else?"

"Please."

He felt the bile burn its way to the top of his throat and the first odious taste in his mouth. "That is all I know. Nothing more. Please, I need—"

Marek leaned forward, doubled over and heaving. The policeman twisted away, but not before his shoes were splattered with vomit. When Marek was done, he fell back on the couch and closed his eyes.

The policeman stood and gazed down at his feet. He rubbed the tip of his right shoe against the side of the sofa, then propped his left shoe on the coffee table and used a sofa pillow to wipe it clean. Then he looked at Marek.

"Now, you see? See what you done?" He drew a black handgun from his belt, grabbed the vomit-stained pillow, and shoved it against Marek's head. "You got puke on my shoes," the policeman said. He pressed the pistol deep into the pillow and pulled the trigger. Marek stiffened, then slowly slid off the couch to the floor, coming to rest in the pool of vomit.

The policeman tucked the gun in his belt and slipped out the door, looked down the hallway. *Always everybody's business.* He turned and walked slowly to Mrs. Lancaster's apartment and pressed the buzzer. From inside came the tapping of her cane as she shuffled to the door.

# 12

A black leather satchel sits on the backseat of his car. A bomb, armed and ticking, is inside. He has no idea how it came to be there, and he cannot find a way to defuse it. He paces the sidewalk in a frenzy, punching phone numbers into his cell phone, searching for help, but no one answers. With every breath, an acrid odor fills his nostrils. Suddenly he hears a ferocious banging from inside the car's trunk. He opens it and an old man, dressed in rags and a battered fedora, stumbles out. They walk to a nearby apartment. Inside the phone is ringing, but they ignore it and sit in the window, staring down at the car, waiting. An overwhelming stench, and the phone rings, rings...

Savella bolted upright, arms flailing, and scanned the darkened room. No black satchel on the backseat. No old man in a fedora. *The phone was ringing.* He lunged across the mattress and snatched up the receiver.

"Yes?"

"You seen the paper yet?"

*Bobby.* "What paper? I'm in *bed.*"

"Yeah, me too, soon. Long night. But you're gonna love this. I stop for breakfast and pick up the paper and wanted to make sure you saw."

"What time is it?"

"Little after ten. You listening?"

The dream panic was almost gone now. "Make sure I saw what?"

"Two found slain in AC apartment house." Bobby spoke the words slowly, deliberately, like a determined first grader.

Savella tucked the receiver under his chin and rubbed his eyes. "Bobby, what—"

"Your super."

It took a moment for the two words to register. "What are you talking about, my super?"

"That's the, what do you call it, the headline. In the paper. Someone killed the super. The dead woman's super. In her apartment," Bobby said. "And another old woman—same floor, same deal."

"Gotta go," Savella muttered, and hung up.

---

The morning paper had found the edge of a murky puddle. Savella gingerly blotted it against his T-shirt as he walked back inside the house. He put on some coffee, then spread the *Post-Herald* across the kitchen counter.

The story about the twin killings and a photograph of police detectives ducking under yellow crime scene tape to enter the apartment building covered the top half of the front page. As the coffee trickled into the pot, Savella quickly scanned the *Post-Herald*'s account of the crime. Marek's wife had found him dead in the Bloom apartment after he failed to return from an errand with one of his elderly tenants, who police discovered lying on the floor just inside the door of her own apartment down the hall. Both victims had been shot once in the head—"execution-style," the *Post-Herald* breathlessly noted. Investigators believed the murders were related.

"No kidding," Savella murmured.

The apartment where Marek was killed had been unoccupied since its tenant's recent death in an automobile accident "that also involved a *Post-Herald* employee." That would be me, Savella thought. He had been out of the office yesterday, trying to find a column. And they wouldn't bother to track him down, not the *Ordinary Lives* writer, not for real news, even if he had been there when Mary Bloom took her last breath.

The paper reported that police believed the victims surprised a burglar who used obituaries to target homes likely to be empty. Maybe, Savella thought as he poured a cup of coffee. Or maybe the super and the neighbor died because it was *Mary Bloom's* apartment. Was it possible their killer had been looking for something in particular? Maybe a beat-up address book. Or some old photographs. Or a class ring.

He went into the living room and from his desk retrieved the envelope containing the photographs, the address book, and the ring. Moving to the spool table in the dining room, he pushed the lamp to one side, folded the envelope, and shoved it into the hole in the middle of the table. Then he placed the lamp back over the hole. No sense in taking any chances.

He returned to the kitchen and his coffee. Through the window splattered with mud from the landscaper's efforts, he could see a bare-chested man in shorts walk by, carrying a surfboard. A UPS truck idled at the curb, its driver making a delivery somewhere on the block. Nothing out of the ordinary. Probably blowing this out of proportion, he thought, willing himself to believe anything, *everything*, if it held out the hope of rescue from the trap he'd walked into at the *Post-Herald.* At the end of the day, Mary Bloom was just a tired old woman who had given up on life long before it left her. And Marek Ravic and the neighbor were just unlucky enough to run into a burglar with a gun.

The phone rang again. Savella reached for the phone on the kitchen wall and jerked the receiver off the hook. "*Bobby*—"

There was silence, then a cough.

"No, sorry," a man said uncertainly. "It's Father Remsen. I wonder if you have time for lunch."

---

An Indian summer afternoon, one last encore before the curtain began to fall. Savella parked in the Caesars garage and walked to the Boardwalk, the envelope containing the Bloom artifacts tucked under his arm.

The beach was mostly empty; only a few bathers lay under a handful of red umbrellas poked in the sand. A dog walker with six animals yapping at their leashes struggled along the water's edge. A group of women in swimsuits, their husbands probably inside at the tables, stood and chatted in the shallow surf, their chalk-white arms folded self-consciously as they studied their feet through the spray.

Savella stretched out on a bench and flung his arms along the railing. This five-mile stretch of glitzy casinos, tawdry T-shirt shops, fortune-tellers, and fast-food joints was the pulsing heart of a city where anything went if there was money to be made. Not what it used to be, surely. The buttoned-down corporations that ran the gambling halls had perfected a reliable formula for separating the people from their cash: endless rows of slot machines, upscale stores, and chef-brand restaurants. Not as much excitement as the old days, when the real estate swindlers and the mobsters and the crooked politicians who built the city and who understood the American truth created a perverse melange of the prim and the prurient, where big-busted strippers, scheming beauty queens, Satanya the Ape Girl, and a diving horse were equally valuable star attractions, and a bed in a rooming house seemed like paradise even if the sea breeze died halfway up the block. Not the same, not at all. But the prospect of money for nothing would always enthrall. A slot machine couldn't hold a candle to a freak show, but there was still kick in the blend.

So they kept coming, Savella thought as he sat on the bench and watched the parade in front of him. Three women in sneakers and fanny packs stood outside Caesars, listening to a guitar player sing off-key, his instrument case open for the odd coin. A convoy of old Asians warily made their way down the boards. Four casino supervisors on break, floor badges hanging from the lapels of suit jackets lying in the crooks of their arms, sipped Starbucks and smoked cigarettes.

And there, just beyond them, trudging up the ramp from Missouri Avenue, wrestling with a brown overnight bag slipping off his right shoulder, a burly man dressed in black, a hint of white at his neck.

*My man of God*, Savella thought as he got to his feet.

---

Church business, Remsen had said on the phone, a conference in Philadelphia, but a free afternoon if you've got time. Let's see now, Savella thought as he watched Remsen approach. A dead woman, Jack Ruby in her drawer, two bodies in her building, and a priest who never heard of her turns up out of nowhere. Oh, I've got time.

Remsen stopped at the top of the ramp and looked about uncertainly. Savella waved, and the priest nodded. Savella studied him as he walked over: mid-sixties, a florid face and close-cropped white hair, blinking furiously in the sunlight as if he'd just been released from captivity after many months in a root cellar. Unremarkable except for a curious shuffle, the dread walk of a boxer who'd been knocked down once and fully expected to be floored again.

Remsen extended his right hand. "Mr. Savella?"

"Michael's fine."

Remsen took in his new surroundings, his head twisting and turning like a sparrow searching for worms. Outside Athena, a man munched on a gyro. A lady with two curlers in her hair staggered out of Readings by Angie and spat three times. A pack of teenagers, baseball caps turned backward, taunted a mime in whiteface until he swore at them.

"Not exactly Monte Carlo, is it?" Remsen said.

"You been to Monte Carlo lately?"

The priest's left eyebrow arched ever so slightly. Savella had seen that look before: sixth-grade catechism class. *Funny boy, aren't you? Well, we'll take care of that.*

"Anyway, it's jobs for a lot of people," Savella said.

"There's always a tradeoff, isn't there?" Remsen said as he watched the man with the gyro meticulously fold his paper plate in half and toss it on the ground. "You think you're getting one thing, and find out you signed up for something else entirely."

Savella clapped his hands lightly. "So you mentioned lunch. What're you in the mood for?"

Remsen shrugged. "A sandwich or something."

"There's a place about a block away. Nothing fancy."

"Anything. I'm not particular."

They started up the Boardwalk, weaving through the crowd.

"So you found it all right?"

"Yes. Your directions were very good."

"You're in Philly for a meeting?" Savella said.

"On church business, yes."

"You said a conference?"

"Yes, I did. A conference."

"How long are you here for?" Savella asked.

Loud rock music blared from two speakers outside Mr. Chang's Tattoos. Remsen massaged his temples with his fingertips. "I have to get back tonight."

"Your conference is over?"

"Yes. Oh, yes."

Up ahead, workmen were erecting a set of bleachers in a clamor of buzzing drills and grinding saws. Remsen closed his eyes, a pained look on his face.

"For the beauty pageant," Savella shouted. "There's a parade."

Remsen pinched the sides of his nose. "The noise."

"I'm sorry, Father. I suppose it's quite a change from Illinois."

"So different. I'm out in the middle of the cornfields. Very peaceful. The clients notwithstanding."

"They're recovering addicts?"

Remsen nodded. "Mostly drugs. It's a last chance for them. The next stop is prison."

"Tough work."

"It is. It is. But I enjoy it." He frowned slightly. "I'm a lousy church priest. If you need me on Sunday, I'm not much help. Can't stand up front looking good, making sense of it all. I tried. I did. It just never took. Thought I'd have to give up, until the farm came along."

Savella stopped in front of Taste of Tuscany, six scarred plastic tables, grease-stained airline posters of sunny Italy on the walls, the kitchen area open to the Boardwalk. He took a seat at the metal counter running along the front of the place and motioned to Remsen to join him.

"It's a nice day. You all right out here?"

"Yes. Fine."

The owner, an Iraqi named Tayyab, was behind the grill, moving sausages and hotdogs with a long fork. He looked up through a cloud of smoke and grinned at Savella. "The usual?"

"Sausage and peppers. And a Coke." Savella glanced at the priest. "You want to see a menu?"

"No, no." Remsen shook his head impatiently and placed his overnight bag on the counter. "What you're having."

"Two of them, Tayyab," Savella called out, resting his elbows on the countertop.

"So how can I help?" Remsen asked.

Savella opened the manila envelope and teased out the funeral photo: the middle-aged Mary, standing behind the counter in her hostess uniform. "This is Mary Bloom."

The priest took it in his hands and inspected it. He blinked rapidly as he moved his left thumb lightly over the photograph. "No, I don't think so," he said. "I don't think I know her."

"Looks a little like this woman, doesn't it?" Savella handed him the black-and-white photo of the older woman in the sweatshirt standing in front of the small house. "They could almost be the same person, don't you think?"

Remsen's breath quickened and he rocked slightly from foot to foot. Then he placed the picture carefully on the counter. "This must be twenty, thirty years old. Maybe more. I don't recognize her, but it could be a girl we worked with. It *could* be."

Savella pulled out GI Joe and Airplane and laid them in front of Remsen. "How about these guys?"

Remsen quickly shook his head. "Where did you get these?"

"From her apartment. Why do you ask?"

The priest tapped the counter with his finger. "You said you attended the funeral?"

"Yes. And I was pretty much it."

"No one else was there?"

"That's right. In fact, the priest didn't know her. She'd gone ahead and planned the thing herself. She left a note laying out the whole deal, right down to the Bible readings."

"Really. Which ones?"

"Hang on, I have it in here." Savella dug out his notebook and flipped through the pages until he found what he was looking for. "Ezekiel eighteen twenty. And Romans twelve, seventeen twenty-one. You familiar with either of them?"

That catechism class look again. "I'm not much of a church priest," Remsen said slowly, "but I've read my Bible."

"They mean anything to you?"

Remsen shook his head. "Strange there was no one at the funeral of a woman who moved out here so many years ago."

"How do you know that?" Savella asked.

"Know what?"

"You said she moved out here so many years ago. *Out* here. That's what you said."

"Oh, I—on the phone, you—"

"No, I said the obit said she was an area resident for many years. That's all."

"Well, she moved here from somewhere. That's the way I took it."

Tayyab placed two tall Cokes in front of them. Remsen unwrapped a straw and dropped it in his drink.

"How about the address book?" Savella asked. "Want to take a look?" He drew it from the envelope and pushed it in front of the priest, opened to the Rs. Remsen ran his finger down the page until he found his name. His brow tightened and his shoulders twitched into a slight slump. His eyes darted from side to side like some defenseless prey fearful of a trap. Then he moved a finger to the page and slowly rubbed it.

"I have no idea why my name is in here," Remsen said, his voice firm, unshakeable. "I'm sorry I can't help."

Savella pointed at the Remsen listing in the middle of the page. "Your latest number. And some old ones as well. You know, when we spoke on the phone, I got the impression that those last two listings meant a little more to you than you let on. The seminary, I mean, and the five-digit number."

Remsen frowned, pulled his finger away. "The seminary was the seminary. I hadn't thought of it in many years. That's all. And I have no idea what the other one was. Look, I don't know why my name is in here. Maybe she needed help. Maybe she needed someone to talk to, and she remembered the help we offered her. If we offered her any. I don't know. In any event, she lived in New Jersey."

"A lot of Illinois numbers in her book."

"It's a big state."

"Just a coincidence, huh?"

"A lot of people."

"You want to take a look at some of the other listings?" Savella said. "Maybe you'll recognize some names." He pushed the book closer to the priest, but Remsen ignored it.

"What did she do?" he asked. "For a living."

"Worked in a restaurant. Retired a few years ago."

"Was there a husband?"

Savella shook his head.

"Or children?"

"Not that I know of."

"So she lived alone."

"Yes."

"Around here?"

"Not too far. An apartment on the beach."

The priest aimlessly tugged at the zipper of his bag. "Are her things still there? Perhaps if I could see her home, maybe something might, I don't know, remind me who she was. If I ever knew her."

"That might be a problem."

"Why's that?"

"It's a crime scene, the apartment."

Remsen looked bewildered. "Crime scene? I thought you said an auto accident."

"Tayyab," Savella said, "you have today's paper?"

The owner ducked under the cash register, came up with a *Post-Herald,* and tossed it along the counter. Savella spread the paper in front of Remsen. A blob of ketchup and spilled coffee had stained the front page, obscuring the picture of the detectives outside the building, but the headline was impossible to miss. Remsen bent down and began to read.

"This is her apartment?" he said, a note of surprise in his voice.

"That's right. And her super and her neighbor."

The priest opened his mouth as if to speak, but instead continued reading. A few minutes later, he slowly refolded the paper. "Very sad," he murmured.

"Just another coincidence?" Savella said.

Remsen stared at him. "What are you suggesting?"

"We talk on the phone, then two people are murdered in Mary's apartment house. And you turn up for lunch."

"I told you. I had business in Philadelphia."

"Yes, you said. A church conference. And you got in a car and drove down here."

"I felt it was my responsibility. I thought if I did know Mary..." His voice trailed off.

*Mary. Finally.*

"A couple more, Father." Savella dipped into the envelope and pulled out the class ring. The priest examined the inscription around the stone, then placed it on the counter without a word. One last shot, Savella thought. He laid Scarf and Night Out in front of Remsen. "I think the girl in the scarf might be the girl on the end in the banquette." He tapped the two images, first one, then the other. "Her and her."

The color drained from Remsen's face. His knees buckled, and for a few seconds he seemed to be struggling to stay on his feet. He pushed the photographs away and turned his back to the counter.

"I have no idea. I have never seen her before in my life," he said, considering each word, every syllable before he spoke, making absolutely sure that nothing in his tone would lead Savella to believe he wasn't telling the truth. And it was precisely the way he spoke that convinced Savella, once and for all, that Father Joseph Remsen was lying.

Savella picked up the photos. "Why don't you take another look?"

"I said no. Let's leave it alone."

"Well, this one's kind of interesting," Savella said, holding up Night Out. "This guy here, this is Jack Ruby. You know Jack Ruby?" Remsen was silent. "Sure you do, a man your age. Ruby killed Lee Harvey Oswald, the man who shot President Kennedy. Remember? And I did a little research. This was taken in a restaurant in Dallas. I don't know why Mary Bloom had a picture of Jack Ruby sitting in a restaurant in Dallas. And if I'm right and that's her, what was she doing there?"

Remsen fingered his collar. "I have no idea."

Lunch, on white paper plates: sub rolls stuffed with Italian sausage, sautéed peppers, and charred onions. Savella carefully slid the photos closer to Remsen, picked up his sandwich, and took a bite. "Very hot," he said, cupping his hand under his chin to catch a stray onion. "You'll want to be careful."

But Remsen wasn't hungry. He gripped the counter edge with both hands, holding on so tightly that his knuckles whitened, his head turned just enough to avoid the sight of the photographs that had upset him. It made no sense, Savella thought. Remsen knew Mary Bloom—that much was certain. So why wouldn't he admit it? All he needed to do was express sadness at her lonely death, say he hadn't seen her in years, and move on. What in the world would prevent him from doing that?

Savella finished eating, plucked a napkin from the plastic holder on the counter, and carefully wiped his hands and mouth. "So can we cut to the chase here, Father? Who was she?"

A pained look crossed the priest's face. "What is it you don't understand?" he said, loudly enough that Tayyab glanced up from the grill. "I tried to help you. I thought I might know her. I was wrong." He reached for his bag, slung it over his shoulder. "Now I have to get back."

"You're not gonna eat?"

Remsen shook his head. Savella scooped up the photos, the ring, and the address book and dropped them in the envelope. "OK. We'll leave it there. For the moment. But it's *Mary* now, right, Father? Not *her*. Not *she*. Mary."

Remsen adjusted the strap on his bag and began walking up the Boardwalk. Savella dropped a twenty-dollar bill on the counter and hurried after him, and they headed back the way they had come, neither pausing to notice the large man in the dark suit on a bench a block away, mopping his sweaty neck with a handkerchief as he pretended to read the newspaper.

---

The colonel stood at the phone, the receiver pressed to his ear, and listened to the boarding calls on the public-address system in an airport two thousand miles to the north. A collect call and the news wasn't good. The cops were involved now. Don Arturo knew finesse. But the fucking son—always with the sledgehammer.

He stood at the phone in a torn flannel shirt, smelling faintly of Bengay and cigarettes, and sorted through the damage. The reporter, let him ask his questions. The phone book and the class ring—a long shot to make a connection.

But *pictures*.

Joey was rattled, no doubt about it. Sounded like he'd just seen a ghost and face it, he had. The colonel talked him off the ledge, but you never know. Then the PA crackled in the background—*final boarding call for US Air Flight 3153*—and Joey hung up and headed home.

The colonel moved to the veranda and watched the tankers making their way east through the Sir Francis Drake Channel. A good day for sailing, he thought, a good day for getting away. Maybe one more beer.

This place—his cocoon, for so long, but that was over now. She had found him, flushed him out after all these years, and already the air smelled stale, the birds sounded flat.

*Pictures.*

He frowned and clawed at his unshaven cheeks.

*Pictures.*

Christ almighty, but that was the jackpot.

# 13

The Key West documents spread across Washington like a summer breeze, darting into a committee chamber on the Hill, lingering at a think tank on Massachusetts Avenue, scattering papers on desks all across town. Richard Miller's offering was good stuff, Grade A prime, Cubans and terror and Commies, and how many of *them* were left to gnaw on? And so phones rang and e-mails beeped, because what's the point of having secrets if no one knows you have them? Miller's voice mail was full, people paying attention, never mind his Gilbert and Sullivan title, undersecretary of who cares what. Richard Miller was *it*—well, we knew that all along.

Miller bunkered in his office, working the telephone, pleading the case against Cuba until the cleaning crews swarmed the floor around ten, sending him home to forage for scraps in the refrigerator before falling in full suit onto the lumpy pullout couch in his study to which Lidia had crossly banished him for the duration. She had never seen him like this.

"Don't you have people?" she whined when he called to say he'd have to miss the Mahler at the Kennedy Center. And no he didn't. Cuba was all his.

But it wasn't enough.

On a rainy Tuesday morning, the task force gathered in his office, a cramped space in a building six long blocks from State, exiled among the purchasing departments and payroll divisions strewn across the government landscape, sharing space with podiatrists and drugstores and H&R Block. The meeting was an unmitigated mauling. CIA set the tone early, referring to the documents as the Crotch Papers. Justice had the room in giggles with a tale of how a ten-year-old with an Apple, an imagination, and some translation software could have done the job. NSA wondered why someone would go to such lengths when any one of the dozens of foreign reporters crawling around Havana these days would have gladly brought the documents back in his suitcase.

It was left to Rodney Keep from Defense to deliver the kill shot.

"You think the Cubans are sitting in Havana this morning plotting war against the United States of America?" he asked, drawing smiles around the table. "Is that what you really, truly believe? The Cubans are coming, the Cubans are coming? In a fleet of Dodge Caravans?"

"I'm not sure you're appreciating the gravity of the situation, Rodney," Miller said. "Not sounding the alarm loud enough, Dick? Let's see, help me out here. Civilians screaming for war, intel saying hold on, no evidence. When's the last time that happened? How'd that turn out? Anybody?"

Richard Miller versus ridicule, and Miller never stood a chance.

His mano-a-mano with the secretary of state was an even bigger train wreck. Lois Elshak demanded his presence at nine sharp, then left him cooling his heels for seventy-nine minutes while she entertained a group of sixth graders—*schoolchildren*, with the national security hanging in the balance. When finally he was summoned, she was on the telephone. An attractive woman, Miller had to admit, elegant in a beautifully tailored pantsuit. The people's diplomat, a columnist once called her, equally comfortable in evening gowns or frayed khakis, negotiating arms deals with the president of Russia or piling her aides into a convoy of Chevy Suburbans and heading out for empanadas. Miller never got an empanada. To Elshak, he was a right-wing spy, and she despised him.

Elshak hung up, came around the desk, sat down on a beige settee, and pointed Miller to a spindly, thinly cushioned chair. "You want to tell me what the hell you're doing over there?" she asked.

"Over where?"

"In your little cave. I'm hearing you're planning the invasion of Cuba."

"Well, we're working on the papers from Florida."

Elshak slowly shook her head.

She gave him the floor and he used it to weave the odd pieces of string he had collected from around the globe into a sinister quilt: the animal feed plant outside Havana that was actually being used to produce chemical and biological weapons; the elite force of special operations troops who vanished from a secret base in Pinar del Rio province six weeks ago; the Cuban cancer specialist who pulled aside an American colleague at a symposium in Tokyo to warn of dark doings—"something soon." And when Elshak shook her head—*not buying this, Richard*—he laid out the consequences, courtesy of a mock-attack exercise in Chicago: germs released in a terminal at O'Hare and a hockey game downtown. People complaining of fever and chills would start trickling into emergency rooms; in a few days, thousands would be dying all over the Midwest. Hospitals would run out of doctors and nurses, beds and equipment, leaving the untreated to wander the streets, infecting others. The final death toll: fifty thousand, maybe more.

When he finished, Elshak was quiet for a moment. Then she sighed deeply, a disappointed mother. "Old news, Richard," she said. "Asked and answered, thoroughly vetted and rejected by intelligence professionals, not college professors. Which is how we do it."

"And the papers? What about the papers?"

"Fakes," Elshak said. "Worthless fakes."

Miller struggled to control his temper. "Where did they come from, you would have to ask."

The secretary shrugged. "Some exile shit, no doubt. I mean, how much sense does this make? Cuba's going to attack us? Aside from everything else, we have a military base on the island. You may have heard of it. Guantanamo? Just because the Castros are old doesn't mean they've gone round the bend."

Miller started to object, but she raised her hand. "Richard, maybe there's a new day in Cuba. Raul's in charge now. It could be he's a different sort. You think Fidel's going to spring out of bed one morning and sprint back to his office—thank you very much, *mi hermano*, but I believe you're in my chair. Uh-uh. Not going to happen. So let's see how it plays out, how Raul handles things. The economy, for instance."

"I didn't fight all this time for lower milk prices, Lois."

Elshak rose and moved back behind her desk, busied herself leafing through a pile of papers. "Here's the thing, Richard," she said, not bothering to raise her head. "I want you to stop this now. No more Key

West documents. No more going to war with Cuba. No more."

"Lois, I cannot stress enough the catastrophe—"

"*Knock it the fuck off.*"

The disappointed mother, furious, and Miller sent to his room.

The talk switched to the weather and then the Redskins before an aide appeared to remind the secretary her next appointment was waiting.

A dead end, Miller thought as he headed back to his office, six long blocks from the center of the action. A handful of people made the big decisions, and Elshak was one of them. And they would cut you off at the knees if you tried to sidestep them, go public with your arguments.

But that was really all she'd left him.

# 14

The list was waiting when Savella slipped into the office a little after two, eleven neatly printed names "From The Desk Of Henry Kipp" placed squarely in the middle of his empty desk. Candidates for the *Ordinary Lives* treatment, if only in the publisher's mind. Savella had seen these names before, made a few perfunctory calls, and forgot about them. But this list served notice that ignoring the suggestions would no longer be possible. On the top, in black ink with an unsteady hand, someone had painstakingly drawn a question mark. *Henry Kipp,* Savella thought. And on the bottom, someone with a firmer grip and less time to waste had messily scrawled the words "See Me" in large, looping red letters. *Janice Garabedian,* Savella knew.

He stole a careful look at the editor's office. The privacy blinds were raised and the lights were off. A busy time of year, he knew: the American Beauty pageant and all its related events seemed to require her constant presence far from the newsroom. With any luck he could hang around the office long enough to be noticed, then slide out before she came in. He hadn't the energy for a confrontation today.

Savella scanned the list again. His job hung in the balance. But these he couldn't do. And now, from Janice, "See Me." He couldn't avoid her forever. One day soon she would come up for air and wonder where the hell he was. There wasn't much he could do about that. Or wanted to. But not today. Not on a day when he awoke with such optimism, a day that started, for whatever reason, with promise, playing out like a movie in his mind, every image so clear, every detail so crisp—the dents in the blue van parked across the street, the gleam on the brass doorknob on the house around the corner, the petals of the last lingering flowers in a peeling window box up the block.

Janice soon enough. Just not today.

He reached into his pocket for Mary Bloom's phone book. Savella worked through it every day, a page at a time, A to Z and back again, dialing and redialing the unanswered numbers, willing someone to pick up. Most of the time, no one did, and when there was an answer, it was always Mary who, or sorry, wrong number, or I'm on the don't-call list. But Savella refused to quit. He ran each name and number in Mary Bloom's address book through every search engine and database he could find. And when all of that turned up nothing, he opened the book to the As and started dialing again.

It surprised him, this insistence on finishing the job. Mary Bloom had become important to him for reasons he couldn't yet understand. The task of tracking her down, no matter how enervating, had taken on the aura of a crusade, especially after the meeting with Remsen. The priest and the reporter had parted with a polite handshake and Remsen's hollow promise to stay in touch. But Savella left the Boardwalk certain that Mary Bloom was no stranger to Joseph Remsen.

"Just the fact that he came out here tells you something," he told Isabella last night. The casino lounge was dark once a week, and she liked to make dinner, her way of relaxing. Last night it had been pasta with a marvelous veal ragu and a leisurely slide through a nice Sangiovese. Afterward, Savella sat at the small kitchen table and debated the merits of opening a second bottle, which stood for the moment on the counter near the toaster. Isabella was at the sink, elbow deep in soapsuds.

"So that's something right there," Savella said. "I get him on the phone and he's polite, but he doesn't know who I'm talking about. Then he turns up here. The guy runs some kind of rehab center in Illinois, and all of a sudden he has pressing business in Philadelphia? Come on."

He was silent for a few moments, listening to the sloshing of the water in the sink, the clash of china as Isabella moved the dishes to the drying rack.

"You want me to get the rest of that?" he asked.

"No, I'm almost done. Finish your wine. Keep talking."

Savella looked around the room. Her Very Brady Kitchen, she liked to call it, the cabinets covered in yellow and orange laminate, the linoleum floor faded and cracking, the appliances straight out of the seventies. Ugly, yes, but the kitchen was her refuge, the one place other than the stage where she felt truly safe. Everything in it had meaning. The smoked blue vase that she filled every week with irises had been brought from Siena by her mother's mother. The ceramic bowl on the windowsill where she kept her rings while she was cleaning had been in her father's family since the turn of the last century. Even the tiny table where they ate had been rescued from the curb after the death of the old man next door for whom Isabella had made coffee nearly every morning.

Savella drained the last of his wine, then got up to open the other bottle. "Then there's our conversation, if you want to call it that. Every question seemed to set him off. And his reaction to the photos—he wouldn't even *look* at a couple of them, and he touched some others like they were religious relics." Savella filled his glass, brought the bottle to the table, and sat down again. "No, Remsen knows more than he told me. The guy didn't want to admit to knowing a dead woman. A *priest*. A priest who lied. What is it about Mary Bloom that leads a priest to lie?"

Isabella rinsed off the last plate and turned off the taps. "So what are you going to do?"

He paused to gather his thoughts. Isabella peered down at him, brushed a wayward strand of hair from her face. A soap bubble appeared on her nose, then burst.

"Keep making calls, I guess. But how it winds up... Look, if I don't come up with something, I'm going to lose my job."

Isabella wiped her hands on a dish towel, retrieved her rings, then pulled out a chair and sat down. Savella held up the bottle; she shook her head. "Did I ever tell you about my uncle Buddy?" she said. "My father's older brother?"

"Uncle Buddy. Jesus, where are you *from?*"

Isabella reached for the candle in the middle of the table and blew out the flame. "Buddy was a salesman, paper goods. When he got older, he started losing his hair and right around the same time, his business started to dry up. His boss told him it was because he was balding. 'Customers don't trust you, Buddy. You gotta do something, Buddy.' That sort of deal. So he got a thing"—she tugged at her bangs—"a hairpiece. And just like that his business picked up. Not like the old days, but enough to get by."

"But he hated it. Hated wearing the thing. And when he died, there was this big debate about whether he should be buried in it. And my dad finally said no, forget it, that wasn't Buddy. That's what they wanted him to be, but it wasn't Buddy. So leave it off. You go out you." She flaked some wax from the candlestick onto the tablecloth and swept it into her hand. "So go out you."

Savella wanted to hug her, hold on tight to every last burns-my-toast and Uncle Buddy in her. *So go out you.* Made sense, if you knew who you were, and he was beginning to think he did. So he would dial.

---

For the next hour, as the newsroom slowly filled, he moved through the book, from A to Z and back again, calling the numbers he hadn't reached, special attention to the handful that carried no area code, working through an ever-expanding circle of possibilities— South Jersey to Central Jersey to North Jersey, then New York, Philadelphia, Wilmington. A disheartening task; it would be Christmas, maybe Easter before he reached Alaska and Hawaii. In ninety minutes he had one conversation, an old man speaking a language Savella couldn't identify, and there was a wait until a neighbor who spoke English came on the line. It was Farsi; the old man was an Iranian who had fled to America last year to be near his daughter, a software consultant thirty years younger than Mary Bloom. One number to cross off, anyway.

Savella pushed ahead until he reached the Zs for a second time, then closed the book. A day that had held such promise, and where had it ended? He surveyed what he could see of the newsroom over the top of his cubicle wall, the colors faded to beige and gray, the sounds muted, the voices strained and worried, what was left of the morning's vibrancy slipping away.

On the edge of his desk, someone had left a copy of the *New York Times*. Savella glanced at the front page, which was dominated by a three-column wire photo of a group of soldiers, children, really, in ragtag uniforms, crammed onto the flatbed of a Toyota pickup kicking up dust as it careered down a bush road somewhere. In a flash the memories overwhelmed him. He had seen them all over the world: bandanas around their foreheads, gold chains on their necks, so weighed down by bandoliers they couldn't balance their bicycles, offering mocking smirks that dared you to defy them. They would give way, but only at the last moment, and only after making sure you knew it was their choice, their decision to let you by. Sometimes, when he was very brave or very stupid, Savella would hold their stares until he saw the flicker that confirmed his suspicions: little boys trying hard to be men. A dangerous game; they could kill in a heartbeat. But most of them wouldn't want to. They were only playing adult.

All over the world: boys with guns, sent to fight the wars, youngsters pushed kicking and screaming into manhood, or what passed for it. Boys with guns, masked boys with rifles and bombs and camo pants and suicide belts, and not a clue in the world about the chaos they would cause. In the end, boys with guns drove him to this place.

But now he had to get away, from the picture, from the publisher's dead friends, from the past the newsroom represented and the future it would never hold for him. As he threaded his way toward the door, he stole a glance at Janice's office: empty, the lights out, Cynthia refreshing her makeup in a small mirror, something she wouldn't dream of doing if the boss were around. Near the reception desk Scott Williams, a smirk on his smarmy face, came toward him with his right hand outstretched until Savella's dark glare made him think better of it, just this once. Savella pushed open the front doors and walked into the fading sunlight. Autumn, he thought, the best season. A cusp, a beginning or an end, or the beginning of the end, you never knew. He took a deep breath and headed for his car. I tried, Savella told himself, Lord knows I tried. And maybe he did and maybe he didn't, but in the end it wouldn't really matter.

A public works truck was parked at the curb in front of Savella's house when he returned home. The sewer on the corner had backed up again, flooding the street, and now, as Savella pulled into his driveway, two workmen in orange safety vests pried off the manhole cover. One threaded a hose coiled on the truck's grille into the sewer; the other man stationed himself next to a control panel mounted on the side of the truck. When the hose had played out, he flipped a switch. A low hum turned to a loud drone as a stream of water shot into the sewer to break up the clog.

Savella unlocked the front door and stepped inside, skirting the stack of mail that had been shoved through the slot. The late-afternoon sun streamed through the windows, a new development since the trees came down. He bent down to retrieve the mail: shopping circulars, the *New Yorker*, a few bills—all of it could wait. Savella laid his keys on the coffee table and shrugged off his jacket, then fell onto the sofa.

He was suddenly aware of a pungent odor hanging in the air. The sewer work? He hadn't smelled it outside. Maybe a dead mouse.

From the kitchen, a muffled thud, the sound of something rolling on the linoleum. Savella lifted his head and listened. Through the open front door came the harsh hum of the water hose. Then a different noise, from the back of the house this time, a rumbling, maybe heavy footfalls, and a soft *thwack*, like something banging into the wall.

Savella rose, took a few tentative steps toward the kitchen.

"Hello?" he called out. There was no answer. He searched the living room for a weapon. The scissors on the desk would do. He made a fumbling attempt to find a comfortable grip, then abandoned the effort. As if he could actually stab somebody.

Another noise from the rear—creaking floorboards? "Who's there?" he shouted, his voice trembling slightly. Now a sound he instantly recognized—the rattle of the back screen door.

Savella tiptoed through the dining room and into the kitchen. The unpleasant odor again, stronger here. Three of his cabinet doors were ajar, and the junk drawer under the microwave was pulled open several inches. Had he left it that way in the morning, when he was looking for a filter to make a cup of coffee that sat now, untouched, at the edge of the sink? As he moved farther into the room, his right foot kicked an empty scotch bottle. He had finished it last night, left it on the counter in front of the kitchen window, which was now cracked open a few inches. It wouldn't be the first time he'd forgotten to lock up before he left. And one gust of wind could have knocked the bottle to the floor—that would account for the rolling sound as it rattled to a rest against the wall.

He placed the bottle back on the counter, then crept past the refrigerator, and ducked through the doorway. Three steps led down to the back door, which was wide open. Couldn't have left it that way, he thought. But maybe he hadn't shut it tightly. He did that sometimes, when he was just running out to the deli for a coffee and couldn't find his house keys. Maybe the wind that knocked over the scotch bottle also pushed open the unlatched door.

Savella slipped down the short flight of steps and out to the driveway. The drone had stopped. The workmen were coiling the hose on the front of the truck. A blue van pulled away from the curb, edged around the traffic cones, and headed down the street. The sidewalks were empty.

Savella went back inside and quickly checked his bedroom, which seemed as he left it in the morning—bed unmade, dirty clothes and wet towels on the floor, scraps of paper scattered across the dresser. He climbed the stairs to the second floor. The doors to the bathroom and two bedrooms were shut tight; the storage space was locked. He was certain no one had been upstairs since the roofer patched the leak.

Downstairs he returned to the living room. The foul odor was beginning to fade. He sniffed the air, trying to identify it. Sweat, maybe, or an aftershave, or a cheap cologne. The creaking floorboards, the footfalls—maybe a neighborhood kid attracted by the open back door? But a kid drenched in cologne? Calm down, he told himself. Maybe the smell had come from the outside after all, from the bowels of the clogged sewer, stirred up by the work crew's water hose. Reassuring to think so. The alternative was alarming: someone had been inside his home, rifling through his things. Still, nothing seemed to be missing.

Unless...

Savella reached the spool table in the dining room in three long strides. He shoved the lamp in the middle to one side and reached down into the hole. The envelope was still there. He let out a long breath and felt himself relax. Let the kids have what they want. Mary Bloom's effects were the only valuables in his life right now.

He plucked the phone book from his jacket pocket and returned it to the envelope, squeezed the package back into its cave. Probably nothing, he thought. Probably nobody broke in, no curious kid, no sweaty body wandered through his home. All the same, tomorrow he would make copies of the Bloom stuff. You never knew about a fire.

"Mr. Savella?" A voice, at the front door. "Michael Savella?"

He moved the lamp over the hole and stepped back into the living room. A woman in a black pantsuit and yellow blouse was standing in the door, holding a wallet open to a gold badge. "It's the police," she said brightly. "Detective Feidy, ACPD. Mind if I come in?"

Confused, he shuffled closer, then stopped. "Is this about the back door?"

"I'm sorry?"

"I guess I left it open. Did somebody call?"

The question was barely out before he knew he was wrong. Police detectives weren't sent out to investigate reports of open doors.

"I have no idea what you're talking about," she said with an apologetic smile. "Can I come in?"

Savella waved her ahead. "Oh, of course, sure. Sorry for the confusion. I just got home."

The woman carefully shut the door. "You shouldn't leave this open like that. Neighborhood's not that safe."

He nodded. "So I'm beginning to find out."

The detective gazed at him, patient, waiting.

"Oh, it's nothing, probably," Savella said. "When I came in, I heard some noises and thought I might have surprised a burglar. The back door was wide open. But I think maybe I must not have shut it all the way when I left this morning."

"Nothing missing?"

"No. Well, I don't know for sure. Nothing *seems* to be missing."

Feidy took in the room, pausing at his desk, a mess, as usual. Had the papers been moved? Impossible to tell. That file drawer, had he left that open? He couldn't remember. The old mahogany swivel chair, was that turned in a different direction last night? Maybe.

The detective ambled through the dining room and poked her head into the kitchen. Savella followed a few steps behind her. For one crushing moment, he saw the place as she must: a loner's refuge, peeling plaster, mismatched furniture, a stack of magazines propping up a table, a liquor-store calendar tacked to the wall, an empty scotch bottle on the kitchen counter. If he'd known she was coming, he would have—done nothing. It was the badge, he decided. If she didn't have a badge, he wouldn't even care.

Feidy glided back toward the living room, an economy of motion that suggested a ballerina, perhaps, or a professional athlete, comfortable with every muscle and tendon, confident of her body's response to any challenge. Late thirties, Savella guessed, pretty in a no-nonsense sort of way: not tall, not short, a practical height; slender but not skinny, a demure hint of generous breasts tucked under her tailored jacket. Her dusky skin bore only a hint of makeup; her hair, chocolate brown with subtle red highlights, was pulled back into a tight ponytail, easy to manage as she ran late out of the house in the morning. Her dark eyes were alert, beds of coal set above a wide, expressive mouth. Only two discordant notes: a pair of earrings you couldn't miss, slivers of irregularly stacked polished stone, like columns of an old wall along a country lane. And she smelled faintly of lavender.

A few sinuous steps and she was at the sofa. "Can I sit?"

"Please." Savella rushed forward to move a pile of newspapers to the floor. Feidy perched on the edge of the cushion, placed her purse beside her. Savella retreated to the armchair across the coffee table. "So you're not here about my door."

"No. They told me at your office that you left for the day." Feidy produced a business card from her jacket pocket and held it out to him. "Marek Ravic's wife gave this to me."

*Ravic. The building superintendent.* Savella leaned across and stared at his card, remembering the chance encounter outside the church.

"You do know he was murdered?" she said.

"Well, yeah. I mean, it made the front page."

"Would you tell me where you met Mr. Ravic?"

"At a funeral. A woman named Mary Bloom. She lived in his building."

"She was a friend of yours?"

Savella shook his head. "She died in an auto accident. A fender bender. I was driving the car she ran into. Guess she had a stroke."

"You didn't know her before the accident?"

"I didn't."

"Why'd you go to her funeral?"

Savella shrugged. "Out of respect, I guess. And I was hoping to write a story about her."

Feidy blinked slowly three times, as if she were trying to clear her vision. "A story about Mary Bloom?"

"Yes."

"Why?"

Savella nodded toward the business card in Feidy's hand. "That's kind of what I do at the paper."

"You write the obituaries?"

"Not actually," he said, with a faint grin.

The detective smiled. "Is that funny?"

"I write the *Ordinary Lives* column. It runs every few weeks. Just stories about some of the...*quirks*, I guess, about otherwise ordinary people who die." He frowned. The explanation made him feel even worse about his job. "Obituaries-plus, maybe."

"What was her quirk?"

"That was the thing. It was her obituary. There was nothing in it. No friends, no family, no jobs, no clubs, no volunteer groups, no place to send contributions in lieu of flowers. Nothing. Pretty strange for a sixty-five-year-old woman. So I went to the funeral. No one showed up there either. Except Ravic. Well, he showed up, but late. And I thought maybe he could help."

"Did he?"

Savella crossed his legs, then uncrossed them again. What did Ravic tell his wife? "Yes, he did. I wanted to see her apartment and he agreed to let me in. In exchange for a ride home."

Feidy scribbled some notes on a pad that had suddenly appeared on her knee. "How'd he seem to you? Was he agitated, nervous?"

"He seemed OK. Well, I mean, he was nervous, I guess. About the apartment."

"Letting you in, you mean?"

"Right. Not wanting anyone to know he was doing it. He kind of stood guard outside."

"Did he mention any problems he was having with a tenant? An argument, maybe?"

"No. I really didn't talk much with him. At the church I asked him what he knew of Mary, and it wasn't a whole lot. He liked her, thought she was a nice person, was sad about her death. Took the time to show up for the funeral, even if he was late. And when he understood that I wanted to write, you know, a nice piece about her, he was cooperative."

"And how about the woman who was killed the same day, Ruth Lancaster? Did you see her?"

"No. Like I said, he took us upstairs, let us in the—"

Feidy raised a hand. "Us?"

"Yeah. A friend of mine was with me."

"Who's that?"

"Bobby Weiss."

The pad appeared on the knee again. "W-?" Savella spelled it for her. "He's another reporter?"

"No."

"What's he do?"

"He manages a T-shirt factory."

"A T-shirt factory."

"Yeah. Eddie's Sportswear. Uptown."

"You always take along the manager of a T-shirt factory when you're working on a story?"

"No. But he was at the funeral and just...decided to come along."

"Did he know her?"

"No, uh-uh."

"So he was at the funeral because...?"

"He was in the car with me when she hit us."

Feidy put down her pen and sighed. "You know, Mr. Savella, this would go a lot faster if I didn't have to drag it all out of you."

"I'm sorry, I am." He spread his hands, palms upturned. "It's just—I'm usually the one asking the questions."

"How do you and Mr. Weiss know each other?"

"We met a few years ago. When I first came to town."

"Mmm. OK, Mr. Ravic takes you upstairs to the apartment. The two of you went in? You and Mr. Weiss?"

"Right."

"And Mr. Ravic?"

"Waited outside."

"What did you do inside?"

"Looked around. Tried to get a feel for the woman."

Feidy laid the pad on the sofa, sat back, and folded her arms across her chest, the pen poking up from her balled right fist. "Did you take anything? You didn't maybe grab a picture to go with your article?"

Savella didn't answer right away, and the detective didn't rush him. Which was fine, because they had reached a crossroads and he had no idea which way to go. He had committed a crime in Mary Bloom's apartment that day, a minor one, to be sure, but he broke the law. Harmless enough at the time—she was dead and who would ever know—but now it threatened to drag him into a *murder* investigation. And try to explain it. Let's see now, me and Bobby—*Bobby!*—and the Polish super go into the apartment of a dead woman, a woman who rammed my car a couple of days before and who I was going to write a column about but never did, and rummage through her shelves, her closets, her *underwear* before stealing a box of pictures from her bed table. Just old snapshots, Detective, I swear, except Jack Ruby's in one of them, you know, the guy who killed the guy who killed the president. Tell the *truth?*

He cleared his throat. "The apartment was kind of weird. She didn't have any pictures on the walls, on the bookshelves, that sort of thing. Struck me as odd, a woman her age."

"Yes, I noticed that."

Savella felt his body relax. He'd somehow escaped the trap and hadn't even really lied. Feidy picked up the pad and jotted another note. As her head tilted, the sunlight caught the earrings, splashing his faded white stucco walls with traces of rainbow.

"Those are nice earrings," he said.

She looked up, her face a blank, as if she were trying to ferret out the motivation for his compliment before committing to a reaction, then dropped her head to the pad.

"Do you own a gun, Mr. Savella?"

"No guns. No knives."

She cocked her head.

"Why would you say that?"

"What?"

"I asked you about a gun and you said no guns, no knives."

Savella struggled to pick up the thread of the conversation.

"No reason. Just...volunteering. Didn't want you to have to drag it out of me." He managed a weak smile.

"You're not a hunter?"

"No. Why would you ask that?"

"The magazines. Under the kitchen table."

The old issues of *Field and Stream*. "Oh, no. No, no," he said, with a short chuckle. "That, those were there when I moved in."

"How long have you been here?"

Embarrassed, he laughed again. "About a year."

Her eyebrows arched as she surveyed the house once more and Savella could read her mind: *I like what you've done with the place.*

"I didn't have a lot of stuff. I was living overseas before this."

"Really. Where?"

"The Middle East, Latin America. Traveled around a bit."

"How about Poland?"

She was relentless.

"No. Never been there."

"You didn't happen to go back for another look, did you?"

"Back—you mean to the Bloom apartment?" Feidy nodded, and Savella shook his head.

"How about your friend?"

"No."

"No?"

"I'm sure he didn't."

She put the pad down again, leaned forward, and fixed him with a gaze that forced Savella to look away.

"Before when I asked you, you didn't say whether you took anything."

She couldn't know. Only he and Bobby knew about the address book and the box. Savella feigned surprise. "I thought I said—"

"No." She shook her head firmly, sunlight on the earrings again. "We started to talk about how she didn't have any pictures on the wall, and then you never answered the question."

"Huh."

"So what's the answer?"

He was past it now. The lie flowed easily off his tongue, almost as if he'd convinced himself of the righteousness of his position, positive she meant money, jewels, antiques, not dusty keepsakes.

"No. Nope. Nothing. Just looked around. Then he threw us out and that was that."

Feidy slowly nodded. "Can you tell me where you were Tuesday afternoon?"

"The day of the murder."

"Yes."

"Let's see. You know, I don't—oh, wait a minute, yes, Cape May. I was in Cape May all afternoon. Doing an interview." The column was finally good for something: an airtight alibi. Grabbing the pictures probably wouldn't have been all that big a deal if he'd thought about where he was when the victims were killed. But too late now.

"With whom?"

"With a woman named Beckham. For a column about her husband. An expert chili cook. The town loved his chili. Gonna miss his chili something fierce."

"You have an address?"

"Not on me. But she's in the book. Under Philip Beckham."

Feidy made a note, then closed the steno pad and tucked it in her purse. "OK then." She slung her purse over her shoulder and stood.

"So what's it looking like?" Savella said.

"Investigation's continuing."

"Ravic surprised a burglar?"

"Maybe. Lots of theories. Anyway"—she handed him her card—"I'm sure you know the drill. If you think of anything else and all that. Thanks for your time."

She was almost out the door when she looked back and touched the earring in her right lobe. "And thanks for noticing," she said softly, an awkward mumble that Savella might have thought he imagined if he hadn't noticed a blush creep across her face.

He followed her out to the front porch and watched as she got into a black Crown Victoria and drove off. When she made the turn at the corner, he stood at the railing, trying to relax.

The landscaper was nearly done. Five small saplings and a handful of bushes were rooted in mulched cutouts, and strips of lush green sod had been laid down. A sprinkler system had been installed, which kicked on every morning at five and drenched the new grass and plantings for a half hour.

"It'll grow quickly," the landscaper had assured Savella. "This time next year, you won't recognize the place." And Savella had to admit, if he was being honest, he was not much missing the haunted house.

He went back inside, locked the door behind him, and fell onto the sofa. Lying to cops—never a good idea. But he made the decision; he'd have to live with it. He sniffed the air. The awful cologne, a fetid odor unleashed by the sewer work, the stench of a dead mouse—whatever, it was gone. Instead, the smell of lavender lingered, a comforting aroma that reminded him of a place far away, a nice memory jammed deep in his subconscious, too far gone to conjure up anymore, and too far gone to help him escape the sinking feeling that he'd screwed this all up.

# 15

Enrique Pena wanted a meeting, in Las Vegas. A descent into hell, as far as Abel Garcia was concerned.

Five hours in a cramped, putrid airliner surrounded by drunks and whores. The dry desert heat that took his breath away when he stepped out of the terminal. Choking on exhaust fumes as he idled through three red lights in a taxi with a broken air-conditioner, wedged between two trucks towing billboards promising GirlsGirlsGirls. And no relief at the Miramar, just a forever hobble through a labyrinth of slot machines, dodging clusters of young women wearing short black dresses, to a door marked Private, where he waited until a security guard buzzed him through.

Still damp with sweat from the cab ride, Garcia shivered in the icy cold hallway that led to Pena's office. The narrow corridor was an ode to loss, a windowless museum lined with photographs and paintings of a long-ago Cuba: Pena's parents on the broad, stone steps of the Havana Yacht Club; cousins clowning for the camera outside the wrought-iron gates of an uncle's sprawling mansion in old-money Vedado; Arturo on horseback, squinting in the sun in front of a drying barn on his tobacco ranch; Mom and Dad and friends, a sea of gowns and tuxes, at El Carmelo for a late dinner after the symphony. The memory stroll ended abruptly in 1959, the year Castro took Havana, and at the end of the hallway was a call to arms: three paintings by the Spanish Impressionist Joaquin Sorolla y Bastida, part of a collection of five assembled by Pena's father and abandoned when he fled the island. The son had tracked down and reacquired these three, but two bare picture hooks hung on the wall just outside his office, waiting, he often said, to be filled by someone with the smarts to find the missing art. Or, and this was always the much preferred alternative, with the courage to kill the Castros and free the country.

Magdalena Ortiz, Pena's personal secretary, a heavy-set woman in her late fifties, was standing just inside the door, her hands clasped expectantly at her ample waist. Garcia liked Magdalena. She wore too much makeup and dressed like a teenager, but her saving grace was an eager smile and an urge to please. *Whatever it takes*, Pena once explained, the hint of a sneer bending his lips. So that was it.

"He'll be with you in a moment," the secretary almost whispered, that smile illuminating her spackled face, and she motioned to a plush gray sofa tucked against the wall. From his perch in a chair by her desk, Oscar the bodyguard looked up briefly, then returned to the magazine in his lap, restlessly turning the pages and flexing his tattooed forearm to make the bloody viper dance. On the other side of the room, swamping an armchair and sipping a tiny cup of Cuban coffee that almost disappeared in his beefy hand, sat Elmer Deets.

Garcia hadn't expected him. He was never prepared to see Deets. He had loathed him since their first meeting. To Garcia, Deets was a grotesque, a huge man, well over six feet tall, more than three hundred pounds. Perpetually perspiring, he drenched himself with cologne—English Leather, Garcia had finally determined—to mask the smell of sweat. The final touch was a mild case of rosacea, which left his eyes red and swollen and led Deets to cake on cosmetics to cover the regular outbreaks of red pimples and bumps on his cheeks and forehead.

And there was the ring. At their first meeting, Garcia had noticed—couldn't *help* it—the rock on Deets's pudgy finger: a 1962 New York Yankees World Series ring. Never mind the absurdity of Deets in pinstripes, or that he was just another obese teenager when the Yankees won the title. Where'd he get the ring, Garcia wanted to know, and when Deets ducked the question, their relationship was over before it began. Deets would never forget the contempt in Garcia's eyes or the implicit accusation of theft that hung in the air throughout the evening.

"Like I ripped the thing off Whitey Ford's fucking finger or something," he groused later to Pena when he thought Garcia was out of earshot. Pena, who had his own questions but didn't care enough to ask them, ordered the two men to work together.

"Jesus, you don't have to *sleep* with each other," he screamed when the jagged edges finally ripped through.

They had learned to coexist, however fitfully. But Garcia considered Deets a thug, nothing more, eager to raise his fists at the barest hint of a slight. And there was nothing redeeming in his violence. This was not a patriot fighting for the liberation of his homeland. The man wasn't Cuban, didn't even speak Spanish. For him, it was about money, and if Castro paid more, Deets would be ironing his fatigues.

What was he doing here, today, Garcia wondered as he dropped onto the sofa. He certainly didn't want him in the room when he gave Pena the bad news about the Key West papers. Don Arturo's little boy wouldn't be happy, and Garcia didn't relish the thought of the hired hands watching his reaction.

---

Miller had been adamant: no phones. He was speaking outside Baltimore. They would meet at the Maryland House rest stop on I-95. Garcia drove down in a drug-induced fog, hugging the right lane for safety's sake, but somehow still arrived early. He bought some Rolaids at the Travelmart and took up a position just inside the door.

Miller was a half hour late, no apologies, dressed incongruously in pressed blue jeans, a yellow golf jacket, and a floppy white hat.

"Who are you supposed to be?" Garcia asked.

"Not Richard Miller," the diplomat whispered.

Garcia looked at the crowds of travelers lined up for food and coffee at Sbarro's and Bob's Big Boy, or trying on sunglasses at the kiosk near the restrooms. Like any one of them would recognize Richard Miller. Washington, Garcia thought, had gone to his head.

"So what have you got to tell me? How are things going?"

"Not so good, Abel. Not so good at all."

They huddled over coffee and Miller mumbled his failure. No one was taking the documents seriously. The task force thought Miller was nuts, a warmonger. And Secretary Elshak—even worse: *Knock it the fuck off.*

The coffee soured Garcia's stomach and he closed his eyes, trying to will away the nausea. For this he had to drive two hundred miles?

But Miller had an idea. "We leak the papers, Abel," he said, his face brightening at the prospect. "To our friends in the media." A prominent exile leader with a talk show in Miami. The conservative host of a national radio program in New York City. A right-wing columnist whose work appeared in papers across the country. "Build some pressure from the outside. The newspapers, the radio—let them have it.

"One thing, though, Abel," Miller said, no more mumbling, with his confession of failure out of the way and a solution—*his* solution—on the table. "It made me think. About the documents, I mean. Because if we get them out to our friends, and then the Cubans can knock them down, or someone *else* even, some reporter or...well..." He paused and played with the handle of his paper coffee cup until it came apart. "You see what I mean?"

Garcia said nothing. Miller leaned in, his silly hat framing his face like a baby's bonnet. "Have to ask. Are we sure they're authentic?"

And it was just then that a man escorting his two young boys to the bathroom stopped abruptly a few yards away and craned his neck to see under the hat. By the time the boys pulled him away, Garcia was on the move. "You'll take care of this, won't you, Abel?" Miller shouted as Garcia headed out the door.

---

A soft chime sounded at the secretary's desk, then again, and Magdalena stood and smiled at Garcia. "This way, please," she said as she opened the door to the inner office and stepped aside. Deets didn't move. He would wait outside with the secretary and the bodyguard.

Pena, his suit jacket draped on the back of his black leather desk chair, was at the computer. Sprawled in a corner, his two brindled Brazilian Mastiffs growled softly and warily clambered to their feet, then slumped to the hardwood floor when Pena raised his left hand and snapped his fingers. In the same motion, he pointed in the direction of a walnut dining table across the room that had been set for two—luncheon plates under metal covers, glasses of iced tea, slices of *panetela borracha* for dessert.

Garcia sat down at one end of the table and glanced around the room. The office reflected its occupant: uncluttered surfaces, soft lighting that created pools of shadow, sophisticated furniture that masked sharp edges. Pena's desk—a slab of opaque glass that held a telephone console, a small keyboard, a mammoth flatscreen computer monitor, and not a scrap of paper—looked out on a faux rain forest filled with lush tropical vegetation surrounding a meandering pool fed by a waterfall that tumbled down the side of the building. In the late afternoons, Pena would sit on a stone bench under palm fronds and smoke a cigar as he watched the clear water splash to earth and snake restlessly through his little paradise. And always alone—Eden was reserved exclusively for Pena, and his dogs.

Pena stood and lifted his suit jacket from the back of the chair, slipped it on, then tugged at the sleeves until his cuff links were properly displayed. "When did you get in, Abel?"

Garcia cleared his throat. "Just this morning."

Pena studied the monitor as if he were confirming the answer.

"And you're leaving...?"

Garcia peeked at his watch. "Four hours. The three fifty flight."

Pena fumbled with the knot of his tie. "Let's eat," he said.

*Ensalada de mariscos,* Garcia noted approvingly, a childhood favorite from Veradero, chunks of lobster and crab, shrimp and bay scallops, marinated in lime juice. He hadn't eaten since the night before, and he was actually hungry, an odd sensation these pill-hazed days. He spread his napkin on his lap and waited as Pena settled in his chair, studied his plate for a moment, rotated it slightly to the right, then left, and right again. Satisfied, Pena delicately plucked a piece of lobster from the pile with his fingers and popped it in his mouth.

The two men ate quietly for several minutes, the silence broken only by the sounds of silverware scraping against china and the two dogs shifting restlessly on the floor. Pena poked distractedly at his lunch, used his fork to rearrange the seafood into separate piles. Finally, he shoved the half-finished plate to one side, leaned back and clasped his hands behind his head, and began to talk. For twenty minutes he held forth on the world— Washington, foreign affairs, the economy, Las Vegas, women—slowing only briefly when he got up to light up a Cohiba from a desktop humidor, sending clouds of smoke billowing over the table.

Garcia had heard this all before. It was the Pena he disliked, the arrogant, blustery zealot who thought his money and his power gold-plated his opinions, gave him an unquestioned right to bend the world to his will, and pity the man who didn't realize it.

The alarm on Garcia's watch finally broke the spell. At the sound of the buzzer, Pena quickly looked around, as if he hadn't realized until that moment there was someone else in the room. Garcia slipped a pain pill from his pocket and swallowed it. He was embarrassed by this dependence, and the presence of Pena, watching him closely, a curious half smile on his face, made it even worse.

The office door swung open and Pena's daughter breezed in. Garcia remembered Marta as a child, shy, stick-thin, weeping over her missing mother until her father turned her anguish into hatred with a fairy tale of abandonment. It was a striking woman who crossed the room now in a tiny black skirt and flaming red heels. She flashed a broad smile at Garcia.

"Uncle Abel, what's up?" The little girl poked through, and Garcia melted.

"Good afternoon, senorita," he replied, rising with a slight bow, and she giggled at his formality, then bent down and kissed her father on the cheek. "Going shopping," she said.

Pena reached inside his jacket for his billfold. "My daughter's hobby," he said. He rifled through a stack of hundred-dollar bills, pulled out ten, and handed them to her, hesitantly, watching to make sure she was satisfied. Marta stuffed the bills carelessly in her purse and kissed him lightly on the mouth. Pena caressed her back and as she turned for the door, he let his hand linger briefly on her buttocks. When she was gone, Pena, all business again, turned to Garcia. "Now tell me about Miller."

To Garcia's immense surprise, Pena took it well. He propped his elbows on the table, his palms pressed tightly together as if he were praying. His head bobbed slowly from side to side—*maybe, maybe not*—as he considered Miller's suggestion. Finally, he stopped and pinched the bridge of his nose between his thumb and forefinger.

"We'll try it. For what it's worth. But get it on television, Abel. The hell with the newspapers. This is America. If it's not on TV, it didn't happen."

He stood and walked across the room to his dogs, knelt and tenderly scratched one, then the other, behind the ears.

"They have such simple ideas about Cuba in this country," Pena said. "An island with rum and cigars. Sunshine and seafood. It's the Bahamas, or Puerto Rico, or Jamaica. It's all the same to them. They don't get it. And our people suffer as a result. A tragedy." He clambered to his feet. "One roll a day. A few pounds of chicken, a half dozen eggs a month. On Saturday night the beer truck comes through, fills the buckets for a few centavos. A tragedy is what it is."

He returned to the table and sat for a moment, lost in his own dark thoughts. Then, somewhere, a decision was made. He clapped his hands together, loudly enough that the dogs' ears pricked. "This is what we do, Abel. When you return to New York, make sure the documents are leaked, like Miller said. And then I want you to call the Russians."

Garcia straightened in his chair as if an electric charge had passed through his body. "What are you saying?"

"What do you mean, what am I saying? Call the Russians."

"Why would we need them?" Garcia asked, but he knew the answer.

Pena cocked his head and affected a sad smile, as if he were dealing with a very slow child. "Now, come on, Abel."

"But what you're asking—this is not so easy. It's a very complicated business."

"I know. I'm aware of that. That's why I have you."

"Too many things can go wrong."

"It doesn't have to be perfect. Who expects Cubans to get it right?"

"Think about this. It is not something to pursue lightly."

Pena toyed with his butter knife.

"Your father knew that," Garcia said.

Pena looked up suddenly. "You mean he *knows* that, right?" He paused, waiting until Garcia grudgingly acknowledged his slip of tongue with a curt nod. "I understand that too. But I'm not gonna wait in line."

"These are different times, Enrique. A different world."

"Not so different, Abel, not really. But listen, don't jump to conclusions here. Perhaps the leaks will work. I hope so. A couple of stories on the news—who knows? But whichever way it goes is fine."

A lazy grin crossed his face, and in that fleeting moment, that smug gesture, Garcia suddenly understood why Elmer Deets was in the anteroom. Garcia once had asked Pena why he kept a man like Deets. "It's very simple, Abel," Pena had replied. "He does things we won't."

And this was where they were. The son had given up on words.

A welling anger suddenly engulfed him. He was tired, weary of the plotting, the meetings, the blood-soaked history. The blood most of all, and for once, Don Arturo's son or not, Garcia could not hold back.

"A tragedy, you called it. Is this what you think the tragedy is? No. The tragedy is still thinking something will change." He didn't recognize his own voice: firm, insistent, brooking no challenge. It had been years. "The tragedy is living your life in the mistaken belief that after all this time, it can be 1959 again. But that Cuba is gone forever. No one's going back there, not me, not you. There's nothing to go back *for*. I laugh when I hear these people say, 'Oh, they stole my farm. I want my cows back.' It's time to forget it. The cows are dead."

He got to his feet and leaned across the table, his palms flat on the glass top. "What do you imagine is going to happen? You think the people living there all these years are going to say, 'Here, take back your house. Please, Senor Pena, your father's hotel, if you wish.' They're going to move out when you knock on the door?"

His face felt hot, but he would not stop, couldn't if he wanted to. He had crossed the line, personalized it—not just any exile, but Enrique Pena, the son of Don Arturo.

"We should have done it ourselves, taken back our country. Our mistake. Castro had a few guys and some old rifles, and he came down from the mountains and won. We sat in Miami and whined for fifty years. We assumed Americans hated Communism so much, they would go in and cut out the cancer. One setback and they gave up. And left us here. We came to leave. But we won't."

The room began to sway slightly, and for a moment Garcia thought he might pass out. He reached behind him for the arms of his chair, sat down heavily, and lowered his head. When he at last glanced up, Pena was standing over him, a puzzled look on his face as if he were unsure how to react. He reached down and touched Garcia on the knee.

"You all right, Abel?"

Garcia nodded and dropped his head again.

"Sure? Want some water? Have some water."

A tumbler appeared in front of him. Garcia shook his head. "A minute, please."

The dogs were restless, stretching, pawing the hardwood floor. Through the thick glass of the door to the garden, he could hear the muffled sound of water falling into the pond. Pena pulled a chair close to Garcia and sat down. Garcia braced for the firestorm, but when Pena spoke, his voice was hushed, almost solicitous.

"An exile's life," he said. "You want to go home so badly, but you don't know how. And after a while, you don't even know where home is, do you?" His hand grazed Garcia's arm. "So you live up here, in the cold and the snow, the heat and the filth. And after so many years, everyone wants you to forget. Maybe even your wife, the woman you love. She wants you to forget home. Wants you to forget it so badly, you start to think there's no world to go back to."

Garcia raised a hand to interrupt, but Pena cut him off. "You spoke, Abel, now it's my turn. You start to think there's no world to go back to. But there is. Of course there is. Do you remember? The farm, the beach at Veradero. Are you forgetting? You remember what it was like, don't you? Of course you do. Just as my father does. It's difficult sometimes, so many years gone by. But he remembers. Just like you do."

Garcia winced. What had Pena wanted that day in the bodega? *One last mission, one final effort to send his father home to die.*

"This isn't a movement, Abel. Don't think of it that way. It's just the two of you. You and Don Arturo. And what would he say if he were here? 'This is what we have to do to get somebody's attention.' And he'd laugh, Abel. Remember how he used to say, you heard him a thousand times, he'd say you'd think being against a dictator would be enough? Right? Isn't that what he used to say?"

Garcia resisted, he fought until it hurt to think, until he was once again lost in the maze of ambiguity where he had spent so much of his life. He stared into the face of this man who had never paid a price, never sacrificed. Havana was old pictures to him, those impeccably framed photos in the corridor or fading black-and-whites carefully taped into dusty albums and tucked away in dark closets, to be dragged into the light whenever the passion started to die. And not for him the old ways. *For my father:* a grand lie. Don Arturo wanted no part of the future, only to reclaim the past, as if a breath of Cuban air would restore his mind and move his legs. *My father:* an obscenity, the way the son used it.

But Enrique was a clever man. He knew the buttons to push.

"Am I right?"

Pena awaited an answer.

Garcia slowly nodded. Pena squeezed Garcia's shoulder.

"OK. Now, listen. We don't have much time. A few days, maybe a week. One way or the other, we have to act. So we try it Miller's way. But just in case, you call the Russians."

Garcia exhaled, the sound of surrender, and Pena relaxed his grip.

"Now eat your dessert," he said, "and we'll get you back to the airport."

# 16

The Clouds, packed for Isabella's second show, the last of her engagement. By the time Savella arrived, a deuce in the corner was the only empty table. Isabella was deep into her final number, and he stood just inside the door and watched her work.

She sat on the edge of a wooden stool, drenched in the soft white light of a solitary spot, a glass of water with a lime wedge bobbing on the surface resting on the piano next to her. Her black hair was pulled back, secured by a violet band that perfectly matched the color of her blouse. Loosely clutching the microphone, Isabella sang low and throaty, her eyes squeezed shut, the audience transfixed. Even her dour piano player seemed impressed, a trace of a smile on his pocked face.

As she sang, Savella took in the room. He'd seen it in daylight, the mustard-yellow carpet stained and threadbare, the plastic-patched banquettes and the gouged and burned tabletops, the floor-to-ceiling windows streaked with grime. The air reeked of smoke and stale beer and cleansers as the housekeeping crew stumbled through their chores, shouting dirty jokes in Spanish. But everything is illusion, and the spots on the carpet, the rips in the upholstery, even the filthy windows disappeared under cover of night, and the well-dressed people in their smart suits and just-back-from-Barbados tans hunched around linen-covered tabletops topped with candles. Only the couple in the back of the room in T-shirts and shorts hadn't got the message: no seedy reality.

Isabella's voice drew him back. This song was familiar, an old standard. What was it called—"Moon River," that was it. Savella couldn't shake the feeling that he'd heard it recently, but where? Isabella...at Max's...on the car radio—and then in a rush he made the connection.

The song Mary Bloom had been humming.

Mary Bloom, as she lay dying. *Moon River.* That was it, of all things. And with her last breaths.

The final notes faded away, drowned in a thunderclap of applause, and Savella headed for the bar. The piano player scrambled off the stage. Isabella waved her thanks and placed the microphone on the stool. Then she spotted Savella. Shading her eyes with her palm, she mouthed a grinning hello, and he caught the curious looks from the crowd knocking knees at the tiny tables as they turned to see who warranted the special attention. Isabella picked up the microphone again and tapped it with her finger to make sure it was still live. "Well, that was *gonna* be it. But let's do this."

A few delighted shouts and more applause as she sat down at the piano, threaded the microphone into a stand in front of her, and began to play.

Savella recognized this one too, a Diana Krall number, "Narrow Daylight." Isabella had sung it for the first time when their relationship was still a giddy mystery. A night like this, but not quite: Savella at the bar a few drinks along, empty tables scattered around the room, Isabella in white light a bit too harsh. But even with the spot washing out her features, she was a vision. And the voice—Savella had closed his eyes and let it engulf him: smooth, subtle beauty, a jumble of emotions, match-ready, just beneath the surface. She played with the lyrics, lingered over them, found in nuance her own definitions, but never stopped telling a story. That first night, the words were lost on Savella. All that mattered was that the ravishing woman on stage was singing to him, whether anyone else in the room knew it or not.

Now he stood at the bar and struggled to shut out the sounds of clinking glasses and scraping chairs around him. Her attention was everything the first time, but tonight he was in a different place. He felt a surge of expectation: the encore, her choice, there was promise in all that. A late dinner, certainly, and then who knew? Forget work, he told himself as Isabella sang him a song. Forget Mary Bloom. For one night, forget it all.

He felt a hand on his elbow: Harold Cobb, at his side from nowhere, looking more haggard than usual, his big belly straining against red suspenders. Cobb put a finger to his lips and smiled, and the two men stood at the bar and listened as Isabella sang.

When she finished, there was silence, then one hesitant clap, and another, and suddenly applause, and Isabella walked out of the light.

"Not bad," Cobb said.

Savella laughed. "You don't know the half of it, Harold."

The bartender leaned across the bar for their orders: Johnny Black rocks for Savella, a milk for Harold.

"Got a call yesterday about a cruise gig," Cobb said. "Last-minute replacement. The other singer's got a sick mother or something. Anyway, some time in the sun, if it happens."

"She'd like that."

Harold glanced at him. "How about you?"

"What do you mean?"

"You're spending a lot of time together lately. That's a good thing, by the way."

Savella didn't answer. The bartender brought their drinks, and he slowly moved the ice around his glass with the swizzle stick. Cobb reached into his pants pocket and pulled out a packet of Oreos.

"Dinner," he said, ripping the wrapper off the cookies. He dunked an Oreo in the milk, held it there for a moment, then popped it in his mouth. "Yep," he mumbled through the chewing, "she's going places."

A hand slipped over Savella's shoulder and darted toward the Oreos before Cobb could move. Isabella, her face still flushed from performance, grabbed a cookie and kissed Cobb on the cheek, then moved around and squeezed in beside Savella. "Hello, boys." She pulled apart the Oreo, scraped the icing off against her teeth. "So how was I?"

"You were"—Cobb made a show of searching for just the right words—"fabulous."

Isabella bowed her head and clasped her hands over her heart. "No, you're too kind." She swept up Savella's drink, splashing the bar with a few drops of scotch. She was always like this after a show: wired, jazzed, inhaling the energy around her in huge, deep breaths, only to collapse a few hours later when the last ounce of juice was gone.

"And you?" she said, staring at Savella.

"Terrific stuff." He nodded back toward the stage. "And the end. Very nice. Diana Krall."

"Elvis Costello's lyrics."

"I prefer to leave him out of the picture."

"Oh, I bet." Isabella tapped his head. "Gets a little messy in there with the three of you, huh?"

She pulled him away from the bar, wrestled his arms away from his sides, and embraced him. "Anyway, I saw you walk in and all of a sudden I got ideas."

"You did an excellent job of letting me know."

Cobb cleared his throat. "I gotta talk some business, honey."

As they fell into easy conversation about the cruise-ship booking, Savella gazed out at the night. The dark suited him. It was his forest, his natural habitat. The exile's lot—skulking through the day, ever vigilant. No one could know him, not really; the risk was too great and no one could be trusted. And so a life of grand performance, a never-ending charade, and in the end playing the part of a man playing the part. Wearying, yes, burnishing and honing a fiction, but it was—what? His life? Well, by now, certainly, the whole cloth had become a second skin, a mother's embrace, impervious to all threats. Hard habit to break, this arranging life instead of living it. But now, after all this time, all these hard years of slipping through the shadows, of *getting by*—now there was Isabella, firmly dragging him back from the edge of the world, showing him the way home.

"Michael?"

She was holding out her hand. "Come with me," she said, and there was never any doubt.

---

A cool night, and she wasn't dressed for it, a thin cream-colored shawl over the purple blouse. Isabella slipped her arm through his. They walked down Pacific Avenue, not talking for the first few blocks. As they waited at the light at Montpelier, she reached up and nuzzled his cheek.

"I like this, you know?" she said softly.

Savella smiled. "So where we headed?" he asked as the Walk sign flashed.

"You'll see, *you'll see,*" she exclaimed. "It's just up ahead." She picked up the pace, and he trotted to keep up. Past John's Cash for Gold, past Il Giardino where the waiters were dragging the tables off the patio, past a trio of hookers comparing notes outside All-Nite Liquors, then crossing against the red, weaving between the cars stuck in Saturday-night traffic. After eight blocks Isabella stopped short at the corner.

"Far as you go, sir," she said, and she untied the shawl from around her neck and wrapped it around his eyes.

"What are you doing?" he said, laughing. "I can't see."

A car horn honked twice, and a man shouted, "Now his hands and feet, babe."

Isabella cinched the knot a little tighter. "There," she said, "now come along."

She took him by the hand and led him a few more yards, then stopped again. "OK, ready," she said, and pulled the shawl away.

She was pointing up, to the roof of a building that sat on a busy intersection. At the top was a huge lighted billboard, bearing an enormous photograph of Isabella Logan, advertising her engagement at the Clouds next month. Savella gaped at the sign, then looked back at Isabella, who stood a few feet away, a shy, expectant look on her face.

"So?" she said.

"Your name in lights. Every little girl's dream."

The smile widened, even as she shook her head, her long hair falling in her face. Savella pulled her to him and kissed her. "You look great. It's terrific."

She stepped back, hands on hips, and studied the billboard. Finally, she tucked her hair behind her ears and nodded. "I think so. OK. Let's eat. I'm famished."

"Where do you want to go?" he asked.

"Well, I'm thinking about omelets. *My* omelets."

"You are, huh?"

"Boy," she said, shaking her head in mock admiration, "always with the lines."

---

He loved to watch her shop. Isabella swept through the all-night market like royalty, inhaling the aromas, bantering with the countermen, who knew her, or were eager to pretend they did. Savella trailed behind, toting a red basket that filled quickly: a dozen eggs, a small log of Chevre, three perfect plum tomatoes, some tarragon, chives, parsley. Mixed greens, two handfuls of crimini mushrooms, and two tiny, delicate lemon tarts for dessert. A feast.

"I've got the wine," she said as they stormed the cash register.

Hand in hand, they walked home, like two teenagers in puppy love, nothing said, everything promised. Isabella's energy was intoxicating. Savella could feel her excitement about the rising arc of her career, and he was eager to share it. Not tonight for the Bloom story, the super's murder, the priest's visit. This was too good. All the rest could wait.

A dirt-streaked van was parked in the alley that led to the carriage house. They squeezed past it, slipped down the narrow passageway, and slowly climbed the rickety wooden staircase to the kitchen door. As Isabella pawed through her shoulder bag for the keys, Savella heard an engine come to life behind him, and turned to see the van's red brake lights flare briefly before it rolled into the street and disappeared.

With a jangle Isabella pulled her key chain from the purse and bent down to the lock.

And stopped.

"Michael?" she said. He followed her gaze. The front door was slightly ajar. Isabella gave the door a push. As it creaked open, she stepped hesitantly inside. She made a sound, *oooof,* the breath running out of her as if she'd been punched, and the groceries fell to the floor.

"What's the matter?" Savella moved past her and found the switch for the ceiling light.

Her refuge, violated.

In the fluorescent glow, mounds of flour, sugar, cereal piled on the yellow countertop; the chrome refrigerator toppled in the center of the floor; a ten-dollar bill and some singles lying in the dry sink; a toaster, its sides crushed, amid the smashed glass of a blender jar. Isabella's old rotary phone had been ripped from the wall. The precious smoked blue vase lay in shards, the heirloom ceramic bowl was in two pieces. A leg was torn off the small table Isabella had saved from the trash.

"Go down. Now," Savella said. "There could be someone in here."

He stepped back onto the landing, slipping on the egg-soaked paper bag. Isabella didn't move. He grabbed her by the hand and helped her slowly down the stairs to the backyard. As Savella punched 911 on his cell phone, she wandered toward the koi pond.

Then, suddenly, a shriek, and everything changed.

---

"Fucking big goldfish," one cop said to another as they stood at the edge of the pool, watching the three koi bobbing in the water hyacinth, thin streams of blood oozing from the deep gashes in their sides. Carp, Savella wanted to say, more like carp. But now was not the time.

Instead he knelt in the grass beside Isabella and slowly stroked her hair. The screams and sobs had only just subsided, but her body still quivered. Savella had gone upstairs for a blanket, but the chunky sergeant in charge of the crime scene ordered him out of the apartment. So he gently draped his sports coat around her shoulders and tried without success to massage the anguish from her trembling body.

The police found no one in the apartment. But from the chatter that drifted down from the open windows, the ravaging was not limited to the kitchen. Sofa cushions in the living room ripped apart. The television a total loss. Nothing left on the walls. And in the bedroom, Isabella's underwear pulled from the dresser and shredded, maybe with the same knife that had gutted the koi.

"She's not living here for a while," one officer declared after a tour of the destruction.

The patrolmen were replaced by detectives and evidence technicians, and camera flashes lit up the apartment windows. Now the discussions on the kitchen landing took on a more curious tone. *How did they get in?* the plainclothes guys asked one another as they slipped out for cigarettes, oblivious to the victim sitting twenty feet below. No windows broken. No doors smashed in.

Either a key or somebody took the time to pick the lock, went to the trouble of being *careful,* if you can believe that, before trashing the place. Isabella, hunched in the wrought-iron love seat, her place of honor beside her cherished pond, gave no sign of having heard any of it. Instead, she lifted her tear-stained face to the apartment building that loomed above, neighbors silhouetted in their windows, gazing down at the tumult in their backyard.

And then it was her turn to be poked and prodded. The two detectives, an older man with a drooping mustache, and a rail-thin kid with slick black hair, were decent about it, but there were forms to be filled out, reports to be typed. Isabella recounted the events of the evening in a low monotone, her voice catching only once, and then only slightly, when she mentioned the stop at the all-night market, when the evening held such promise. Did she have any enemies, they wanted to know, anybody else with a key, a former lover, maybe, anyone suspicious around recently, here or at work, and she shook her head each time. A few questions for Savella, biography, mostly, and it was over. After asking Isabella to send along a list of missing property, they walked up the drive to their car. The evidence technicians were finishing too, stowing equipment in their van.

The cool night had turned cold. "Isabella, you want to go in?" Savella asked softly, rubbing her shoulder.

"Not just yet." The voice of a survivor, devoid of emotion.

"OK, no rush. We'll just sit here a little longer."

In the driveway, the two detectives stood at their car, the older one with the driver's side door open and one foot inside, talking to someone. A few moments later, the younger one pointed in the direction of the house, started back toward them. Then a raised voice, the words indecipherable, and he returned to the car and got in the passenger seat. The driver slid behind the wheel and backed onto the avenue. And into the light walked Sylvie Feidy.

---

A different look tonight: a hint of lipstick, her brown hair down around her shoulders, red-framed eyeglasses, a soft raincoat draped over a black evening dress. She nodded at Savella, then moved to the stairs, floated up the staircase so smoothly she could have been riding an escalator. He was reminded of the way she had crossed his living room that afternoon. *That afternoon.* He flailed against the memory, but the connection had already been made. Someone *had* been in his home that day. Nothing out of place, not like this, not the mindless destruction. But no room for coincidence, was there? Someone *had* been there, in his home, and now someone had been here, in Isabella's. So what were they looking for, and he knew the answer before he even finished asking the question.

Feidy reappeared on the landing, surveyed the ground below her, then descended the stairs and crossed the lawn to the love seat.

"I'm Detective Feidy," she said to Isabella. "Sorry for all this. Some mess," she said to Savella, and caught his quizzical look. "I heard your name on the dispatch call on my way home from dinner. Can you handle a few more questions?"

Savella stood and looked down at Isabella. "She needs to get out of the cold."

"They're almost done up there," Feidy said. "Just this, I guess—when you came home tonight, what did you see? Exactly. Don't leave anything out."

Savella shrugged. "Garbage pails along the side of the building"—he pointed at the apartment house—"some lights on the first floor. A van parked in the driveway."

"Tell me about the van."

"There's nothing to tell. A van."

"Color?"

"Dark. Blue, maybe black. I wasn't paying attention. Anyway, it pulled out while we were going upstairs. I mentioned this to the other officers."

"OK. And then what?"

"And then...nothing. We walked up the stairs, the door was ajar. I poked my head inside and saw the kitchen and called the police."

Feidy nodded and turned to Isabella. "How long have you been living here?"

"About two years," she said in a reedy voice.

"And no problems like this before? No trouble with kids in the neighborhood, that sort of thing?"

Isabella shook her head. Feidy pulled a pad and pen from her purse and scribbled a note. "And you can't think of anyone who might have done this? Something at work, or problems with a relationship? A jilted lover?"

Isabella, her face a stone mask, gestured toward Savella. "He's it."

Savella raised his hands in protest. "Look, she answered all this already, with the other two."

The detective examined him for a few moments, then made another note. "How long you been seeing each other?" she asked.

"About a year," Savella said.

"And you stay here often?"

"How is that relevant?" he asked, a little annoyed.

"Often enough that someone might think you lived here? That this was *your* place too?"

Isabella's head jerked up.

"Wait. Wait a minute," Savella said. "You think this was about *me*?"

"Could be," the detective said. "You don't know. The timing is interesting, don't you think? After whatever happened at your place the other day."

Isabella got to her feet. "What do you mean?" she asked Feidy, her voice stronger now. She looked at Savella. "What's she talking about?"

He quickly moved to her side. "It's nothing. I came home and thought somebody might have been inside. But there was nothing. It wasn't important."

The last of the technicians clambered down the staircase and with a wave to Feidy stalked up the alley. Isabella slipped Savella's jacket off her shoulders, shuffled closer to the koi pond, and stared at the dead fish bobbing on the surface. In the faint light, Savella could make out a stunned look on her face, as if she had just figured out what all the commotion was about.

"There was somebody in my home, Michael," she said, with an intensity that caused him to take a step backward. "Somebody killed my koi and there was somebody in my home."

Feidy dropped her pen and pad in her purse. "You have someplace to stay tonight?"

"How bad is it?" Savella asked.

"You're not gonna want to go up there tonight. Get some sleep and deal with it in the morning."

"So we'll go back to my—"

Isabella shook her head vigorously. "No. No way. No one's driving me out. This is my home," she said, her arms crossed at her chest. "I'm not going anywhere."

"OK," Feidy said. "Again, I'm sorry you have to deal with this."

"I'll walk you out," Savella said.

---

A stiff breeze had sprung up, sending the season's first fallen leaves swirling along the asphalt. Savella was anxious to be rid of the police, to help Isabella deal with this horror. But Feidy was taking her time, strolling along at a pace that seemed designed to frustrate him. Or to give him a chance to tell her something. He slowed to let her catch up.

"So you don't think kids? Drugs?" he said.

Feidy raised an eyebrow. "Let's see now. You're involved in an accident and the other driver dies. You decide to write a story about her, and you get her super to let you poke around her apartment. He gets killed, along with a neighbor. Now you come home with your girlfriend and find her place tossed, and somebody knifed the fish. And this"—she waved back at the carriage house—"this is *kids*?"

A truck rattled past on the avenue, its cargo bouncing loose on the flatbed. At her car Feidy slipped behind the wheel and started the engine. The window on the passenger side rolled down, and Feidy leaned across the seat, looked up at Savella on the curb, hands in his pockets.

"Seventeen dollars in cash in the sink," she said. "Couldn't have missed it, kids, or even a crackhead. And not a window broken or a door pushed in. Somebody was looking for something. But this was also meant to scare. Sending a message—we can get in anytime. For you, for her, I don't know. And why, I also don't know. Maybe you'll tell me."

He briefly held her gaze, then looked away.

"Well," she said, and drove off.

---

Isabella, grim-faced, was standing barefoot in the pond, the hem of her skirt grazing the surface of the bloody water, gently lifting the savaged koi into a large black plastic trash bag. A brutal, wrenching scene: Savella remembered how much joy the fish had brought her. The time one of the two Kohaku, *the black ones, Michael, with the red and white patches,* leaped out of the water into a rhododendron bush, or the hot summer morning when the Tancho Showa, *white with the red spot on its head—c'mon, get it straight,* caught a curious cat's paw in its mouth and dragged it into the water. The fish were her peace of mind.

She stepped out of the pond and quickly tied a knot in the bag, then put her shoes back on and trudged slowly to the garbage cans. A moment of hesitation, and the bag was trash. Isabella moved to the staircase. One hand on the railing, she stood for a moment, staring up at the now-darkened windows of her neighbors. In the moonlight, her cheeks were shiny with tears, and she rubbed them with her palms.

"There was somebody in my home, Michael," she said softly, anguish almost strangling her words, and then they climbed the stairs in silence.

# 17

The cell phone, around ten, buzzing in place on the hardwood floor.

Savella silenced it before Isabella could be disturbed, then studied the number on the display: *Cynthia.* For a moment he considered going back to sleep. But the woman was relentless.

He crept out of bed and tiptoed to the bathroom. Evidence of the home invasion was everywhere: shaving cream smeared over the vanity mirror, a wooden cosmetics rack torn from the wall, three bath towels cut to pieces and strewn across the tile floor. Closing the toilet lid, Savella sat down and pressed Talk.

"Michael. It's Cynthia. At the office." Brusque, no nonsense; the boss had unleashed her. "Janice wants to see you this morning. Eleven thirty."

"Not sure I can make it, Cynthia," Savella said, even as he realized there was no point in resisting.

"Michael, she made it clear. No excuses. And please don't be late. Janice has a very busy day."

A very busy day, he thought as the call ended, and still time to squeeze me in.

He showered quickly, drying himself with the towel shards, then dressed and let himself out, trying not to awaken Isabella.

They had spent the night on the thin mattress of the rollout sofa in the living room. She wouldn't turn the lights on, not even for a moment, and they tumbled into bed awkwardly. Isabella, exhausted by the night's drama, fell asleep immediately. Savella was grateful for the silence. Isabella would have questions, about the break-in at his house, about why he hadn't mentioned it. And when she awoke, it wouldn't be long before she made the connection to the artifacts in Mary Bloom's tin box. It would hang over them like humidity, making it difficult to even breathe until they talked it through. But they could survive it, Savella told himself as he climbed down the stairs. They could make it to the other side.

---

His parking space was empty, waiting for him, a security guard hovering nearby. The newsroom was quiet. In the middle of the room, Scott Williams was holding court, surrounded by a few of Janice's other babies and a starstruck intern. For once, he ignored Savella's entrance.

Cynthia waved him inside without a word. Janice was at her desk, sorting through a pile of folders. She offered a quick smile.

"You want a coffee or something?" she asked, and when he shook his head, she looked relieved. All business today, and Savella was glad of it. A chance to get in and get out, run back to Isabella and help her regroup.

Savella pointed at the folders. "More pageant bullshit?"

"Not bullshit, Michael," she said, her eyes narrowing slightly. "Maybe for you. But people love it."

"What people would that be, exactly?"

"Well, *somebody's* watching it, reading about it," she said. "Or it wouldn't be on TV. And we wouldn't write about it. Don't be such an elitist."

Savella shrugged. He wasn't interested in Janice's analysis of the American Beauty pageant.

"Anyway," Janice said, "that's actually why I wanted to talk with you. We could use your help on the coverage, your unique perspective."

He jerked to attention, suddenly on to the game, but too late.

"I mean, really, these are all human interest stories, aren't they?" she said. "How they got here, what they hope to do, their backgrounds."

"I remember," Savella said. "That girl from Maryland. She taught her cat to sing."

Janice forced a short laugh. "You see? That's exactly what I mean. Taught her cat—well, they're kids too, let's not forget, but…"

She smiled broadly at Savella, waiting for his surrender.

"Look, I know my job here, but beauty pageants?" Savella said. "You read the paper today? The president wants a jobs bill, we're fighting a war, some kid shoots the next-door neighbors with his dad's gun…"

Janice picked at a loose thread on her jacket sleeve. "You know something?" she said. "You're not in the Middle East anymore. Or Washington. You did that already. Now you're back in Atlantic City. And this is the news here, OK? Not wars. Not guns. And not the president, not unless he wants to put the goddamn tiara on Susie's fucking head."

They sat quietly for a few moments, the whirring of her computer fan the only sound in the room. Through the glass wall, Savella could see the gaggle of staffers gathered around Scott Williams, sipping coffee and stealing glances toward the editor's office. Now he understood why Williams hadn't bothered to run through the ritual. Savella was heading for the gallows. Someone, probably Cynthia, had tipped off Williams, and the chosen few had been summoned to witness the execution.

"So Allie Wozniak is coordinating the coverage," Janice said. "Why don't you check with Allie, see what she might need, how you might fit in. OK? And then we can talk about it some more. If you feel the need. But speak with Allie first."

The last mile. A final meal. And he had already passed on the coffee.

"I don't think that's something I want to do," he said evenly.

The telephone buzzed and she snatched up the receiver—"Yes?"

Savella stood and walked to the window, spread two slats of the blinds with the fingers of his right hand. Across the street, where the *Post-Herald* complex gave way to woodland, two men in hard hats were studying a set of blueprints spread over the hood of their truck. The future home of, what, *Post-Herald* Estates? Savella wondered. And if that worked, hell, you could throw up million-dollar waterfront mansions on the land where the newspaper building stood. *Of course* Janice wanted him to write about beauty queens, and see you later if he wouldn't. That's what the paper needed to survive. All these years later, different hair color, better wardrobe, same driven woman. She was used to getting her way. And she wanted him to write about beauty queens.

He heard the receiver drop into its cradle. He put his hands on his hips, straightened his shoulders, and turned to face the hangman.

"I was hoping this would go differently," Janice said. "But you're just gonna have to trust me. What do you think? This one time."

So he told her about Mary Bloom and the picture of Jack Ruby, about an old address book and a priest who lied, and a ransacked apartment and a pond full of dead fish. She listened, visibly bored, and when he finished, she sat back, her mouth set in a sullen pout, her fingers drumming a haphazard rhythm on the armrests of her chair.

"I don't know, Michael," she said, in sorrow or sounding like it anyway. "Not what I wanted, not at all."

The drumming ceased. She rested her elbows on the desktop, and slowly clasped her hands. "I'd say clean out your desk, but you never really moved in, did you?"

"Yeah," Savella said. "I think we're done."

Janice came around the desk and touched his arm. "I really *was* hoping this would go differently," she said, and opened the door.

The little group around Williams had swelled as the drama in the editor's office played out, a performance best appreciated from a distance. Savella went to his desk and retrieved his passport from the bottom drawer. It was all he wanted from this place. He felt no rancor at his dismissal, the real surprise being how long he had managed to survive.

As he headed for the door, Williams moved in front of him, a sly grin on his face.

"Everything all right, Mike?" he asked, jockeying for the best position to give his fans a good look.

Savella tried to walk around him, but Williams blocked his path. Savella took a deep breath. "Get the fuck out of my way, Scott," he said, the anger in his voice surprising him.

"What happened in there? Looked pretty serious."

"I'm not going to ask you again."

"Hey, I—"

His punch caught Williams on the chin and sent him stumbling backward into a cubicle wall. As his colleagues rushed to his aid, Savella, his fist in agony, made his way to the exit.

"No, no, it's OK, let him go," he heard Williams say. "Forget it." At the door Savella glanced over his shoulder. Janice Garabedian stood in the window of her office, arms folded tightly across her chest. He glanced at Williams. The intern was holding a cold can of Diet Coke to his bruised chin. When Savella turned back to Janice, her office blinds were shut tight.

---

It hurt to grip the steering wheel, but not so much that he didn't appreciate the pain. Savella couldn't remember the last time he'd been in a fight, not that Williams ever had a chance to get involved. Sixth grade, maybe, when he decked Jimmy Tuttle over who got to wear the snorkel gear in the school pool. But Jimmy got back up, and Savella wound up swimming laps by himself in the shallow end. This was a much better result, never mind the swollen knuckles.

He parked on Atlantic Avenue, took his time locking the car, then headed toward Isabella's place, flexing his throbbing fist.

In the full light of day, the extent of the damage from the rampage was clear. The stream of water gurgling over the rocks in the koi pond was stilled; a cloudy reddish sheen covered the surface. A pile of debris was mounded at the foot of the staircase: a slashed mattress, a television with the screen kicked in, three broken chairs, pictures torn from their frames and ripped in half. Trash bags sat in the grass, filled with the contents of the kitchen cabinets, bras, and panties, a shelf of paperback novels.

From the apartment came the deafening sound of cleaning equipment, and when Savella reached the top of the stairs, the antiseptic smell of a hospital ward momentarily gagged him. Inside, a man in a blue uniform was wrestling with a commercial steam cleaner, pawing at the drapes in the living room. Isabella, in an old pair of paint-spattered khakis, was furiously scrubbing the floor with a mop, a bucketful of soapy water at her side. Seeing Savella, she looked up and waved a brief hello. Savella crossed the room and leaned forward to hug her.

"I need to talk with you," Savella said, raising his voice to be heard over the din, which had crescendoed into a strained high-pitched whine.

"What about?" she shouted back.

Savella glanced at the cleaner, who was moving methodically along the bank of windows overlooking the koi pond. "Something's happened. I met with Janice this morning, and it didn't go too well."

"Didn't go what?"

"I said"—the steam equipment abruptly shut down— "I got fired."

The words exploded in the sudden silence. The cleaner cringed and offered Savella an apologetic look before switching on his machine again. Isabella pointed at the door, and the two of them walked outside. She clambered halfway down the staircase, then sat down; he perched on the step above her.

Savella quickly recounted the events of the day. As he described the punch, Isabella turned to him, amazed. "You hit somebody?"

He held up his swollen hand as evidence.

"Who was it again?"

"Scott Williams."

"What'd you hit him for?"

"I don't know. It just felt...right."

"You *hit* somebody," she said, struggling to understand. "Gosh, Michael, I just don't know..."

Savella massaged his fist. Isabella's reaction annoyed him. He'd lost his job, fought with a tormentor, and come looking for—well, sympathy would have been too much to hope for, but some ice would have been welcome.

"So now what?" she said.

"I don't know. I—I need to think about that." He reached down and took her hand. "I guess what I'm most concerned about is us. I'm sorry about all this, you know."

The steam cleaner was silent again; they could hear the operator clomping around the apartment, his work boots thudding against the hardwood floors. Isabella pulled her hand from Savella's and meticulously brushed some twigs off the step. "You never mentioned it," she said. "Your break-in."

"I wasn't sure. And I didn't want to worry you."

"Well, that worked well, don't you think?"

A cell phone jangled, and for a few minutes the cleaner stood by the window complaining to someone about his schedule. Isabella glanced up the stairs.

"I have to get back," she said. "He doesn't know what's next."

"Hard to believe there's *anything* left to clean in there."

A half smile flitted across her face. "Let me ask you something. Did you tell the police about the stuff you took from that apartment?"

He shook his head.

Isabella took his aching hand, carefully, as if she were cradling an egg.

"Michael, it's going to be OK. You didn't even like the job, so what the heck. Although why you needed to get fired to get out of there, I don't know. But it's for the best probably. It's the stuff we never see coming that saves us in the end."

With the chipped nail of her forefinger, Isabella traced a route through the sea of black and blue around his knuckles. "But go tell the police about the pictures and address book. This isn't a game."

She leaned in closer and examined his bruises. "Jeez Louise," she murmured. "Michael, Michael, Michael. What have you done?"

# 18

The detectives were on the third floor of police headquarters, shielded by a wall of clear bulletproof glass
that could be breached only by invitation or arrest.
Clutching his battered manila envelope, Savella waited
patiently in a plastic chair while a civilian aide went off
to track down Sylvie Feidy. Twenty minutes later he returned and with a crook of his finger ushered Savella
inside.

The detective bureau was a stuffy sprawl of a room
blazing with overhead lights even as the midday sun
poured through the sweeping windows. Savella followed
the aide's zigzag path to a dented gray metal desk in a
far corner.

"Sit there," he said. "She'll be right with you."

In the drab surroundings, Sylvie Feidy's work space
sparkled. Two philodendrons, green and healthy, sat
atop her filing cabinet, their leafy tendrils tumbling
to the grime-stained floor. Her chair, listing slightly to
the right, an armrest missing its padding, was draped
with a lipstick-red quilted slipcover. Pictures covered
the desktop, color photographs in white wood frames,
and slightly out-of-focus snapshots encased in drug-
store plastic—girlfriends, all smiles and arm in arm on
a white, sandy beach in sunglasses and not much else,
Feidy in the middle of the pack; a tall Marine in dress

blues, hugging a woman, her face obscured by a floppy wide-brimmed hat—was that Feidy, yes it was; two women in a bar, shot glasses raised over a bottle of Tequila, and that was her too. Off to one side, out of the fast lane, a black-and-white image in antique silver filigree, an old couple dressed formally in black and posing stiffly in front of a modest home with whitewashed stone walls.

"Hey, Syl." Savella turned to see Feidy, resplendent in a salmon-colored pantsuit. Another detective, a trim man wearing horn-rimmed glasses, stood between Feidy and her desk. "Listen, I got a computer file on the hotel job, but I can't get it open," he said. "You got a sec? Now?"

"Yeah, all right," she said, then, to Savella: "Give me another minute?"

She was back in ten. "Like I'm Bill Gates now," she said, leaning back in the broken chair. She brushed through her hair with one hand, straightened the papers on her desk with the other. "Anyway. The widow Beckham said she enjoyed your little chat. She's waiting to read all about the late Mr. Beckham. So what can I do for you?"

Savella fingered the flap of the envelope. "Listen, I wasn't being exactly truthful with you the first time we talked."

"Or the second."

"Or the second," he conceded.

"Nobody ever greets me with a band and cake." She pointed at the envelope. "That for me?"

"This is some stuff I found in Mary Bloom's apartment." Savella handed her the envelope and watched as she carefully removed the contents.

"Pictures. An address book. A ring. Quite a little treasure chest you have here, Michael—can I call you Michael? You made yourself copies of everything, yes?" She chuckled at his surprise. "Do yourself a favor. Don't play poker. You found all of this where?"

"In a box in her dressing table, whatever you call it."

"And what was your point?"

The question confused him, and when he didn't answer right away, she looked up. "I mean, what did you expect to do with this stuff?"

"I called a lot of the numbers in the book looking for someone who would talk with me about her."

"The column thing again."

"Right. Pretty much struck out, except for one guy. A priest, it turns out, in Illinois." He stood and reached across the desk for the book, then flipped through the pages until he found Remsen's listing. "He said he didn't know her, but if you look at it"—he ran down the page with his forefinger—"she kept updating his numbers over the years. He said she never called, but I don't know about that. And then he came here."

Feidy picked up the ring and buffed it with her thumb. "He was here? When?"

"The day after the murders, as it happened. He said he was in Philly for a meeting and was curious about this woman with his numbers in her book."

"So what did he tell you?"

"Nothing."

"What did you talk about?"

"Nothing, really."

Feidy shook her head. "Uh-uh. He comes out here from, where did you say?"

"Illinois."

"Illinois. And you meet with him and he's got nothing to tell you? This is what you want me to believe?" She dropped the ring on her desk. "This from a guy who hid potential evidence in a murder investigation. What am I supposed to do with that? What I'm thinking, I don't know, is maybe I should read you your rights."

"Wait a minute." Savella threw up his hands. "We sat up on the Boardwalk for a half hour or so. I bought him lunch, which he did not eat, and he looked at the pictures, which he did not recognize. Or so he said. Didn't know anything about a woman named Mary Bloom. And that was it. Really."

"But he went home knowing you had the address book. And the pictures."

"And one of them's particularly interesting," Savella said. "The one of the people at the table." He waited until Feidy picked up Night Out. "The picture was taken at a hotel in Dallas. The guy in the dark suit? I'm pretty sure that's Jack Ruby."

"The Kennedy guy?" Feidy jabbed a finger at Ruby's image. "This one?"

"The guy who killed Oswald," he said. "And I think the young girl on the end there might be Mary Bloom."

Feidy studied the photograph. "Since we're being honest now, what have you found out about her?"

Savella laid out his disappointing research results. "My next step was going to be that ring. It would be nice to know where she got it. Maybe find somebody who knew her that way, fill in the blanks."

The detective slipped the ring on her pinkie and held out her hand to examine it.

"You coming to work for us now? Is that it?" she said. "Anyway, I wish I had all this sooner." She took off the ring and dropped it back in the envelope, then added the photographs and the address book and bent the metal clasp to close the flap. "But we go on."

"Listen," Savella said hesitantly, "I know I'm not in a position to ask this, but any chance you could give me a heads-up if you find anything here?"

She fixed him with a hard stare. For the first time, Savella thought, she looked like a cop.

"Here's what I don't get," she said. "Why didn't you tell me about this the day you thought someone was in your house? Or after the break-in at your girlfriend's? Especially after that. You're a bright guy. You had to figure there was a connection."

Savella pulled a face. "I was wrong. But I didn't want to upset her, I suppose."

"She winds up getting hurt, upset would be the least of your problems. You think that was smart? Bad enough you committed a crime. I could charge you right now for taking this stuff. But after the break-ins, the murders, you didn't think maybe that this was what they were looking for, what somebody was willing to *kill* for?"

"Look, I couldn't be sure there was a connection. My house, hers, it could have been—"

"Kids, yeah, I heard you the other night." Feidy leaned forward, elbows on her knees. "You want a heads-up? Here's one—there were knife marks on Ravic's body, stab wounds on his arm, stab wounds on his cheek. Somebody had some fun with him before he died.

"Two break-ins. A couple of bodies. You can blame it on kids all you want, but I think you know better."

# 19

It began the way these things do, with a phone call to a friend at the radio: how's Bianca, *y los ninos*, the kids are fine? The Dolphins need a quarterback, and oh by the way, I got something you're gonna wanna hear. And just like that, the Key West papers were the flavor of the day in Little Havana, flogged relentlessly, morning drive, afternoon drive, all-night talk, until you couldn't live in Miami and not know about them.

A simple phone call, and then a trip across the river, to a midtown Manhattan office building and upstairs to a long cheerless corridor, and at the end of the hall, the high priest of television talk, nibbling at a tuna-on-that-Arab-bread and scowling through the *Times* for evidence of treason. No time for small talk here. It was a buyer's market: if television didn't cover it, it never happened. But Abel Garcia did his job and by evening, just as soon as the producers could deep-six the saga of this month's missing coed, Cuba was the topic du jour.

Garcia was lucky this time: the monster needed feeding. Its usual fare—mother drowns babies, pop star goes crazy, tornado destroys town—was missing from the larder. The stomach growled for sustenance and here it was, crawling across the bottom of the screen—*Cuba Planning Terror Attack?* The lacquered blonde on MSNBC, the retread with the comb-over on Fox, and

CNN's kid-of-the-month panted out whatever was at hand—new twists, old turns, mindless rumors—to finish the picture. An army of retired spies and generals shared split screens with file footage of Cuban military exercises, a victorious Fidel at the Bay of Pigs, and ominous-looking laboratories. Scientists were summoned under the blinding lights to describe the intricacies of a chemical or biological attack. The network stables of political strategists, more familiar with vote counts than terror tactics, were suddenly instant experts on all things Cuban.

The frenzy peaked two days later in a hotel ballroom in Miami when the chairman of the Senate Armed Services Committee warned a meeting of aging Cuban exiles, pucker-faced men with fading hopes, that Castro's agents were already in the country, having slipped into California through a concrete tunnel that snaked from Mexicali to a shabby ranch house in Calexico. And for good measure, the senator wondered if Venezuela and Iran were helping Cuba mount the attack.

Venezuela, Iran, and Cuba. Oh Lord in heaven, *the fucking trifecta.*

Just not true, the president's spokesman said, and Secretary Elshak rushed up to the Hill to reassure Congress. But the denials couldn't cut through the media clutter. Hour after hour, the hosts churned the story, whipping up a frothy brew of anger, fear, and outrage, laced with a lethal dose of uninformed speculation and malevolent conjecture. Midway barkers driven by one rule: no one talks for more than half a minute without being interrupted. Now the Cubans were everywhere. Limbaugh had two men taken off an Amtrak train in Delaware after passengers reported jittery Latins. Hannity heard five Cubans were in custody after a police raid on an apartment owned by a leftist community organizer in Jersey City. Beck learned a plane was delayed on the tarmac in Houston for four hours while the FBI grilled its pilot and copilot. Dirty bomb threats against a football stadium in Phoenix. A plot to blow up the Harbor Tunnel in Baltimore. A weird smell in New York City, and the IRT subway shut down. An unceasing torrent of imagination, all of it carried live across America.

And just when the shows began to acquire the feel of a wedding hall after the band has gone home, the Cubans snapped at the bait. Before dawn one morning, wheezing Soviet-era buses packed with the faithful and the forced poured into Havana, dumping their cargo along the Malecon. A quarter-million people marched on the US Interests Section, roaring, "*Cuba, si, yanquis, no, patria o muerte.*" *Fatherland or death*: a good day to be Cuban, never mind what came next. But it was a bit different this time. Raul, not Fidel, took the open-air stage, and not for him his brother's olive green fatigues and white sneakers—a gray suit and silver tie set off by gold-rimmed glasses, a CEO addressing his executive board. None of Fidel's six-hour stem-winders either; Raul wrapped it up in forty-five minutes, and in truth his heart didn't seem all that much into even that. But he had a message: Washington was trumping up false allegations to justify an invasion of Cuba. And he had news: a massive military exercise, involving a hundred thousand soldiers and a half million reservists, to prepare for the assault.

Drearily familiar stuff, the marches, the inflamed oratory, the revolutionary fervor. But it was enough to jump-start the chatter. The Cuban army on the move?

The navy put out to sea and the sky dark with MiGs? Where in the world would this all end?

Abel Garcia tuned in every night, enveloped in a baggy blue tracksuit to ward off the chills that came over him more and more frequently lately. Sipping a cup of tea, he put the remote through its paces, flipping between channels until the shows began to morph together into one miasmic cloud of impending doom. He should have been proud of what he'd accomplished, pleased he still had the touch, knew the buttons to push. But it was different this time. The thrill of the cause was strangely missing. Who were these people, he wondered, these faces who filled his screen every night? Strangers, almost all of them. Only Buchanan he recognized, an old friend, an ally from way back. He seemed to live on television, shuttling from show to show, morning, noon, and night, offering his dark and gloomy predictions. Garcia imagined his dressing room—a well-stocked liquor cabinet, the closet filled with dark-blue suits and red-striped ties, a quiet place to sit and wait until they came to whisk him off for another few minutes on-air.

Buchanan, he knew. The rest? Not journalists, not hardly, not like the old days anyway. They were entertainers, using words to enrage and frighten and amuse and ridicule, like all good showmen. It wasn't about the politics or the policies, and that, in the end, was the problem. Just as it was for Pena—the son, not the father—this was business, plain and simple. Abel got the point: make sure no one touched that dial. Lots of speculation; throw it out there and see what sticks. Two days later, when somebody says how do you know, it might have been the *New York Times* or the *Washington Post,* or did the secretary of state make that point on *Meet The Press?* And now the rumor hardens into fact. Marauding Cubans would do the trick nicely, thanks very much, and until it didn't work anymore, they would never let it go.

All Cuba, all day long. Quite a thing, but a lie all the same, and that was no cause for applause.

Still, maybe now they wouldn't need the Russians.

---

The four o'clock ferry from Red Hook was crowded— maids and waiters heading to work on St. John, schoolchildren on their way home, a horde of early season vacationers. The colonel stood outside on the bow and let the warm Caribbean breeze flow over him. He never grew tired of the forty-minute run to Cruz Bay, around the rocky cliffs of Long Point, through the aquamarine waters of Great St. James Island, its white sandy beaches shaded by sea grape trees, then a straight shot to St. John. He was always a little bit disappointed when the ferry docked.

It was a weekly deal, his Wednesday-afternoon trip to St. Thomas. Once there had been a woman down the hill, Ruthie Reynolds from Pittsburgh, a few years younger, all pearls and sensible clothes. She would drink her wine, he would nurse a beer, and then he would pull her close and kiss her roughly, and she would push away with a coy smile, wait, wait, oh wait, the same damn dance every time. Ruthie, see, she wanted to *talk* first, about his past, mostly about his goddamn wife, as if simply hearing about that relationship could give the two of them a lifetime of their own. So he stopped calling. He liked her all right, as far as that went. She'd flown up to Miami to visit him when he got sick. But Ruthie liked to talk, and it was a small island.

So now it was Evangelista who served his needs, a chocolate mountain of a woman with huge breasts that spilled out of her Technicolored blouses, an aging wonder with a wide smile and a Caribbean lilt. He had never paid for it before, not in all the years in Latin America or in Asia, where that was what you did. But now it was just...easier this way. Lately, though, lying in her engulfing arms, listening to the tape player next to the bed offering mood music in languages he never understood, the muddied sounds of midafternoon traffic bubbling up from the street below, he found himself...talking. Idle chatter, nothing more, but wouldn't Ruthie be surprised. Ever the good sport, Evangelista tried everything, but after a few minutes it was more of an irritation than anything else, and he would abruptly buckle his pants. She said it was a phase, it would pass, suggested a pill. But he knew he was done and impatiently waved off the help. So they would talk. Somehow it was different with her. Maybe it was the crisp new bills he left on the plastic card table in the kitchen.

The ferry shuddered to a stop in the harbor. He beat the stampede to shore, walked quickly across the dock, and ducked into Café Iguana, where he slid onto a stool in the corner. His stool, his corner, and if someone happened to be sitting there when he arrived, the day was shot.

The bartender, a stringy kid with limp blond hair, uncapped a bottle of Budweiser and placed it on the bar—no glass. The television over the bar was tuned to CNN, but muted. On the screen a picture of Fidel Castro appeared. The colonel pulled a pack of Camels from his jacket pocket, lighted one with a lime-green Bic.

"Neil," he said, a command, "turn up the TV, please."

The bartender glanced at his three other customers. Probably wouldn't mind. And the colonel—a regular, two beers every Wednesday afternoon, two singles for the tip, then out the door. He grabbed the remote control and punched up the volume.

For the next ten minutes, the colonel listened, slowly sipping his beer, as the world rattled sabers. He listened, scratching off the red-white-and-blue Bud label with a fingernail, his mind racing back across the years. He was in Guatemala, with the CIA and three thousand angry exiles, the second wave, ready to go, and left with their dicks in their hands when Kennedy said no to air cover. And then he goes on the TV and tells the fucking world he made a mistake. A mistake? *Betrayal.* Sitting at the bar, the colonel could feel the bile rising, and he washed it back with beer. They kept training, sure their time would come, because the man said so, General Lyman Lemnitzer, the fucking chairman of the goddamn Joint Chiefs of Staff—they don't come any higher, and this was sixty-two, when Americans loved their soldiers, believed every last damn thing they said. But soon as he flashed some balls, they packed him off to Europe to watch the Russians.

The hell of it was, it would have worked; the colonel believed that to his core. Operation Northwoods, they called it: a boat full of refugees sinks, or a plane is hijacked, or someone shells Guantanamo, or maybe John Glenn never makes it back—take your pick. Point is, Cubans get blamed, and next thing you know, the marines are in Havana, Castro's hanging from his heels on the Malecon, and the colonel's little army is shipping out from Guatemala to take back its country.

But instead, it was Lemnitzer in Brussels and the colonel on the night plane to Phnom Penh, halfway round the world, almost as far as they could send him before he started circling back. And Operation Northwoods with a dagger through its heart.

"You done with that?" Neil was motioning at the television. The colonel looked up at the screen; the day's stock prices flashed where Castro's face once loomed. He nodded, and Neil clicked the remote.

The colonel drained his beer, letting the last few lukewarm droplets linger in his mouth for a few extra seconds before he swallowed. The boy on the boat—a fool's errand, a senseless favor for an old friend. And Jesus, it's a long way from television bullshit to boots on the ground. But maybe Arturo's kid actually knew what he was doing. His breathing caught a moment at the prospect. Just don't let's fuck it up this time.

He glanced at his watch. Early yet, just past six. Maybe he'd give Ruthie a call.

---

Inside the barn Father Remsen could hear the boys, their voices rising in taunt and challenge as they tinkered with the balky engine of the ancient John Deere tractor, which had broken down during morning chores. Remsen had been supervising, sweltering in the heat, nearly overwhelmed by the musky smells of the horses pawing the straw-covered floors of their stalls, when the news crackled over the portable radio, and all of a sudden he needed some air.

Put it together, the priest told himself, swatting away a swarm of flies, what do I know? *There's another project,* the colonel had told him, and a dead Cuban turns up with a set of war plans. *We can't let her fuck things up,* the colonel had said, and someone searching for something in Mary's apartment murders her super and her next-door neighbor. Then somehow—and this didn't surprise him, not at all, because he knew these people—somehow the plans leak and the country's on high alert.

Remsen rubbed the back of his neck, slick with perspiration. It cannot be, he thought despondently, not again, not this time.

Because there was a *last* time.

The faces changed that summer—transfers, build-ups, stand-downs—but they all shared the same vocabulary, words like treason and treachery and sellout, and when the white-hot anger dwindled to a bitter-cold fury, retribution, revenge, and reprisal. Even the amusement had a hard edge. The two Agency interpreters, Nathan and Steve, came out of the jungle with a half dozen human ears on a string and a blue-bellied monkey named Penelope. Every night they would pile bananas in the corner of the dining room and fill a bucket with cold beer. Penelope would eat her fill of the fruit, then lap up the beer until she fell into the bucket, drunk out of her monkey skull. Bread and circuses, the colonel called it, and how they roared when Penelope took her tumble. But even before she licked herself dry, their rage returned. The anguished howls, loud enough to be heard above the monsoonal rains pounding on the bamboo shutters, were frightening testimony to that.

The colonel calmed them. They were still in the game, just playing on a different field. And that worked for a time, until, to his evident shock, he stumbled on the next play. Obsessed with Castro and now too close to Diem—that was the bill of particulars against him. Too many trips to Saigon for who-knew-what. Suddenly, again, it was time to go, and this time, no monkey to relieve the pressure.

But first, foreboding: Nathan and Steve oversleep, miss their Tiger Airlines flight out, and the plane crashes in the South China Sea. No coincidences, not in the colonel's mind.

"They want us all gone," he warned that night, and Remsen never doubted him.

A sharp crack echoed through the barn, and the priest flinched. Only a backfire, he quickly realized, the tractor, and he relaxed, but too late to shove away the memories. Up from Phnom Penh for a few days in the jungle, temporary assignment, the colonel called it. Nathan and Steve, swilling lager from two oversized German steins, organized the Colt Olympics. They liberated a case of Heinz Franks N' Beans and set up a row of cans along the back fence, the idea being whoever blasted the most into the jungle got a three-day pass to Saigon. Remsen's first shot with the heavy .45 missed so badly the mules grazing thirty yards up the road kicked and brayed in fear, and the recoil almost dropped him in the dust, much to the loud amusement of the Agency guys. But no laughter from the porch, just an acid-laced bellow from the colonel, glaring out at him in disgust: "What are you *afraid* of?" Remsen put his head down and kept it there the next time the pistol kicked. "Not afraid of nothing, sir," he shouted out through gritted teeth as the can exploded in a cloud of red, but that wasn't the truth, and they all knew it.

The tractor engine sputtered, and Remsen heard shouts of elation. Esterhaz, most likely, he thought, the car thief from Carbondale. The tractor ran roughly for a minute, then died again with a loud bang. "Shit," someone shouted, and a voice demanded, "What you fuckin' do, Omar?" Remsen allowed himself a slight grin. Give Esterhaz another shot at it. The boy was a wizard with a screwdriver.

And so a midnight run out of Saigon, to Manila and a month in a barracks at Clark, working the phones for a clue to their fate, sitting on the tarmac day after day waiting for a plane out. But the calls weren't returned, and everything with wings was going the other way. Finally, orders: Alaska, *Alaska*, but it almost didn't matter at that point, they were moving. A cargo plane dropped them in frigid Juneau, and it was another week before the weather changed again: the draining heat of East Texas, Fort Hood. No assignment, just a chance to stew and seethe while the army tried to figure out where to stash them. The colonel, for one, never forgot, never forgave.

But that bill had been paid, or had it? A panicked shudder convulsed Remsen's body, a stab of ice on the stifling hot afternoon. There was more death in the offing; he didn't need the headlines to tell him that. He had heard this talk before—angry voices, demands for action—and he knew where it ended. The killing had started again, and the trail of blood had found him in his rural hideaway. The police had already called, wanted to know about the address book, about Mary. There was no escaping this time. To run away would mean more death; he was sure of it. And it had to stop.

His mind drifted back to Mary's funeral, the readings she'd requested, Romans 12:17–21: *Do not be overcome by evil, but overcome evil with good.* He had tried, Lord knows he had, burrowing in his cornfields to offer help and hope to men as young as he was when the train went off the tracks. To give all that up, to walk away from the calling, to violate the sanctity of the sacrament, which is what it would take to stop them, to clear Mary's name, to protect her from what came next, as he hadn't done so many years ago—was it worth it?

The enormity of the sacrifice frightened him. Even the thought seemed a transgression. And yet.

Remsen dropped to his knees in the dusty barnyard, made the sign of a cross: *Bless me, Father, for I have sinned.*

The heat was unbearable.

He removed his collar and scratched his neck.

Inside the barn, the John Deere rumbled back to life, to cheers.

# 20

Isabella got the cruise-ship gig.

"Standards for blue hairs," she said, waving a travel brochure. "But hey, Barbados, Antigua, St. Kitts. If they let me off the boat. Ship, boat, what do you call it?"

"Ship," said Savella. "Congrats. Really."

"Well, the timing's right, you know? I scrubbed the heck out of my place, Michael, but...I don't know, it just doesn't feel right. Doesn't feel like home, I guess."

"Now, see, I wouldn't have had that problem," he said, but the joke fell flat.

They sat on the tiny outdoor patio at Cameron's, shrouded in a fine mist pierced only by the headlights of passing cars. Not really outside weather, but Isabella had called it a little adventure and led him to a small table slick with condensation. She had come straight from a run; perspiration glinted on her face, and her shorts and T-shirt were dark with sweat. She dabbed at her brow with the white towel around her neck.

A waitress in a black skirt, looking unhappy about working outside on an inside morning, dropped two menus and a stack of paper napkins on the wet tabletop and dashed back inside. Isabella snatched a menu and opened it. "Are they still serving breakfast?"

"When do you leave?" Savella said.

"Well, that's the thing," she said. "Tomorrow."

"Tomorrow?"

"Yeah. Gotta meet the ship in Miami tomorrow."

"*Tomorrow.*"

A delivery truck with a red lobster logo splashed across its side stopped in front of the restaurant. The driver slid open the side door, pulled out a large basket of clams, and carried it inside.

"You need a ride to the airport?" Savella asked. "I'll drive you."

She wrinkled her nose. "Michael. It'll be too early."

"How too early?"

"I don't know. Too early for you. Harold's gonna take me."

She pushed back from the table, leaned down, and retied the laces of her running shoes. "You OK with this? It's only ten days, but..."

Savella nodded, a bit too vigorously. "It'll be a nice break for you. And you're right, ten days. Just...*tomorrow.*"

"'Cause if you're not OK with it...," she said, and he knew in an instant she would stay if he asked. He wanted to, for a million reasons. He'd lost his job. He'd lied to the cops. And someone wanted something he'd stolen from a dead woman, wanted it badly enough to kill. Isabella would help him find a way, Isabella who believed everything was possible. *Stay,* he wanted to cry out, *stay.*

But what he said was, no, go ahead. What he said was, I think maybe I'd like a cheeseburger. What he said was, I'll be fine. And, to his great surprise, he meant it.

Across the table, Isabella smiled.

Isabella, who believed everything was possible.

Even Michael Savella.

The mail was poking through the slot in the front door—some bills, two magazines, and a plain envelope with his name and address printed in block letters, no return address. He ripped it open and an unmarked tape cassette tumbled out. No note, no invoice. The postmark indicated the envelope had been mailed in Philadelphia two days earlier.

Savella turned the cassette slowly in his hand. He didn't have a tape player. Only a CD player in the Altima. Who used tapes anymore?

He ran an inventory of the neighbors. The only one he'd even spoken with was Mrs. DiLorenzo next door. He had met her, briefly, just three times, once at the curb with their garbage cans on trash day—"You're the one who writes about dead people," she said, accusingly, and what could he say—and twice when she knocked on his door to complain about his dog and didn't seem to understand when he explained he didn't have any pets. They didn't know each other, but she knew his face. And he'd heard music in her place. Maybe a tape player.

Savella slipped the cassette into his pocket and walked around the corner. The neighborhood was quiet on this wet afternoon. He'd have to move, of course. Fifteen hundred a month—too much rent for a man without a job. Isabella's apartment was a possibility; they'd discussed it before. But maybe not now, when it didn't even feel like home to her.

Mrs. DiLorenzo answered the door in a housecoat and slippers, her hennaed hair done up in a kerchief, a cigarette in her right hand.

"What, is it my turn?" she said loudly, her eyes arched in surprise.

"Hi. No, no. It's not about work. Sorry to bother you, but would you happen to have a tape player?"

"A what, hon?"

He held up the cassette and wiggled it. "You know, to play one of these. It came in the mail this morning, and I don't know what it is. And I don't have a tape player."

"Oh, no. I don't think so. Unless…that?" She pointed to an ancient silver-and-black boom box on a table in the corner of the sunporch. "My nephew's kids. For the beach. The noise…" She shuddered and sucked on her cigarette.

"You think I could borrow it for a few minutes?"

She exhaled slowly, the smoke curling toward the ceiling. "Well, use it here, I guess. If it's only gonna be a few minutes."

"You sure? I wouldn't want to bother you."

"No, go on ahead," she said, and stepped aside to let him in.

Even with the fan turning quietly on the ceiling, the front room was stifling, as if she'd been running the heater. The decor was shore casual: a long sofa with a slipcover featuring seagulls; a lamp with a miniature lifeguard stand as a base; a table littered with plastic bottles of suntan lotion. Mrs. DiLorenzo leaned against the doorjamb and puffed on her cigarette as Savella crossed to the boom box and inserted the tape cassette. He pressed Play and the tape whirred into action. There were several seconds of silence, then an abrupt click and an older man's voice, raspy, caught in midsentence:

"*—what I mean? That's how you can tell.*"

The sound was muffled, as if the microphone was wrapped in something.

*"You'll let me know when you need me to leave? You will do that, won't you? No sense in overdoing it."* A younger man, polite. Savella closed his eyes, tried to identify the voices, but came up empty.

*"I can take care of myself."*

*"I know you can, I know. Just checking."*

A door creaking open, a faint burst of distant laughter.

*"Hi, yes. We'll just be a few more minutes, and then I'll come and get you. Is that all right? Thanks."*

The door, closing.

*"How much longer is this gonna be?"* The older man, irritated.

*"Well, of course, it's really up to you. This is about you."*

*"If it's about me, I'm done. Get her back in here."*

A phlegmy throat clearing.

*"Are you sure? Because I think there's a few other things we need to discuss, you need to talk about."*

*"So who's this for? You or me?"*

*"What do you mean? You."*

*"But you're directing the show, aren't you."*

*"Well, helping you through it."*

*"What else, then?"*

*"How about Mary? We haven't talked about her."*

Mary. Savella pressed Stop, then Rewind, and played the tape again.

*"How about Mary? We haven't talked about her."*

Savella paused the tape, fumbled in his pocket for a pen, looked around for something to write on. A paper napkin blotched with lipstick lay on the arm of the sofa. "Would you mind?" he asked, holding the napkin aloft. "I want to make some notes."

Mrs. DiLorenzo shrugged. Savella pressed Play again.

*"What about her?"*

*"Well, let's start with why was she there."*

*"What the hell's the difference?"*

A racking cough, then another.

*"Can I get you some water?"*

*"I can get it myself."*

*"You sure?"*

The sound of water trickling into plastic.

*"What the hell was I gonna do with her?"*

*"You could have left her behind."*

*"And I should have. Would have raised some questions. But goddamn right I should have. My mistake. But it doesn't matter anymore. Hasn't mattered for a long time."*

*"So she was, what do we say, wrong place at the wrong time."*

*"She was, what do we say, like gum on the shoe. Couldn't get rid of her. All that bullshit about wanting out, and when I left her alone, she went nowhere. Don't you forget that."* The older man was getting angry. *"Her choice. You remember that. Her choice. And afterward we were in a hurry."*

A hand slapping wood. *"Missed it. Fucking thing. What's a fly doing in here in the first place?"*

Chair scraped floor.

*"You know something, this sure as hell isn't the way I remember these things going. Not one fucking bit like what I remember."*

*"Well, it's a little unconventional, I grant you."*

*"You grant me, huh? A little unconventional?"*

*"I'm only trying to get it all out. Get it straight."*

*"Get what straight? Goddamn it, I told you this, now. What are all these questions about Mary? She's got nothing to*

*do with it. With any of it. She had no idea the son of a bitch was gonna die.*"

"*Yep.*"

"*Now let's go. I need—*"

The tape ended suddenly. Savella scribbled furiously on the napkin. *Listen to me*, Mary Bloom had said as they awaited the ambulance, but she ran out of time. He might have been desperate for a column, but his instincts were right. All those duck decoys and elderly Boy Scouts, and it turns out Mary Bloom was the one with a story to tell. If he only knew what it was.

"Friends of yours?"

Mrs. DiLorenzo was standing over him, cigarette lighter in hand. He forced a laugh and pressed the Eject button. "I have no idea," he said. "Maybe. Anyway, thanks for the help."

"All that dirty language," she said, fishing a pack of Kents from the folds of her housecoat.

Savella pulled the tape from the machine. "Just some friends, probably, you know? Rehearsing a play, or fooling around. That's all."

Mrs. DiLorenzo chewed on her lip. "Funny," she said finally, and lit her cigarette.

Funny, Savella thought, as he stumbled out of the hothouse into the cool breeze. Mary dead, the super dead, the neighbor dead. And maybe a fourth—*no idea the son of a bitch was gonna die.*

Yeah, funny. Fucking hilarious.

---

*Gonna get her at six*, Harold said. *Need to make it to Philly before the morning rush. You want to surprise her, don't be late.*

Savella arrived fifteen minutes early. One light burned upstairs, and he sat in the love seat and watched her pass in front of the window, back and forth, as she prepared to leave, his own private shadow puppet show. Then the light died and a few minutes later Isabella appeared at the front door, gripping a suitcase in her right hand.

She spotted him in the shadows as she reached the bottom of the stairs. "Michael?" An easy smile. "It's so early."

"I know. But I wanted to wish you luck."

"Aw, that's so sweet." She dropped her bags and hugged him.

"Don't let it get around."

The high beams of Harold's Mercury caught them in mid-kiss as it pulled down the alley. The agent got out of the car and winked at Savella. "If I knew you were going to be here, I'd have stayed in bed."

Isabella rolled her eyes. "Who you kidding, Harold?"

He laughed, grabbed her bag, and loaded it in the trunk, closed the lid. "We'd better get a move on, hon. You miss your plane, that boat ain't gonna wait for you."

"Ship, Harold. It's a ship." She hugged Savella. "Sure this is OK?"

"Go, go. You'll be back before we know it."

Savella followed the Mercury as it backed down the alley, then stood on the sidewalk and watched the taillights creep slowly up the block. And as the car passed under the glare of the streetlight, he was certain, would swear to it, that Isabella twisted in her seat, craned her neck, and looked back to where he stood, looked back for him.

Always the easy way out, forever his weakness. But not this time.

This time he would be there when she came home.

# 21

No waiting this visit: the civilian aide muttered his name into the phone, and before he could tell Savella to take a seat, Sylvie Feidy was at the door, waving him inside. As they shook hands, Savella noticed a purple bruise across her right cheek, a streak of mud down one leg of her pantsuit.

"Guy ran, and we went and got him," she said when his gaze lingered on her face a beat too long.

At her desk, she pointed to a chair, then leaned over and straightened the photograph of the old couple standing in front of a whitewashed building.

"Your parents?" he asked.

Feidy ran a finger along the top of the frame. "Grandparents. Back in the old country."

"Where's that?"

"The Middle East."

"Feidy," he said slowly, trying to make a connection.

"Lebanese." She motioned again at the photo. "My grandfather's house. A long time ago."

"No kidding. Where was it? I worked over there for a while."

"To tell you the truth, I forget. He was Palestinian. He lost it, the house, after one of the wars. They wound up in Lebanon and eventually he brought my grandmother over here, but his heart wasn't in it. He told me once it was like they were permanently on a trip. Very strange."

"Those are sad stories."

She stared at the photo for a moment, then offered a dismissive wave. "An old house. That's all." She sat down, pulled a file folder from her drawer and spread it open in front of her. "I talked to your priest. He wasn't a lot of help. You forget to tell me something else, or what?"

Savella took the tape cassette from his pocket and held it out. "This came in the mail yesterday. No return address, no note. It's part of a conversation between two guys talking about someone named Mary, and one of them says something about this Mary not knowing someone was going to die."

"Really." Feidy reached across the desk and plucked the tape from his fingers. Holding it by the edges, she examined it closely. "Where's the envelope?"

Savella grimaced. "Sitting on my desk. I guess I should have brought it."

Feidy opened her desk drawer and rummaged through its contents, triumphantly held up an old Sony cassette player. "Let's see what we got." She sat down behind her desk, slipped on a set of headphones, inserted the tape, and pressed Play. "Shit." She snapped open the battery compartment and scowled. Opening another drawer, Feidy found three new batteries and loaded them in the cassette player. She pressed Play again and after a few seconds began scribbling notes on a yellow legal pad.

It hadn't even occurred to Savella to keep the tape from Feidy. Two people dead, a lying priest, a ransacked apartment, and now, in his mailbox, a voice on a tape talking about someone else dying. He was in the deep water now. Feidy was right: this wasn't kids. Savella was it. He'd tried hard to hide, but a fender bender had flushed him into open ground. Two choices now: slip back into the shadows and hope no one noticed, or find some answers and live his life.

No choice, really: he was tiring of the dark.

Savella looked around the squad room, half empty in midafternoon. A knot of detectives was gathered around a coffeemaker in the back of the room, one of them telling a story, the others laughing loudly every few sentences. Near the door a young woman pounded on a computer keyboard. And always, insistent, the muted chirping of the telephones. It felt like a newsroom, drowsy a few hours before deadline, the pace bound to quicken as night fell. The passing thought triggered a spasm of regret. The way it ended at the *Post-Herald* bothered him. Not just quitting, but setting himself up for the fall, waiting for someone else to pull the trigger. Again the easy way out. Where had he heard that before? The answer came in a babble of reproving voices, teachers, bosses, lovers, undimmed by the passing of time. His guilty burden, and he recognized them all, every single one. The intensity of the memories surprised him. He was supposed to meet Bobby later for a few drinks. But somehow that didn't quite seem like the thing to do anymore.

"Hey. Michael. You with me?"

Feidy, the tape rewinding, headphones lying on the desktop. "I said, these two guys. I don't suppose you recognized the voices."

Savella shook his head.

"And no idea why someone would send this to you?" she asked.

"None. Someone maybe wants me to know that Mary, and I'm guessing that's Mary Bloom, didn't have anything to do with, what, a killing? But that's pure speculation."

"Any thoughts about who might have sent it?"

Savella spread his arms wide. "The numbers in her book. I must have talked to fifty people. Could be any one of them, I guess."

"OK then."

"So what are you thinking?"

"We'll see. This could be related to the killings, or maybe not. Could be related to the break-in at your place, or your girlfriend's, or maybe not. We'll see."

"Oh, come on," Savella said. "What did you say outside Isabella's that night? Someone sending a message, to me, or to Isabella. I mean, I don't want to be melodramatic here, but..."

Feidy popped open the cassette player and extracted the tape.

"In addition to which, I could use a little help," Savella said. "There might be a pretty good story in all this."

The detective dropped the tape into a plastic bag and zipped it shut. "Who you gonna write it for?"

Savella offered a faint smile. "You guys don't miss a thing, do you?"

"We try not to," Feidy said.

A slight man with a tired face, the gun on his hip the only giveaway that he was police, placed a slip of paper on Feidy's desk. She snatched it up and began reading.

"This our guy?" she asked.

"And he's asking for a lawyer."

Feidy studied the paper. "Abdul-Hakim? What happened to Willie Thomas?"

"You know how it rolls these days, Sylvie. Put 'em in jail for a couple of years, and when they come out, they're not eating pork."

Feidy's head snapped up. "That's great, Ron. Nice approach. Very tolerant."

"What? What'd I say?" He grinned and walked away.

"And they wonder why we've got problems," Feidy said. With a tired sigh, she stood and clapped her hands twice. "Anyway. That's where we are, Michael. You're gonna get me that envelope?"

He was halfway across the squad room when she called out his name. He turned and she held up the ring he had taken from Mary Bloom's apartment. "Western High School," she shouted. "Macomb, Illinois. Maybe fifty miles from your priest's farm. Go figure."

Then she was sitting again, and reaching for a file.

———————————

A place to start, anyway. Three names with Macomb addresses in Mary Bloom's book, but only one of them was still listed, an Alvin Lemke, and Savella hadn't yet reached him. Sitting at the kitchen table, Savella picked up the phone to try again, then paused. He'd made a mistake with the priest; he realized that now. Remsen knew more about Mary Bloom than he was willing to share. He might have been surprised by Savella's call, stunned, even, but the brief chat had tipped him to the game, gave him time to fix his story, and by the time he came East, for whatever reason he did, the priest was prepared to fend off every inquiry. This was no time for a repeat performance.

Savella rose and walked to the kitchen window, pulled open the blinds. At number twelve, a crew of day laborers was tearing into a first-floor front room, a veranda once, but shuttered long ago to make space for some exploding family. The windows were already missing; shards of glass and broken frames poked over the sides of a Dumpster parked on the sidewalk. The five workers—Mexicans, probably, from the makeshift shape-up that gathered every morning outside Home Depot—were well on the way to finishing the demolition, knocking down walls, clambering up a metal ladder to rip out the plaster ceiling. The room would be a porch again, open, airy, the ocean breeze blowing away the past, sea salt scrubbing out the stifling odors that had seeped into the walls over decades.

Savella turned away from the window. On the Internet, he dragged up a map of Illinois and located Macomb. A college town, Western Illinois University. Twenty-odd thousand residents, thirty miles from the Mississippi River. He widened the scope of the map slightly, then leaned into the screen and combed the surrounding area until he found what he was looking for: Lemoine, Illinois. A dot on the map, smaller than Macomb. And the home of New Beginnings treatment center, the Reverend Joseph Remsen's prairie redoubt, his safe haven for lost boys.

The good father, hard at work saving souls, just fifty miles south of where Mary Bloom attended high school. And absolutely no idea how his name wound up in her address book.

---

The Rendezvous Grille was another of Bobby's dives: last year's Christmas decorations drooping from the ceiling, all Sinatra all the time, one dyspeptic waiter, and an old pay phone in the rear over which hung a placard that read "Dreams Do Come True." A little after seven, five ironworkers at the bar matching shots and beers; a gaggle of hospital orderlies celebrating a birthday. Savella took a seat in the corner. At the bend of the bar, Bobby was deep in conversation with the Filipino hostess, a morose woman in her forties with a mole on her right cheek.

"Nice neighborhood, I guess," she said, tugging at the hem of her too-tight red skirt. "I'm not prejudicial, but no black people there."

"You married?" Bobby asked.

"No."

"Goin' out with anyone?"

"No," she said sadly, and she rubbed her face with both hands, as if she could wipe away the wrinkles.

Bobby drained his vodka tonic. "Well, get one of those nice guys who live out by you now. Lots of bucks. Then you don't need this shit."

A wistful look crossed her face. "Money not worth it sometimes."

Bobby laughed, and she went off to answer the telephone.

"Money not worth it," Bobby said, and he laughed again. "A little confused, is all."

The waiter bumped through the kitchen door, and Sinatra was drowned out by the clatter of pots and pans. Bobby signaled the bartender for a fresh drink and pointed at Savella. "My friend here too."

"Just a club soda," Savella said.

Bobby squinted at him. "You sick?"

"No, just working on something."

Bobby slid along the bar to Savella's place. "Since when did that ever stop you?"

"Oh, it's just this Mary Bloom thing."

"This Mary Bloom thing. What Mary Bloom thing? When did Mary Bloom become a thing?"

Savella frowned. "It's a little complicated. That's all."

"Not so complicated," Bobby said. "Two bodies and the cops looking for a killer. Not where you want to be."

"They're not looking at me or you."

"And you know this how?"

"What do you mean? You said your story checked out."

Talk about miracles—Bobby had an honest-to-God alibi. At the time of the murders, he was someplace where people were actually willing to admit they saw him: at work, *what were the odds*, making T-shirts.

The bartender placed a club soda in front of Savella, and he took his time squeezing the lemon.

"One thing I learned," Bobby said. "Same with cops as it is with everybody else—figure they're lying to you. You don't trust nobody."

"Not even you, Bobby?"

Bobby turned back to his drink. "Just saying. Words to live by."

"Well, I don't know anymore. I'm starting to think that's a hell of a way to live. I'm starting to think you either take some chances, trust some people, or spend your life hiding in the closet."

Bobby shook his head. "Your girl singer, huh? Man, what they can do."

The men drank silently for a moment. "So what Mary Bloom thing?" Bobby said. "She died in an auto accident. I was there, remember?"

"But then there were two murders in her building. And I come home and maybe surprise an intruder. And someone definitely breaks into Isabella's place. Looking for something. You see where I'm going?"

"You're thinking it's the pictures."

"And the address book."

Bobby swirled the fruit in his glass with his forefinger. The music suddenly spiked—*Sinatra at the Sands*— and Savella leaned in to make sure Bobby heard the rest of it.

"It gets better. Today in the mail I get a tape of two men talking about someone dying. And there's this whole conversation about someone named Mary knowing nothing about it. They don't say Mary Bloom, OK, but what do you think? And the cop I shouldn't trust, she tells me the ring I took was from a high school in a town in Illinois up the road from the priest's farm. The priest who never heard of Mary Bloom."

Bobby watched the old waiter deliver a platter of burgers to the hospital party. "This Mary," he said. "You're almost taking it personal."

"Maybe. I guess I don't like mysteries. Or people lying to me."

"So you're gonna chase this some more."

Savella nodded.

"Now that you've got the time."

"I'm going to check out this town in Illinois. There's a name in her phone book, Alvin Lemke—he might remember something. And while I'm in the neighborhood, maybe drop in on Remsen. See if his memory is clearing up."

Bobby sighed. "You want some company?"

"You kidding?"

"What the fuck. Like the man said, don't die wondering." Bobby finished his drink and frowned at Savella's glass. "Club soda," he said. "I'm liking this already."

# 22

They found a space in the short-term garage at Philadelphia International and were almost at security when Bobby held up a hand.

"We gotta go back to the car," he said.

Savella looked at his watch.

"Just come on," said Bobby, and he hoisted his bag and headed back toward the garage. At the car, he asked Savella to open the trunk, then looked up and down the aisle. Satisfied no one was watching, he pulled a blue steel revolver out of his bag, lifted the cover off the spare tire compartment and shoved the gun into the wheel well.

"Forgot it was in there," he said. "You wanna bet they'd have some questions at the X-ray thing?"

"What are you even doing with that?"

"Dangerous world out there," Bobby said. "In case you haven't noticed."

---

The drive up had been easy enough, and the slow shuffle through check-in and security wasn't too bad either. But trouble began, as Savella knew it would, when the flight attendant slammed shut the cabin door. Within seconds he began to squirm nervously in his seat, flinching with every change of direction, each new unfamiliar noise. As the plane roared down the runway and left the ground, he pressed hard against the headrest, closed his eyes, and slowly began counting to three hundred. The first five minutes, he had read somewhere, were the most dangerous of all.

"Jesus," Bobby muttered. "You flew all over the goddamn world."

Savella forced a smile. "I never said I liked it."

In fact, there was nothing he hated more. It had been like that for years. Strapped in and trapped, he flew in dread from the moment the plane backed away from the gate until the pilot ended the terror by touching down. But you couldn't very well tell them you wanted to cover the world and then refuse to fly. So he gritted his teeth and prayed to God they wouldn't run out of whiskey.

The Embraer banked sharply and headed west. Two hours in the air. Savella pulled the seat belt tight and death-gripped the armrests until his fingers cramped.

---

In Saint Louis, they rented a car, crossed the Mississippi, then turned north, the radio spitting out the headlines—*Markets down on unemployment news, White House calls Cuban invasion papers a fraud, governor signs abortion bill*—until Bobby took control and punched up sports talk, then psychobabble from a smooth voice, and finally seventies rock. After the terror of the plane flight, Savella was reassured by the feel of the tires gripping solid ground, but still there was something edgy about the journey. He had been here before, on a glide path into the unknown, to a place where a boy with a

Spiderman doll gets blown to bits because someone wanted to make a point. And now, once again, far from his moorings. It made no sense. Why was he pursuing any of this? Never mind the pictures and the priest, or Mary Bloom's life and death. He could pick up and go, find another place in another city, another country. It was what he had always done. But not this time. Something was pushing him into the middle of this one. *She's got nothing to do with it.* So here he was, because two cars collided and Savella leaned in the window to hear her: *Listen to me.*

---

They reached Macomb just after dusk, checked into a Comfort Inn, and headed to a restaurant down the street for a drink and some dinner. Savella and Bobby took seats at the bar, empty except for an old man with a double chin huddled in the corner. A waitress at the cash register looked up from her magazine, flashed a quick smile, and called out "Frank," and a young man came out of the kitchen to take their orders.

While he made the drinks, Savella asked him whether Western High School was nearby.

"Western?" Frank asked. He wiped his hands with a towel. "Never heard of it. You got the right town?"

*The right town?* "I'm pretty sure, yeah," Savella said. "Western High School. Macomb, Illinois."

Frank shook his head. "One high school in town. Macomb High. And it's been Macomb as long as I know, anyway." He glanced at the waitress. "Marie? You ever heard of Western High School?"

She put down her magazine. "Nope. *Macomb* High School."

The bartender turned to the old man. "Hey, Jimmy, you ever heard of Western High School?" The old man didn't move. "Jimmy. *Jimmy*. Western High School?"

Jimmy raised his head. "Sure."

"Really? You heard of it?"

"Western. It was up at the university. Closed maybe thirty years ago."

"No kidding," said Frank. He looked at Savella and Bobby. "There you go."

"Not good," Savella muttered, reaching for his scotch. "Not good at all."

"Well, there gotta be records, no?" Bobby asked. "Goddamn school can't just disappear without a trace."

"Old paper. I don't need old paper. I need someone who knew Mary Bloom."

Bobby finished his drink and waved the empty glass at Frank. "I'm starving. Let's get some menus."

---

Alvin Lemke lived in a large red split-level home set under a canopy of old oak trees, one of which divided the driveway, in a quiet neighborhood of expensive landscaping, two- and three-car garages, and roofs bristling with satellite antennas. Savella parked at the curb in front of the house, and the two men crossed the lawn to the front door. Bobby pushed the doorbell, and a chime sounded inside. There was no answer. After a few moments, Bobby punched the bell twice more, harder, as if extra effort would change things.

"They're not home."

Savella twisted around to find the voice. In the next yard stood a man with a rake in his hand. "You looking for the Lemkes, they're not home."

"Any idea when they'll be back?" Savella called out.

The man lifted his rake and halfheartedly pawed at the pile of leaves at his feet.

"They went to the grocery store. Probably an hour or so."

Savella waved his thanks.

"We'll get some coffee," he said. "Stop back in a bit."

———————  ———————

The neighbor had disappeared by the time they returned, his rake left leaning against a tree next to a plastic garbage bag overflowing with fallen leaves. A late-model Acura was parked to one side of the oak-divided driveway. Perched on the Lemke porch was a small brown-and-white Jack Russell terrier, which barked loudly as Savella and Bobby walked up. Through the open screen door, a male voice shouted, "Baby," and the dog fell silent.

Savella carefully reached around the terrier and pressed the doorbell. A tall, trim, older man with blond hair matted down as if he'd only just taken off a baseball cap appeared in the doorway, wearing a white polo shirt and long maroon shorts that reached to his knees.

"Mr. Lemke?"

The man studied them warily.

"My name's Michael Savella and this is Bobby Weiss. We're reporters with a newspaper in New Jersey." Bobby grinned slightly at his unexpected hiring.

"OK," Lemke said, and he placed his hand on the doorknob, just in case.

"I think you might be able to help us with a story we're working on." Savella reached into the envelope and drew out the photograph of the young girl in the white raincoat and scarf. "Do you recognize her?"

Lemke stared down at the picture. His mouth fell open.

"Oh," he said softly. "My."

From inside the house came a woman's voice: "Who is it, honey?"

Lemke took the photo from Savella. The voice, closer: "Alvin?"

He turned slightly and answered, "It's Mary."

"Mary?" The voice sounded surprised, even alarmed. "She's here?"

A woman loomed behind Lemke now, short and stocky, in a red floral print sundress and sneakers. "She's here?" she repeated, with more urgency.

Lemke looked at Savella, who cleared his throat and shook his head. "No, she's not. I'm afraid I've got some bad news. She died in an automobile accident a few weeks ago."

The woman's hand moved slowly to her mouth, the tips of her fingers pressing against her lips. She leaned into her husband, their hips touching. Lemke's face registered nothing, but his shoulders had visibly tensed.

"Who are you again?" he asked, and Savella told him.

"I'm Alvin. This is my wife Brenda. Why don't you come on in?" He held the screen door open, turning aside to let them pass.

They descended a short flight of stairs to a large living room with a beamed ceiling and windows overlooking a lawn that sloped down to a meandering creek. "Sit anywhere," Lemke said with a careless wave, and moved to the windows. An athlete once, Savella thought. He walked with the confidence in his body that comes from playing games.

What's it all about, the Lemkes wanted to know, and for the next ten minutes Savella told them the story of the accident, the empty church, his desire to put flesh on the bare bones of a death notice, to create a memorial to a woman who few apparently knew. A life well lived, that's what they were after, and no need to mention the murders down the hall, the break-ins, the tape in the mail. Never mind the photos stashed in a tin box in the back of a bed table drawer, or the desperation of a dying woman as she implored him to listen. When he had finished, Savella sat back, laid the manila envelope on the table, took a notebook from his hip pocket, and waited.

The Lemkes settled into a white leather sofa. No one spoke for a long while. This was the hardest part. But if you did your spadework, if you set the stage, then you were in business. People couldn't stand the quiet. They needed to fill it up. They talked.

From the mantel over the fireplace came the ticking of an antique clock. The terrier slipped down the staircase and, pausing long enough to sniff the strangers, scampered across the polished wood of the living room floor, and nestled at Brenda's feet. The curtains on the windows giving on to the river rustled slightly as a warm breeze blew through. Lemke leaned forward and played distractedly with a bouquet of roses sitting in a glass pitcher on the coffee table. A few petals fluttered to the floor.

"Guess they've had it," Brenda murmured.

Lemke leaned back and folded his hands across his stomach, his eyes fixed on the dog.

"Years ago, when I was growing up, this was all farmland," he said softly. "Right out there, other side of the creek, was one of the biggest, the Moffett place. Then the university started growing, people needed housing, so...I grew up about two miles from here. All my life.

Went to high school here, and after went into the bar business. Never left. I was 4-F, so the army didn't want me. I just never left. Well, Chicago once or twice, St. Louis. But I'm still here. Didn't go far. From over there to over here. A couple miles. Not much of a story there, huh?"

He looked up with a pained smile. Brenda raised her chin and crossed her arms. "We like it here," she said firmly. "Just fine."

Lemke glanced at the notebook on Savella's lap, then turned to Bobby. "And what about you? Don't you take notes too?"

Bobby tapped the side of his head with a finger. "Photographic memory," he said, but Lemke wasn't listening. He looked down at the floor and rubbed his hands together, squeezing them so tightly they squeaked.

"Mary," he said, shaking his head once.

He glanced quickly at his wife, who hesitated for a moment, then patted him softly on the arm and stood.

"It's all right, Alvin," she said. "I'll put on some coffee."

# 23

He saw her for the first time in early '63, during home-room, sitting in the second row when classes resumed after Christmas break, at the desk that belonged to Tom Reinhardt until his family moved to Galesburg. The seat had been empty ever since, and then one morning it wasn't, and she was in his life.

That first day Mary was already a mystery. She didn't look like anyone Alvin had ever known, certainly not the girls he'd grown up with, with her long brown hair, the bangs that fell carelessly in her eyes, the strange, exotic earrings, and a strand of tiny seashells around her neck. She was in her seat before the bell, bent over a note-book, and never looked up until Mr. Blanchard asked her to stand as he introduced her. Brushing her hair from her face, she surveyed the classroom, murmured "Good morning," and offered a perfunctory wave as if she'd been told this was what you just did in these situations.

Alvin looked for her in the cafeteria at lunchtime, but she never came in. When he snuck outside for a cigarette, she was sitting under a tree, distractedly nibbling on a sandwich. Alvin waved as he approached.

"I'm Alvin. From homeroom," he said, and she smiled politely.

"Don't like the cafeteria food, huh?"

Mary shrugged.

"So what've you got there?" he asked, pointing at the sandwich.

Mary turned the sandwich over in her hand, looked at it, then at Alvin. "Cream cheese and olive," she said, and he was hooked.

For three weeks he tried to draw her out, to connect somehow through enigmatic hallway chats, awkward lawn monologues as he grabbed a smoke, a chance encounter in the classical section of Ray's Music one Saturday afternoon. Mary gave up little, only the barest of back stories. She lived outside of town with her mother. They'd only just arrived, her mother accepting an offer to teach history at the university. Her father was away, and that was it. Where she'd come from, what she thought of Macomb, her likes, dislikes, hobbies—all dry holes, no matter how far down Alvin drilled. And the haze that swirled around her only made Mary that much more alluring.

One day, as she finished her lunch, he summoned his courage and asked her for a date.

"Hmm," she said, dabbing her lips with a red cloth napkin as she looked him over, and then, much to his delight, she said yes.

Alvin arrived early and spent fifteen murderous minutes in the cluttered living room with her mother—"Call me Mimi, honey, everybody does"—as she graded papers, kept an eye on the television, and rattled him with questions about school, the town, his parents, his plans.

When they were safely in the car, Mary asked, "Did you enjoy that?" and she chuckled at his stammered attempts to convince her he had.

She picked the movie *The Manchurian Candidate,* not Alvin's cup of tea, really, especially with John Wayne and a hundred other stars fighting Hitler in *The Longest Day* down the street, but he was still flush with gratitude that Mary had actually agreed to go out with him, so he sat stock-still, trying to follow the action, pausing every so often to steal a puzzled peek at the rapt look on her face as she sat mesmerized in the darkened theater. When he tapped her forearm and held out the bucket of popcorn, she shook her head, annoyed at the interruption, and turned back to the screen. By the time they spilled out into the street and tumbled into his father's Corvair, Mary seemed drained, but the good kind, almost exhilarated, which kept Alvin off balance.

"Kinda confusing," Alvin said as they wolfed down cheeseburgers and root beers at the A&W. "Brainwashing and all. Do you really think that can happen? I mean, if you don't want it to?"

Mary was silent for a moment. In the neon light of the drive-in, he could see her face, always so confident, self-assured. "Yes, and you would never know it," she said, toying with a french fry. "No one would. You'd be walking around looking perfectly normal, and all the time you were quite the opposite."

She turned to him. "Sometimes, Alvin, things aren't what they seem."

He had no idea what she was talking about, but it didn't matter.

Friday night became a standing date, then Saturday too, and by the time school let out for the summer, all week long. It was the three of them, a lot of the time, Mimi, Mary, and Alvin. Mimi was a corker, he decided, the first adult who wanted him to use her first name. She was right off the drive-in screen, a brash platinum blonde who drew icy stares from women and covetous leers from men. But she had her diplomas too, and had been around the world, or so she said, and dressed like it, even if Alvin could never quite pin her down on exactly where she'd gone, and what she'd seen and done.

Mother and daughter were more like sisters. They exchanged clothes, swapped makeup tips, gossiped endlessly about people they knew and others they didn't, and ferociously debated the issues of the day. Mimi was very interested in China—*Red* China—and was forever organizing lectures and attending readings, which didn't make her the most popular woman on campus, let alone in town. Not that she cared.

"Don't close your eyes to anything, guys," she cautioned. "Warts and all, I mean." The magazines and books that arrived in the mail almost daily piled up around the little house. The television was on constantly, the sound off until some image on the screen, the news, or a documentary, caught Mimi's eye, and then she was off on a running commentary, words of praise for her heroes, streams of obscenities for her enemies, words Alvin had never heard uttered by any adult, much less the mother of a friend. To Alvin, it was freedom unleashed and he couldn't get enough of it.

"Oh no," Mimi would protest when Alvin turned up, "you don't need me around. I'll just be in your way." But he'd insist and after an appropriate struggle, she'd give in, beaming.

"My mom doesn't like to be alone," Mary told him one day. "In case you hadn't noticed."

They would sprawl on the ratty sofa or the misshapen armchair, furniture that Alvin's mother would have thrown away years earlier, drinking Cokes and blasting 45s from the large collection of records that Mary kept in five pink cases stashed in the back of the hall closet, the two women bellowing the lyrics as Alvin grimaced at their off-key efforts. It was a summer of unsettling rhythms and beguiling lyrics and singers he'd never heard of—the Angels and Little Stevie Wonder, Lesley Gore and Sam Cooke, Ray Charles—scratched out by the needle in the stylus of the Montgomery Ward Airline phonograph until the grooves finally wore out.

When the last record was played, they would grill steaks or burgers and sit outside in the fading sun while Mimi talked about Monk and 'Trane and a concert she saw in New York City in '57, or a club in San Francisco where the headliner was someone named Lenny, a comedian except he wasn't just ha-ha-ha, and a folk singer out of Minnesota, Bob something, Alvin could never remember, "and he's not much older than you two." She would talk about Bull Connor and his hoses, which he had heard about, and a tiny country halfway around the world called Vietnam, which he hadn't, "but you will." The point was, there was a world on the other side of all this corn, and she wanted them to go out and find it. Just in case they weren't listening, Mimi would drop her own record on the turntable—Andy Williams crooning "Moon River," her gentle if pointed reminder: *Two drifters, off to see the world, there's such a lot of world to see.*

And when Mimi saw they'd had enough, she'd give them their space, slip-sliding off to bed with a knowing grin and leaving them to the dark and long, deep wet kisses and groping hands in unfamiliar places until they reached the edge of the cliff and backed off. Puppy love, teased Alvin's mother when he came home floating, but it was so much bigger than that, and she could never understand.

———————————————

A week to go until school resumed. Mary and Alvin could taste it now—a senior year to navigate, and then freedom. The U of I at Urbana-Champaign, they'd decided, not quite the world but a good start down the road.

Mimi and Mary had spent a sweltering, sticky day at the university pool. Alvin, who had a summer job as a janitor at the Travel Lodge, joined them when he got off work. By the time he arrived, Mimi was involved in a heated discussion with one of her colleagues, a man named Loomis who appeared to have been drinking.

"What are they arguing about?" Alvin whispered to Mary, who was sprawled on a beige chaise lounge a few feet away from the debate.

"Not sure," she said, shaking water from her hair. "China, I think."

Just then Mimi stalked toward them, waving back at Loomis. "Can you believe this bastard?" she said.

Loomis pretended to stagger backward.

"My goodness, Professor," he said, smirking. "And in front of the children."

Mary rose on one elbow and looked at the professor. "Asshole," she said, and Loomis stormed off. Mimi kissed her daughter's forehead. "Probably cost me a contract for next year, honey, but it was worth it."

And grounds for celebration, she announced as they crammed into her Ford. On the way home, she pulled into the A&P parking lot and they swept through the supermarket like an invading army, gathering chicken and potatoes and salad, a chocolate cake for dessert. While Mimi headed to the checkout, the kids stole a moment for themselves, one eye out for shoppers turning the corner into the cereal aisle as they hugged and kissed against the Sugar Pops.

At the house Alvin manned the grill, stoking the flames engulfing the charcoal in the Weber, the chicken pieces mounded at his side, steeping in Mimi's special marinade—Oriental, she called it, but it didn't taste like anything Alvin had eaten at the Imperial Gardens on the square. Mary waltzed through the yard, snapping photos with her new toy, a gray and silver Brownie Fiesta. From inside the house came the sound of the television, occasionally drowned out by Mimi's indignant shouts as she set upon another target.

"This is nice," Alvin said, laying the first pieces of chicken on the hot grill. Mary leaned over and kissed him on the cheek, clicked the shutter one more time. The telephone rang inside, and they could hear Mimi, in full voice, walking across the living room to answer it.

"Hello," she said, and then there was silence. A few minutes later, a murmured pleading voice, and then the television was turned off. Mary ran up the front steps and went inside. She was gone for what seemed like an hour. When she came back outside, she dropped heavily to the steps, ashen-faced. Alvin rushed over to her.

"Did somebody die?"

Mary shook her head.

"Then what the hell…"

She stood up. "It's my father. My father's coming home."

Alvin could smell the chicken burning, but he knew enough to let it go.

"She doesn't want him here," Mary said, her voice ice. "He wasn't supposed to come back. But he is."

---

Lemke had been talking for forty minutes, growing more animated as the memories flowed. Now he sat back on the couch, quiet, lost in his thoughts. Brenda brought in a fresh pot of coffee and filled their cups, then passed around a tray of doughnuts. Only Bobby was hungry, and Savella watched as a shower of powdered sugar fell into the napkin draped over his lap. Brenda sat down next to her husband, crossed her arms, a look of resignation on her face.

"Go on," she said. "Tell them the rest of it."

Lemke drank some coffee and cleared his throat. "About three weeks after school started again, Mary wakes up and Mimi's in the kitchen making her lunch, cream cheese and olive, don't you know. We'd been eating lunch at a diner down the street, so she didn't really want the sandwich. But her mom insisted. 'Take it. I want you to have it today.' That sort of thing. Mary couldn't figure it out, but she took the sandwich. And just as she's going out the door, her mom calls to her to stop. She comes up and hugs her, then holds her face in her hands and says, 'Remember, honey. Warts and all.' Mary tells her she's getting spooky and they both laughed.

"When Mary got home, she called out for her mother, but there wasn't any answer. She looks through the house—no sign of her. Then she notices the car key is missing from the hook by the back door. So she goes to the garage to see if the car is around.

"Mimi was lying on the front seat, with the end of a garden hose duct-taped to her mouth. The other end was stuffed in the exhaust pipe. The engine had stopped running, out of gas, but the radio was tuned to the college classical station, her favorite, and she had a kind of smile on her face. It was peaceful, anyway.

"Mary went inside and called the police, then she called me and told me to come quick. And she hung up, went back into the garage, and sat down on the floor and waited with her mom. I asked her later why she did that. 'She doesn't like to be alone,' she says." Lemke rubbed the corner of his right eye with the tip of his finger. "Can you beat that?"

He reached into his pocket for a handkerchief. "No note. Just a lot of problems," he said in a whisper. "And her husband wasn't supposed to come back."

———

Mary spent that night at Alvin's house, in the spare bedroom. After everyone had gone to sleep and the house was quiet, she eased down the hallway, the floorboards creaking, and slipped into his room. They wrapped themselves in blankets and huddled together, shivering in the bay window that looked through tall elm trees to Jackson Street, deserted in the middle of the night. They talked about Mimi and the future and how frightening it all seemed. As the sun's first rays streaked the eastern sky, Mary stood to return to her room.

"You're all I've got now," she said, her voice breaking. "Please don't leave me."

When he awoke, she was gone. Her father had come for her, his mother said, but don't be upset, she promised she'd write. Mimi's body was packed into a coffin and shipped off, somewhere south, Alvin's mother heard. Ten days later, strange men with a truck packed up the house and hammered a For Sale sign on the front lawn.

There never was a letter.

Lemke needed water, and he left the room. They could hear him in the kitchen, taking down a glass, then the sound of the tap running. Brenda began stacking the coffee cups and saucers.

"I'm sorry to dredge all this up again," Savella said.

"No, no," she said. "I know all about Alvin and...We were in the same class, actually."

*Brenda Radcliffe. Right above Remsen and Rincon, in cursive hand and faded with time.*

"You know, your name was also in her book," Savella said.

Brenda arched an eyebrow. "How strange. I didn't really know her. She kept to herself," she said, then with a glance toward the kitchen, "mostly."

She placed the stack of china on the coffee table. "A while later, I met Alvin again, at a dance, and we eventually got married," she said, as if it were the only possible outcome. "But even then, he spent some time trying to find her. Late at night he'd call information in different cities, look for a listing. He'd get out of bed, think I was asleep. But I heard. And it still comes up, nearly every year, around, you know, her birthday."

Right on cue Lemke returned, holding a small creased black-and-white photograph. "April twenty-sixth," he said, and Brenda flinched as if she'd been slapped. Lemke handed the photo to Savella: a young Alvin with his arm around the shoulders of a willowy brunette, the same pretty girl who found herself in an evening gown at a dinner table in Dallas. "Mimi took it," he said quietly. "We had a picnic. Gave her my class ring that day. You know how kids do. Or did. Different world back then, I guess."

Savella handed him the photo of the ring from Mary Bloom's box.

"Oh my Lord," Lemke murmured. "She kept it. All this time."

The woman in the sweatshirt was next.

"Mimi," Lemke said, smiling at the memory. "That was her."

Finally, Savella handed him Night Out. Lemke examined it closely.

"The one on the end," he said. "Mary. All dressed up. Never saw her that way. Jeez, but she was—" Brenda finished for him, a touch impatiently. "She was very pretty, Alvin. All right."

"Do you know anyone else in the shot?" Savella asked.

"No. Should I?"

He handed back the pictures. Savella drained his coffee as he recalled Mary Bloom's last moments: a dying old woman humming a memory of a happier time, *two drifters off to see the world,* and then, no time left, *listen to me.* He was listening, and Mary Bloom was talking to him, through the bread crumbs she left along the trail: an address book, then a ring, and now a boy who loved her still.

Savella nodded to Bobby and stood. "Well, I don't want to take up any more of your time. You've been very helpful and I know it was difficult. Let me ask you, is there anybody else around here who might have known the Blooms?"

Lemke looked up, puzzled. "I'm sorry?"

"The Blooms."

Lemke shook his head.

"Can't help you there," he said. "Don't know anybody by that name."

# 24

A looming sky, and thunder rumbling in the west. Tinder-hot weather for the last month, something had to break. Perched on the top step of the front porch, Jaime Figueroa sipped a Coke and watched the boys in the barnyard tossing a football, the dogs in the kennel barking as they tried to claw through the chain-link fence to catch up with it.

A good day, this one, always was when someone made it out. Graduation, for Francisco. Mom come to pick him up, hot dogs and lots of tears and he was gone, hopefully that's it. This one, no one figured to make it through, but Father, he knows different. And he was right. He was always right. Although he got mad at you if you told him that.

Jaime peeked over his right shoulder. He was still there, in the picture window, hands in his pockets, all dressed in his priest clothes. That was good too, seeing Father in his priest clothes again. He was in a mood a lot lately, and when he was in a mood, he didn't wear them so much. What do you think, it's not about the clothes, Father would say, in that mad voice, like when Jaime asked if he should unpack the overnight bag inside the door. Sounded like those dogs in the kennel when he said no, leave it be. But that was Father. An hour later he was your best friend.

Out by the highway, a car slowed, then turned into the farm, kicking up a cloud of dust as it moved up the entrance drive. Late for visitors, Jaime thought. He got to his feet and looked back for Father. He was already at the screen door, hands at his side now as he watched the car drive past the barn and the old warehouse where the boys and their counselors slept, then pull into the yard and park next to Father's Chevy Silverado, breaking up the game. One of the players tossed the football away, and it bounced harmlessly against the kennel fence. The dogs barked louder.

The driver cut the engine and got out, a tall man with dark hair, holding a manila envelope and reaching up to straighten the collar of his sports jacket. A moment later his passenger, heavy-set, clutching his knee and grimacing in pain, struggled out of the front seat. He sniffed the air and made a face.

"It's a *farm*, Bobby," the driver said.

The screen door screeched open, and Father came out onto the porch. The driver drew a photograph from the envelope and quickly approached, his passenger limping behind him. Father edged back toward the front door. Jaime had never seen him like this. His face was flushed and his hands trembled. His eyes widened, and he stole three quick glances behind him, as if he were measuring the distance to the safety of inside. Father's scared of these guys, Jaime thought, amazed, and he moved onto the steps to prevent the two men from coming any closer.

At the foot of the stairs, the driver stopped and held up the picture.

"Your sister," he said, and waited.

Father sagged, and took another step back.

"You don't understand," he said.

The driver put a foot on the bottom stair.

"Hey," Jaime shouted, and at that three of the boys in the yard trotted over to the porch.

"You sent me the tape," the driver said. "What's it about? What don't I understand?"

Father raised his left hand, and then let it drop.

"What was she doing in Dallas with Jack Ruby?" the driver asked again, louder. "What don't I understand?"

He started up the stairs. Jaime turned for the door, but Father grabbed him by the arm. "No. No, Jaime. No more guns."

The big man groaned. "What'd I tell you?" he said.

The driver brandished the picture one more time. "Mary Remsen. She was your sister. She lived with your mother. Why wouldn't you say so?"

Anguish flashed across Remsen's face. "You're asking for answers you don't want to hear," he said. "You will never be the same if you do."

"I won't? Or you won't."

Remsen hesitated for a moment, then walked inside, the screen door clattering closed behind him. The big man moved forward; two more boys climbed over the railing. The driver shoved the photograph into the envelope and waved to his companion. "Let it go, Bobby," he said. "We'll get him later."

---

Father's study was dark and quiet. The door wasn't locked, but Jaime didn't bother knocking. He knew what he'd find inside: Father on the hard chair, staring out the bay window. At times like this, better to let him be, so Jaime sat at his desk outside and waited. Finally, a button on the telephone console lit up: Father's private line. It glowed for twenty minutes, then the connection was severed. A few minutes later, a second light lit up, but only briefly. Then the door opened and Father emerged.

"I have to leave for a few days. Father Anselm will be coming tonight to look after you all. Help him, Jaime, will you?" Without waiting for an answer, Father picked up the small brown suitcase that he wouldn't unpack, and walked out of the office.

Jaime scrambled to his feet and rushed to the door. Father crossed the yard to his pickup and dropped his bag on the front seat. He stood for a minute, turning slowly as he surveyed his little world—the farmhouse, the boys' dormitory, the kennel, the tractor shed. Then he got in the truck and drove off, up the road the strangers had come down, between the rows of corn awaiting the late harvest.

A few hours later, the rain came, finally, a drizzle to begin with, then a deluge, thick droplets thudding on the wooden planks of the porch. Tinder-hot weather for the last month, something had to break.

# 25

Jorge—*Georgie,* he preferred now, another one with the English—leaned against the counter, fingers splayed on the Formica as he studied the *Daily News* sports section.

"This Jeter," he said, licking his forefinger and turning the page. "The best. He could have played in Cuba."

Abel Garcia ignored him. He hated baseball, and Jorge knew it. A friend from the Guatemalan jungle, he stopped by most days to read the papers, to spell Garcia when the pain was too much, and to talk endlessly about baseball. Just his way of being playful, but Garcia wasn't in the mood today.

He stared at the four letters arched across the glass of the front window in flaking paint, the remnants of the store's original name. *KAM* at the top of the arc and an *S* at the end of the line. Was it the old owner's name? Easy enough to ask the nephews, but Garcia had come to appreciate the distraction, wondering who the owner might have been—an immigrant, maybe, escaping tyranny, hunger. And did he ever go home?

Jorge got up and retrieved a *Post.* Cuba had fallen off the front page, thanks to a relentless counteroffensive waged by the White House. Still a hot story in Miami, but buried inside the farther north you went—four paragraphs at the bottom of A22 in the *Washington Post* this morning, a World brief that Garcia missed the first time he went through the *Times*. Not even the chilling specter of Cuban terrorists with dirty bombs tucked away in their carry-ons could compete for very long with the public's need for fresh. The news marched on. A brain-damaged cop in New Mexico woke up after eighteen years and asked for a Pepsi. The pope visited a mosque in Turkey. Eleven-year-old twins in Missouri tried to sell their four-year-old sister. An earthquake swallowed a small island in the Pacific. And suddenly it was what invasion, unless you had something more than a sketchy sequel to *The Mouse That Roared*.

But there was unfinished business in Washington. Someone had to pay a price for all the tumult, and that, Garcia knew, would be Richard Miller. His name was all over the Cuba story. The White House and its allies had made sure everyone got the message. Miller was the guy driving this nonsense. Miller was the one man in Washington who *believed* in the documents with near-religious fervor. Obsession was a word that popped up a lot around Miller's name. Fanatic was another. Garcia knew the game. You can survive a debate on the issues. But when they start making it personal, as if you were someone from a completely different tribe, that crazy one, from the village just over the mountains—well, then you were gone.

The bell above the door tinkled softly, and a tall young man with wavy black hair, his face outlined in groomed stubble, pushed through the door, carrying a small package wrapped in brown paper and tied with string. He placed the package on the counter, reached into his hip pocket, and drew out a wad of cash and a bar napkin.

"You will please, Lotto," he said in a thick accent, waving the napkin in the air, and looking expectantly at the two men.

Garcia moved to the machine. The customer slowly surveyed the nearly empty shelves. "You will close?" he said, gesturing at the room.

Garcia frowned. "Your numbers."

"Five dollar. Mega Millions," the man said slowly, as if he'd worked hard to memorize the lines. "These." He handed the napkin and a five-dollar bill to Garcia, who punched in the numbers and dropped the ticket on the counter. The customer studied it closely, nodding as he confirmed his selection. He tapped the top of the package and looked intently at Garcia, then bolted out the door.

Jorge tugged on his Yankees cap and craned his neck to peer out the front window. "He left his package," he said.

Garcia struggled to shake off an icy tingle of dread.

*The accent.* Slavic. Eastern European. Russian.

He stretched across the counter and slowly, tentatively, rotated the parcel, turned it on its side, then upside down, looking for an address, a store logo, an identifying mark, something that would tell him he was wrong. The brown paper wrapping was pristine, unmarked.

*The accent,* he thought again.

Garcia picked up the package, heavier than he might have expected, and walked slowly to his office. Drawing the curtain behind him, he carefully placed the package on his small wooden desk, then rummaged through the drawers until he found a pair of scissors.

He snipped the string, then methodically tore away the wrapping paper to reveal a dimpled metal box with Cyrillic lettering on three sides and a red-and-yellow radiation warning sign on the fourth. Garcia lifted the lid. Inside, shielded in lead, lay two sealed canisters, each five inches long, bearing a radiation logo and the notation Cs-137.

He gazed down at the contents for a moment. Garcia could not translate the Cyrillic. He had no idea what Cs-137 might be. But the radiation warning was all the answer he needed.

Pena was tired of waiting.

He had called the Russians himself.

A Georgian, actually, not that Pena would know the difference, or care, but it mattered very much to Nikolai Gromoff, archenemy of all things Soviet. Garcia had last seen him a few years ago, a long dinner one night in a French bistro in the city, two old warhorses swapping stories from their murderous pasts. Gromoff had helped Garcia build the bomb that brought down the Cuban airliner. Over the years they had scrambled to find the tools of their trade: a greedy soldier, perhaps, or a government official with secrets to hide. Relics of the past, Gromoff scoffed, and over plates of cassoulet and a fine Gascon red, he told Garcia how it was now: a ramshackle barn, high in the Lesser Caucasus, a few hundred kilometers from Tblisi. At the front gate, a young boy in a disheveled uniform shirt, an automatic rifle across his knees, sits on an upended packing crate. The weapon is unloaded, but no need to confront him; the rear is wide open. Hop a crumbling stone wall, stroll across an overgrown soccer field with the goal netting torn away from the stanchions. One rusty lock on the back door, and inside, the terrible treasure: a chemical and biological nightmare, abandoned by the Soviets when the empire collapsed. Take what you can carry to the beat-up Lada idling on the dirt trail, then a slow drive down the mountains to the coast, the trunk sagging under the weight of the booty, where the right price in Bat'umi has it on a boat to America. Dock at dawn across the Hudson, Port Elizabeth, so poorly guarded, even after 9/11, that you want to cringe. A freight clerk takes the hand-off from the captain, bypasses the radiation detectors, and by nightfall, the box is in Brighton Beach, waiting for a call.

And Pena had dialed the number.

Garcia slowly closed the lid, then fell into his recliner. The office reeked of rotting garbage from the pizza place next door. Tuesday, Garcia remembered. Always worse on Tuesday, the day before the trash hauler rolled through the alley.

His job was the trigger. Simple enough for a pro like Abel Garcia. They'd talked about it briefly just before he left Las Vegas, Pena playing with his dogs, Garcia nibbling at his dessert, and Deets, summoned after lunch for his marching orders, watching closely in case some cake was left unfinished. Pena wasn't sure what he wanted, if it came to that. But one thing he knew: Americans don't pay attention until their neighbors start coming home in body bags. And when Garcia raised an objection, Pena cut him off.

"I'm getting tired of telling you this, Abel. We don't have more time. We do this, they blame it on Castro. And we go home."

Garcia glanced around the spartan office, his eyes coming to rest on the map of Cuba. He left the recliner and shuffled across the room. With his forefinger he traced a route from west to east, silently reading the names in sorrowful tribute to a life he'd never really known: *La Habana, Matanzas, Santa Clara, Sancti Spiritus, Ciego de Avila, Camaguey, Las Tunas, Santiago de Cuba, Guantanamo.* "We're Americans now," Pilar had decreed after Honduras. Had she been right all along? Garcia winced, the pain in his gut and something more: deadly memories—three dozen Cubans when the airliner fell from the sky over Bermuda; seven more outside the embassy in Caracas; two soldiers in Panama, the bomb that was supposed to take out Castro; the Bahamas, El Salvador, Colombia—a trail of blood. And the mistake, the horrible miscalculation: the busload of children in Guatemala City, on a school outing to the zoo.

And then Garcia's finger was moving again, west this time, along the coast, the names in small print evading his aging eyes until, as if directed by some unseen force, his finger stopped: Veradero. Garcia leaned into the map until his vision blurred, pressing insistently on the smudge of black in the blue of the Bahia de Cardenas. He stood stock-still for an eternity, or was it half a minute, and remembered: a full moon, the long nets of the fishermen groaning with black mullet ambushed on their run down the Canimar River to the ocean. Or the break of dawn at the end of summer, when the north winds would bring the *langostas*, armies of tiny brown lobsters fanning out across the beach, easy pickings for even the youngest children. But did he really remember any of it? Or was it simply that he needed to if he was ever to make sense of a lifetime?

Returning to his desk, Garcia rewrapped the package with the string and the torn brown paper. The bell above the front door tinkled again, and he heard the murmur of conversation, unintelligible, someone asking for a phone card, perhaps, or a pack of Winstons.

And Jorge—*Georgie!*—answering in English.

*Forget it, Abel,* Garcia thought to himself as he pushed through the curtain. *The cows are dead.*

# 26

The Chevy pickup truck was gone when Savella and Bobby returned to the farm the next morning. The boys playing football in the yard were nowhere to be seen, and the window shades in the farmhouse were drawn tight. A different priest met them on the porch, a fidgety man with a gloomy aspect. Remsen would be away for several days, he said, don't know how long, was there something he could help them with? And all the while, the Hispanic kid, walking circles in the dust, ready to pounce.

After fifteen fruitless minutes, they got in the car and drove back to the highway, pulled over on the shoulder, and hunkered down to wait under a towering oak tree, sweltering in the heat unbroken by the overnight deluge. Several times the Hispanic kid and a couple of buddies sauntered down the dirt drive and stood at the wire fence, glaring at them, chattering in a Spanish punctuated with threatening gestures. By nightfall Savella realized he was wasting his time. Remsen was spooked by something that trumped family. He wasn't about to open up, even if he did return.

Dinner, then a quick scotch and a restless sleep, Savella tossing in sweat-drenched sheets, kicking himself about the visit with the Lemkes. A rookie mistake, he thought, not having set the playing field before the coffee and the trip down the rabbit hole, not having mentioned the name, the *full* name—*Mary Bloom*—to begin with. Instead, he and Alvin had danced a confused jig until finally they stumbled on the heart of the matter—Mary *Remsen*—and when, astonished, he timidly asked whether she had ever mentioned a brother, he knew the answer before Lemke opened his mouth: "Might have. Yes, I think so. In boarding school. Or some such." A rookie mistake, Savella thought one last time, before the steak and the whiskey finally did the trick.

The next day brought little relief from the heat and even less from Savella's frustration. Leaving Bobby at the hotel pool, Savella drove around town in search of traces of Mimi and Mary. It was, as he had suspected, a futile effort. The leafy lot where Mimi's house once stood had long since been paved over for a strip mall. The university's records showed Mimi had been a visiting professor of history for eight months until her death. "Wasn't going to be asked back, anyway," the clerk volunteered, as if that somehow made a difference. At the local newspaper, an assistant editor found a short item on the suicide, nothing else on the family. "Those were kind of private matters back then," he explained. The name Remsen drew a blank screen on the police computer. There might be paper—death certificate, incident report—somewhere in the bowels of the county courthouse, the duty captain suggested, although they were probably destroyed in that fire back in 1986. And more to the point, no one was offering to look.

Savella drove back to the hotel around three. Bobby hadn't budged from the pool, sound asleep in a lounge chair, four empty Heineken bottles on the table beside him. Savella sat down and made one last call, to Macomb

High. A secretary in the principal's office passed him along to a guidance counselor, who gave him a telephone number for a woman who had stayed in touch over the years with a number of Western alumni. Eppie Simms didn't remember the name Mary Remsen. There were yearbooks, she said, but in storage, maybe a week or so before she could get to them. And why exactly did he want them, again? Savella left his number, told Mrs. Simms he'd call again in a few days, and hung up.

Bobby yawned loudly and sat up. "Jesus, it's hot." He glanced at Savella. "So what's up? Solve the riddle?"

"Yearbooks," Savella said. "Maybe."

"Yeah, I heard."

"They're in storage."

"I heard that too."

Savella took a deep breath. "Well, it's something, I guess."

Bobby lifted the dark-green beer bottles one at a time, searching for a last sip. "Oh, it's something, all right. A fucking dead end, you know what I mean? You got, what, a crazy priest and his dead sister and some farmer who never got over a high school crush. Trust me—this ain't happening. Is it time to go home?"

Yes it was, Savella thought, as they bounced through the skies later that night, engulfed in a thunderstorm. But no dead end. Mary Bloom, nee Remsen, existed. She had a life, people who loved her, a family, even if that wasn't necessarily the same thing. And all of that somehow brought her to a table at the Adolphus Hotel, a banquette where she didn't belong, don't ask me how I know. She didn't have a choice, and Savella couldn't explain how he knew that either. But the answer was in the photograph. Three women—a teenager from Illinois, a Doris Day blonde, and a dark-haired porcelain doll.

Two men—one young, who gazed into the lens with all manner of suspicion, and one older, with slicked black hair, a shiny suit, and a five o'clock shadow. And on the edges of the frame, a man's hand wearing a gold band set with an impressive black stone, and a man's pant leg, perfectly pressed.

What was it, Savella asked himself one more time, what were the connections between these people? How had Mary, she of Top Forty hits and cream cheese and olive sandwiches and Friday nights with a farm boy at the Odeon Theater and afterward the A&W—how had she wound up at this table? And where was brother Joey, the priest who all these years later would not even admit he knew his own sister?

A priest who lied. What was it about Mary that would lead a priest to lie?

The picture was it. So, start there: A fading black-and-white photo, so important to an old woman with nothing on her walls that she tucked it in a painted box and stuck it deep inside a drawer. Start there: A girl from the heartland and her big Night Out amid the balled-up napkins, the overflowing ashtrays, and the empty high-ball glasses. Start there: Mary Remsen, sad-eyed Mary, a frightened child squirming in her big-girl clothes and having dinner with a killer.

# 27

There was an old reporter, nice enough guy, who for years would make the rounds of Washington newsrooms, talking conspiracy. No one wanted to offend, but eyes would roll whenever he turned up. As the years passed, junior staffers got the assignment, then copy desk interns, and finally he was stopped at reception. Kooks, after all, were kooks.

Savella could recall seeing him only twice: standing in the back of a hearing room one frosty morning, and a few months later at the funeral of an old Johnson administration insider, both times lugging a well-worn leather briefcase crammed with papers. What the hell was his name, probably dead by now, anyway. But a few phone calls turned up a pleasant surprise: Randall Emmons, very much alive, and still living in Washington.

He was a name once, a Pulitzer Prize for his coverage of the labor movement, trolling the murky lakes where union bosses and mobsters swam together, two best sellers, his choice of jobs. Then Kennedy was killed in Dallas, and life turned upside down. Emmons never believed the Warren Commission, plunged into the shadows for three decades, sifting through the detritus of an American tragedy, searching for the tiny nugget that everyone else had missed. But Americans like endings and when Emmons couldn't deliver, the spotlight shifted elsewhere.

The voice on the other end of the line cracked with age, but Savella's call was obviously a tonic, a prayer answered: *a reporter on the phone, after all this time.*

---

Emmons lived in a tired brownstone sandwiched between an Ethiopian restaurant and a French bistro in Adams-Morgan. A palm reader occupied the ground floor; the windows of the apartment above it were covered with bedsheets. The vestibule stank of urine, the tile floor was strewn with a ratty blanket, a Seagram's bottle, and a half-eaten Big Mac. Savella pressed the intercom button for Emmons and the front door quickly clicked open to a steep flight of stairs. "I'm up here," said a watery voice from on high. Almost like he was waiting next to the buzzer, Savella thought as he climbed slowly upward.

Emmons was a wisp of a man in his eighties, thinning gray hair swept straight back, thick square-framed glasses. In his frayed gray slacks, brown sandals over black socks and a short-sleeved white shirt with two pens poking out of the breast pocket, Emmons looked every bit the mad professor.

"Welcome," he said, and waved Savella inside, with a curious glance at the envelope in his hand. "Please forgive the mess. My wife passed two years ago and I'm afraid I'm not much of a housekeeper."

A maze of cardboard boxes lined the front hallway. Stacks of books and cairns of yellowing newspapers and magazines covered every available surface in the living room. Shaky towers of plastic baskets stuffed to overflowing with folders leaned against the walls. Wandering through the muddle were cats, three or four of them, Savella couldn't be sure, all the same shade of brown. "Brothers. Maybe sisters. Elizabeth found them in the alley," Emmons said. In the kitchen an old dog, its white coat matted and tangled, staggered to its feet to give Savella a mail-it-in sniff, then slumped to the lino-leum and shut its eyes. "All right, Harley, enough now," Emmons said, a beat late. He pushed open a screen door next to the refrigerator. "I thought we'd talk on the porch."

A pitcher of iced tea and two glasses sat on a small white table overlooking the alley. A sad place to find an old man, Savella thought as they settled into canvas deck chairs.

"How long have you lived here?" he asked.

"Since 1970," Emmons said. "The neighborhood's changed quite a bit. Very trendy these days. Lots of young people. But I'm not moving. Do you know Washington?"

"Not so well, really. Just passed through a few times." Savella quickly outlined his career, omitting his dismiss-al from the *Post-Herald*. Emmons had agreed to see a newspaper reporter pursuing a story, not an out-of-work writer grasping at straws. As he spoke, Emmons studied him closely, head still, eyes riveted on his guest.

A door opened below them and for a moment, a particularly pungent Chinese spice odor engulfed them. Savella wrinkled his nose, and Emmons offered an apologetic smile. "I stopped smelling it eleven years ago," he said, "when it was Mexican."

"Pretty tough."

Emmons moved to stand up, a look of concern on his face. "Would you like to go inside?"

"No, no. This is fine. Really."

Emmons unsteadily lifted the pitcher and began to pour, ignoring Savella's offer of assistance even as a thin stream of tea missed its mark and splattered the tabletop, raining drops on the envelope in Savella's lap before he could whisk it out of range. Emmons made a halfhearted attempt to soak up the liquid with a wad of paper towel.

"Not many visitors now, you see," he said. "It's just me. And my papers." He cleared his throat. "There was a photograph, I believe you said?"

Savella opened the envelope and drew out the restaurant picture. Emmons took the photo and briefly studied it, moving it within inches of his face and lifting his glasses to eliminate any chance of obstruction.

"Where did you get this?" he asked.

*I stole it from a dead woman. No, that wouldn't do.*

"It was discovered in the home of someone who recently died. She's in the picture. The girl on the far left."

The old man's eyes were glued to Night Out. From below came the sound of boots on concrete and gravel, and a chorus of voices that faded as footsteps moved down the alley. Finally, Emmons let the picture drop to his lap. He adjusted his glasses on the bridge of his nose and sat back in his chair.

"Of course, anybody with a computer can put together a convincing forgery these days."

Savella shook his head. "No forgery here. Whatever it is, a little old lady had it stuck inside a box in her bed table drawer. So am I wrong, or is that Jack Ruby sitting with them?"

Emmons placed the picture on the table, rose slowly, and walked back into the apartment. Through the open door, Savella could see him running a finger across the spines of a row of books stacked against the wall in the living room. Finally, he plucked one volume from the shelf, leafed through its pages until he found what he was searching for, then returned to the porch. He handed the book to Savella and pointed to a picture of a pretty young woman in her twenties, a shy smile for the camera as she held back her hair on a windy day. Emmons picked up Night Out, slid it onto the facing page, and tapped the image of the dark-haired young woman with the snow-white complexion. "What do you think?"

Savella compared the two photos. A match, no doubt about it.

Emmons sat down heavily, the legs of his chair scraping the deck wood. "You're correct about Ruby. That's him. With his girlfriend, the blonde. But that's not the real significance of your photograph." He leaned forward, picked up Night Out. "The woman sitting next to him is Svetlana Lyakhov. The cousin of Marina Oswald."

"Marina Oswald? Lee Harvey Oswald's wife?"

"The same. The wife of the man Ruby shot in the basement of the Dallas city jail."

Savella was stunned. The idea of Mary Remsen with Jack Ruby had been enough of a mystery. But this took it to an entirely different level. *Mary Remsen having dinner with Jack Ruby and the cousin of Lee Oswald's wife.* His mind reeled.

"And this much I know." Emmons paused to sip his tea. "In all my years of doing this, I never came across any solid evidence that Ruby and Oswald might have met before that morning in the police garage."

"When do you suppose it was taken?"

"I can't say." Emmons's voice was suddenly stronger, as if he'd shed fifty years. "But it raises some interesting questions. One of the most intriguing things about the assassination is Marina's role. This is a nineteen-year-old pharmacist from the Soviet Union, Marina Prusakova, living in Minsk in 1961. One night at a dance, she meets Oswald, an American defector who's trying to go home. A couple of months later, they marry. Oswald gets permission to return to the United States, and the Soviets allow Marina to go with him. They settle in Texas in June 1962."

The dog shuffled onto the porch and stood in the corner, noisily lapping water from a plastic bowl. When the dish was dry, he took a few steps and dropped to the deck at Emmons's feet.

"Svetlana Lyakhov follows Marina and Lee within a month or two. She goes to Texas, reunites with her cousin, finds work in a laundry. Marina stays home with their daughter, Lee goes from job to job, is in and out of trouble. Svetlana is something of a party girl, I guess you'd call her. The more English she learns, the more time she spends in bars and clubs. In November 1963 Oswald supposedly shoots the president. The police find Marina within hours. But no one's seen her cousin, Svetlana, since that afternoon. She disappears. Gone. A clean break, no traces."

Emmons reached down to scratch Harley's ears. "She's always been a minor irritation. The timing of it, the idea that she vanishes that afternoon. No one's ever suggested she had anything to do with the assassination. But people have wondered what she knew about Oswald and what he might have been up to in the days and weeks beforehand.

"And now here she is with Ruby. Could be a coincidence, certainly. There are lots of those in this case— Ruby lived less than a mile from Oswald, Marina took English lessons from Ruby's neighbor, Oswald was heading in the direction of Ruby's apartment after the assassination. But this—it's something else entirely."

Savella shook his head. "It just seems so, I don't know, *unlikely*. A Russian laundry worker and this guy, this mob wannabe? Wasn't that his thing? He ran a strip club?"

"A string of burlesque houses, each of them seedier than the last. Catered to off-duty policemen, soldiers on weekend leave from the military bases around Dallas, truck drivers. Low-rent operations, including amateur nights where he tried to entice adventurous young women to give stripping a try, or even a little prostitution. Secretaries, housewives…maybe even Russian émigré laundry workers."

Emmons reached for the photograph and settled back in his chair. "Mister Ruby. He of the flashy cuff links, the diamond stickpins, the pinkie rings. An emotional, even volatile man, prone to violence. And as you say, organized crime ties. More of a hanger-on, really, somebody who tried his best to insinuate himself into that world, with varying degrees of success. An errand boy for the mob, moving their gambling money around. Running cash and girls down to Havana in the days when the mob ran things there. An unforgivable character, even if he hadn't murdered Oswald."

"Did he ever offer an explanation?" Savella asked. "Did he say why he did it?"

Emmons waved off the question. "Enraged by the murder of his president, wanting to spare Mrs. Kennedy the ordeal of a trial, trying to impress his police friends—take your pick."

"You don't believe any of that?"

Emmons leaned forward and rested his elbows on the table.

"That this was some spur-of-the-moment decision, an emotional reaction? The story of his life tells us one thing: Jack Ruby was all about Jack Ruby, no one and nothing else. Forget about patriotism or widows. He was in that garage with a gun in his pocket because it was going to benefit Jack Ruby, burlesque king, mob groupie. A little nobody who wanted to be a big deal. And he got his wish."

"What, then?"

"Oh, now, it's a lifetime of work," Emmons said hesitantly. "You probably don't have the time."

Savella shrugged off his jacket, slid his glass across the table.

"I could use a refill," he said, and an old man's eyes lit up.

———————

Two hours in another world, a parallel universe where up was down, right was wrong, day was night. A bizarre, confusing journey across the globe—Saigon, Moscow, Marseilles, Havana, Las Vegas, New Orleans—amid a whirlwind of names: Khrushchev, Castro and Diem, Giancana, Rosselli, and Lansky. Garrison, Shaw, Ferrie, Johnson, Warren—different actors, disparate roles in a play with a tragic, world-shattering ending. Once, the telephone jangled, two, three, four times, Emmons kept talking, five, six, seven, he didn't seem to hear, and then it fell silent. Once, Savella got up to use the bathroom, and when he returned, Emmons was in the kitchen making cheese sandwiches—"Cupboard's a bit bare," he said sheepishly—but the food sat untouched for another hour until Emmons stripped off a crust and leaned down to feed it to the dog.

Dusk approached, the clatter from the restaurants along the alley signaled the start of the dinner hour, and still Emmons talked, his voice cracking in the evening air. Grassy knolls, single bullets, sixth-floor snipers' nests, and 26.6 seconds of 8mm home-movie footage taken with a Model 414 PD Bell & Howell Zoomatic Director Series Camera with a Varamat 9 to 27mm F1.8 lens. Emmons never wavered, grateful for this unexpected opportunity, this most fortunate of circumstances: *a reporter again, and after all this time.* The theories tumbled out in mind-numbing detail: gunned down by Cubans, rubbed out by the mob, terminated by the CIA. "Crazy stuff, some of it, but some of it makes a lot of sense," Emmons said, and he looked a little hurt when Savella wondered how anyone could tell the difference.

In the end, a maddening riddle, and then they were back where they began: Emmons engrossed in Savella's photograph, scrutinizing it in the light that streamed from the kitchen through the open porch door, searching the faces for one missed clue.

"The Warren Commission spent less than a year to come up with an eight-hundred-and-eighty-eight-page report that concluded Lee Harvey Oswald, acting alone, killed President Kennedy, and Jack Ruby, acting alone, killed Oswald," Emmons said quietly. "And for all my efforts, I haven't turned up evidence to prove otherwise. This picture"—he shook it lightly—"is something new, maybe adds another dimension. But we probably won't really know the truth until the commission files are finally opened. By which time, I shall very likely be dead."

From below came the screech of a rusty screen door, then a high-pitched woman's voice. "What you doin' out here, huh? You in the garbage?" The screen door slapped shut. "Ain't no handouts tonight. Get the hell out of here." Metal clanged, and leather scuffled against concrete as someone moved heavily down the alley. "Fucking bums," the woman muttered, and then unleashed an irritated torrent in an unrecognizable language. Savella leaned over the railing, looked both ways, but there was no one. Had somebody been eavesdropping on their conversation? He glanced back at Emmons, who smiled.

"One of the hazards of this work. You always think someone's coming to get you," he said. "But it's nothing. The homeless are regulars in this alley, looking for scraps. Still a national disgrace."

The smell of cigarette smoke drifted up through the deck slats. Emmons sniffed twice, and fanned the air in front of his face. "That is also a disgrace. Filthy habit." He ran his fingers around the edges of Night Out. "The woman who had this—who was she?"

"Remsen, Mary Remsen." Savella sat back down. "Although she lived for years as Mary Bloom."

"Tell me about her."

Savella quickly recounted his efforts to trace the life of a woman who lived alone in an apartment by the sea, the priest who lied about knowing his sister, and the Illinois farm boy who never stopped loving her. Emmons sat quietly, chin resting in his right hand, the photograph lying in his lap. When Savella finished, he picked up the photo and got to his feet, wavering slightly as he sought his balance. "Must feed the cats," he said, and walked back inside. Savella glanced at his watch: after seven, and four hours of driving still ahead of him. He slipped on his jacket, pocketed the envelope, and joined Emmons in the kitchen.

The old man was leaning against the small counter, watching the cats jockey for position in front of two plastic bowls filled with wet food. "Always the little one there who gets in first," Emmons said.

He held the photograph up to his face and reexamined it closely. "Svetlana Lyakhov. And this young man at the end, he looks vaguely familiar too." He laughed. "Another occupational hazard. A tendency to obsess over the bit players. You start to think that some obscure character is going to be the key to the mystery. Lyakhov, Marina, this man, Marina's *English* teacher, the babushka lady."

"Who?"

"You don't remember her?"

"I'm afraid not."

"You weren't paying attention. There's a well-known snapshot, grainy, out of focus, showing people in Dealey Plaza as the president drove past. One of them is a woman with a scarf like an old Russian peasant woman might wear, a babushka. There's a school of thought that says she holds a camera, from the way her hands are positioned, but who can really tell?"

Savella reached into his envelope and pulled out Scarf. Emmons studied it for a moment and smiled. "As I said, an occupational hazard. Sometimes a woman in a head scarf is just a woman in a head scarf."

He put Night Out on the counter, picked up the empty cat food cans, and dumped them in the trash.

"Any suggestions on where I go from here?" Savella asked.

"Oh, you don't need my help," Emmons said, and for the first time since he'd seen the photograph, he sounded his age. "Haven't you heard? I'm just an old man who wasted his life searching for conspiracies that never existed. But you're young. You've still got legs. You'll find your way." He took a long brown dog leash from a hook on the wall, then picked up the photograph. "Come on, I'll walk you to your car."

They descended the stairs slowly, one at a time, Emmons hesitant in the dark hallway, the dog even more so. At the bottom Harley strained at the leash and pulled them out the front door. The sidewalk was dense with office workers on their way home, couples headed for drinks and dinner, clumps of milling teenagers.

"I'm just across the street," Savella said. The two men stood awkwardly for a moment, and then Savella held out his hand for Night Out.

"Oh yes," Emmons said with a rueful chuckle. "To find a new piece, after so long..." His voice trailed off, and after one last glance he handed over the photo. "If you should learn anything more, I'd be interested to hear about it."

Savella gave Emmons his telephone numbers, shook hands, and trotted across the street, pausing briefly to avoid a blue van pulling away from the curb. At the car Savella turned to wave good-bye, but Emmons and his dog had already disappeared, swallowed up by the passing crowds.

# 28

Thirty-seven million, the number this week, thirty-seven million dollars. For that kind of money, they were coming in all day and all night. Jorge perched behind the counter in his Yankees cap, looking up from his *Daily News* long enough to punch in the numbers and hand over the tickets. Thirty-seven million. A lot of money, could change a life.

Abel never played. What kind of a chance did you really have? And what difference would it make now? Six months, the doctors gave him, a year at most. And that was around the time Jorge's daughter Miranda got pregnant. Last week, Miranda had her baby.

The rotating fan on the shelf up front blew a whiff of cigarette smoke and the odor of stale beer into Abel's backroom lair. He needed water. He was parched, again, thirsty all the time now, nausea and diarrhea every day, no appetite. No way for a warrior to live, or die, more to the point. Not to mention the worst of it, the nightmares that kept him awake until dawn, moving from room to room as if he could escape them. The man with the list was the worst, his face hidden in a cloud, his hands clutching a clipboard so thick with papers that the clasp threatened to explode. Every night he would read from the papers, not the proclamations of thanks Abel had always expected from the liberated, but a bill of particulars, a laundry list of sin: *September 16, 1967, bomb aboard a Spanish ship in Puerto Rico; October 9, 1969, bazooka attack on a Lithuanian tanker in Miami; July 15, 1971, bomb in a Montreal theater where a Cuban ensemble was appearing,* on and on, until Abel awoke and sought distraction in the living room television.

It was the pills, nothing more, he would tell himself. Sometimes he'd forget and take one too many, and then there was no sense in being awake; he couldn't think straight enough to change the channel on the remote. Happened just this morning, on the way to the store. Pilar told him to stay home, but the Lotto, he knew it would be busy. And there was something else he needed to do today, something the man with the list couldn't know about. But he slipped up, took a second pill, or was it a third, and when the light turned green, three blocks from the store, he couldn't move, sat in the middle of the intersection, head resting on the steering wheel, hands gripping the edge of the seat as if the pressure alone would keep him from slipping under.

Through the narcotic fog he heard the honking and the angry shouts from drivers forced to go around him and finally the *whoop-whoop* of a squad car, a cop rapping on the window. "You OK, sir?"

Even with the drugs surging through his veins, Abel felt the chill of alarm, and worked to muster an apologetic smile. "The engine stalled, Officer," he stammered: *just an old man with a problem.* To prove it, he got out, and opened the hood, made a show of adjusting the wires. The engine fired when he turned the key in the ignition: *back in business, officer, and many thanks for your kindness.*

As if he knew anything about engines, Abel thought. Well, wires he knew, proof of which was sitting in a dimpled metal box under the blanket on the backseat.

Now the box was safely hidden in the crawl space under the floorboards in this ratty office, right over there by the back door. "*Somos listos?*" Pena had asked on the phone the other day. Of *course* we're ready, Garcia wanted to shout down the line. Never let it be said that when it came time to act, Abel Garcia was missing in action. Ready to go, he'd done his job, and truth be told, it felt good, to know he still could. A soldier, not a shopkeeper. But too many sweaty nights, too many nightmares he couldn't share with anyone, not even Pilar, who thought he was finished with all that. Did he want to add a page to the clipboard, this close to the end? And not for Cuba, but for Enrique Pena—a difference there, all the difference in the world, when you thought about it.

Abel struggled up from the recliner and slowly reached out with both hands for his glass. At home, Pilar would be hovering over him, ready to grab for the tumbler should it slip. But he could do it, even if it did require more attention than ever before. He slurped the water, then carefully placed the glass back on the footstool he used as an end table, and slid his shirtsleeve up off his wrist to check his watch. Ten fifty-nine. One minute and the Lotto machine would lock up: *no more tickets*.

At the front of the store, Jorge was ushering the last players out the door, back to their homes or the bars where they would crowd around the television during the eleven o'clock news to find out, as if there had been any doubt, that they were still poor, still desperate. And still here, *still here,* after half a century.

"Abel, you ready to go?" Jorge called out. A broom brushed the floor in quick, sure strokes. Abel closed his eyes. Not long now.

The bell over the door tinkled one more time. "Closed," Abel heard Jorge say, brusquely, determined to cut off any challenge, and then the broom stopped and his tone softened. "Oh, good evening, Father," he said, now little-boy polite. "Hope you're not looking for the Lotto."

# 29

The Reverend Joseph Remsen flashed his best Sunday Mass smile and fingered his collar. "My name's Remsen. I'm looking for Abel Garcia," he said, and the man in the Yankees cap disappeared through the curtain in the back.

Remsen looked around the store. After all the struggle and turmoil, the fearless young soldier wound up peddling cigarettes and phone cards. He stepped around the counter and straightened the photo of the Holy Father pinned crookedly to the wall behind the register.

His reflection in the display window was a revelation. Four days of chin stubble, egg yolk on the lapel of his badly wrinkled suit, and—the worst—his white collar askew, thrown on in haste before he got out of the pickup. Remsen needed a shave, a long shower, and a pillow. And then maybe he could figure out exactly what it was he was doing.

A week on the road, seven days of hard questions and no answers. The first night, in a room in a Motel 6 near Springfield, the television barely loud enough to drown out the party next door, he made the call he dreaded. The colonel wasn't happy, not that Remsen had expected that he would be, not when he found out the reporter knew about *sister* Mary. And of course he was drunk, the way he could get, the liquor unlocking a ranting, venomous rage that no one could control. *"You were supposed to take care of this."* And when Remsen tried to explain, the bitterness and hatred deepened: *"Don't start with the hand washing, you son of a bitch. Way too late. Too far gone for that. This is bigger than anything you can imagine and you're not gonna fuck it up."*

The conversation haunted him as the music and laughter in 207 gave way to grunts and groans and a headboard banging against the wall. The Cuban stuff, all over the news, that was it, had to be. Remsen knew these people. He'd lived their worst. The question was, what could he do about it? What *should* he do about it?

And then, as dawn broke, the eureka moment: always a chance for redemption, he told his boys, no matter what they'd done.

Somewhere in Indiana Remsen stopped for lunch and while he waited for his tuna melt, he took his cell phone outside and called again, reassuring this time, no one's gone wobbly here, you don't have to worry. It's just this reporter keeps nosing around. He's been in touch with the police. A hesitation, and Remsen could imagine the thought: *better he's inside the tent.* The receiver smacked a tabletop, ice tinkled in a glass as it was set down. Then he was back, with an address for Abel Garcia. "He'll take care of you," the colonel said. "Remember him?" A stupid question. Only a few years apart back then, but separated by a gulf of experience. Garcia had guided him through the rough patches. Perhaps he could again. But whose side was he on now? And what would he think of the plan slowly taking shape in Remsen's mind?

So he wandered, searching for firmer ground. At a truck stop outside Indianapolis, he drank a cup of coffee with a washed-out hooker who tried to close a deal until, embarrassed, he pulled the collar from his pocket. "That's not fair, Father," she protested. "How'm I supposed to know?" In a river bar in Columbus, Ohio, he traded shots with an unemployed carpenter eager to vent about an ex-wife who emptied his bank account and moved to Costa Rica. Under an I-70 overpass, he shared a cold bottle of Coors with a motorcycle convoy of Iraq War veterans headed for a funeral in Delaware as they took shelter from a blinding rainstorm. Exhilarating, after all these years in seclusion, a reminder that there were honest lessons to be learned from real people who had lived lives good and bad outside cloistered walls. But in the end, no solution to Remsen's central dilemma: *Was it too late?*

And so he moved on, but always the road led him east and back five decades. And always the memories, long hidden away where they could do no more harm, but now spewing forth, mile after unholy mile, an unceasing deluge.

*Was it too late?*

In the end it was Mary who decided it for him, her choice of Scripture, the second reading, Ezekiel 18:20: *The soul who sins is the one who will die. The son will not share the guilt of the father, nor will the father share the guilt of the son. The righteousness of the righteous man will be credited to him, and the wickedness of the wicked will be charged against him.* A message, Remsen finally realized when he stopped for gas at a Shell station in Bayonne. As she prepared to die, Mary sent him a message.

The counterman poked his head through the curtain. "Come on back, Father," he said, waving him back. "Can I get you a beer?"

He recognized Garcia immediately; the slender soldier who wore his camos like a second skin was long gone, but the aquiline nose, the crooked smile, the meticulously barbered mustache, even coated in gray, were dead giveaways. Remsen crossed the room, his right hand outstretched. With a pained grunt, Garcia stood and wrapped him in an awkward hug, then pulled away. Hands clasped at his waist, the priest stepped back and studied the Cuban.

"It's good to see you, Abel. You're looking well."

Garcia snorted. "*You'll* need confession."

It was true, Remsen thought. Garcia had the drawn look of a man who'd lost too much weight much too quickly. His blue warm-up suit hung on him like a tent. His eyes were red-rimmed and dull, and his skin had a chalky pallor that Remsen had rarely seen outside a hospital.

He pointed to the ring on Garcia's finger. "And you're married?"

"Pilar."

"Children?"

"We were never blessed. It was just as well. There was no time." Garcia dropped into the recliner and motioned toward a folding chair. "And you—the church."

"A place to hide, at first." Remsen moved the chair to face Garcia and sat down. "And then I thought, well, I can do some good here. It's been a satisfying life."

Garcia lifted his water glass and took two delicate sips, wiped his mouth with the back of his hand. "Do they know?" he asked quietly.

An inevitable question, the answer an indelible stain of shame. The lie had lasted a lifetime. The priest slowly shook his head. Garcia let out a breath. "How did you find me, Joey?" He threw up his hands. "*Joey*. What am I saying? Not Joey now, is it. Do I call you Father?"

"Joey's fine."

"Father Joey," Garcia said.

"It was the colonel. He told me to come see you. There's a reporter asking questions about Mary." He paused. "You *do* know about Mary?"

"Yes." Garcia rubbed his jaw. "I was sorry to hear of your loss."

The curtain rustled and the counterman came inside. "Abel, you want to do the register?"

Garcia glanced at the back door and for a moment, he appeared undecided about something. Then he nodded at his guest. "A moment, please. We were just closing." He stood and followed Jorge to the front.

Remsen rose and slowly circled the room, stopping in front of the map of Cuba. What that yellowed, fraying paper meant to Abel Garcia *today* would make all the difference. *Bigger than anything you could imagine.* Nothing that big, not without Garcia's involvement.

As he drove across America, Remsen had tried to plan this moment. What would he say to Abel? Where were the words that would enlist a man from another time to a new cause? Every gesture, every aspect of his appearance was important. Collar or no collar—he'd debated until the last minute, until he was parked outside the store, before finally choosing to wear it. The collar, after all, was what had saved him for so long. Would it be enough? The room suddenly felt close. He walked to the back door, opened it, and stood in the doorway, sucking in the night air.

"What are you doing? Please get away from there."

Remsen turned around. Garcia stood at the curtain, frowning.

The priest quickly closed the door. "I'm sorry, Abel. Just needed some air."

As he stepped toward the desk, his toe caught a loose floorboard. Regaining his balance, Remsen tried to push the board into place with his foot.

"That's not necessary," Garcia said, his voice tense. "Please."

"Listen, I'm very sorry, Abel."

Garcia glanced down at the floor near the back door, then up at Remsen. Finally, he shook his head. "No, no. It is I who should be sorry. It's all right, Joey. No harm done."

The counterman reappeared at the curtain, holding up a bank deposit bag. "I'm leaving, Abel. I'll make the drop. If you're sure you don't want me to hang around."

"No, that's fine, Jorge," Garcia arched his back. "The father can help me close."

Remsen and Garcia sat quietly until Jorge left, pulling the front door shut and twisting the handle to make sure the knob lock was set. When he was gone, Garcia looked around the small room and chuckled. "A shopkeeper," he said. "Would you ever have thought it?"

Remsen smiled. "A shopkeeper and a priest."

For the next half hour, they took refuge in the awkward small talk of two people who knew each other much too long ago: antiseptic sketches of their lives, humdrum narratives free of wrong turns and unintended consequences. Garcia dwelled on Pilar and the store, ignoring every lapse in chronology, gaping holes that he would not close, not even under Remsen's polite questioning. *La lucha,* the struggle, Garcia shrugged in explanation as he leaped ahead a decade here, nine hundred miles there. Remsen was no more forthcoming. His autobiography began at the seminary, not a word about what prompted him to answer the call, much less how he even came to hear it, and ended in safe haven at New Directions.

"A farm for delinquent boys," Garcia said. "You were so"—he groped for the words—"a little bit headstrong. You wanted action. A mission."

"And now I have it. Helping young people, showing them a better life, a way out." A picture of the farm formed in Remsen's mind. "My life, this calling. I've been blessed."

Garcia took a sip of water, eyed the priest over the rim of his glass. "A little more to it than that, don't you think?"

"What do you mean?"

"Penance, perhaps."

"Penance?" Remsen considered the idea. "Maybe some of that too. But you know, Abel, you talk about missions, actions. Why do I get the feeling you haven't spent your life selling lottery tickets?"

Garcia didn't answer. Remsen leaned forward, elbows resting on knees. "Something big happening. 'Bigger than anything you can imagine.' That's what the colonel says, why he's so worried about Mary and what she might have left behind. And then he tells me to come see you. The shopkeeper. Of all people. And this Cuba stuff all over the news. Familiar, I thought, a story I've heard before, but I couldn't remember when.

"And then the other night, it came to me. I heard this story twice, actually. Once from you. Do you remember?"

His face a mask, Garcia drank some water and placed the glass on the footstool.

"Remember Fort Hood, that hot, hot summer, the stories you'd tell me about Cuba? About the Spanish-American War? How it started when the American ship blew up in Havana harbor, and how it later came out that maybe the Americans blew up the ship themselves to get things going? 'Remember the *Maine.*' Right?"

Garcia lay back in the recliner, closed his eyes.

"So that was the one time," Remsen continued. "The other time it was the colonel who told the story. In the early sixties, the military was hell-bent on getting Castro, but there wasn't much of an appetite for that, not after the Bay of Pigs. About the only people who still wanted to try were a few generals. Well, and the exiles, of course, guys like you. But first they had to set the stage, fool the people into believing Castro was trying to get them. And they were willing to do anything to make it look good. Whatever it took. Blow up ships, hijack planes, set off bombs, maybe even kill their own troops if it came to that. Just as long as they could tie it back to Cuba. You remember when we heard about it, Abel? Sounded good, didn't it? Made us feel like we were part of the real deal, if we could handle stuff like that.

"But then Washington canceled the operation. The colonel was always going on about it. Not his usual ranting either. The real ugly stuff. And now I turn on the radio and hear this controversy over these Cuban war plans. And I begin to wonder, is that what's going on here? Is that the something so big I can't imagine?"

Garcia opened his eyes and stared at Remsen, then looked away. The priest allowed himself a moment of satisfaction. *On the same page now, Abel. Time to move to the next chapter.*

Remsen reached over and laid his hand on Garcia's shoulder. Garcia started at the touch, but didn't pull away. *A good sign.*

"This exile is a horrible thing," Remsen said quietly. "But to spill any more blood to make up for it, that's just as wrong. Maybe worse. I wish I'd known this back then. But we were kids, you know?"

Garcia looked impassively at the priest. Then he slowly stood. "I must go," he said. "Pilar will be worried."

"Of course," said Remsen.

"Tell me how I can contact you."

Remsen found a pencil and paper on the desk and scribbled his cell phone number. As Garcia stuffed it in his pocket, he suddenly doubled over, his eyes tearing. The pain again, no early warnings this time, no twinges to prepare him for the agony.

"Abel?" Remsen said.

Garcia pulled his pills from his pocket, swallowed two caplets, and washed them down with a large gulp of water.

"What is it, Abel?" Remsen asked.

"I'm not well," Garcia said weakly. He placed his hands on the desk and braced himself.

"What—"

"I'm dying," he said impatiently. "Simple. I'm dying."

"Of what?"

"Cancer. I have cancer."

"What do the doctors…"

Garcia shook his head violently. "Hopeless."

"Never hopeless. You have to have faith."

Garcia's pallid face flooded with color and his eyes flickered with anger, and Remsen suddenly saw the fierce idealist who stalked the barracks one hot summer long ago.

"You do not want to involve yourself here," Garcia said. "These are not the same men you remember. For them it's not a question of liberty, freedom. It is money, nothing more. The men they hire to fight their battles are not patriots or liberators, they are hoodlums, and for them this is blood sport. If you get in their way, you will die."

Then the fervor ebbed and the spell was broken, and Garcia was a broken old man trapped in the unforgiving fluorescent glare of a life of sadness and regret, sorrow settling over him like a thick black veil. He winced at the last vestiges of pain, his face drained to chalk, and his chest heaved as he struggled to catch his breath.

When he spoke again, his voice was shaky.

"*Ayudeme, Padre.*"

"Of course I'll help you, Abel." Remsen picked up the water pitcher, but Garcia shook his head.

"No, not water."

"Anything."

Garcia leaned heavily on the desk and closed his eyes.

"I'm having a problem, Joey," he said. "Can you get me home?"

# 30

The morning after his return from Washington, Savella tried to reach Sylvie Feidy three times, but her cell phone went straight to voice mail. In the afternoon he called her office; a bored voice at the other end of the phone told him the detective was in the field and only reluctantly took Savella's name and number. He was searching his desk drawer for a takeout pizza menu around six when Feidy finally called back.

"Four messages in one day," she said, her voice desert dry. "You're getting to be a full-time job."

Savella flooded the zone, the words tumbling out in no particular order: *the priest and Mary Bloom are brother and sister, something truly amazing about one of the pictures, Father Remsen's disappeared, we have to talk.* When he had finished, she was silent for a few moments.

"Can we do this tomorrow?" she asked, but offered no argument when he said no.

"Mississippi Avenue and the Boardwalk, in an hour," she said finally. "But you're gonna make it quick."

Feidy was sitting at a table outside a Greek restaurant when Savella arrived, a half dozen teenage girls wheeling and fluttering around her like a flock of gulls.

She pointed at the video arcade next door, and the girls rushed away, quickly swallowed by the bright lights.

"One of them yours?" Savella asked.

"Oh, no, no—the neighbor's kid, the tall one with the red hair," Feidy said. "I promised her mom I'd bring her up for the parade. My neighbor's the nervous type."

"What parade?"

Feidy looked at him oddly. "The pageant."

American Beauty. After his firing Savella had erased it from his mind. Now he looked around him. People carrying cameras and wearing badges and buttons bearing images of smiling women stood in small clumps up and down the Boardwalk; a few blocks up the beach a crowd waited in bleacher seats, a public address announcer doing his best to entertain them. Savella knew the drill: every contestant in a classic convertible for a parade up the Boardwalk. Fifty states, the District of Columbia, and Puerto Rico. Five miles an hour. It would take awhile.

"I guess I don't get it," he said. "My boss called me an elitist. Maybe I am."

Feidy waved toward the arcade. "The girls don't care about it either. Just an excuse to hang out and maybe meet boys. But we won't tell Mom about that part." She swallowed a yawn. "So what couldn't wait?"

Bright stars in a brilliant sky, the light of the moon tracing the tide as it swept to shore. A few minutes apart, the cars drove slowly past, cherry-red Mustangs, gleaming white Corvettes, buffed black Cadillacs, each bearing a beautiful young girl in a skimpy halter top and micro shorts. As they arrived at the grandstand, the names of the states crackled through the scratchy loudspeakers like some mind-numbing grammar school drill: *Miss Indiana...Miss Kentucky...Miss Louisiana...*

An eye out for her giddy charges, Feidy listened as Savella told the story of his visit to the Lemkes, pushing him forward when he bogged down in the details. "The *Reader's Digest* version, OK?" she said as he described the meeting in the living room. "I don't need to know about the doughnuts." But when the scene shifted to New Beginnings, the detective leaned across the table, her hands clasped in front of her. And when Remsen had fled to the sanctuary of his farmhouse, screen door slamming behind him, his last words lingering in the air—*You're asking for answers you don't want to hear. You will never be the same if you do*—she eased back, distractedly tracing a line along her cheek with the fingers of her left hand.

"No idea what he meant by that, right?"

"Not a clue," Savella said.

"I guess I need to have another chat with him."

"Well, we tried. We went back in the morning, but he was gone, or so they said. We sat outside in the car for the rest of the day, but he never showed up."

"Wow," Feidy said, deadpan, "a stakeout."

Savella offered an embarrassed grin. "Anyway, we thought of pushing the point, demanding to see him, but..."

"Oh, come on," she said with a dismissive frown. "You did the right thing. The other is movie shit."

Screams, shouts, and applause swept down the Boardwalk. "Miss New Jersey," the announcer cried. Feidy fumbled with the strap of her shoulder bag. "I promised them pizza," she said. "You want a coffee?"

He watched her shepherd the girls to the takeout window and dig in her purse for a pair of glasses to read the menu board. Makeup slightly faded, smudged, her hair lank, gritty, the regulation blazer wrinkled—just a working girl at the end of an exhausting day, if the working girl carries a gun and a badge. When the girls were fed, Feidy returned with two cardboard cups, and Savella followed her across the Boardwalk, where they leaned against the iron railing, watching the girls giggle down their slices. Feidy pulled off her glasses and dropped them in her bag.

"OK," she said. "You probably have a theory about why Remsen lied about his sister."

"It's the pictures," Savella said. "It has to be." He tugged Night Out from his jacket pocket. "This one in particular. I went to Washington yesterday and showed this to a guy down there. Randall Emmons. He's a Kennedy assassination expert."

Feidy looked away. "Come on, Michael."

"I know, I know. Crackpots. I get it. But listen. I showed him this picture. Wanted to see if I was right about Jack Ruby. He takes one look and starts acting like it's Christmas morning." He pointed to the woman sitting next to Mary. "Forget Ruby. See her? That's a Russian named Svetlana Lyakhov."

Feidy examined the photo for a few seconds, then sighed. "I'm going to regret this, I really am. Who is Svetlana Lyakhov?"

"She is Marina Oswald's cousin. Marina Oswald, Lee Harvey Oswald's Russian wife. That's her cousin, sitting at a table with Mary and Jack Ruby, the man who would wind up killing her husband."

"Sylvie! Look what I found!" A slim woman with a riot of curly blonde hair flowing to her shoulders was approaching them at a rapid pace, waving something in her hand.

Feidy started to laugh. "I don't believe it."

"Best I could do," said the woman.

"Let me see it." A wedding cake topper, maybe five inches tall, a woman in a tuxedo and another woman in a wedding dress holding a bouquet of red roses under an arch decorated with tiny flowers, ribbons, and lace. Feidy turned it over in her hands.

"It's great, Jenny. Perfect. Where'd you get it?"

"Girard's," Jenny said as she took back the decoration. "Believe it or not, they had them in stock. Handmade porcelain, the man said."

"Belinda and Jackie are gonna love it. Listen, I'm almost finished here. Could you..." Feidy pointed up the Boardwalk. The girls, engrossed in chatter, had begun to drift away.

"Not a problem. Ladies!" Jenny shouted and started off after them.

"She a cop too?" Savella asked as she caught up with the pack.

"Who, Jenny? No."

"Just the girls tonight, huh?"

Feidy looked amused.

"I mean, no husbands."

She cocked her head.

"The picture," Savella said. "On your desk. The guy in uniform."

"Ah. My *brother*." She waved at Night Out. "So what is it you think you've got here?"

This is where it gets tricky, he thought.

"Look, I never heard of Mary Bloom until she banged into the back of my car. The only link is the stuff in the tin box. That's the common denominator. She had it and now I do, and someone knows that. And how do they know that? The priest told them. He's the only one I showed them to. Outside of you."

"Eventually," she said.

"Eventually."

"And your pal Bobby."

"Bobby's not involved."

"You're sure of that?"

"As sure as I can be. And so are you."

Feidy ignored his conclusion. "And the tape? Also the priest?"

"Maybe, maybe not. But where it comes from isn't really the important thing. What *is* important is that it's two people talking about what Mary knew or didn't know about…whatever *it* was. We don't know. But think about it. She was in Dallas, Texas. With Jack Ruby. And Oswald's wife's cousin. Sometime before November twenty-second, 1963."

The detective raised the cardboard cup to her lips and finished her coffee in two slow, deliberate gulps. She tossed the cup into a nearby trash can, patted her hands dry on her pants. "All very interesting, Michael, the sister and brother, this picture, the cousin. I'm gonna think about it.

"But understand something. I'm investigating a double homicide in Atlantic City, New Jersey, a few weeks ago. If you want to go off and solve the Kennedy assassination, God bless. I'll look for you on CNN. But I've got two bodies, right here and right now, and that's what I'm focused on. Period."

Miss Wyoming drove past, in a cowboy hat and not much else, followed by a squad car. Feidy looked down the Boardwalk. "Jenny," she called out. "Time to go."

*Wyoming*, Savella thought. *The end of the line.*

He spread his arms wide. "Look, this has everything to do with your two dead bodies. This is motive, don't you see? The murders, the break-ins at Isabella's, at my place, these weren't random acts of violence. You said it yourself. You said it was someone looking for something specific, or sending a message." He held out the photo. "This is what they were looking for. Someone didn't want this out there. Think of the questions it raises. What was Mary doing in Dallas? What was she doing in a bar with Marina's cousin and Jack Ruby?"

The detective found her car keys in her bag. "Interesting theory, but that's all it is. You have nothing to back it up. You don't know for sure that woman is *anyone's* cousin. Or that girl is Mary."

"Alvin said it was."

"Alvin being..."

"The boyfriend."

"Alvin, right. Very nice. Touching story. But it's ancient. The guy hadn't seen or heard from her in decades. He's got nothing to tell me about something that happened a couple weeks ago."

"And Remsen?" Savella said. "He gets antsy when I show him the pictures, and leaves town without mentioning it's his sister who died."

Feidy shrugged. "I'll follow up with Remsen, why he didn't want to admit his relationship with his sister. But it's probably just one of those family things."

Jenny and the girls were hanging back, letting the detective finish her work. Feidy lifted the strap of her purse to her shoulder. "Listen, time's up. I gotta get going."

Savella trailed the women down the ramp to the street. As they reached the bottom, the girls raced ahead. Jenny held up the cake topper, slipped her arm around Feidy's waist, and whispered something that made the detective smile. Then she ran ahead to catch the girls.

Feidy brushed a stray hair from her forehead and watched her go. She waited until Savella caught her, and they walked on in silence. As they reached the corner, Savella stopped.

"Look, can I ask one favor?"

"You can *ask*."

"Can you see if you can find Mary's father? Alvin said she left town with him. I don't know if he's still alive. But if he is, he might be able to answer some of these questions. Maybe even what she was doing in Dallas. And I'm telling you, if you know that, maybe you can find out who wanted that picture bad enough to kill for it."

Feidy pulled a face. "I don't have time to waste on craziness. I'm not saying no, but...Anyway, have a good night." She started up the street, then stopped and turned back to Savella with a slight grin.

"Just the girls, huh?"

"Aw, shit." He cringed at the reminder. "But hey, what a country."

"Oh no," Feidy said as she walked away. "Not just yet."

# 31

A postcard from Isabella was in the mail when Savella returned home: a glossy photo of a mammoth cruise ship on the front and on the back, scrawled in green ink, "I ain't sunk her—yet." Savella laughed out loud, imagining the scene in the Caribbean, Isabella taking charge. The cruise line would never be the same. He dropped the card on his desk, then reached for his BlackBerry to check his messages.

A call from Washington, while he was on the Boardwalk.

*"Yes, this is Randall Emmons."* In the background, the clatter of pots and pans and shouted Chinese. *"Something's wrong with my phone, so I came down to use the phone in the Chinese, but they're asking me to hurry, so let me—the other man in the photo is a Cuban exile named Abel Garcia. That's A-B-E-L. And Garcia, G—well, common spelling. Long career as a bomber, a killer. A terrorist, you'd call him today. Or yesterday, for that matter. No idea where he is, if he's even alive. Anyway. Perhaps this will be helpful. Now I have to go. Good-bye then."*

Savella laid the Night Out photo on his desk. Three women, two men. Ruby on the right, Emmons was talking about the young man on the left, sitting stiffly next to the disembodied hand with the unusual ring. Handsome, Savella thought, and he knows it: a barbered plume of lush hair, a full mustache trimmed just so, a fine suit and a starched white shirt, a striped necktie knotted perfectly beneath the upturned chin. And now, finally, a name: Abel Garcia.

Savella switched on his computer and drummed his fingers on the desktop as he waited for the screen to come alive.

---

Google put bloodstained flesh on the bone. Stories in *Vanity Fair*, the *New Yorker*, newspapers around the world—you could track a career. Garcia was an unmatched sharpshooter, a genius with explosives, a propaganda artist who could drink all night and still bounce out of bed in the morning and kill.

A protégé of the rabid anti-Castro zealot Arturo Pena, the darkest of marks had been laid against Garcia's ledger over the years. The takedown of a Cubana Airline jet, all souls lost, Cubans, yes, but also four exchange students from Malawi and three South Korean missionaries. A hotel bombing in Havana that claimed a French tourist and his nine-year-old daughter as they returned from an excursion to the park for ice cream. Attacks on Cuban interests in Santiago, Quito, Caracas, Panama City; the victims included a night watchman, a bus driver, an ambulance crew, and two street cleaners. Bombings at US government offices in Miami, a warning against any deal with Castro, and a hazy suspicion of involvement in the assassination of a former Chilean diplomat in the heart of Washington.

Garcia denied it all, of course, but with a smile that said don't believe me.

Then the eighties, and for a time his name dropped from the headlines. And when he did resurface, it was a different Abel Garcia—older, naturally, but less sure of himself, the past tense creeping into his remarks. The patriot who devoted his life to the pursuit of liberty was reduced to hiring himself out for a thousand a week to ferry guns to the Contras in Nicaragua. Finally, the denouement: a garden-variety ambush, nothing a young warrior couldn't have smelled before he reached the pavement, but altogether too much for an older man who never even spotted the shooters who left him for dead in a flooded gutter outside a hotel in San Pedro Sula, watching his blood stain the fetid rainwater.

It was late that night when Savella found what he had been looking for, even if he hadn't really known it. A grainy television news magazine piece from fifteen years earlier, taped off a home set and squirreled away on YouTube by someone who offered the name Dospesos. The network wasn't identified; Savella had never seen the reporter before, a tall redheaded woman named Patsy Herz, whose English carried an accent. She was in search of answers about the exiles' struggle, she said at the outset. Abel Garcia was the next stop on her journey.

He was a garrulous host. On the veranda of a friend's place in Key Biscayne, Garcia bragged about the old days, mustered the strength to flirt just a bit, and she let him go to keep him talking. Not so careful anymore, he reminisced loudly about past triumphs and lamented old defeats. Later, in Little Havana, a few other dinosaurs crossed the street to shake his hand and sing his praises as he and Patsy strolled through the streets, Garcia in embroidered guayabera, the reporter in tailored khakis. And when lunch at Versailles was on the house—*the least we can do for Senor Garcia, un patriota, we don't forget*—he accepted his due with practiced nonchalance.

It wasn't until they sat down in a studio, knee-knocking close on a bare set, that the smiles faded. As Patsy confronted Garcia with his legacy of bombings, his mood soured, his answers grew shorter, hinting of fury. Finally, she turned him toward a monitor to watch the film of a burning bus in Guatemala City, the frantic sirens and screams of the dying the only soundtrack to the carnage on the screen. Someone thought it was a group of Cuban Embassy employees headed for an office picnic, Patsy said softly when the final image had faded. Someone—*was it you, Abel?*—was wrong. Instead of diplomats, the bus carried three dozen schoolchildren headed for the zoo, their outing cut short by the C-4 explosives packed in a two-liter bottle of RC Cola and tucked inside an ice chest.

Suddenly Garcia was on his feet, ripping open his shirt to reveal the ugly scars from bullet wounds, one just inches from his heart.

"Who do you think did this?" he raged as the cameramen scrambled to keep pace. "Where did these bullets come from? The tyrant. The tyrant sent them. It's a war. In a war people die. All kinds of people. Even the innocent. Especially the innocent."

But the bombs in Miami, she wanted to know. The attacks in Washington, New York. Even the Americans? Even your allies?

"A warning," he said bitterly. "We will never forget that he betrayed us once."

*He.*

Not they.

Not it.

Not them.

*He.*

The dimensions of the betrayal were that narrow. Kennedy.

With the exile army pinned on the beach at the Bay of Pigs, he ordered the air support to stand down, consigning them to humiliation. When he stood in the Orange Bowl a year later with the veterans of Brigade 2506, held aloft the flag they had carried to defeat, and vowed to return the standard "in a free Havana," he had already promised the Soviets he would leave Castro alone if they took their missiles home. The rest—halfhearted attempts to kill the dictator or make his beard fall out, anyway—was light opera.

Betrayal? Kennedy.

"But these were your patrons," Patsy persisted. "They gave you money, supplies, training."

Garcia's sweaty face glistened in the harsh studio light. "They purchased the chain," he hissed, "but they do not have the monkey."

---

Some things are too dangerous to think about, a wise editor once told Savella. Because the closer you get, the greater the risk.

So keep them separate, these gleaming pearls he had collected. Isolate them, swaddle them in cotton, and whatever you do, for God's sake don't let them rub up against each other. Abel Garcia was just an angry Cuban. Jack Ruby was only a mob bagman. Svetlana Lyakhov was a Russian party girl, and Mary Remsen was Alvin's sweetheart. And there was absolutely no reason why they found themselves crammed around a banquette at the Hotel Adolphus one night in Dallas. Better that way. Because the alternative, well, too damn dangerous to think about.

Abel Garcia's trail effectively ended in the television studio. His name popped up from time to time in other accounts of the exiles' war, like a baseball player who put together a season or two of excellence, then faded from view, a footnote to the history of the game. But when he walked away from Patsy, he disappeared. No more patriot. No more dead innocents. No more Abel Garcia.

Savella fell back in his chair. After a few minutes, the monitor screen went black. He got up and poured himself a drink, took a seat in the window, and watched the pear trees on the corner sway in the breeze. It had been awhile since he had felt the thrill of the hunt. But now he was deep in the forest, unsure of his footing, afraid he'd turned the wrong way a few miles back, and left with nothing to do now but push forward. No obituary for Garcia; you'd think a man with a past like that would rate a few paragraphs somewhere, so maybe he was still alive. Savella made a note to check the Miami phone directories. If he still even lived down there. Perhaps Feidy could help him. But would she? Remember her sarcastic reaction to the discovery of Marina's cousin? *I'll look for you on CNN.*

And what the hell, maybe she was right. Maybe there were no conspiracies. Suppose there were good reasons for everything, rock-solid explanations that turned the bizarre into the mundane. His picture was no smoking gun, no missing link. An auto accident hadn't led him to the Holy Grail, the one piece of evidence that had somehow escaped legions of JFK investigators for years. And did he want to move into the province of crackpots and nut jobs, handpicking facts and smashing them into unrecognizable forms that could be easily blended to suit a purpose? Did he really want to end up like Emmons, stumbling around Washington to a chorus of snickers before heading home to his cats?

Repeat after me: The Cuban just wanted to go home. The Russian came to see her cousin. Ruby was a small-time hood. And Mary—well, what about her? *The closer you get, the greater the risk.* Because the Cuban was a killer with a grudge against America, a lacerating hostility that still smoldered decades later. Here was motive, and everyone else had a link to it—Ruby, the errand boy for gangsters seething over the loss of their island gold mine; Svetlana, her cousin married to an assassin; and Mary—damn it, there she was again. What was in it for Alvin Lemke's precious sweetheart, a kid who had spent the previous year necking at the movies, listening to 45s, and daydreaming about her future?

But stop it now. One more time, until you get it right: The Cuban just wanted to go home. The Russian came to see her cousin. Ruby was a small-time hood. And Mary—*what's she doing in this picture?*

A strange coincidence. It's possible. But you couldn't leave it there. The Cuban felt betrayed by a president. The Russian's cousin was married to the man who would murder him. And the guy with the stripper would shoot the shooter.

And that still left Mary.

Some things are too dangerous, the man said.

# 32

Enrique Pena kept offices in New York City on the twenty-seventh floor of a glass-and-marble palace on West Fifty-Eighth Street. He had been rejected for space initially, but that only served to set him off on a frenzied crusade, badgering, threatening, until he forced his way in.

For all the effort, however, Pena was rarely there, and it showed: a few travel posters hanging on the walls in the sprawling reception area, months-old magazines on the coffee tables, a wafer-thin receptionist sitting at a computer, which she never seemed to use, and a phone, which she did, and often. A buzzer-controlled door led to four more offices, two forever empty, a third occupied by Leonard, Pena's gnomish assistant, and at the end of a narrow corridor, Pena's hideaway, an oblong room with two mammoth tropical fish tanks and floor-to-ceiling windows that looked west to New Jersey and north to Central Park, but only if you craned your neck just right.

In the end the New York City office of Miramar Holding Co., Ltd., was very expensive wasted space. But the point wasn't whether Enrique Pena needed it. The point was he could have it if he wanted.

Abel Garcia had been ushered to one of the vacant rooms down the hall when he arrived shortly after ten thirty. Leonard, sniffy as always and scratching for information, had called a few hours earlier to summon him across the Hudson.

"*Estas listos*, Abel? Mr. Pena says it's time. He says you'll know what he means. Do you?" And when Garcia didn't answer, wouldn't play, Leonard sighed. "He says to tell you to pack a bag."

A trip, especially for Pena, was the last thing Garcia needed, or wanted. He hadn't slept well since the encounter with the priest two days earlier. The meeting had ended poorly. Too sick to drive himself, Garcia had slumped in the front seat of Remsen's pickup, offering directions in a strained monotone as they rushed through the Battery Tunnel, up the West Side Highway, and across the George Washington Bridge, Remsen chattering all the while about ancient history. When at last they pulled into the driveway, Pilar was waiting just inside the screen door. At the sight of her husband stepping down from a stranger's truck, she rushed out and encircled him, a lioness protecting her cub, almost dwarfing Abel as he staggered up the porch steps and into the house. Garcia raged inwardly at the indignity, to be cared for like a child, but he was helpless to resist, and by the time he fell onto the brocaded sofa in the living room, breathing shallowly as Pilar fetched more pills, he was grateful for the help and wanted only sleep. Through the haze, he could hear his wife in the kitchen interrogating the disheveled priest with the crooked collar, and after Remsen mentioned he went back decades with her husband, she showed him to the door without even a cup of coffee for his troubles.

Garcia had spent the next day at home, leaving Jorge to open and close the bodega. His cell phone rang on the hour, Remsen every time. He let it go unanswered, hoping the priest would disappear just as abruptly as he had arrived. He knew what Remsen wanted, but didn't know what to do about it. And now, before he could sort it out, Leonard, on the phone: *Pack a bag.*

Pilar was shopping at the mall in Short Hills; afterward, there would be a long lunch with her girlfriends. Garcia was relieved—no risk of a scene when she demanded to know where he was going and he refused to say. He went into the bathroom and turned on the shower, stripped quickly, and stepped into the stall, recoiling as the hot water rained down upon him. He washed carefully for fifteen minutes, his skin reddening in the steamy heat. When he was finished, he dried himself thoroughly and returned to the bedroom with a towel wrapped around his waist.

In the closet he found a pair of black slacks and sorted through the hangers on the rod until he found his snow-white guayabera. He laid it across the bed, pausing for a moment to admire the exquisite tailoring. How long had it been? Fifteen years? He lightly stroked the fine linen, his hand lingering for a moment as he brushed the pleated front. Then he went back to the closet for his best hand-tooled leather shoes. In a bureau drawer he found silk socks and underwear and a shiny black belt. He dressed slowly, examining himself in the mirror after each step, Pilar's framed picture of the Virgin Mary staring down at him from its favored position on the wall. When he was finished, he stepped back and studied his image. The clothing hung loosely on him; that was to be expected. But otherwise he was pleased to see he looked much as he had all the other times the telephone had rung. He placed a change of underwear, a fresh shirt, his razor, and a toothbrush in a small valise, stopped in the kitchen for a glass of orange juice, and left the house.

Halfway to the bus stop, he remembered he hadn't left a note. A phone call later would do, he decided. Too late to turn back.

Now he sat in the small office, waiting. Pena felt as if he had been entombed. The faint blare of car horns occasionally drifted up from the street, and once he heard the screech of a winch and opened the blinds to watch two window washers move higher on the building next door. But otherwise the office offered no signs of life. The room was empty except for a desk and chair still wrapped in plastic and set haphazardly in the middle of the floor. The air smelled of paint. A telephone lay on the carpet in one corner, but when Garcia lifted the receiver, the line was dead.

A half hour after he arrived, Garcia heard a murmured voice just outside. He stepped hesitantly into the hallway. The door to the adjacent office was ajar; inside, perched atop a conference table, sat Marta Pena, a lipstick in her hand, talking into a cell phone. A beautiful young woman, Garcia thought, but just beneath the delicate surface, he knew, lay a hard edge. Her father's daughter, certainly, and the evidence was everywhere: the mocking smile, the dull eyes, the warning posture that said *stay away*. A woman after Pena's own heart. Perhaps too much so, the way Pena treated her—not exactly paternal, Garcia always thought on those occasions when he saw the two of them together. Las Vegas, a few weeks ago, sprang to mind. Garcia shook his head, anxious to banish the thoughts. What a peculiar obsession, this morality of his now, after a life of broken promises, practiced lies, and blood-soaked resolutions.

Marta hung up the phone and busied herself with the lipstick. Garcia pushed the door open a bit more and coughed. Her face broke into an amused grin at the sight of him.

"Uncle Abel."

"Marta."

"How are you?"

*Dying, Marta. Not much longer now. And you speaking English.*

"Ah, old age," he said. "There is no use complaining."

"Come on, Abel, you're still a young man," Marta said, teasing. "Still run your wife around the bedroom, no?"

Garcia forced a wan smile. "Not as often as she would like."

Marta laughed and raised the lipstick to her face.

A door opened and closed somewhere along the corridor, and a few seconds later Enrique Pena pushed into the room with a questioning glance at Garcia. "Didn't Wanda put you in the other office, Abel?" Before Garcia could answer, Pena crossed to his daughter. "You're here," he said, his voice cozy, satisfied.

"Only for a minute." She stood, fumbled through her purse, and pulled out a purple compact.

"But you'll be at dinner."

"Yes, of course. At—"

"Eight," Pena said. "Anyway, I'll be right back." He hugged her, tightly, his hands in motion. After a moment she wriggled free. "Daddy, my blouse," she said, with a schoolgirl's pout. Pena chuckled and with one more quizzical look at Garcia, walked out of the room.

Marta opened her compact. Garcia watched her intently. Did she seem upset? Did her father's behavior bother her? Garcia didn't know. But he had wondered too long.

"May I, may I ask you a question?" he said.

"Sure," Marta said, her eyes fixed on the mirror.

"Do you think sometimes your father is..." *No, he couldn't.* He searched for the right words, but they wouldn't come. Instead he reached out and gently touched her shoulder. Marta looked down at his hand, curious now.

"My father is what?" she said. When he didn't answer, she turned her attention back to the mirror and checked her mascara.

"No, of course not," she said. "That's Daddy. That's just his way."

"What's my way?"

Garcia and Marta spun around, startled at the sound of Pena's voice. He stood in the doorway, this time with Elmer Deets looming behind him in the corridor. Marta's face reddened.

"Oh, nothing," she said, forcing a laugh.

"No, what's my way?" Pena said, his eyes fixed on Garcia, who shuddered inwardly. What had he done? He had seen the man this way before, the chilling glower. It never ended well.

"No, I—" Abel began.

Marta closed her bag, threw it over her shoulder, and headed for the door. "I will see you at eight," she said, leaning in to kiss her father. Pena draped his arms around her, then looked back at Garcia, daring him to speak. But he was an old man, dying. His moment of bravado had passed, and Pena marked it with a faint sneer.

"Eight, then," he said, releasing his grip on his daughter slowly, only when he was ready. "At the restaurant."

Pena watched her walk away. When the door at the end of the corridor clicked closed, he turned back to Deets and Garcia. "We'll talk in my office," he said brusquely.

---

No lunch this time, no how-was-your-trip, no *ensalada de mariscos,* not even a frosty glass of iced tea. Pena sat behind his desk, hands resting lightly on the glass; Garcia and Deets stood in front of him, facing the undraped windows, squinting in the fierce glare of the midday sun. Pena's dogs, the two great beasts, squatted on either side of their master. Ugly things, Abel thought, and on cue, the one on the right eyed him and growled.

"Here's what I want, Abel," Pena began. "We need some extra manpower. You'll help Elmer find it."

"Hunting Cubans today, Abel," Deets said. "My favorite thing."

Pena ignored him. "Then you're going to go with Deets. You're going to do what he says."

"Where are we going?"

"You'll know when you get there."

The dog on the left began to whimper. Pena reached over and scratched his ear, but the dog continued to cry.

"And what is the target?" Garcia asked. "I need to know this. It makes a difference."

Pena took a deep breath and exhaled slowly. "You just make the bombs," he said in his mind-your-own-fucking-business voice, "and Deets will take care of the rest."

The dog on the left pawed the carpet and looked up at Pena, who reached down and stroked its head. Garcia shifted uncomfortably from foot to foot.

"But the target matters. If I don't know the target, I cannot tell you how effective the devices will be."

"Effective?" Pena frowned. "How many bodies—is that what you mean? Where have you been, Abel? The world's changed since you were roaming around Latin America with your sticks of dynamite and an alarm clock. It's not about numbers anymore. It's about fear."

He stood and walked to the window and pointed down. "You want to make people afraid to live their normal lives. Make them look over their shoulder when they go to the grocery, stop at a restaurant, fill the gas tank, when they get in the elevator. Wherever they go, they're thinking the guy behind them in line might have a gun, might be carrying a bomb."

He turned back to his desk and sat down. "You make them afraid, you scare the people badly enough, and the government will do anything to make them feel better."

The dog on the left shuffled to the door, stopped, and looked back at Pena. Then he squatted on the carpet. An acrid smell quickly filled the room. When the dog rose, a pile of feces lay on the carpet.

"Ah, Jesus, Rodrigo," Pena muttered. He reached under the desktop and moments later, Leonard appeared at the door, looked down at the mess, and left again, to return with a broom and dustpan and a can of disinfectant. The three of them watched as he worked, as if cleaning a pile of dog shit was the most interesting thing they'd ever seen. In short order the pile was gone, and the room smelled of pine. Leonard stood smiling in the doorway, proud of his accomplishment.

"That's all, Leonard," Pena said. "And take them with you."

Leonard herded the dogs out the door and closed it behind him. Pena looked at Garcia. "This has been a nightmare from the beginning. The colonel kills Marta's boyfriend. For what? That wasn't supposed to happen. And you"—he looked at Deets—"the mess in Atlantic City, bringing the police into it. Then Miller doesn't get the job done in Washington. A disaster. And the reporter's still out there."

"You wanted me to leave him alone," said Deets. "You said we don't know what he knows, who else he's told. You said it yourself. And you wanted the pictures back."

"Well, that was then."

"So now I'll take care of it."

Garcia looked at Deets. *He does things we won't.*

"He had the pictures with him?" Pena asked. "In Washington?"

"I think so," Deets said. "But it doesn't matter now."

Pena shook his head. "It's getting late. Wrap this up, Elmer." He held up the *Daily News*, angling the paper so Garcia couldn't see it. "They're waiting for us."

Garcia grappled with what he'd heard. What plans had Pena concocted for the three bombs hidden in the crawl space of the bodega? Garcia had promised Don Arturo an attack on Cuba or Cuban interests or Cuban allies. Military targets. Government offices. Not civilians, not after Guatemala. He remembered a reporter in Miami, his anger at her audacious challenge. *In a war people die. All kinds of people. Even the innocent. Especially the innocent.* It made sense then, or maybe it never really did.

And now a priest appears.

*Estas listos?* Was he ready? He didn't know anymore.

Pena dropped the newspaper on his desk and pointed at Deets. "You call me tonight. Abel? Anything else?"

Garcia shook his head. It was pointless, he realized. He was at the mercy of men who knew just enough to be dangerous and not enough to be scared, a lethal mix. But what could he do? What would he do? The promise to the old man trumped all. He had given his word.

They were headed for the door, halfway across the room, when Pena stopped them. "One more thing, Abel. What's my way?"

For a moment, Garcia had no idea what he was asking. "I'm sorry?"

"You were talking to my daughter before. And she said that's Daddy, that's just his way."

"OK." He should have known the episode wouldn't be forgotten.

"So what's my way? What were you talking about?"

*My pills,* Garcia thought. *I need my pills.*

"I don't remember," he said. "I...don't know. What we were talking about."

Pena stared at Garcia for what seemed an eternity, then glanced back at Deets and nodded once, firmly. As they filed out of the office, their shoes tapping a parade-grounds rhythm on the polished marble tiles, Elmer Deets was grinning like he'd just won the lottery.

---

Cubans, and only Cubans, two of them. Young, old, sick, healthy, black, white, brown—it didn't matter.

"Just as long as they're real Cubans," Deets growled. "From Cuba. You get it?"

Garcia didn't get it, didn't know why they had to be Cubans, couldn't understand why they needed help in the first place. As these things went, this was child's play; he'd done a dozen all by himself over the years. But Garcia was tired of asking questions that were never answered. So it would be Cubans and only Cubans, two of them. Easy enough to find at his store, but then Jorge would be snooping around and that wouldn't do. Instead they drove across the river to Union City, which, if you wanted Cubans and only Cubans, two of them, was as good a place as any to look. *Little* Little Havana, they called it: outside of South Florida, the largest Cuban population in the country.

For almost two hours, they cruised Bergenline Avenue, the community's twisting spine, jammed with traffic on a sultry autumn afternoon—cars and delivery trucks and senior citizens' buses creeping between stoplights, police cars, and ambulances trying to squeeze through on the strength of flashing lights and sirens. Drivers leaned on their horns, and the pounding rhythms of a dozen different tunes rose from the gridlock. Deets hunched over the steering wheel, stinking of English Leather, sweat, and onions, crumbs from his lunch dotting his lapels. Garcia rolled down the window and scanned the teeming sidewalks for possibilities. He could usually spot the new arrivals. They stood awkwardly on the street corners, stealing amazed glances at the wealth around them, absorbing their New World, turning away out of habit when a patrol car cruised by. In a few months or maybe a few years, they'd wonder what they'd done, not regrets really, just questions they'd never be able to answer. But for now, fresh from their island prison, this was fine. And if a chance to make some real money presented itself—*dollars!*—that was even better than fine.

Garcia knew them, but today he couldn't seem to find them. They rolled the length of *La Avenida*, then back again, stopping so many times to approach groups of young men that it was a wonder they hadn't been attacked as perverts. Nobody fit the bill. Mud-caked Timberlands was Puerto Rican. Ripped blue jeans was Dominican. Green knapsack was from Ecuador. And even when they found a Cuban, no one wanted day-work.

"Si, Cubano, who are you?" said the man at the counter when they stopped for sodas. "I'm here twenty years, so get out of my store."

It wasn't until Deets started a third pass down the avenue that Garcia understood the problem. Bergenline wasn't *La Avenida* anymore, or at least not the slice of Havana that it had been for decades. Oh, the old men still lolled outside the Jovenes Unidos social club, talking politics. And *pan con bistec, café Cubano, dulche de leche* were all over the restaurant menus. But it wasn't the same. Once every business was Cuban-owned, every store's name evoked the homeland. Now there was a Colombian restaurant, a Spanish bakery. A Puerto Rican Muslim owned the jeweler's, and his customers sent money home to Peru. The Chinese ran the corner shoe store, and these days a kid could walk down the street in a Che Guevara T-shirt and live to tell about it. Little Little Havana was slowly slipping away.

And Deets was getting angry. "Running late here," he grumbled as he tried to edge around a sanitation truck moving at glacier speed. "Could've sat in your place in the city and got this done in an hour."

Garcia's cell phone beeped. "No phones," Deets said. Garcia glanced down at the display. The priest, again. Not Joey Remsen, but Father Joseph, all grown up and urging him to rethink his life. A lot of living and dying since they'd last seen each other. How could a priest ever hope to understand? How could Abel Garcia even begin to explain it to him? Better that he went away with his suspicions, his judgments. Garcia cleared the screen and jammed the phone into his jacket pocket.

The traffic lurched forward briefly, then stopped.

"Go down another few blocks," he told Deets. "The empty lot near the Dunkin' Donuts. Sometimes they wait there for work."

---

Not many left at three in the afternoon. The morning shape-up started early, ended early. The contractors looking for day labor were done by seven. But the stragglers often hung around, playing cards, dominos, pooling their change for a quart of beer, waiting for nightfall, putting off as long as possible that emasculating moment when they had to return home and explain to the kids that Papa came up empty.

Deets pulled the van to the curb and surveyed the lot. A young boy in painters pants lay sleeping on the ground in the shade of an elm tree, using his backpack as a pillow. Next to him sat an older Hispanic who spotted them and halfheartedly pulled a wad of papers from his pocket.

"His immigration documents," Garcia said. "Wants us to know he's legal."

Deets pointed across the lot. "What about those?" He gunned the engine and pushed the van over the curb and into the lot, stopping just short of a group of men watching four others playing dominoes. "Those two, the red shirt and the Mets jersey. With the brand-new sneaks."

Garcia glanced down at the board. A few dozen *fichas*. They were playing double six, the favored game in Santiago de Cuba, on the eastern side of the island. He leaned through the open window, snapping his fingers. "*Ustedes desea a un trabajo?*" In a flash, the spectators were at the window, pushing and shoving, arms outstretched.

"Hey, they're gonna scratch the fucking paint job," Deets said crossly.

"*Solamente dos*," Garcia shouted, and he pointed at his two targets, who smiled in triumph as the rest returned to the dominoes.

Garcia opened the door and stepped out. "*Cubanos, si?*"

The smiles vanished. The two men began to turn away.

"Guess that answers *that*," Deets said with a harsh laugh.

"*Espera, espera. No soy la migra*," Garcia said quickly. He looked at Deets and shrugged.

"They'll do," Deets said.

"How much?"

"Tell 'em two hundred bucks apiece for the deal. Make it more if you need to. What the fuck, five hundred, whatever."

"What do you mean?"

"Just tell them, huh?"

Garcia quickly translated the offer, and the man in the Mets jersey responded in Spanish. "They want to know how long we need them."

"The weekend. Back by Sunday."

The weekend? Garcia thought. What would he tell Pilar?

"They don't have their things."

"They won't need clothes. We'll give them clothes."

"Toothbrush, a change of underwear…"

"OK, we'll get it," Deets said impatiently. He pulled an envelope from the sun visor and handed it to Garcia. "Write down their names."

"For what?"

Deets glared at him. "You gonna ask me questions every time I tell you to do something, it's gonna be a long day."

Garcia found a pen and took down the information, and the two Cubans hopped in the back of the van. Didn't know where they were headed, or what they would be doing, and probably didn't care, Garcia thought. There was money to be made and they had each other to lean on. In exile you stuck together, and that's what mattered.

Deets adjusted the rearview mirror and watched them for a moment. The man in the red shirt looked up and grinned, then nudged his friend, who smiled and waved at Deets.

"Don't understand a fucking word of English," Deets muttered, maybe to himself. "*Perfecto.*"

---

They headed for the Lincoln Tunnel, Deets bullying his way through the early rush-hour traffic. The Cubans in the rear struggled for a secure grip to keep from sliding into the sides of the van. Garcia ducked his head to peer out the windshield for a glimpse of the New York City skyline. A spectacular sight, especially at this time of day, with the sunlight glinting off the buildings. He could still remember the first time, a trip up for a meeting in '65. Angry about the sellout, disillusioned with the promise of democracy, yet still awed by the power and the wealth and the promise that those buildings represented.

As they sat in traffic, inching their way down to the tunnel entrance, Garcia checked off the landmarks, the Chrysler Building, the Empire State Building, until he came to the hole at the tip of the island. Not about numbers anymore? Pena was wrong. Tell that to the three thousand who died in the attacks. Tell that to the soldiers killed in the wars that followed, and to the innocents caught in the crossfire on battlefields across the globe. The numbers mattered, they always did.

Pena was right about one thing, though. You win when you make people afraid to live their lives. In the old days, when the war was over, things returned to what passed for normal. But not anymore. Today the battle never ended. Always the threat of another assault when you least expected it, the threat of one more bomb. Like the three he had hidden in the back of the bodega. What did Pena want? An attack on civilians? How many? How many was too many? How many was not enough?

In the tunnel now, humming under the river, flickering lights guiding their path. Garcia closed his eyes and tried to forget about it all.

---

Fifty minutes later the van jerked to a halt in front of the bodega. Through the window Garcia could see Jorge perched on the counter, sipping a soda and talking with Francisco, the coffee man. Garcia unbuckled his seat belt and opened the door. Behind him he heard the rear door screech open.

"No, no, no," Deets said, "they stay with me." Garcia turned and motioned the Cubans back inside, then stepped out of the van. "Don't take forever," Deets said.

Jorge and Francisco—*Georgie and Frank, Dios mio*—shouted greetings as he came through the door. Garcia stopped briefly to reassure them about his health, then walked back to his office and drew the curtain shut. Bending down, he pried up the floorboards near the alley door. Buried under a pile of old newspapers was a green duffel bag. Inside, wrapped in an old blanket, was a metal box with Cyrillic lettering and a red-and-yellow radiation warning sign that now contained the twisted culmination of Abel Garcia's dark and savage career.

It hadn't taken long for Garcia to understand exactly what Pena was after. The night of the visit from the young man with the stubbled face, *maybe Slavic, maybe Russian,* Garcia had feigned sleep until Pilar had her fill of television. When she was softly snoring, he slipped out of bed and went to the kitchen, switched on the Dell laptop computer his wife used for her Internet shopping. A few minutes later, his worst suspicions were confirmed.

Garcia was a world-class bomber, a master of the Czech-made plastic explosive Semtex-B, a wizard with state-of-the-art Goma 2 Eco dynamite. But what Enrique Pena wanted from his cold warrior was a twenty-first-century dirty bomb.

The two small canisters under the flooring of the bodega contained cesium-137, a radioactive isotope produced by nuclear reactions and used in cancer therapy and atomic clocks. A harmless-looking powder, almost like talcum, Cs-137 was a forever killer. It would lodge deep in human muscle tissue; anyone exposed to it would be consigned to a lingering terror—the knowledge that the chances of cancer in the next ten, twenty, thirty years had gone dramatically up. And the powder could cling to any imaginable surface—roofing shingles, concrete blocks, soil, grass—rendering an area uninhabitable for decades. The entire zone, everything in it, would have to be destroyed.

The ultimate weapon, Garcia realized. He had killed people, blown up property. But to force your enemy to destroy his own society, that was genius. Pure evil genius.

*But what was the target?* What did Pena have in mind? Was it New York City? The possibilities were endless, especially since Pena had made it clear that civilians were in bounds. So, what, Yankee Stadium on a sunny September afternoon? A concert at Madison Square Garden? Maybe a Broadway show, or Macy's, or a hotel, or Wall Street, or one of the tunnels, or a jam-packed subway, or the Central Park Zoo. Or simply set off the bombs on a Midtown street corner and let the breeze decide. The possibilities were too horrifying to contemplate, like nothing Garcia had ever confronted.

But he did his job, did it well, in fact. Now he sat in the back of his store inspecting his handiwork in the box at his feet. Not bad for a dying old man, he thought, and for a moment a frisson of pride replaced the anguish that now defined his days.

Pena wanted something compact, small enough you could hide it anywhere. Garcia had fashioned two bombs, the lead-encased cesium attached to a small amount of explosive and a cell phone that would trigger the explosion. A simple timer would have been better. No paper trail, unlike the cell phone with the embedded memory chip, which carries a wealth of information. But Pena had said no. He wanted to control the timing of the explosions, to change his mind and order a delay at the last minute if things weren't just right. So there you were. And Deets needed something for himself. Dynamite charge, also triggered by a phone call. A diversion, Deets had said.

Up front, Jorge and Francisco were flirting with a customer. Garcia took one last look at the explosives. Then he removed the dynamite and placed it in a paper bag. He secured the lid of the box, zipped the duffel bag, and lifted it carefully out of the hole. After pushing the boards back in place with his foot, Garcia started for the front door. At the curtain he paused for a moment. A soldier, he thought, heading off to battle. There are certain standards. From the bottom drawer of the desk he drew a black .45-caliber Colt automatic with a brown stock. A gift from long ago, one of two Colts that belonged to an old friend, a man with whom he'd gone to war, for whom he'd risked his life. Garcia tucked the gun in his belt, the cold steel brushing against his scarred abdomen. He glanced at himself in the wall mirror. Satisfied the weapon was concealed, he marched out of the back room and, with a curt nod to Jorge and Francisco, left the store.

At the van, Deets was pacing in front of the cargo door. "They keep trying to get out," he said. "Let's get going."

# 33

The target wasn't in New York City.

Garcia should have known Pena wouldn't foul his own nest.

Instead, Deets bulldozed onto the Brooklyn-Queens Expressway—gridlocked on an average afternoon, imagine the scene after a terror attack—and over the Verrazano Narrows Bridge into Staten Island. One by one he crossed off the options. Not a tunnel or a bridge, not JFK, LaGuardia, not the Statue of Liberty. They crossed into New Jersey and limped onto the Garden State Parkway—heading south, not north to Giants Stadium, or the Elizabeth refineries. *Or Pilar,* Garcia thought.

But there was no relief. With each passing mile, Garcia felt worse. Everywhere he looked were shopping malls, hospitals, McDonald's, cul-de-sacs in tony suburbs. Like the missing piece in the Manhattan skyline, it depended on the statement Pena wanted to make.

An attack on America, he had crowed.

Which could mean McGuire Air Force Base, or Blessed Mother Roman Catholic Church.

As they headed into the twilight, Garcia glanced over at Deets, who was deep into a tuneless hum.

"How far?" he asked, taking one last stab.

"You're gonna love it," said Deets, and hummed louder.

---

The few last rays of afternoon sun filtered through the tall trees that flanked the parkway. It was dark earlier every day now, Garcia realized, another winter approaching. He glanced back at the Cubans. They had fallen asleep, leaning on each other, lulled by the rhythm of the road. Would this be their first winter? The shock of it all: the snow and ice, the clothes they'd never worn before, the odor of the furnace fumes. Why hadn't they gone to Miami? Family here, probably, or a wife, a girlfriend, maybe a promise of a job, a piece of solid ground. And instead, a van on a strange highway, heading who knows where, and they sleep like babies. For a moment Garcia wished they would never wake up, that their last memories would be their first glimpses of a magical new world. If only he could end his own film there, Garcia thought, just turn off the projector and walk out of the theater for good.

Up ahead a pack of small deer nibbled the grass on the road shoulder, oblivious to the speeding traffic. Nice to be so innocent, so trusting. Like the two boys in the back. Strangers offer you a few dollars, and you climb in the back of a van and fall asleep. Well, maybe it would work out, Garcia thought as he dozed off.

---

The brakes, metal on metal, woke him. He blinked once, twice, then sat up and looked at his watch. Just past seven. He had been asleep for maybe an hour. Dark out now, and Deets was steering the van toward an exit. Garcia glanced up at the sign: Atlantic City and Shore Points.

The van wound slowly along the ramp, then merged onto another highway, thick with traffic on a Friday night. Billboards announcing hot singers and loose slots replaced the dark forests of the parkway. In the distance Garcia could see bright lights glowing on the horizon.

The traffic. The billboards. The lights.

Atlantic City's casinos. Thousands of visitors. Public spaces.

Got to hand it to Pena, Garcia thought as the van rolled down the road toward the ocean. An attack on America, and if he happened to cripple a few competitors on his way to war, so much the better.

In the parking lot of the Oceanside Motel, Deets jerked to an abrupt halt, rousing the Cubans and sending them tumbling into each other.

"End of the line," he announced, and dropped two room keys in Garcia's lap. "Keep 'em in the room. Get some sleep. Busy day tomorrow."

Garcia toyed with the keys for a moment.

"Let's go, let's go," Deets said. "I got things to do."

Garcia reached down for the duffel bag and the paper sack, but Deets quickly pulled his arm away. "Uh-uh," he said. "I'll take those. You just watch the Cubans."

"When will you be back?"

"When I'm ready. You keep an eye on them."

Garcia's cell phone began to ring, and he brought it to his face to read the incoming number. Deets swiped at it. "I told you—no phones."

But Garcia held the phone tightly against his ear and thumbed the button to answer the call. "I need to let my wife know I'll be away."

"No, no, no way. We don't let anyone know where we are."

"I am talking to my wife," Garcia said coldly. "Or you can handle this yourself." He jammed the phone even closer. "*Pilar, es Abel. Yo soy en Atlantic City.*" He paused. "*Si, dos, tres dias, no se.*" He could hear Deets muttering under his breath. "*Bueno, hasta luego.*"

Garcia ended the call and sat back, trembling slightly, his mouth dry as dust. Was it the right thing? He didn't know. But perhaps his movie wasn't quite over. Maybe one more reel.

———————————

Two hours to the north, Joseph Remsen snapped shut his cell phone and reached for the keys to his truck.

# 34

Finding a Garcia in South Florida wouldn't be a problem. Finding *the* Garcia might be more of a challenge.

And that was if he still lived there. Or if he still *lived*.

Savella needed help.

Sylvie Feidy didn't hang up on him, a huge relief. And after he laid it out for her, he was actually rewarded with a quiet chuckle.

"That's quite a photograph you got there," she said. "Every time I think you're through, you find Waldo again."

In the background he could hear the sounds of the squad room—ringing phones, raised voices, raucous laughter.

"Garcia?" Feidy asked. "How do you spell the first name?"

And with that, Abel Garcia, longtime terrorist, onetime tablemate of Mary Bloom nee Remsen, joined Sylvie Feidy's to-do list.

---

Bobby called around two.

"Need a favor," he growled down the line. "You gonna be at Max's tonight?"

A favor. Another errand, Savella thought. Not gonna happen. He loved Bobby, God knows he did, but not right now.

---

A fire truck was parked outside the restaurant, and two firemen were hosing down the street when Savella pulled into the parking lot a little after eight. A few children stood on the curb, watching the water sluice toward the sewer drain on the corner. As he walked to the front door, Savella asked a boy in a ripped Sixers jersey what had happened.

"Steve's dog got ran over. He's dead," the boy said, then looked up. "Raffles. Not Steve."

Savella studied the street. A cardboard box covered a misshapen pile. Raffles, he figured, awaiting Public Works. "Too bad," he said.

"What?" The boy stared at him in confusion.

"No, no," Savella said, holding up his hands. "Not Steve. You know, sorry about the dog."

The boy tugged at his jersey. "He was always trying to get away," he said as the firemen sprayed the patched asphalt. "Raffles, I mean."

---

The bar was almost full, a Friday-night crowd. Savella squeezed into a seat at the end, ordered a club soda, and stared blindly out the wide picture window, his mind hostage to a dead woman. Mary was under his skin, this bold teenager with a world to conquer, who had instead gone to ground in a shabby beach resort. He knew her, this woman who died in front of him, begging someone to take notice. They had a bond that any two country-men stranded in a strange land might form after stumbling upon one another, relieved, finally, to share the misery of exile. He knew the dizzying panic that engulfed her as she sat alone, night after night, desperate for the dawn. A bond, yes, but Mary was different. Both had lost something, but she had proof—photographs, a ring, an address book. The detritus of exile, bits of a life that, pieced together, might form a recognizable mosaic, might help him make sense of her shattered life.

You could look at it another way, though. What the philosopher said: Sometimes you had to go far out to sea to find firm ground to stand on. Mary had made the voyage, but hadn't survived; Savella was still out there, and maybe now, up ahead, he could see a not-so-distant shore.

"Really, I want to know," Isabella had asked. "What are you even doing here?"

Mary, that was it. A chance to get us home.

---

Drops of rain dotted the bay window, streaking the glass. A thick bank of clouds scudded across the sky, shrouding the half moon. Across West End Avenue, seagulls feasted on food scraps dumped at the water's edge. Savella sipped his soda and swiveled in his seat in time to catch a fleeting glimpse of the face of Randall Emmons filling the screen of the television over the cigarette machine. Savella bolted from his seat and settled under the TV, his thumb on the volume button.

A busboy taking out the garbage was the first to notice the smoke wafting from the porch over the alley. By the time the fire department arrived, the building was in flames. Emmons's body was discovered in bed, his dog lying dead on his chest, as if he'd been trying to wake his master. The CNN anchor said the "legendary assassination buff" fell asleep with a cigarette in an apartment crammed with papers.

*No, no, no. Not so fast,* Savella thought. Just the other day, leaning over the railing, looking for a homeless man run off by a restaurant worker, Emmons gagging on the smell of cigarette smoke rising from the alley. "Filthy habit," he had called it. Don't tell me he crawled into bed and fired up a Marlboro.

Donna the hostess brushed past and smiled hello, but Savella was two hundred miles away, running down the rest of it. Emmons's phone is out, all of a sudden, he's calling from the Chinese restaurant to make sure Savella knew the young man at the edge of the banquette was a killer. And a day later, his apartment up in flames, an old man and his dog lying in bed and no way to call for help. The cops would find the burned-out cigarette that did the damage right where it should be, bank on that. But Savella knew better.

"One of the hazards of this line of work," Emmons said. "You always think someone's coming to get you."

Well, sometimes someone is.

---

And now Bobby walked through the front door in black leather, dressed for an errand. He glanced around the bar, spotted Savella, and headed over.

This wasn't the time. Bobby, God bless him, but not now.

"Drinking?" asked Bobby.

"Nothing for me."

"All business, huh?" Bobby tapped his arm. "Wanna take a ride?"

Savella shook his head. "I told you last time. No more."

"Well, let me use the car, then." Bobby drew a piece of plastic from his pocket and held it out. "Got my license back. Legal again."

*This wasn't the time.*

"Jesus, Bobby, are you fucking kidding me?" Savella could feel the anger rising even as he struggled to control his voice. "I can't deal with you tonight. Not tonight, OK?"

Bobby stepped back and stared at Savella for a few moments. "Well, hell," he said finally, "whose shit don't stink now?"

He'd gone too far, Savella realized. Bobby was a friend. The guy got on a plane and flew halfway across the country to watch his back. Tell him no more errands, OK. But tell him he's in the way—that's just not right. The license was probably a fake, or Bobby would have asked for the keys to begin with. But there were other things to worry about.

"Look, I'm sorry," he said. "A lot on my plate."

Bobby considered the apology, then nodded.

"And you need the car, take the car," Savella said. "Just let me get my house keys. In case I head out before you get back."

A grin spread across Bobby's face. "Who said you weren't a pal?"

They walked out into the drizzle. The fire truck, its cleanup mission accomplished, was pulling around the corner and heading down West End Avenue, followed closely by a Public Works pickup carrying away the remains of Raffles. The Nissan was in the far corner of the parking lot. Savella unlocked the passenger-side door, tossed the car keys to Bobby, and bent down to retrieve his house keys from the center console.

Bobby slipped behind the wheel and punched on the radio.

"How long you going to be?" Savella asked.

"Not long. Hour, maybe two. Depends. I gotta—"

"Call me on my cell when you're done. I'll probably grab some dinner inside."

Bobby sniffed the air, turning his head from side to side. "Man, something fucking stinks in here," he said.

"So roll down the window. And bring it back in one piece."

Bobby broke off a crisp good-bye salute and started the engine.

"I must be nuts," Savella muttered.

He hurried across the lot and slipped in the kitchen door. Niccolo, Max's Florentine chef, was stationed in front of the cluttered range, shuttling between pots and pans. He smiled at Savella. "You hungry tonight?"

"I could eat. What's good?"

Niccolo spread his arms wide. "Easier to say what's not."

Savella took in the sweet aroma of garlic and onions bubbling up from Niccolo's red sauce. Nothing smelled better or offered more comfort than a good red sauce. And Niccolo's was a masterpiece. He leaned down and breathed deeply.

*Man, something fucking stinks in here.*

A mouse, a rotting mouse, maybe under the refrigerator. Or cologne, cheap stuff, slapped on heavily to mask the odor of sweat. A man, or kids. But someone broke into his house.

And now his car.

"Bobby," Savella said. "No."

He ran to the back door and surveyed the parking lot. The Nissan was gone. He turned and raced through the kitchen, into the dining room, and out to the bar, to the rain-streaked window overlooking the bay.

The seagulls that had been feeding near the shore suddenly rose in a black cloud, wings flapping frantically. Then a muffled *whoomph*, and a moment later the building shook. A window shattered, spraying the tile floor with fragments of glass. No time to move, no way to avoid it. Savella dropped his head and covered his face with his arms. Silence, broken by a low moan and a man asking for Karen, then a high-pitched shriek. Outside, a car alarm went off, then another, and one more. The restaurant filled with panicked shouts as the customers stampeded the exits.

Savella followed them to the street. The Nissan had come to a halt just short of the bay. Flames shot up from underneath the car, licking the windows. The hood had buckled, the trunk lid was blown open, and two tires were flattened. Inside the car, the air bag had deployed, pinning Bobby in his seat. In the intense heat, the bag began to melt, draping him in toxic goo. In seconds his head slumped to his chest. A tire exploded, and then there was only the crackle of flames.

The fire truck made a U-turn and sped back up the avenue, all lights and sirens, narrowly avoiding a blue van that fishtailed off the wet shoulder and sped off in the opposite direction. A police car pulled around the corner and braked sharply in the middle of the street, blocking traffic. The patrolman switched off the engine and jumped out. "Get back," he shouted to the crowd. "That thing could explode."

But this wasn't the movies. That much Savella had learned from a young Palestinian kid in Nablus one day. The danger was on the inside, where nearly everything would go up in flames—the carpets, the plastic cup trays, the foam cushions, even the wiper fluid. And human beings. Especially human beings. Which of course was the whole point.

An odd calm engulfed Savella as he watched the firefighters work. An ambulance arrived, and Savella could hear the snap of plastic as the paramedics donned gloves and raced inside. A white cat emerged from the reeds, ears pricked to the cacophony of car alarms and sirens, then scurried across the street to safety. A police officer approached and placed a hand gently on his chest.

"Sir, you want to get back now."

"My car," Savella said, and the sound of his voice surprised him.

"What's that?" the officer asked.

"I gave him my keys," Savella said. "He wanted my keys."

"This is *your* car? Who was driving it?"

"Bobby. Bobby was driving it."

The patrolman put his arm around Savella's shoulders. "Come on, man. Let's go inside." Savella let the officer steer him back to the restaurant. As they walked away, he turned his head and searched the ground for a dirt-streaked Spiderman.

---

Savella patiently related the story of his last conversation with Bobby, about the smell in the car when he handed over the keys, then repeated it to the next wave of blue. But there was a nagging confusion, a sense that something about his story wasn't exactly right. He couldn't put a finger on it and it began to frighten him. As he struggled to cooperate, it suddenly occurred to him to mention Sylvie Feidy. She'd be the one to talk to, he told his interrogators. She knows me, knows Bobby. We've been involved in another one of her cases. Maybe she'd know who would want to kill Bobby. That he couldn't figure. But Bobby, he played the edges, the angles. Or maybe it was just that he knew me. I'm the angel of death, he told the officers with a strained laugh. You come into contact with me, you die. They asked if he'd been drinking, and he said not nearly enough.

While someone went to call Feidy, Savella wallowed in the nightmare. On one tabletop an untouched raspberry filet with garlic mashed, on another a half-eaten Greek chicken and an empty wine bottle. A large piece of carrot cake with four forks leaning on the plate in the corner booth. Soft music, and candles in their holders. Friday night, interrupted: overturned chairs, broken glass, bloodied linen, a dozen bandaged victims, wondering what the hell just happened. A dozen wounded once before, Savella remembered, at a checkpoint near Jerusalem, but the medics there knew the toll would climb higher. The bomb had showered the survivors with shrapnel, which fell from the sky like black rain. But some people wouldn't know they had been hurt for a while, not until strange pimples appeared on their bodies. Tiny pieces of flesh and bone, explained the doctor who cut open the pimple on Savella's forehead a few months later, leaving a faint scar just above his right eye. The flesh and bone of a boy and a girl, driven into Savella's body by the blast that killed them in a flash of orange one brutally hot afternoon.

Twenty minutes later Feidy joined the huddle of investigators, who briefed her, then listened as she talked. Once, she pointed in Savella's direction, and the patrolmen turned and looked at him. Finally, she broke away from the pack and walked over to where he was sitting.

"How you doing, Michael?" she asked quietly, and he gave her a look. "I know, stupid question. You got my friends over there extremely worried."

"About what?"

"They think you know more than you're saying. Or that you're a head case. Something about the angel of death?"

"Yes."

"Did you say something about that, Michael?"

"I don't know. I might have. I'm a little confused."

She nodded slowly and patted his arm. "I know, I know. And I'm very sorry about Bobby."

He brushed his fingers through his hair. "He was playing with some bad people."

Feidy looked puzzled, then her shoulders slumped as it dawned on her, and she exhaled slowly.

"*He* was playing? Michael, this wasn't about Bobby. They were looking for you, man. *You* were supposed to be behind the wheel. *You* were supposed to be dead."

Savella opened his mouth to argue, but the words wouldn't come. It made sense, what she said. He drove up alone, and when the car left the lot, on a rainy night, there was no one inside except the driver. And the smell from the house, in the car. He'd known it since the gulls took flight, but tried to make it not so by ignoring the obvious. Now it was out there, and the confusion began to clear.

"So it was a bomb?"

"Yeah, pretty likely."

"No chance of an engine malfunction or something?"

"They'll check it out."

He chewed his lip. "It's the pictures, isn't it?"

"The pictures, the tape, the address book. I don't know."

He sat silently for a moment.

"So you heard Randall Emmons is dead?"

Feidy nodded.

"They said it was smoking, but...That's what I meant, I guess. The angel of death. I meet the guy, and he's gone. Mary Bloom taps my fender, she dies. Marek Ravic and...and now Bobby. And I should have known. The smell. The inside of the car smelled like my house that day."

Feidy got to her feet. "Stay with me, Michael. Hang on a minute and I'll get you out of here. You got someplace to stay tonight? Other than your house, I mean."

He shook his head firmly. "I'm going home."

"Jesus, you and Isabella. Spare me the bullshit, OK?"

"I mean it. I'm going home."

She glanced out the window. "Well, you're gonna need a ride, at least."

Savella followed her gaze out the window, where the firefighters were dousing the last remnants of the blaze.

He felt a chill: the world, again, and this time there was no panic.

The easy way out, his weakness.

Not this time.

## 35

"*Garcia.*" A thud against the door, and the knob jiggled. "Where the fuck are you?"

Stretched out on the torn vinyl of the motel room sofa, Garcia glanced at his watch: eleven forty-five in the morning. Too early to deal with Elmer Deets. But a sharp rap on the door shook the wooden frame, and Garcia knew he was lost. He got up and cracked the door. Deets pushed his way inside, his arms draped with men's clothing.

"There's nobody answers in the other—" he began, then noticed the two Cubans sprawled on the double bed, sound asleep in their sparkling white Nikes. Deets dropped the clothing in a pile on the floor and surveyed the rest of the room. The yellow curtains were drawn tightly against the morning sun. A dozen empty beer bottles sat on the desk in the corner. The morning newspaper, its pages ripped and crumpled, was strewn across the worn brown carpet. A greasy pizza box, a handful of crusts propping open the lid, lay on the television set, SpongeBob SquarePants dancing silently across the dusty screen.

"What, you got them *drunk?*"

Garcia shrugged. "They were hungry. We had dinner. We talked."

Deets placed a hand on the mattress and shook it. "Hey. *Hey*," he said loudly, pulling at the bedspread until the Cubans blinked awake. "Almost noon. Let's go. Things to do." Tomas and Guillermo climbed out of bed, yawning.

Garcia leaned against the door, his arms folded across his bare chest, as Deets pawed through the clothing pile. The red pimples and the spider web of red veins that usually marked his face were gone. The disease must be in remission, Garcia thought. Or maybe he was cured. Lucky Deets. Lucky man.

Deets plucked two shirts, two pairs of pants, and two jackets from his pile and held them out to Garcia.

"Tell the tall one—"

"Guillermo," Garcia said quietly as he took the clothes.

"—tell him to try these on. And these for the other guy."

"Tomas."

"Just tell them."

Garcia relayed the instructions. The two men exchanged baffled glances, then took the clothes and headed for the bathroom. "Modest little bastards," Deets said as the door closed behind them.

Garcia stared out the window. The rain overnight had swamped the motel parking lot and collected in puddles on the tiny balcony outside the room. Even now, an insistent drip fell from the eaves. Like a ticking clock, Garcia thought. He returned to the sofa and sat down. Across the room, the front page of the paper, wedged between the legs of the desk chair, taunted him as it had since the desk clerk dropped it outside the door around five thirty. From where he sat, the funeral-black letters of its headline were clearly visible: **Car Fire Kills One; Bomb Suspected.**

*Deets's diversion.* The bomb had missed the reporter, destroyed his friend. And why did either have to die? Civilians, both of them. Garcia had killed his share of innocents. Some were deliberate—the Cubana jetliner. Others were horrific mistakes—the school bus in Guatemala that haunted him to this day. But no more. He was out of that business. "*Everything's* a target," Don Arturo had once told him. But not *everyone*. If he could talk, the old man would agree, Garcia was sure of it. Especially now, in such a different world. Especially now, when everything had changed.

Don Arturo would agree. He knew the world. The son knew only money.

The room was warm, and Deets was perspiring heavily. Garcia peered closely at him. A hint of red was now barely visible on the right side of Deets's face. And some sort of goo—was that makeup? Could this creature be so vain? As if to answer, Deets pulled out a handkerchief and lightly dabbed his face, then inspected the smeared cloth and frowned.

The bathroom door sprang open, and Tomas and Guillermo shuffled back into the room. Tomas's pant cuffs drooped around his heels. Guillermo's right shirtsleeve covered half his palm. Both men were swimming in their jackets. Deets walked around them, reaching over to straighten the shoulders of Tomas's jacket, tucking Guillermo's shirt deeper in his trousers. Finally, he stepped back and nodded in satisfaction.

"OK," he said, and he leaned into Guillermo. "You look good," he said, and when Guillermo seemed puzzled, Deets raised his voice and repeated the compliment, pronouncing each word slowly. Guillermo glanced helplessly at Garcia.

"Oh, for Chrissakes," Deets said. "Tell them to take the stuff off and hang it up proper. I want them looking nice tonight."

"What are these for?" Garcia asked.

"They're gonna see a show."

"What kind of show?"

Deets swept up the rest of the clothes into a manageable pile. "I'll be back at six. How long you gonna need?"

"For what?"

Deets looked disgusted.

Garcia cleared his throat. "Not long. Ten minutes, perhaps. To set the triggers."

"OK. Show starts at eight. Six should be plenty of time. But don't be keeping me waiting. And make sure they're dressed right."

"The jackets. They're too big."

"Nah, nah. Just right." Deets glanced over at the Cubans. "Nice. Almost like they didn't come from the jungle." He jerked open the door and left the room, a pair of pants dragging the floor in his wake.

Tomas and Guillermo were tugging at their new clothes, searching for comfort. Garcia went into the bathroom and quietly closed the door. His guayabera and dress slacks hung carefully from a hanger hooked over the shower rod. A half-empty pill vial stood on the side of the sink. He drew a glass of water from the tap and swallowed one and then another—the pain was unusually severe this morning. When would the pills no longer be enough? The doctors couldn't be sure. But until then, there was no sense in suffering. He sat down on the edge of the bathtub to await relief. Only then would he be able to deal with what lay ahead.

―――――――――

The cell phone had rung as the boys were finishing the last of the beers the night before. *I'm in town, Abel.* Remsen wanted to meet. *We don't have much time, do we, Abel?* No, we don't, Garcia thought, but the morning would be better, would be soon enough. He had things to take care of. *As you wish, Abel,* said Father Joey. *I'm at the Days Inn. Let me know when you're ready. Sleep well.*

*Sleep well.* Was that some sort of joke? Garcia had called Pilar to tell her he wouldn't be home, but she had figured that out already. The short conversation ended with her slamming down the receiver. He curled up on the sofa, watching the two boys wrestle for the remote. Good kids, he thought: Tomas, the little one with the jumpy eyes, and Guillermo, tall and pale, an easy laugher who loved to tell stories. Strangers to the language, but lost in the images that flashed before them until their eyes closed and they fell into a deep slumber. A peaceful moment, for Garcia, the television finally muted, only the occasional shouts of guests returning to their rooms to break the spell.

And then the newspaper: **Car Fire Kills One; Bomb Suspected**

Bad enough, but that wasn't the story, not all of it. The big news was everyone was expendable. A nosy apartment-house super. A friend borrowing a car. Even good kids, he thought. Even me. Especially me.

The air in the motel room seemed thick as wool. The ocean, Garcia remembered, a block away. He opened the bathroom door and walked out. Change your clothes, he told the boys, and we'll go eat.

---

They found breakfast in a coffee shop, all splintered plastic and grease-stained plywood. In a booth near the bathrooms, the boys inhaled eggs, pancakes, bacon, washed down with large tumblers of Coke. Garcia settled for a glass of milk. When Tomas and Guillermo could eat no more, they went outside and headed down the Boardwalk.

The overnight storm had given way to a beautiful day, blue sky dotted with puffs of white cloud, the flags and banners that lined the railing moving in a warm breeze. They walked slowly, Garcia bent and brooding, staring out to sea, the Cubans racing ahead, turning in circles, crying out in delight at the sights and sounds in a wondrous new world. Kids, Garcia thought again, as they stood ogling the women on a poster hawking a beauty pageant. Just two stupid kids, and now here they were, the walking dead.

It was Tomas who found it first: *Havana,* one word among dozens on the wall of advertisements outside the Tropicana. Startled, he leaned closer to make sure, then pulled away and jabbed at the glass.

"*La Habana, La Habana,*" he shouted, until Guillermo broke away from his review of the picture menu outside an ice-cream parlor and ran to his side. The two of them huddled around the poster, searching for another familiar word.

Garcia made the connection, disagreeable as it was: The Quarter, the casino called it, restaurants and shops with an Old Havana theme. The original advertising campaign had featured billboards of a youthful Fidel Castro wreathed in cigar smoke and the slogan *The Next Revolution.* Cuban-American outrage brought down the image of the dictator, but The Quarter remained. "*Un insulto, no?*" Garcia asked the boys after he told the story, but to his dismay, Tomas and Guillermo insisted on seeing for themselves. Freedom has its limits, Garcia muttered to himself as they headed inside. On the other hand, he needed to sit.

The escalator dumped them in the middle of a cheap movie set, some designer's stab at recreating the inimitable. A midday sky, plastic palm trees, ersatz chirping birds, faux island music, much too loud. The passage to the casino was a three-story streetscape, *Calle de las Oficios,* they called it, lined with lingerie shops, men's clothing stores, an expensive chocolatier, restaurants and bars, including Cuba Libre—*Cuba Libre,* free for what, from whom?—and Red Square, where the vodka and caviar flowed behind a statue of Lenin. How fitting, Garcia thought. Cubans and Russians side by side, where America left them. And all to amuse *los Yanquis* in their suits and ties, shorts and T-shirts, jeans and sneakers, *los Yanquis,* who had forgotten about Cuba long ago, if they ever really knew.

The boys darted away and disappeared, and Garcia slumped on a bench in the middle of the bedlam. He felt disoriented—the extra pill or this ghastly apparition—and he fought the urge to leave his body, to float above this nightmare until the lights were dimmed and the music silenced. He began to slide off the bench, his right hand flailing for a grip, catching himself in time to see a security guard eyeing him. I'm an old man, Garcia thought, leave me be. I'm in Havana, dreaming, and a dream would have to do. Because now there was no denying the icy reality. He was never going home. He had been right all along. There was no home to go home to. It was too many years, too late in the day.

The boys last night didn't have the faintest idea what he was talking about during his nostalgic ramble. Garcia's Cuba was Mars to them, and truth be told, to their fathers. His Cuba was a brittle memory, falling to pieces in the minds of old men. Garcia forced himself to look around The Quarter. This hallucination, this obscene fantasy, would be the new Cuba: Russian vodka, French lace panties, the black plague of the dollar. Men like Pena knew no other way. Before long Cuba would be theirs, and then anything was possible, any stain on the memory of the fallen—even a misty photo of a tyrant, filtered to erase the warts and wrinkles, puffing on a Cohiba. The tourists would surely expect it.

Guillermo and Tomas were moving his way, ambling down a fake street, surrounded by fantasy, two young guys here for girls or baseball or a job, whatever young guys seek these days. But not freedom, Garcia thought. They think they came here for freedom, but not really.

He reached for his phone, found the call log, and pressed Redial. As he awaited an answer, Garcia felt his chest tighten. Had he imagined the conversation the night before? Had he really come, was Joey here? No, no, no, not Joey, not any longer—Father Remsen. *Where was he?*

Then a voice on the other end—*Abel, is that you?*—and the cloud began to lift. *At the Tropicana,* he heard himself say, his voice far, far away. *In Havana, do you believe it, after all this time...No, of course, I'm not serious. Just someone's bitter joke. You will see.*

Garcia rang off and tried to stand, but his legs buckled. The cell phone clattered to the floor and skidded away. The boys grabbed his arms, held him up. Garcia caught his breath. He would need their help getting back. Tomas retrieved the phone and handed it to Garcia, an eager-to-please smile plastered on his brown face. A nice kid, Garcia thought again as he nodded his thanks. He gave the boys the last of his cash and sent them off to explore, then settled back on the bench to wait. Twenty minutes, Joey promised. *All right, Father,* he thought as the pills finally vanquished the last of the pain. *All right, I'm ready.*

# 36

The man, again, in rags and looking...used: the scratchy growth, the scuffed and dented fedora, bleak eyes sunk deep in their sockets. He gets up and goes to the kitchen, and Savella spots the limp, the balky knee, and he's *alive*, dammit, it was all a big mistake, he borrowed the car and is just late running an errand. But the man shouts for help and Savella runs into the kitchen to find water seeping out of the wall between the stove and the refrigerator, spreading across the linoleum. He searches in vain for a cutoff valve under the sink; the water keeps coming. He finds some towels and tries to staunch the flow, but it's no use and he runs into the living room to call a plumber. The man is gone, the used man, nowhere to be found. Then suddenly here is Isabella, trying her best to get his attention—*Michael, Michael*—but the water's followed him, and it's rising, lapping against the pictures on the wall, splashing his cheeks. And Isabella wants to help—*Michael, Michael*—her voice in echo.

Wait a minute. *Wait* a minute. It *is* her, Isabella, on the phone—

"Michael, can you hear me?"

Savella struggled up on one elbow. His face was damp, and when he licked the corners of his mouth, he tasted tears.

"Michael?"

He cradled the phone under his chin and fell back into the pillows. "Yeah, I'm here. Where *are* you?"

"On the boat. The ship."

"Why does it sound like you're at the bottom of a well?"

"It's this ship phone. My cell's not working down here. The captain let me use this for a few minutes. I had to call. Are you OK?"

"Fine, fine. What time is it?"

"It's a little after ten here. I don't know if it's different up there. Morning, anyway. Are you really all right?"

"Yeah, yeah. I'm fine. Where are you?"

"Cozumel."

"No kidding," he murmured, and palmed his face.

"Yeah. But oh my God, Michael, I am so sorry about Bobby."

He pulled himself up, sat on the edge of the bed.

"How did you—Harold?"

"He saw it on the news or in the paper or whatever and got the cruise people to get me a message. I'm so, so sorry."

"How much did he tell you?"

"I didn't talk to him. They slipped a piece of paper under my door. What a horrible thing."

"It…it was pretty rough."

"How could anyone have known he would be in your car?"

It took Savella a few moments to understand. He squeezed shut his eyes. "You're not getting it, Isabella."

"What do you mean?" Savella didn't respond. "What do you mean?" she asked again, and then a gasp. "Oh. Oh my God, Michael. You?"

"That's what the cops think."

"Why?"

"I don't know, Isabella. I don't know. Mary Bloom? I don't know."

"Is it, is it, you know, connected to the break-ins and all that? My fish?"

"They're looking at that. Especially your fish."

"Michael, it's not funny."

"You're telling me?"

"You know what I mean."

"I know. They're looking at that. They put a cop on the house just the same. My house."

More voices from the bottom of the well. "Hold on a sec. Michael, can you hold a minute?" He heard her talking with someone in the background. "Michael, I have to go. They need their phone. But I just wanted to hear your voice."

"How're things going out there?"

"Oh, you know. The Great American Songbook."

"Seeing much of the islands?"

"Not really. We're sailing in a little bit. Grand Cayman. But I hardly ever get off the damn boat. Ship. Anyway, I'm sorry about Bobby. Please, please take care of yourself."

"I'm trying."

"Good-bye, Michael. I miss you."

Pause.

"Yeah, me too."

She was hanging up.

"Isabella, wait."

But she was gone.

Savella lay back down, shaking off the remnants of the dream. His mind flashed for an instant to a burning car on the edge of the bay, and just as quickly he erased the picture. Bobby was dead. Not running an errand, or doing a favor for a friend. He was dead. Savella could cry in his sleep all he wanted, it wasn't bringing Bobby back.

From the living room came the low static of a radio. For a moment he started at the thought of intruders, then it came back to him. Feidy's idea, her orders: a guard overnight, if he insisted on sleeping in his own bed, which he most certainly did. So they had returned to the house around eleven, Savella and the detective and a small army of patrolmen who searched the place thoroughly, every room, all the closets, the crawl space in the basement, the eaves under the roof, casting looks at Savella all the while as they wondered how anybody could live like this, or why.

By one it was only Savella and Feidy and two babysitters off the overnight tour, sitting in the living room, watching the fifteen-inch Panasonic that someone had wheeled in from the bedroom to keep everyone awake. For an hour they made desultory small talk, one of the cops switching channels with a practiced thumb, the other paging through one of the fishing magazines he'd rescued from the pile propping up the kitchen table. No one mentioned the events of a few hours earlier, but it hung in the air like the smoke from the bomb blast until Savella couldn't stand it anymore.

"No chance they were looking for Bobby?" he asked Feidy, and immediately regretted the question. What the hell was he thinking? He'd be relieved if Bobby was the target all along? Like death was what he deserved for playing with matches all his life?

But if she found the question odd, Feidy didn't let on. Instead she gently let him off the hook with an answer he already knew.

"This wasn't some Coke bottle filled with gasoline they tossed in the window," she said quietly as the patrolmen debated the relative merits of rods and reels. "Somebody planned ahead, planted this thing, waited to trigger it from a distance. Pretty sophisticated. They just made a huge mistake."

*A huge mistake.* Savella's chest pounded as he recalled her explanation. Which is why I'm lying here in bed and Bobby or what's left of him is stretched out in cold storage at the coroner's office. Beads of perspiration began to dot Savella's cheeks. They would try again. He had come here to hide, but the world had come crashing back into his life.

*A huge mistake.* They would try again until they got it right.

He got out of bed, slipped into a pair of jeans, and padded in his bare feet to the living room. Feidy stood with her back to the room, gazing out the front window; a patrolman and a sergeant talked quietly on the sofa, an assortment of cups and mugs on the table in front of them.

"Morning," Savella said, and he sniffed the air. "I see you found the coffee."

Feidy pointed to an oversized thermos on the desk. "We come prepared," she said.

"What, no doughnuts?"

"How to make friends, huh?" Feidy said. "We did help ourselves to the cups."

She looked tired, probably hadn't slept. Her hair was pulled back in a messy bun. The maroon blazer, the black slacks—she'd been wearing them the night before. But weary or not, there was a seriousness about her this morning, a steely resolve that would tell anyone, in case they ever doubted it, *not again, not on my watch.*

Feidy had made the most of the night.

She'd leaned on the lab guys for an early read on the bomb and they came through at dawn: Goma 2 Eco, *might have been, Sylvie, can't swear to it,* a gelatinous high explosive used by the Spanish mining industry. Not to mention, Feidy felt obligated to point out, although she wanted no one drawing any conclusions—*and that means you, Savella*—the occasional Basque terrorist cell, and maybe the guys who blew up that train in Madrid a few years back.

She'd done her due diligence in the field, supervising a canvass that spread to six square blocks and lasted well past midnight, much to the annoyance of the neighborhood, but turned up exactly nothing.

And then she turned her attention to all things Remsen. Mary Bloom's tragic death had been followed by a crime wave—murders, break-ins, now a bombing—that could only be related to the discovery that she was in fact, and always had been, despite her amazingly successful effort to hide it, Mary *Remsen.* So Sylvie Feidy returned to her office, sat in her broken chair surrounded by her plants and pictures, and dug. She found gun permits in two states issued to an Edward Remsen, US Army (Retired). By breakfast she was on the phone with an old friend at the Pentagon, and a couple of hours later she had her man: Remsen, Edward, career army, wife deceased, nineteen sixty-three, two children way back when, but no longer listed as next of kin.

Remsen spent twenty-seven years in uniform, all over the map. Three tours in Southeast Asia in the sixties, military attache in a half dozen Central American countries for a decade after that. *Not infantry so much, Sylvie,* Belinda at the Pentagon said as she puzzled through the record, *lot of special assignments, you might call them.* Now living in the Virgin Islands, St. John, or at least the checks go there. *With these guys, Sylvie honey, you never know.*

And there was a picture: a fax copy of a black-and-white photo showing a severe-looking man in uniform with short-cropped hair, staring into the camera with a frown on his face. Savella had seen him before, only he was standing under a palm tree, squinting into the sun. So Mary had a picture of her dad. But it meant nothing. Not yet.

Feidy saved the best for last. She had cajoled the Illinois state cops into driving out to the farm for a little chat with Father Joseph Remsen.

"He wasn't there, but they hung around making pests of themselves until one of his little darlings gave him up," Feidy said. "Remsen's been gone a week or so. He called back to the office yesterday. You'll never guess where from."

Savella sipped his coffee. "It's too early for games."

"Right here."

Savella slowly put down the mug. "Remsen's here?"

"Registered at the Days Inn."

"Remsen?"

"The very one."

"What's he saying?"

Feidy shook her head. "Haven't had a chance. His stuff is in the room, but he's not."

"I want to come with you," Savella said. "To see Remsen."

"Put some shoes on. I wouldn't have it any other way. I don't even know what this guy looks like."

———————————

Mrs. DiLorenzo and a few other neighbors drawn by the police cars stood on the corner as Feidy and Savella jumped in the blue Crown Victoria and drove off, past two Asian kids dueling with broomsticks on the sidewalk, past a Honduran blackjack dealer on his way home with a loaf of bread, and past a large man in a black suit sitting in a blue van on the corner, his face a malignant glower.

# 37

The noise in The Quarter had swelled, Garcia could hardly bear it. A sort of madness, he thought, watching a rowdy group wind its way down the staircase from the faux-Irish pub on the second level. He scanned the crowds for some sign of his Cubans. The cash couldn't last forever, not even in America.

But there, at the railing above him, the old man in a blue windbreaker—was it Remsen? Yes, it was, and quite a disheartening sight: grease stains on his gray trousers, ripped canvas sneakers, shirt open at the neck, exposing a thin gold chain. You could tell a lot about a man by the way he presents himself to the world. And Garcia wouldn't have been surprised if Remsen had picked that moment to hurl himself over the side and plunge to eternity on the Calle de las Oficios. Not a man of God. Not Abel Garcia's savior.

Remsen suddenly spotted him, waved, then bounced down the stairs, a folded newspaper tucked under his arm.

"Abel, I'm glad you called," he said as he reached the bench.

Garcia scratched his neck with the tip of his forefinger. "Where's the collar?"

Remsen's right hand floated to his bare throat. "It seems to make people uncomfortable."

"Aren't there rules?"

"It doesn't matter."

The priest sat down, motioned for Garcia to join him, then carefully laid the newspaper in his lap, the front page folded to the photograph of a smoking Nissan Altima nose-first in the bay. When he was certain Garcia had seen it, Remsen slowly rubbed a palm across the paper, smoothing the wrinkles.

"I once knew someone who could do this," he said. "Better than anyone in the world, perhaps."

Abel shrugged. "Anyone with a chemistry set," he said, "or a soda bottle, some gasoline, a rag, and a match."

Remsen placed the paper on the bench.

"Abel, you called me. You wanted help. Do you need my help?"

Garcia said nothing for several moments, then nodded.

"Are you sure?"

"Yes, yes," Garcia said impatiently.

"And I want to. But that starts with truth."

"The truth." A short, weary laugh, and Garcia's eyes narrowed. "Whose truth, then? And where does it end? With this?" He plucked at the newspaper, and it fell to the floor. "Or do we go back further? Do we tell all the truth? Who decides? Me? Or you, a priest with no collar?"

He slumped back on the bench, his eyes closed, an old man, dying. He had earned the right to ask the questions, but what was the point? The past was past, and nothing could be done about that, no matter how much truth we told. But today held out the hope of something better.

He opened his eyes and looked hard at Remsen.

"Without the collar. It changes nothing?"

"Nothing, Abel. I told you—it doesn't matter."

Garcia nodded, tentatively at first, then firmly, answering a question that only he had heard. "I want you to hear my confession."

"Of course," said Remsen. "When?"

"Now."

The priest arched his eyebrows. "Now?"

"Now, yes."

"Then let's find a quiet place," Remsen said, and got to his feet.

"No, no. Here is good enough." Garcia glanced again at Remsen's neck, the thin gold chain draped across the space where a collar should have been. "Father, hear my confession."

"All right, Abel," Remsen said, and in his voice was the end of something.

---

The Cuban spoke for almost an hour; the priest listened intently, the color slowly draining from his face. The confession, with its litany of murders past and future, had relieved Garcia of a burden, but Remsen was now saddled with the punishing load, and he seemed staggered by the weight, and more. For the first time since their reunion, Garcia saw the priest not as a cleric nestled in the protective bosom of the mother church, but as a tortured soul whose own past still haunted him.

Garcia finished, and Remsen whispered a final prayer. When he spoke again, his voice was strangled, a man struggling to breathe.

"It was supposed to be over," he said. "My God, it was over."

"It never ended, Joey."

They sat quietly for a few minutes, the noise washing over them.

"Tell me again about this Deets," Remsen said finally.

"An animal. And like any animal, he does his master's bidding."

"What does he look like?"

"An ugly man. Very tall. Very fat. Greasy hair. And a red rash on his face."

"And the Cubans?"

Garcia pointed down the hall. "See for yourself." Tomas and Guillermo stood in front of a shop window, giant plastic drinking cups in their hands.

"So young," Remsen said. "And the target. He hasn't told you?"

"No. Only to be ready at six, *y los Cubanos* will see a show. Supposed to start at eight."

Remsen glanced at his watch. "That gives us, what, four hours? Abel, we can't sit back and let him do it again."

Which him, Garcia wanted to know, but in the end it didn't make much difference.

"Call me when you know the target. Abel, do you understand? And we'll stop it this time."

Garcia shifted in his seat and suddenly felt a stabbing pain, but not the cancer: the butt of the Colt, tucked in his belt, jabbing him when he moved. He repositioned the gun to relieve the discomfort. Seeing the weapon, Remsen frowned and held out his hand.

"You don't need that anymore."

Perhaps not, Garcia thought. It wouldn't do to meet God with fresh blood on his hands. But he made no move to give it up. He was still a soldier, after all.

The boys were headed back. Not much time now. "My penance, Father," Garcia said. "Give me my penance."

Remsen rose, placed his hands on Garcia's shoulders, and shook him slightly. "Stop this," he whispered. "Stop this, and then we pray."

# 38

A housekeeper's trolley propped open the door to room 617, and a vacuum cleaner roared from within. Sylvie Feidy squeezed past the cart and moved down the short foyer into the bedroom. Catching sight of her, the Filipino maid looked up and smiled. The detective offered a friendly wave and flashed her badge.

"Can I come in?" she shouted over the din, and when the maid said nothing, Feidy moved to the middle of the floor.

"Silly things, those warrants," Savella murmured as he joined her.

If Remsen had spent time in 617, he hadn't made much of an impression. The bed was neatly made; the fresh linens stacked on the small sofa by the maid offered evidence that he hadn't used it. The closets and dresser drawers were empty; except for the telephone, a lamp and a hotel notepad, the bed table was bare. On the desk the folder of tourist brochures and hotel guides was placed precisely in the middle of the brown blotter. The only sign that Remsen had ever checked in was a scuffed brown suitcase on the luggage rack, unopened, and a stained toiletries kit, zipped shut and lying next to the bathroom sink.

Feidy unclasped the valise and sorted through it. "One shirt, black. A pair of pants, black. Some mints.

Some clean socks and underwear. Guy comes halfway across the country with basically the clothes on his back. Must have been in some kind of a hurry."

"Or he didn't think he'd be gone too long," Savella said.

"The Illinois cops say he left a week ago. I mean, even priests need something to wear."

She closed the bag, then wandered through the room, glancing behind the curtains, inspecting the trash cans, unlocking the minibar, finding nothing. The maid tracked her every movement, running the vacuum brush over the same patch of carpet, a worried look on her face. Finally, she dropped to her knees and began to clean underneath the bed.

Feidy shook her head in amazement. "Either she thinks we're from the manager's office, or I should hire her to do my place." She pointed toward the door. "We'll wait downstairs. For a little while, anyway."

———

They found two seats in the lobby facing the elevator bank, and settled in, Savella watching the revolving front doors for a glimpse of the priest, the detective studying Savella for a sign the wait was over. The hotel was swarming with families—the pageant crowd, Savella finally realized, but only after noticing the buttons and ribbons festooning their jackets and sweaters, all bearing photographs of smiling young women who hailed from all over but looked remarkably alike. Not such a bad fit anymore, though, he thought. In the time it took a car to burn, he had found himself in a vastly different world.

Images of Bobby trapped in the Altima played over and over in his mind, like a trailer for a trashy horror movie. And the realization that he was the intended target threatened to suffocate him. Crowds had always been his safe harbor. Now, even with a police detective at his side, a woman with a gun on her hip, Savella felt exposed, at risk. His life was on hold. Everyone who passed was a threat. To be expected, he knew: how many other people in the lobby had somebody trying to kill them?

"So how you doing , Michael?" Feidy asked.

He watched a contingent of Miss Missouri supporters board a red minibus parked at the curb. "Not every day you lend a friend your car and watch him burn to death."

Feidy exhaled slowly. "Keep an eye on the elevators, right?"

---

About three thirty a patrolman cruising the hotel parking garage spotted a Chevy Silverado pickup with Illinois tags parked crookedly in a space on the third level. Feidy left Savella on duty with instructions to call if Remsen turned up. She was back a half hour later, her once-bleary eyes suddenly sparkling. She pulled two sandwiches wrapped in foil from her jacket pocket.

"Chicken or chicken?" she asked, and dropped one in his lap.

The Chevy had been empty, aside from a Bible and an owner's manual in the glove box and a carpet of fast-food wrappers and drink cups.

"But we got him now," Feidy said, unwrapping her food. "I left a guy on the truck. He's not leaving without his wheels. Or his Bible."

"The truck, maybe," Savella said. "But never the Bible."

———————————

And just before five, here he came, at a half trot through the doors and across the lobby. Savella nudged the detective and pointed.

"Which?" she said, scanning the floor.

"The blue jacket. The windbreaker."

Feidy followed Savella's finger to its target, an over-weight man in need of a shave scurrying toward the elevators, chest heaving, stained pants sagging below his waistline and pooling around torn sneakers, jacket un-zipped to reveal a shirt open at the collar.

"And to think I stopped going to church," Feidy said. "Hard to believe."

The priest was jabbing at the Up button when the detective tapped him on the shoulder.

"Father Remsen?" she asked quietly. He stiffened, but kept his eyes on the floor indicator: not a car be-low the fifteenth. Feidy reached over and dangled her badge in front of his face. "I'm Sylvie Feidy. We spoke on the phone." She glanced at the hotel guests waiting to go up to their rooms. The badge had caught their at-tention. "Let's take a walk," she said, and took Remsen by the elbow.

The priest jerked his arm free and pivoted away from the elevators. But at the sight of Savella, he took a step back and stumbled. With a soft ping, an elevator car reached the lobby, and the detective and the priest were quickly caught in a crosscurrent of passengers. Feidy pulled Remsen clear. "Let's get out of the way, huh?" she said.

He shook his head. "I can't do this right now."

"You're not understanding me, Father. This isn't a favor I'm asking for. We need to clear up a few things, OK? Won't take long." She guided him to a sofa near the lobby windows, motioned for him to sit down, and relaxed her grip.

In a flash he was on the move again, toward the revolving doors. Savella grabbed his right arm and spun him around. Feidy slipped behind him and pulled back on his windbreaker, pinning his arms against his sides. Remsen lunged forward, straining against his shirt until the buttons began to pop, one by one, the tiny discs flying through the air and landing with clicks on the stone floor. The pendant on the gold chain around his neck whipped the air as he struggled to escape.

A security guard jogged to the edge of the melee, muttering into his walkie-talkie as he watched for an opening to break up the fracas.

"It's OK, it's OK," Feidy called out. "I'm the police." With one arm around Remsen, she fumbled in her jacket pocket for her badge and held it up. "It's OK. We're fine."

"Can you take it out of here? I mean..." The guard waved his hand at the bustling lobby.

Feidy reached behind her back, unclipped a set of handcuffs from her belt, and held them up. "You want to go out in these, Father?" she said. "Or do we walk out like civilized people. You call it."

"You don't understand," he said quietly, the fight leaking out of him. "There's something I need to take care of."

"So let's talk and then you're on your way. How's that?"

Remsen attempted to close his buttonless shirt, then gave up and zipped the jacket. "All right. All *right.*"The last, impatiently: a man with more important things to do.

---

A pavilion on the Boardwalk, roof sagging, paint peeling off the buckled columns, seagulls pecking away at a spilled bucket of popcorn and a paper tray of french fries. Remsen sat stiffly on a weathered bench, arms locked across his chest. Feidy moved beside him.

"Michael, why don't you wait over there?" she said. "When I'm done here, I'll get someone to run you home." She was finished with him, Savella realized, but he wasn't about to walk away.

Feidy turned back to the priest. "So, let's see, where do we start? How about what you're doing back in town?"

Remsen pursed his lips and looked away. "I'm not sure it's any of your business."

"Oh, it's my business. It most certainly is my business."

Remsen took a deep breath. "I came to see to my sister's affairs," he said in a measured tone, as though it was all he could do to control himself.

"Her affairs."

"Yes."

"And what exactly would those be?"

"Her...things. Her things. That's all."

"Really," Feidy said. "Have you been over to the apartment?"

"Not yet."

"Where have you been, then?"

"I don't know why I should have to tell you that."

"Now, see, that's just not gonna get us anywhere," she said, shaking her head. "This question about whether it's my business."

"Maybe I need a lawyer."

"Maybe you do. Your choice."

They sat quietly for a minute. Feidy brushed a piece of lint from the lapel of her blazer, then crossed her legs and clasped her hands behind her head. Savella shuffled a few feet closer. Once again he admired Feidy's technique, one professional to another. Sometimes it was better to let them move at their own pace. And in the end it was Remsen who resumed the conversation, his tone less confrontational, as if he'd just figured out how to work through this unpleasantness and be on his way.

"How did you know I was here?"

"The boys at your farm," Feidy said.

He smiled. "Ah, I see. I've not taught them too well, perhaps. The importance of honesty, they get, but not the occasional necessity of the social lie." He stole a glance at his watch. "I drove out here from Illinois. I arrived last night. My first visit, after getting the call from"—he waved in Savella's direction—"was very brief. I was stunned, shocked, you could say, not having seen my sister in so many years, and now she was dead. And I may have been—I *was* less than forthcoming. So after his visit to the farm"—again a wave toward Savella—"I decided to come back and clear up whatever needed clearing up. And that's it, really."

"When did you say you arrived?" Feidy asked

"Last night, I said."

"Yes, but when? What time?"

"I don't know. About six. Seven, maybe."

"From where?"

"From northern New Jersey."

"What were you doing there?"

"Visiting friends."

"Do your friends have names?"

"Of course."

"I'll need them. What did you do last night?"

"I checked into the hotel. Then I watched some television."

"That's it?"

"I went downstairs and got something to eat. A Greek salad and a club soda and one or two pieces of very stale bread." He stared her down: *enough detail for you?* "Then I walked around a little bit, until it started to rain."

"Talk to anybody?"

"No one in particular. The waiter. Listen, isn't this the sort of thing you ask a—"

"A suspect? Yeah."

"And what am I suspected of doing? Not spending enough at dinner? Failure to gamble?"

"Well, that's the thing. We had another killing last night. Did you see a paper today?"

"Yes, the bombing."

"The point is, Father, we think Mr. Savella here was the target. It was his car. But something got screwed up, and it was his friend who died in the explosion. You knew him too."

Remsen looked up at Savella. "The other man? From the farm?"

"Yes."

"I'm sorry."

"But Mr. Savella was the target," Feidy said. "This guy, who called you about your sister. This guy, who called you about the woman you lied about not knowing. Who found the pictures you lied about not recognizing. And who confronted you with your lies out there in Illinois. Now someone tries to kill him and, what do you know, you're just around the corner."

"And you think I had something to do with it?"

"I don't know. Did you?"

"Of course not. I'm a priest. Don't be absurd."

"So what would you call it?"

Remsen toyed with his watchband. "A coincidence."

"Interesting thing with you, Father. Every time you turn up, somebody's just died. Is that just a coincidence, you think?"

"What are you talking about?"

"Well, last time your sister, of course."

"I knew nothing about her death, which in any event, if you are telling me the truth, was an accident. An *accident*. And me a thousand miles away."

"And her super and a neighbor. And last night. But you don't know anything about it?"

"No." He slowly rubbed his eyes and unzipped his jacket.

"Like you didn't know who Mary Bloom was?" Feidy asked. "Let's talk about that lie. Why didn't you tell me Mary was your sister?" She sounded wounded, Savella thought, as if the slight was personal. "You'd think that might be something I'd like to know. I mean, wouldn't you?"

The priest folded his hands, squeezed his palms together. "Now, I'm sorry I didn't tell you about Mary. It was just—I hadn't seen her in many years. I didn't know what she might have been doing, and I wasn't sure I wanted to be, I don't know, associated with her at this point. Without knowing what she'd been doing. Can you understand that?"

"Then why are you here today?" Feidy said.

"I told you. To straighten out her affairs." Remsen stared at his watch. "Look, am I under arrest?"

Feidy shook her head slowly from side to side. "Not yet."

"Because if I'm not under arrest, then I really have to get going."

"To take care of your sister's things."

Textbook, Savella thought. The detective, skirting the perimeter, alert for a break in the barbed wire, ready to move in when Remsen least expected it. And he was coming undone, his face flushed, his voice pitched higher, arrogance giving way to anger, at Feidy, at himself, who knows who else, as he realized his predicament. One good shove and he'd fall.

Remsen gathered his torn shirt tightly in one fist and tugged it closed, as if to ward off a draft. Savella spotted a glint of gold between his fingers. The necklace—an odd touch for a man sworn to poverty. If they still even did that.

"And then there's this tape." Feidy, jumping from nowhere again. "This tape that Mr. Savella got in the mail. No note, no return address. You know anything about that, Father?"

"What tape?"

"A tape of two men talking."

"I don't know what you're talking about."

"You don't? Two men talking about a woman named Mary? This doesn't ring a bell?"

Remsen fingered his watch again.

"You have an appointment?" Feidy asked.

"As a matter of fact, I do."

"Can I ask who with?"

"No."

Feidy shook her head. "I don't know, Father." She was silent for a moment, then her face brightened. "Speaking of which, have you been in touch with yours lately?"

"In touch with who?"

"Your father. You know. In the Virgin Islands? You must have called him about his daughter."

Remsen put his head in his hands. "I don't see my father. We haven't had much of a relationship. What does this have to do with anything?"

"Is that his voice on the tape?"

"What tape?" the priest said.

A small man with a wooden cane hobbled slowly into the pavilion, followed by a woman clutching a small purse. He stopped at a bench in the back and pulled a handkerchief from his hip pocket. "Here, I'll just dry it off for you," he called out.

The woman smiled. "A nice day, it turned out," she said. "How long until the bus?"

Feidy stood and held up her hands. "Folks, can you take the next one, please? We kinda got a situation here." The old man bent over to wipe down the bench. Badge in hand, Feidy started toward him.

Remsen rose quickly and headed back toward his hotel, forcing a bicyclist to swerve sharply to avoid a collision. Feidy called to him to stop, and he began to run, the detective and Savella on his heels. A half block on, his toe caught on a loose board, and he fell hard to the ground, his right knee grazing a popped nail and ripping a gash in his pants. He struggled to his feet, but

Feidy was quickly on him, pulling him off to the side and cuffing his left hand to the Boardwalk railing.

"You just made this a lot harder than it needed to be," she said, her hands patting him down roughly. "We'll do the rest of this at the office."

The pieces don't fit together, Savella thought as he listened to Feidy on the radio requesting a car to transport a prisoner. The guy is all wrong. A killer? Doubtful. Does he know what happened to Bobby and the others? Maybe. But why would he cover it up? What were they missing? People are always telling you something, even when they don't know it, but you have to be listening to hear them. What wasn't he hearing from Remsen? Who was he, really? An army brat, living on military posts all over the world, in the global turmoil of the sixties, no less. Mother killed herself. Dad away a lot of the time doing God-knows-what. Hell of a way to grow up. Is that what brought him to the priesthood? Sanctuary from a violent world? Priests were made of less.

Savella watched Remsen at the railing, jerking on his shackle every few moments as if he really thought he could break free and escape. People are always telling you something—their posture, the clothes they wear, where they live, all of it. A priest in a panic, a thousand miles from home, dressed like a man whose life has just collapsed. And that chain around his neck, something dangling from it, something round and hard that had almost cut Savella during their brief struggle in the lobby. Not a pendant, a…ring? A large ring. He'd seen it before. Savella stared at Remsen's neck, hoping for another glimpse. He fought to remember, hazy images slowly pulling into focus. A table in a restaurant. Three young women and two men, dressed for the evening. Neckties, pearls. And on the edge of the frame, a man's cuffed hand, a gold ring inlaid with a large black stone on his finger.

*Night Out. Dallas.*

Savella pushed past Feidy in three bounding steps and lunged at Remsen. The priest cowered against the railing as Savella reached inside his shirt collar and ripped the chain from his neck before Feidy could drag him away.

"What the hell are you doing?" she shouted. "Get away from my prisoner!"

Savella held the chain aloft and waved it at Remsen. "This is the ring in the picture of his sister. The restaurant in Dallas, with Ruby and the Russian woman." He pushed against the detective, trying to reach the priest. "Was that your hand? Were you there too? I showed you that picture. You said it meant nothing to you. Why did you lie about that?"

"Is he a policeman?" Remsen shouted at Feidy as he rubbed his bruised neck. "Because if he's not a policeman, I want him arrested. You saw him attack me. I want him arrested. And I want my chain."

Feidy twisted Savella's arm behind his back. "Everybody calm down. Father, take a minute and catch your breath. I don't want to have to call an ambulance. Michael, I don't know what you think you're doing. Give me that chain." He reluctantly surrendered it. "Now stay away from him. It's over, you hear me? What is it with you guys? Dallas, Ruby, Russians. Call Oliver Stone if you want to talk about that. I got three bodies right here in Atlantic City, New Jersey. And that's all I want to hear about."

# 39

A *prisoner,* chained to a railing. In a few minutes, a car will show up and then more questions. Won't, *can't,* answer them, but she'll pick at the stray threads until the fabric unravels. Won't, *can't,* allow that.

Look at her now, playing with my chain, twirling it in her hand. Look at these people stopping to stare at the zoo animal. And look at the reporter, slouched on the bench, watching everything I do. He's not done yet either, oh no, more trouble there.

*He recognized the ring.*

And any minute now, a police car and that's it, last chance for redemption gone.

*Unless.*

But that would mean the end of everything. The seal of the confessional is inviolable. Betrayal is forbidden. Not to right a wrong. Not to save a life. Not to avert disaster. It would be sacrilege.

*Unless.*

What was the exception: the penitent grants permission, and his identity is never revealed. Abel would agree, of course he would. Abel would welcome the help. Why else had he reached out to a priest?

But even the exception required the blessing of the bishop, or maybe even Rome. And there was no time for that.

*Unless.*

Oh Lord, what should I do? What led me to this place? Why did I come to know this horror if there is nothing to be done? I cannot, must not, sin again. What must I do? Oh Lord, Lord Almighty.

And here's the car, coming up the ramp, moving through the chattering crowds. Such a beautiful day. But when the sun goes down, hell unleashed.

No bishop then, no Rome, no time, just my own sense of justice.

I can shoulder this guilt if it comes to that. I've lived with worse. But forgive myself if hundreds die and I did nothing? The canon be damned. Stand up this time and say no.

No names, not Garcia, *especially* not Garcia. But give her this Deets, and the two Cubans. Give her the operation. And maybe then she'll forget about pictures and rings and the past. You heard her—she doesn't care about all that.

So. A prayer of absolution.

*Dominus noster Jesus Christus te absolvat …*

Not too loud, they'll think you're crazy.

*… ego te absolvo a peccatis tuis in nomine Patris, et Filii, et Spiritus Sancti. Amen.*

It doesn't count, OK. You can never absolve yourself of your own sins. But at least the heart's in the right place. God, I sound like the kids, the shortcuts, justifying the unjustifiable. Too much time with thieves, all my life. But I should never have left them. I should never have driven off the farm.

And now look: The car is here.

# 40

Remsen could tell a nice story, Savella had to admit it, a hell of a yarn.

He had his villain: a sadistic bomber named Elmer Deets, a monster straight out of Grimm with greasy hair and a blood-red rash across his face. He had his victims: Guillermo and Tomas, two hapless lambs lured to slaughter by the promise of a few hundred bucks. He had a plot: an attack on America by a man named Pena, a remember-the-*Maine* operation to spark a war and reclaim his dying father's empire. And he had a ticking clock: a dirty bomb to be triggered by a simple telephone call, with devastating results.

"In a couple hours," Remsen said in a haunted, round-the-campfire voice, "a lot of people will die."

Feidy unlocked the handcuffs, and the words tumbled from the priest as if she had freed his very soul. *Deets murdered my sister's neighbors, Deets blew up your friend. This is the Cuban attack on America the TV's been talking about.* Remsen begged her to believe, beseeched her to act, veering wildly from panic and alarm to a fretful wail that her best efforts would be futile. Which it was, he couldn't decide. So he kept talking. None of it made sense to Savella, and when he glanced at Feidy, her arms crossed, head cocked to one side, he felt sure she shared his skepticism. But they listened to the priest, because they still smelled a car in flames and they still saw a good man dying.

The detective bore in, hard and nasty:

*Who told you this?*

*A friend.*

*What's your friend's name?*

*I can't tell you.*

*Can't or won't?*

*Can't and won't.*

*Who are the bombers?*

*A man named Deets and two Cubans.*

*What do they look like?*

*The man is big, has a red rash. The Cubans have clothes, coats, that don't fit them.*

*Where are they staying?*

*A motel.*

*Which one?*

*I don't know.*

*What time will they attack?*

*My friend will call me.*

*When?*

*When he knows the target.*

*And he doesn't know the target?*

*An attack on America, is all he said.*

*Nothing else?*

*They're going to see a show.*

*What show?*

*I don't know. It starts at eight.*

*And nothing about the target?*

*He didn't know.*

*The airport, the train station?*

*He didn't know.*

*The water supply, the gas lines?*

*He didn't know.*

*Who's he?*
*My friend.*

And around they went again. Savella fidgeted on the sidelines, eager for a turn at bat, a chance to break Remsen. But after the business with the chain, Feidy had mentioned an arrest for hindering a police investigation, so he kept his silence. They had different agendas, he and the detective. He wanted answers about a photograph. She wanted to know who tortured a Polish janitor, executed a neighbor, and blew up the wrong man. And the badge was all the leverage she needed. But even that couldn't push Remsen any further, and finally she had enough.

"This friend—you wouldn't be this friend, would you, Father?"

"My God, no." He looked horrified at the suggestion. "Of course not. It's true, what I'm telling you—it's true."

"You couldn't blame me for wondering."

"I'm telling the truth."

"Except you can't tell me his name."

"I...I cannot."

"So, what, I'm supposed to drive around looking for two Cubans and a fat guy with skin problems? Uh-uh. Don't think so." She waved over the patrolman, a tall man with flaxen hair and a bodybuilder's physique. "Officer Malinowski here's going to take you down to the office. I'll be back in a while and we can pick this up again."

She started to walk away. The patrolman took hold of Remsen's arm. The priest struggled to break free.

"Wait a minute," he shouted. "*Wait* a minute."

Feidy turned around.

"You've got to believe me. He'll *call.* I know he will. When he knows the target, he'll call."

She gazed at the priest, then shook her head and paced a few yards along the Boardwalk, hands on hips. For a few moments, she stared out at the ocean. She checked her watch, shook her head again, then turned and walked slowly back.

"That phone had better ring, Father," she said, waving off the patrolman.

"It will."

"How are you so sure?"

The priest frowned. "For you, it's three murders. For him, it's not that simple. It's much more complicated than you could ever imagine."

Savella had heard that before, in Hebron and Managua, in Grozny and Pristina. And it was true: there was often a lot to talk about, religion and land and money and power, and it could be tangled. But in the end, not so difficult, nothing that couldn't be quickly understood. In the end, it always came down to the killing.

# 41

Deets's van pulled into the motel parking lot just after six. Garcia and his charges had been outside, dressed and ready to go, for a half hour. Leaving the engine running, Deets staggered out of the driver's seat and adjusted the black leather gloves on his hands.

"We ready?" he asked.

Garcia silently pointed to the Cubans, and Deets moved in for a closer inspection. He fixed the top button of Tomas's shirt, smoothed the fabric bunched around Guillermo's waist, leaned down to straighten the crease of his pants, then froze.

"Fuck," he said. "The shoes."

The unblemished Nikes, blinding white, barely out of the box.

"Nobody dresses up in those," he said. "Not even Cubans."

Garcia fought the urge to laugh. "That's all they have. You didn't give them anything else."

Deets stomped a few yards away. The Cubans looked anxiously at Garcia. But Deets moved back to the van and jerked open the rear door.

"No time for this shit," he said. "Get in the back."

The Cubans clambered inside. Garcia started toward the front passenger seat, but Deets placed a hand on his chest. "All of you," he said, and Garcia knew there was nothing to discuss.

The cargo bay was dark; the windowpanes in the rear door had been painted black, and Deets had hung a blanket from the ceiling behind the driver's seat that blocked most of the light from the front. The Cubans squeezed in together on one side, gripping the steel ribs, searching for a firm hold. Garcia found a space on the floor next to the green duffel bag, jammed up against the wheel well and tied to the side of the van with red bungee cords. As he settled in, his hand grazed a piece of fabric. He lifted it to the weak light: a pair of frilly panties. Garcia tossed the underwear away in disgust. What had this pig been doing back here? Who was the woman who had the misfortune of being with him?

The van lurched forward into traffic. In the dim light, Garcia could see the two Cubans bracing themselves for another wild ride. Must be frightening, he thought, a painful reminder of the trip to freedom, another dark space, perhaps the hold of a leaky boat, rocking in the rough seas, strange voices above them. He leaned forward and waved his hand to get their attention. *"Esto está como el viaje aquí, no? El barco? Pero ninguna agua, por lo menos."*

Guillermo chuckled and nudged Tomas. *"No, no, no barco,"* he whispered to Garcia. *"Volamos a Miami de México."*

Garcia shook his head. He should have known. No waterlogged boat. No twenty-foot waves. No harrowing trip dodging the Cuban Navy and the US Coast Guard. Just a plane to Miami from Mexico. Probably a sandwich and a soda, maybe a movie, the headphones, anyway, for the in-flight music. He laughed, softly at first, then louder. The war, *his* war, was over—he could say that now. As the Cubans watched in confusion, he began to bang his fists against the side panels in noisy celebration until the blanket parted and Deets's face appeared in the opening, shouting at him to shut up.

---

A right turn and quickly another right, then two lefts. The van slowed and the horn sounded. Muttered curses from the front, then the *tick-tick-tick* of the turn signal. The van crawled forward and eased to a stop for a moment, then another right, and they were moving, up, up, up, twisting up, before finally leveling off. Garcia smelled gasoline and exhaust fumes. The van eased to the left and stopped, and Deets engaged the parking brake. Garcia could hear him breathing heavily in the front seat. Then the driver's side door creaked open, and the van's suspension sprang up with the loss of Deets's weight. Moments later he was standing in the open rear door.

"Come out of there," Deets said.

Garcia pulled himself along the floor of the van and dropped to the ground. A brightly lit parking garage, nearly every space filled. He swiveled until he spotted a name: Sultan's Palace Hotel–Casino.

So he had been right. Now the question was how.

Deets reached inside the van, unclasped the bungee cords securing the duffel bag, and pulled it to the edge of the cargo bay. He glanced around the garage to make sure no one was watching, then opened the metal box. Garcia peered over his shoulder; the dynamite was missing.

Deets walked around to the front seat and came back with two black cloth belt packs. He carefully withdrew the two devices and placed one in each of the pouches.

"Tell them to put these on," he said. "Under their shirts and jackets." At Garcia's direction, the boys clipped on the pouches, complaining all the while in Spanish about the discomfort.

"Where's the phone?" Deets asked.

"I have to make the final adjustment."

Garcia reached into his pants pocket and retrieved his pill vial, fiddled with the cap before slowly extracting a tablet. How many had he taken this morning? A second, he was sure, because the pain had been so severe. A third so soon might be too much. Or perhaps what he needed. He placed a pill on his tongue and swallowed hard several times. Only then did he draw the small black Nokia from his jacket pocket. He busied himself for a few minutes with the telephone, removing the battery, inspecting the SIM card. He had underestimated Pena—Deets too. Now he saw it: simple, but clever. Somewhere in the casino, the phone triggers detonate the explosives in the devices, ripping open the lead containers and releasing the cesium. A few casualties in the immediate vicinity; the Cubans, of course, would be the first to go. But in a matter of minutes, most people in the area would probably begin feeling the effects. The lucky ones would get away with runny noses and blurred vision. The less fortunate might lose consciousness or suffer paralysis, go into respiratory failure—some would die. And who knows how many might be injured or killed in the panicked stampede for the exits? Garcia remembered the witness accounts of the Tube bombing in London. A pop, like a bottle of champagne opening, and then the odor of rubber burning, and suddenly people were knocking one another to the floor and walking across the prostrate bodies to get off the train.

Simple, but clever. What was it Pena had said in his office in New York? *You make them afraid, you scare the people bad enough, and the government will do anything to make them feel better.* And it wouldn't take long for the authorities to trace the Cubans back to the island. Write down their names, Deets had ordered in the lot on Bergenline Avenue. Their friends and families would report them missing in a few days, or maybe a friendly reporter would get a tip about their identities. And when the authorities matched the DNA, the link to Cuba would be established.

He looked over at the boys, squirming to adjust the pouches. Guillermo and Tomas, starring in somebody else's show, playing the part of clues. And Abel Garcia had cast them in the roles.

"You done?"

Deets was losing patience. Garcia reassembled the phone. Then he moved to Guillermo and Tomas, reached inside their belt packs, and spent a few minutes adjusting the wires connecting the trigger phones to the explosives before zipping shut the pouches.

The Cubans exchanged nervous glances. Guillermo plucked at Garcia's sleeve and spoke quickly to him in Spanish.

"What's he saying?" Deets demanded.

"He wants to know what's in the pouches. He doesn't like the wires."

"Oh, for Chrissakes. Tell him it's a tape recorder. Tell him they're going to a show and they're gonna make a tape of it. Bootleg. They know bootleg in Cuba?"

Garcia translated the explanation, and the boys relaxed.

"Can we go now?" Deets said.

From his pocket Garcia plucked a slip of paper bearing a telephone number written in pencil. Slowly, like someone learning to dial for the first time, he punched the number on the keypad of the Nokia and hung up. He ripped the paper in quarters, tossed the scraps under the van and handed the Nokia to Deets.

"You press Redial," he said. "Then Send."

Deets juggled the phone in his hand. "Let me test it."

"Not unless you want to die. I just armed the devices."

Deets hesitated, but he couldn't argue. He took three tickets from his pocket.

"See?" he said, handing them to Garcia. "You're gonna see a show."

Garcia read the back of his ticket. Oh yes, he thought as he gave the others to Guillermo and Tomas. *Si, si,* he thought as they peered at the printed words, which for all they knew might have been Egyptian hieroglyphics. But Abel understood only too well.

A jetliner packed with tourists over Bermuda.

A bus full of school kids in Guatemala City.

Clever indeed. *Si, si.*

# 42

Follow the signs to the theater, Deets said. I'll be watching.

Garcia figured it out: Deets wanted to avoid the surveillance cameras, didn't want the police to examine the video later and find him marching off to war with two boys in ill-fitting coats. So, follow the signs to the theater. I'll be watching.

Saturday night, the place was packed. Garcia felt disoriented, lost in the wide corridor, dodging the hordes wandering along the red-and-gold carpet, casting jaded looks at this parallel universe whose anthem was the steady flow of come-ons over the public address system and the relentless *ding-ding-ding* of the slot machines.

Follow the signs, and they turned a corner, and the neon of the theater came into view. A long line of ticket holders snaked along the corridor to the front doors, where six security guards were making cursory inspections of women's purses. Garcia glanced up at the box office marquee. *Joey.* Must tell him. And then maybe the penance.

He stopped in the middle of the corridor, the crowd breaking around him. I'll be watching, the animal warned, but he couldn't be everywhere. Garcia drew a gray Samsung phone from his pocket and switched it on, the Cuban flag unfurling on the screen, and dialed the priest's number.

What the surveillance tapes would show later was two men, one big, one old, colliding in a busy corridor, the big one grabbing the other by the elbow to keep him from falling and smiling while he leaned in to say something. The encounter was fleeting, the two men quickly sinking back into the stream of customers flowing toward the casino. Sort of thing that happened all the time, when the place was busy, as it very much was on that Saturday night. Nothing unusual about any of it.

Except the cameras hadn't seen the fist hard to the ribs that sent the cell phone tumbling to the carpet. The cameras couldn't smell the gagging odor of English Leather that enveloped the old man as the black cloud loomed over him. The cameras didn't hear Elmer Deets hissing, "What did I tell you about that?" before he disappeared. And when Abel Garcia turned to look for his phone, it was gone, swallowed up by a hundred pairs of feet.

---

The call, when it came, surprised them all. Feidy's eyes widened slightly. Savella let out a short disbelieving laugh. Officer Malinowski, who had kept the handcuffs out in absolute confidence they'd be needed again, returned them to his belt. Even Remsen, despite his fervent assurances, seemed unsure about what to do. For a few long seconds, he studied the number on the screen, then looked up and slowly nodded, pressed the phone to his right ear, and stalked several yards away. The detective let him go.

"What do you think?" Savella said as the priest cupped a hand over his left ear to block out the Boardwalk noise.

"Probably a lot of bullshit," Feidy said. "But maybe there's a pony buried in there somewhere. If not, Father Remsen's got some problems."

"*Father* Remsen?" the patrolman said. "This guy's a priest?"

"For now," Feidy said.

Remsen was shouting into the receiver. "Is that you? Are you there?" He shook his head helplessly. "Can you hear me? Are you there?" Finally, he held the phone aloft. "There's no one," he said, his voice cracking a little. "There's no one."

"Give it to me." Feidy moved quickly to his side, grabbed the phone, and listened for a moment. "It's like someone left it open in his pocket. Or left it sitting somewhere. A lot of noise, maybe people walking past." She closed her eyes, straining for a hint to a location. "Some kind of announcement in the background. Kinda muffled, but something about a cash giveaway or...I can't make it out. But it must be a casino." The detective turned to Remsen. "And that was your friend calling?"

The priest nodded.

"No doubt about it?"

"It was his phone number on the caller ID," Remsen said.

"It makes sense," Savella said. "They're going to see a show, the man said. Where else in town are you going to see a show? A casino."

"If that's what he meant by a show," Feidy said. "And even then, which one? We've got less than an hour."

They stared down the Boardwalk, lined with giant billboards, ads for all-you-can-eat buffets, looser slot machines, bigger craps payoffs, and occasionally some entertainment, names writ large to cut through the clutter. A Beatles tribute act. KC and the Sunshine Band. Jay Leno. Blue Oyster Cult. Earth, Wind & Fire. A martial arts competition. Sinbad. The American Beauty pageant. Which is where he would be right now, Savella thought, if things hadn't gone...right. His mind wandered back to the parade: vintage convertibles, pretty young things perched on backseats, Alabama, Alaska, Arizona...Michigan, Minnesota, Mississippi...West Virginia, Wisconsin, Wyoming. Girls from every state. Homecoming queens, class presidents, 4-H champions, stars of the spring musical, track stars. Somebody's daughter, someone's sweetheart, the girl up the street, the sexy thing on the downtown bus.

*An attack on America,* the man said.

*We're gonna see a show.*

Savella grabbed Feidy by the sleeve and pointed up at the billboard.

"It's the Sultan's Palace," he said. "If this guy's telling the truth, it's the Sultan's Palace."

The detective scanned the advertisement. "The beauty pageant?"

"An attack on America, right? A girl from every single state. Maybe four thousand people in the theater, from all over the country, and how many watching on television? It's terror on the cheap."

"Boy, you really don't like that thing, do you?" Feidy gazed at the billboard for a long moment. "OK," she said finally, her voice firm. "Let's start there."

For the next few minutes, she thumbed the keyboard on her cell phone, bringing her shift commander up to date and arranging for a platoon of support troops: an emergency response unit, the bomb squad, more cops.

As she worked, Savella looked down the beach. The last rays of sunshine were fading; the night would soon belong to the neon. The smell of beer and suntan lotion and fried food hung in the air. The enervating thud of the music from an open-air bar echoed along the sand. The Boardwalk was teeming, bands of gamblers wandering past the T-shirt shops and pizza stands, drifting in search of one moment of good fortune or at least the promise of the sort of evening you couldn't find back home in Erie or Elkton or Elmira.

Another Saturday night, Savella thought, except for this priest and his wild tale. Which might just be true.

Remsen was slumped against the railing, the air out of the balloon. A thin sheen of sweat glistened on his cheeks and forehead, even in the cooling breeze. He looked up to find Savella staring at him, the promise of unfinished business in the unsparing glare, and he turned away.

"And somebody call the security guy over there and tell him to meet me in the lobby," Feidy was saying. "You know his name?" A pause, then a soft groan: "This is gonna be a mess."

She ended the call. "The pageant goes on the air at nine," she said. "How about that?"

# 43

The Iguana had a television and besides, the colonel reasoned, an audience might be nice. For a while he thought he might bring along Evangelista, let her see what real power was, never mind the bed. But an invitation like that, she'd have called it a date, and that wouldn't work.

Ruthie, of course, was out of the question. She liked to talk, and people might wonder why the colonel had dragged her to this dive to watch a beauty pageant. So he would settle for the company of strangers.

Precious few of them tonight, though, especially for a Saturday. In the window one guy reading the paper and nursing a drink, the ice rattling in his glass as he raised it to his lips. Two older couples at a table in the middle of the room, hunched around a pitcher of margaritas and a basket of chips—tourists who had ventured out of the Westin to sample real island life and had made it as far as the Iguana before the ladies got skittish. In the back three tanned frat boys, their snorkeling equipment piled on a chair, the table covered with drained Dos Equis bottles.

The colonel liked it like this, relaxed, unpretentious, without the rich and the lazy who fucked up his refuge year-round now, no time off for hurricane season. But tonight even they would be welcome. The next ferry from Red Hook would dock around eight thirty and the place would get a rush then.

Neil was behind the bar, riffling through the cash in the register, his lips moving silently as he counted the take. The colonel assumed his position on the stool in the corner and watched as Neil lifted a twenty and a ten from the till and nonchalantly stuffed them in his pants pocket. He turned to pick up a mahimahi taco and found the colonel, crew cut mowed, blue blazer buttoned against the night, watching him chew.

With a sheepish grin, Neil loped down the bar. "What, is it Wednesday already?" he said, scratching his chin as he struggled to regain his composure. He withdrew a bottle of Budweiser from the beer box. "It's on us," he said, setting the bottle on a paper coaster.

The colonel slapped a wad of cash on the bar. "Take it out of here," he said. Nobody was buying him, not ever, but especially not tonight. He drank some beer and pointed at the darkened television. "You get CBS on that?"

"Sure," Neil said.

"Then put it on. And leave it there."

"OK." Neil played with the remote control and found the proper station. "What're we looking for?"

"Just leave it alone," the colonel said, fishing a Marlboro out of the pack in the pocket of his blazer.

Neil moved to the other end of the bar, picked up a newspaper shoved in the space next to the register, and turned to the TV listings. CBS. The usual crap. And then the American Beauty pageant. Guy had to be kidding.

"A beauty pageant?" he called out. "You gonna watch that shit?"

"Yeah."

"You?"

"That's right."

"Your granddaughter in it or something?"

The colonel ignored him.

"Really not that kind of place, you know?"

"It is tonight," the colonel said, and took another sip of his beer.

Neil studied his face: a tuft of whisker on the chin that had escaped the razor, the taut skin, worn and brown as saddle leather, a fine webbing around the lips. And the eyes, boring back at him, icy blue pools, deep, insensate, unforgiving. He started to speak, then thought better of it, and walked down to the other end of the bar to clean some glasses.

# 44

The run to the Sultan's Palace took ten disquieting minutes, a harrowing dash to the very tip of the island in a squad car reeking of cigarettes and Big Macs and sweat. Remsen seemed particularly unnerved. He gripped the slick plastic of the backseat, struggling to keep his balance as Malinowski wove between lanes on Pacific Avenue, leaning on the siren to get them through the worst of the gridlock.

Savella braced himself against the door as he watched the city zip past. He almost hadn't made the trip. Feidy had ordered Remsen into the car—*you're gonna stay with me until we find out what's going on*—but hesitated before bringing Savella along. In the end she had no choice. There wasn't time to find another babysitter, and she couldn't cut him loose. Someone, after all, was trying to kill him.

Malinowski swerved to the right, and the gaudy onion domes and fiberglass minarets of the Sultan's Palace suddenly loomed, shimmering in the dusk. The car drove quickly through huge white gates guarded by two-ton stone elephants bathed in spotlight and began the slow descent to the beach along a serpentine drive lined with shrub pine.

"You guys all right back there?" Feidy asked.

"You could sell tickets for this," Savella said.

At the bottom the car crested a slight rise and the ocean filled the windshield. The patrolman swung past an enormous flowing fountain and turned hard into a porte cochere shrouded by still more blanketing foliage. The car slid past a line of limousines idling at the sea wall that separated the entrance from the beach, and pulled to an abrupt stop at the curb. The detective jumped out, pulled open the back door, and helped Remsen from the car.

"Keep an eye on these guys, Malinowski," she said. She fixed her shield to the breast pocket of her blazer, and, pushing past a television crew interviewing pageant-goers, led her entourage through the revolving doors and into the hotel.

As many times as he had been inside the Sultan's Palace, Savella never ceased to be amazed at the ridiculous extravagance of the place. Fourteen million dollars of German crystal chandeliers. The entire two-year output of the Carrera marble quarries in Italy. Almost five times as much steel as the Eiffel Tower. Gold mirrors, flickering neon signs, acres of purple carpeting. The place had seen better days; duct tape held up the tusks of the elephants at the entrance, and a faulty drain in the fountain regularly made the basin a breeding ground for mosquitoes. But it was still a sight, and on a night like this, thousands would pass through the doors to gamble, eat, drink, see a show. The scene would be repeated across town, and in cities and Indian reservations across the country. A problem here, a single act of terror, would ricochet through the industry like a modern plague, costing billions of dollars. The perfect target, Savella thought. How fast would it all end if people began to worry that they'd be blown to bits when they came in to play the slots?

Outside the lobby bar, the welcoming committee had already gathered, led by Albert Bottach, the hotel's security director. Ex-cop, and the worst kind, Feidy had complained to the patrolman during the drive, a retired captain pushed out the door by a new chief committed to modernizing the department. Savella knew the type—pining for the days when police work meant white men, and you could only imagine what he felt about Feidy.

Bottach was a medium-built man in his early sixties with a shock of white hair shaped into a pompadour that made him seem all the more dated. In an expensive dark-blue suit, he stood in the center of an uninspiring covey of security guards—two grandfathers in sweater vests, three gaunt young men, each sporting a light fuzzy mustache, and a tiny middle-aged woman. Bottach watched Feidy cross the lobby, the pained expression on his face never wavering. Only when she was standing in front of him did he bother to remove his right hand from his pants pocket and reluctantly extend it.

"Sylvie, nice to see you," he said in a polite monotone. "You dating boys yet?"

"Same old Albert," she said. "How do we get along without you?"

Bottach plunged his hand back into his pocket. "So what's up?"

The guards pressed against Feidy as she recounted Remsen's story. When she was finished, Bottach looked as if he'd swallowed something foul.

"Shit, Sylvie," he said. "It's a big night. TV show and all."

"I don't know, Albert, you think that's maybe what they had in mind?"

Bottach stiffened at the sarcasm. "You don't even know it's us. The call could have come from anywhere."

"We've got people going to the other places too. But this seems like the most likely. Like you said, TV show and all."

Before Bottach could reply, half a dozen police officers burst through the front doors, followed by two dog handlers, their German shepherds prancing on their toes. A few arriving hotel guests stopped short of the registration desk, waiting to see what might be coming next.

"Jesus, can we tone this down a little, honey?" Bottach said. "You're gonna spook the whole fucking place."

"We got a *bomb*, Albert," Feidy said.

"Or not."

"You want to take a chance?"

Bottach turned to the guard at his shoulder. "Jerry, see if anyone found a phone in here tonight." He adjusted his shirt cuffs and shook his head. "Wish you had something more concrete, Sylvie. It's like looking for a needle in a haystack. Fifteen hundred rooms. Twenty separate entrances. Couple thousand doors to knock on. Eleven hundred surveillance cameras to check." He pointed down the broad corridor. "And that casino's the size of two football fields. What are we supposed to do with all those people, pat 'em down? It's a casino, not an airport. We start that shit, they'll go somewhere else."

For all his bluster, he had a point, Savella thought. That's the way these things go: unless we're really lucky, or someone gets a conscience, not a damn thing we can do about it. But there was no chance Bottach could walk away, not after he'd been warned. And his guard, when he got off the radio, ended the debate. "Lenny Brezinski found a phone a little while ago, Al. By the theater."

"The theater," Savella said quietly.

"I heard," Feidy said. "OK, Albert?"

"Ah, Christ." Bottach swatted at the air in frustration. "Jerry, tell him we're on our way over."

"He's going on break."

"Tell him to stay the fuck there." Bottach glared at Feidy. "So there was a phone. Big deal. A needle in a fucking haystack, Sylvie. That's what you're looking for."

# 45

The pouch around Guillermo's waist was slipping.

He reached inside his jacket, tried to hitch it up, but as soon as he took a few steps, it slid again. Garcia offered an encouraging wave. Velcro, he thought. Just a strip of Velcro holding it up, but he's fumbling around for a belt buckle. At this rate the pouch would be around his ankles by the time he passed through security.

Garcia sluiced through the line to Guillermo's side. He flashed an apologetic smile to the ticket holders standing behind him and held up one finger: *forgive me a moment.* He hugged Guillermo, slipped a hand under his shirt, and tightly cinched the strap. It would hold until the boy was inside. "*Esperaré afuera,*" he whispered. "*Usted puede decirme todo sobre las mujeres bonitas.*" *I'll be waiting outside. You can tell me all about the pretty women.*

An acceptable lie, Abel decided as he walked away. He doesn't need to know that we'll never have the conversation.

He pushed through the crowd, swimming against the tide, allowing himself to be caught in a knot of women heading for the bathroom. Twenty yards down the corridor, he found space against the wall and stopped to watch the boys' progress. *Take them to the door and make sure they get inside,* Deets had ordered, *then meet me in the hall.*

Garcia glanced ahead to the security desk near the entrance. It was largely what he expected: bored guards giving women's purses a quick glance, another guard at a metal detector flirting with a cocktail server balancing a tray full of dirty glasses, a fourth man in a suit with a casino identification badge trying to pick up the pace with a traffic cop's automatic wave. Not that the lack of attention made much difference, Garcia knew. The screening equipment was designed to maybe—*maybe*—spot some gangbangers trying to smuggle their TEC-9s into a dance at P.S. 56. But not this stuff. Not anymore.

So very like the Americans, Garcia thought, such short memories. After 9/11, they were willing to put up with anything: take off your shoes, remove your belts, four-hour lines at the check-in, automatic weapons on the train. But that was eons ago. Dinosaurs walked the earth back then. Man made fire from sticks.

Did they really think it would be jetliners the next time? When it came, and it would come, they would remember a little man reading the *Daily News* on the F train, swaddled in a parka on a warm spring day, or a frazzled housewife dragging a heavy shopping cart and squeezing the cantaloupes in the Shop-Rite, or two teenagers dribbling basketballs on the sidewalk in front of the synagogue. Or a Cuban boy meeting an old friend in the line to see a beauty pageant.

Abel knew better. He had learned the lesson: *forget nothing.* The past was painful, the future bleak, it didn't get better. *Forget nothing.*

A pretty girl with big brown eyes waltzed past. *Pilar, when she was younger.* Her voice, just once more. But his phone was gone.

The boys were almost at the security desk. Still time to pull them out of line, give them back their lives. But Deets was lurking, monitoring every move.

And then it was too late. First Tomas walked through the metal detector without a beep, then Guillermo with a self-conscious tug at his waist, and they disappeared inside. As if to mark the moment, the noise in the corridor crescendoed, gleeful laughter, loud voices alive with expectation, *celebration*, pinballing off the walls, floating to the ceiling. Too much, Garcia thought. He wanted quiet, the comfort of home, the sofa with Pilar, sitting at their TV trays, watching her silly *telenovelas*.

*Pilar.* But he was out of time.

The last pill was making him woozy, a final indignity. The hall shimmered, as if he were watching the world through gauze. But even the haze couldn't obscure Deets, lying in wait farther along the corridor, his face turned to the wall. Pena had given Deets the trigger; they didn't trust Abel Garcia, and he knew how that would end. Again the idea of escape crossed Garcia's mind: turn back inside before Deets spotted him, slip out a back door, disappear. But it was futile. He couldn't run fast enough or far enough to elude Enrique Pena. The order had been given and it would be carried out.

But not for him a lonely death at the side of a road, the body dumped in the ocean or left to rot in the marshes. Garcia would write his own ending to this show. He too would be a clue: the old Cuban freedom fighter, the unrepentant rebel, dying in one last byzantine attempt to topple the dictator. There would be no question, in the end, who was behind the attack.

Garcia ran his fingers hurriedly through his hair, then straightened his guayabera. He threw back his shoulders and marched, or so he hoped, to Deets.

"We will do this here," he said quietly.

Deets nibbled on his lip as he considered Garcia's ultimatum. For some reason he no longer looked the least bit threatening. Was it his face, Garcia wondered, red and splotchy, the makeup he used to cover up his malady washed away by sweat, exposing his vanity? Was it that the dance they'd played over the years was finally drawing to a close? Or was it simply that a man who knows his fate has nothing more to fear?

Deets tendered a curt nod. "Makes no never mind to me," he said.

Garcia had counted on it, bloodlust overwhelming his common sense. Deets looked around, his eyes coming to rest on a men's room door down the corridor, guarded by a metal Out of Order sign on a chain stretched between two yellow rubber stanchions. He took hold of Garcia's arm with his chubby fingers and nudged him forward.

"Won't take but a minute," he said, the words soothing, echoing through the buffering haze, and offering, at long last, rest.

# 46

Bottach's man waited by the cash machines, bouncing lightly against the wall, hands clasped behind his back. He came to attention at the sight of suits and badges, and held up his hands in self-defense.

"Al, I didn't think it was anything but lost and found, or else I—"

Bottach cut him off. "Just give it to her, Lenny," he said, pointing at Feidy.

The guard fumbled the gray Samsung out of his pants pocket.

"Guess we won't be worrying about prints, huh?" Feidy said. "Where'd you find it?"

"A woman. A woman found it."

"What was her name?"

Lenny reached in his breast pocket for a small green notebook and flipped through the pages for a name that almost certainly wasn't there.

"A woman," he mumbled. "I got it somewhere—"

Feidy sighed. "Just show me where she found it."

"In the hallway here." The guard gestured aimlessly down the corridor.

"Jesus, Lenny," Bottach muttered.

"What? It was a lost and found, Al."

Feidy turned to Remsen. "What's your number, Father?" He recited it and the detective quickly scrolled through the list of recent dialed calls until she found what she was seeking. "The one and the same. Right number, right time." She moved closer to Remsen and held the phone screen directly in front of his eyes. "We've got him now, Father. One call, and I know who it belongs to. That part's over. So what's his name?"

Remsen looked down at the floor. Feidy slowly shook her head. "Well, we're gonna find out. It'll just take a little longer, is all." She slipped the phone in her jacket pocket. "Meanwhile, Albert, we've got ourselves a situation."

"What you *got*," Bottach said, "is a lost cell phone."

He was right again, Savella thought, and Feidy knew it. Remsen had his story, and the phone call had come from the discarded phone, but that wasn't a lot to go on. And the uniforms and the dogs were already attracting too much attention. The police couldn't linger forever without questions being asked.

The detective stalked the corridor, inspecting the line of people waiting to enter the arena. Then she returned to Bottach. "For starters, get somebody up to the surveillance room to review the tapes, maybe spot whoever dropped the phone. Then turn this line around. And we have to clear the theater."

"Are you nuts? Where am I going to put them?"

"Take them out the other way to the beach. Just until we can check the room. Look, we don't have time to evacuate the whole casino. So we take a chance and focus on the theater."

"I got a few thousand people in there. What am I supposed to tell them, Sylvie?"

"Think of something. A problem with the air-conditioning."

"And what about the show?"

She waved him off. "First things first, Albert. We need to check the room. And I don't know how the hell we do this, but we have to do it quietly. If the trigger guy's around here, and sees us moving, it's over."

"*If* there's a bomb," Bottach said.

"I *get* it, Albert."

"*Detective.*" A stout man in a starched white shirt, gold captain's bars gleaming from his collar, escorted by two aides in elegant blue suits and soft leather Italian loafers. Feidy's face soured, but Bottach rushed forward to greet the new arrivals.

"Hey, Marvin. Thank Christ you're here."

The captain looked through him, nodded at Feidy. "What the hell's going on?"

---

There was a problem with hearing stories like this too often. The first time around, the reaction was genuine alarm. But listen to the details again, and then again, and it began to sound like the start of a bad joke: *Two Cubans and a fat guy with a rash walk into a casino.* Which is how, Savella thought, you get from 9/11 to complaining about taking your shoes off at the airport.

But Captain Marvin Hamill was a virgin, and Feidy's hasty rehash left him properly shaken.

"Let me get this straight—this is that Cuban bullshit they've been going on about?"

"Sounds like it," Feidy said.

"We gotta call the feds."

"OK." She pointed at Remsen. "But if he's telling the truth, we don't have time to wait for them."

Hamill glanced at Remsen, who stood at Feidy's elbow with Malinowski glued to his side.

"This is?" Hamill asked.

"Father Joseph Remsen," Feidy said.

The captain studied him closely. "He's a priest?" he asked Feidy, as if Remsen wasn't there.

"Yeah. He brought us all this."

"Uh-huh." Hamill looked at Savella, hovering over Feidy's shoulder. "Who're you?"

Feidy took Savella's arm and pushed him out of the way.

"The car bomb. His car."

"The reporter?"

"Ex-reporter."

"So what's he doing here?"

"Needed him to find the priest."

"And you found him." Hamill waited for an explanation.

"Captain, somebody tried to blow this guy up last night. I thought we should keep an eye on him. There hasn't been time to make other arrangements. But if you've got a better way..."

"Marvin." Bottach had edged his way into the meeting. Now he held up his hand, like a schoolboy seeking the teacher's attention. "Marvin, here's the thing. Saturday night, right? We're sold out. My *mother* couldn't get a room. And we got this TV show, this pageant, on top of everything else."

Hamill's gaze fell first on the priest, moved to Savella, and finally settled on Feidy. With a quick nod, he patted Bottach on the shoulder.

"Relax, Alfred. Detective, do what you got to do."

---

They did not like it, not one bit. Here they were, come all the way from Visalia and Beaver Creek and Caruthersville and Martinsburg, come all this way to see their girls in their crowning glory, and now just outside the theater, so close they could see the Big Stage after all these years of preparation, they're told the air is on the blink and they'd have to leave. The duct tape on the elephant's tusks was one thing, and who cared about the soiled carpet and the chintzy chandeliers, and why anyone would want to tart up a place like some kind of bordello—but you couldn't make sure the air was working on such a big night?

But a badge was a badge, so they grumbled and they whined, and headed for the exits, slouched reluctantly toward the lobby, tossing puzzled glances over their shoulders at the confusion behind them, and taking care to keep the kids clear of the German shepherds heading the other way, into the theater. And come to think of it, what was that all about? Who needed dogs to fix a balky chiller? And while we're on the subject, what were all these cops doing here, anyway?

Sylvie Feidy walked the line, peering closely at the face of every overweight giant, and Lord, there were a lot of them: *didn't anyone work out anymore?* She stepped over Pepsi cups and fast-food wrappers discarded by the departing disgruntled, and then she retraced her steps, alert to the laughter, the complaints. Listening but not hearing—no time to smooth the rough edges, like the nauseous look that crossed Bottach's face when she mentioned evacuating the whole damn place. No time for any of that. She needed someone to call the phone company, see if they could take down the cell signal, needed the theater cleared so the dogs could sniff it out, needed wide-awake patrolmen in the lobby and at the beach exit, eyes peeled for the two dumb mules and the trigger, this horror movie character with some kind of skin thing on his face. She needed all that, and five minutes ago. But what Sylvie Feidy needed most was a little bit of luck.

It was the priest who found him.

---

"You don't twitch a muscle, Father," his police minder had ordered, just before he went to the rescue of a blonde who had fallen in the crush. Remsen had plastered himself against the wall, afraid to so much as scratch his nose, his eyes focused on the Out of Order sign in front of the men's room across the way. Which was how he came to see the large man in the dark suit edging through the door of the broken bathroom, his gelled hair glistening in the chandelier light. His eyes widened slightly as he absorbed the commotion in the corridor, then, having seen his shadow, he ducked quickly back inside. A few minutes later, the bathroom door again swung slowly open, and this time the groundhog emerged, joined the exodus, head bowed, obscuring his face, but not before Remsen spotted a flash of red.

Along the corridor, plywood partitions had been erected to shield a renovation project, and a bottleneck formed where the hall narrowed. As he neared the choke point, the big man slowed his pace, trailing two couples in the midst of a chilly quarrel. He checked his watch, stepped out of the pack, and headed back toward Remsen.

The priest searched in vain for his police guard. Feidy was also missing; Remsen had last seen her maybe ten minutes earlier, entering the theater with the dogs.

Now the man had drawn abreast of him, lobby bound, passing so close that Remsen could have reached out and grabbed him by the sleeve. He felt a fleeting relief that the danger had ebbed, but that couldn't be the end of it, not with lives in the balance. Something must be done.

The reporter, who had been drifting aimlessly along the hallway, returned to his position at Remsen's elbow. The priest hesitated. He wanted to put a country between himself and this man who seemed to know too much already. But as the big man loped toward escape, Remsen tapped Savella's arm and said quietly, "What about him?"

Large enough, Savella thought, ten yards past them by now but still towering over the throng even as he hunched over to blend in. Savella suddenly became aware of a faint odor, an acrid, unpleasant stench he couldn't quite identify—dried sweat, maybe, or fried onions, or bad cologne. "I can't see his face," he said.

"I did."

Savella glanced back at Remsen. "Anything on his skin? A rash?"

"It was red. Something red."

Savella sniffed the air, and this time came memory: *The house, the day it was tossed. The car, the night it exploded.* He started down the hall. "Find Feidy," he shouted over his shoulder. "Let her know."

---

No way to lose Deets here, not with his brilliantined head bobbing fitfully above the crowd, like a Macy's Thanksgiving Parade balloon threatening to tear loose from its moorings. The job here was merely to tag along, hang with him until the cavalry came over the hill. Every few steps, Savella glanced back, hoping to find Sylvie Feidy closing on him, but they were approaching the lobby, and Savella was still alone. There were cops up ahead, but he had to be sure. No time for false alarms, and Remsen was hardly a reliable witness. *Turn around, damn it, let me see the face.* Savella wove through the line, jostling for position.

Then, just in front of the Sweet Shoppe, Deets moved to the outside to skirt slower traffic. He raised his wrist to check the time, and for a fleeting moment, his profile came into view: *a slash of scarlet across his right cheek.*

And right on cue, here was Feidy, but *ahead* of Savella, huddled with Hamill and his two aides. Savella waved his hands above his head until he caught the attention of one of the aides, who said something that caused the little group to turn around. Savella pawed at his right cheek and pointed up the corridor as he pushed his way to Feidy's side.

"What're you *doing*, Michael?" she asked.

"Deets."

"Where?"

"The big man up ahead. A rash on the right cheek, just like Remsen said."

Feidy took a quick look. Savella's suspect was approaching a set of double doors that led to the lobby. The guy fit the bill. A little luck never hurt. With the captain and his aides in tow, they pushed ahead, Feidy speaking into her radio. Deets was through the doors and into the lobby. Another fifty yards, Savella thought, and he's on his way.

"You need to stop him *now*," Savella said.

"No, no. Too many people. We take him outside." She glanced sideways. "We got him, Michael. Just not here."

# 47

No policeman. No reporter. Nobody paying attention to the man in the stained pants and ripped sneakers, standing rigidly against the wall.

Across the hall, a little boy in baggy shorts slipped out of line, ducked under the Out of Order chain, and tugged on the brass bathroom door handle before his mother called him back. Then a young man carrying a giant cup of beer hurriedly stepped over the chain to the hoots of his pals and pulled open the door, only to be driven off by the inky darkness inside. No one was going inside, Remsen knew. They weren't meant to. It was his job, and only his, to open that door, ask the question: *If that was Deets, then where was Abel?* He knew the answer, even if he couldn't bring himself to admit it. But this was how it was supposed to be. There were expectations; he was a priest and he had promised absolution. And so, reluctantly, despair tearing at his gut, he crossed the hall.

The bathroom was pitch-black and reeked of disinfectant. From speakers somewhere in the dark came the voice of Marvin Gaye: *what's going on?* Remsen slid his hands up and down the walls until he found a light switch. He stood, blinking furiously, as the fluorescent bulbs flickered to life. The room was empty, the floor bare save for a cleaning bucket in the corner, a mop left soaking in the dirty water. Piles of paper towels were stacked neatly by the sinks, and a wicker tip basket for the washroom attendants lay next to a tray filled with bottles of mouthwash.

"Abel?" Remsen called out. "Abel, you in here?" The sound of a dripping faucet was his only answer.

But the room was empty—that was the essential point. There was a chance he was wrong, that he still might be able to answer the question as he would have preferred. Or a toilet in the rear would flush any minute now, and Abel Garcia would step from the stall, zipping his pants, flashing the kind of cocky smile that used to illuminate his young face in the old days, in Texas—the last time, really, that everything still made sense. Or his phone would trill, and it would be Abel, wondering where Father Joey was, impatient to go home. There was still a chance, if he stood here and waited, and the possibility lifted his spirits. Because the room was empty—that was the key bit.

"Abel?" he said, and moved toward the rear.

The dripping faucet was at the fifth sink, the one closest to the urinals, water forming at the mouth of the spigot, then falling into a stainless steel basin filled with suds. Crumpled paper towels cluttered the counter. The soapy water was tinged a faint red, dark smears blotted the discarded towels. *If that was Deets, then where was Abel?*

Remsen picked up a wad of towels and let them flutter to the floor.

"Abel?" His voice trembled slightly. "Are you in here, Abel?"

From the back of the room came a thud, and an arm draped in the exquisitely tailored sleeve of a snow-white guayabera skidded out from under the door of the last stall on the left.

# 48

Somewhere in mid-corridor, Deets had attached himself to what seemed to be, judging by the badges they displayed, Miss Georgia's family—mother and father, two brothers and a sister, aunts, uncles, and cousins, and a grandmother in a wheelchair. With the exception of the old woman, all were extremely tall, and towered over the crowd like skyscrapers on a desert horizon.

As they streamed out of the lobby, Deets stayed close, ignoring their quizzical glances. He knew what he was doing. The cover the giants from Georgia afforded him made things a little more complicated for the police.

Standing at the valet booth, Hamill spelled out a plan. His two aides, Monck and Witherspoon, were former narcotics detectives who knew a thing or two about taking bad guys off the street. They would shadow Deets until he strayed from the pack, then swoop in and grab him.

Feidy rubbed her forehead. "Captain, I—wouldn't we be better off with a few more people? I mean—"

"You want to tip this guy that's something's up?"

Feidy looked around her. Several police cars were parked at awkward angles around the porte cochere. Two ambulances had arrived, their bay doors open as paramedics readied first-aid equipment. A fire truck sat at the curb.

"I think he's probably got a little hint," Feidy said.

"Or he thinks there's a problem with the ventilation," Hamill said.

"With all these police? The dogs?"

"He hasn't bolted, has he? No, my guys can handle it."

His aides' faces registered not a hint of enthusiasm for the strategy. Narcotics, maybe, but light-years ago. Now they traipsed around in thousand-dollars suits, not T-shirts and jeans, trailing a captain, not drug dealers in the projects. Cops, sure, Savella thought. But odds are their real strength was politics.

Hamill patted Feidy's shoulder. "Look, Sylvie, I've been here before—we all have. We don't need an army. And besides, we don't want to upset Bottach's night any more than we already have, do we?"

Feidy held up her hands in surrender. Hamill was Hamill, or, more importantly, a captain. "OK, if you think," she said. "But listen, guys—whatever you do, get his hands. Don't let him near his phone." As if to reinforce the point, Deets, now securely positioned in the midst of the Georgia delegation, jammed his right hand deep in his pocket.

"They get it, Detective," Hamill said, and jerked a thumb at Savella. "And why is he still here?"

------

Stretched along the driveway, a line of Sultan's Palace security guards guided the crowd around the row of limousines and onto the beach on the other side of the low seawall. Children raced ahead toward the water; some adults slipped off their shoes in sand still warm from the afternoon sun. Miss Georgia's contingent stopped on the sidewalk that bordered the beach. For the first time since he joined them, Deets drifted away from the group, only a few feet, but an opening, and the detectives moved to seize the advantage. Monck circled the crowd, angling along the beach to flank Deets on his right. Witherspoon took up a position at the end of the limo line, chatting with a driver washing his windshield.

Deets checked his watch, then glanced up the beach. Throngs of pageant-goers were piling out of the two Boardwalk exits. He turned slowly in a lazy circle and when he had finished, he reached in his jacket pocket for a peppermint and popped it in his mouth. For the next few minutes, he sucked contentedly on the candy, twisting its cellophane wrapper in his fingers.

"What's he waiting for?" Hamill asked.

"I think he's got orders," Feidy said. "He's supposed to trigger the bombs when the pageant's on the air, on live TV. That's why he keeps checking the time. On top of that, he still can't be sure his mules are in position. We might have caught a break."

The candy gone, Deets dropped the wrapper and watched it blow away on the breeze. He stepped off the curb, took a half dozen steps, and stopped abruptly. Another quick glance at the time, and he walked back to the sidewalk and stared up the beach again.

Feidy looked along the sand: all that stood between the casino and the tip of the island was the Sultan's Palace gargantuan fifteen-story parking garage. "It's his car," she said. "He wants to get his car in the garage. He's not taking any chances. He'll be out of here and on the road as soon as he hits the trigger."

Another peppermint for Deets, but a bit more hasty this time, the wrapper wafting away long before he was finished with the candy. Then he edged off the curb for the second time.

"OK, guys," Feidy murmured, "let's do this thing."

Deets navigated another deliberate circle, agonizingly slow. Scanning the beach, his gaze came to rest on Monck, who had one foot on the first step of the stairs to the Boardwalk. Feidy tensed slightly. Monck made a show of bending down to brush some sand off the top of his loafer. After a moment Deets moved on, reviewed the Boardwalk, then focused his attention on the limousines. Witherspoon, deep in conversation with the puzzled driver, folded his arms across his chest and casually turned away in midsentence.

Suddenly Deets whirled around and found Monck again, just as he reached the top of the staircase. The detective froze and teetered backward. As he grabbed the handrail, his jacket flew open, briefly exposing the revolver holstered on his belt.

Feidy groaned. "He's got them," she said. "The son of a bitch made them both."

———————

For a big man, Deets moved well. He headed down the sidewalk at a dead run, arms pumping furiously, straight for Witherspoon. Slow to react, the detective fumbled for his weapon. Suddenly Deets veered and climbed over the seawall, his sweaty face bathed in neon. Feidy figured it out in an instant.

"The limos," she shouted. "He's going for the limos." If Deets couldn't reach his car, he'd find the next best thing.

At the front of the line, a short balding man in a black suit stood at the open door of his long white limousine, a cigarette tucked between the fingers of his right hand. Deets barreled over a traffic stanchion and lunged at the driver, knocking him to the pavement with a forearm to the neck. He squeezed behind the wheel and slammed the door shut. A moment later the limousine was moving, clipping the bumper of a police car parked just ahead and skirting the fountain in herky-jerky spurts before squealing off up the long entrance drive.

Feidy sprinted across the driveway, the radio raised to her mouth. "Top of the drive, limo coming your way," she said. "The white limo is our guy."

The driver, bleeding from the nose, struggled to his feet. "He's got the kids," he said.

"The what?" Feidy asked.

The driver pulled a handkerchief from his pocket and motioned toward the portico. A woman in stiletto heels and a sequined T-shirt and carrying a slim leather briefcase had just walked out of the building, her mouth agape as she surveyed the confusion.

"She's some executive," the driver said. "I picked up her and her children at the airport and she wanted to swing by here to get some papers. Left her son and daughter watching a movie."

"They're still in the limo?"

The driver dabbed at his bloody nose. "In their car seats."

Feidy lifted the radio. "And there are two kids in the car. You got that? Two kids." She looked over at the woman, who was waving for the driver's attention. "Somebody go give her the good news."

The limousine twisted through the dunes, its head-lights playing off the tall trees flanking the road, red brake lights flickering intermittently through the foliage. Ahead, at the top of the drive, a faint trace of blue strobes whipped the sky above the tree line.

"Is there another way out?" Feidy asked one of the casino guards.

"It's like a giant U. He'd have to come back down here, run along the water, then head back up the other way, past the garage and the surface lots on the other side of the building."

Feidy glanced at Hamill, who stood to one side with his aides. After the botched capture, he was through giving orders. "Get a couple cars across here," she told the officers gathered around them. "Block it off."

At the top of the drive, the brake lights on the limousine flashed, and stayed on. Deets had just discovered there was no way out, Savella realized. Decision time, and not a lot of options. The brake lights faded, and suddenly the limousine was heading back down the drive in reverse, a squeal of rubber as Deets navigated a bend in the road, a low thump when he lost the road and side-swiped a tree. A blue strobe appeared behind him, then a second, and a third, moving slowly, maintaining a distance, forcing Deets back into the box. Halfway down, the limousine's red running lights disappeared, and for a moment there was no sign of the car, as if Deets had left the road for good. But then a white beam from a single headlight pricked the trees, marking the resumption of his frantic descent.

The crowd on the beach had drifted up from the water, pressing eagerly against the seawall, as if this were just another casino attraction, an entertainment for their amusement: an exploding volcano, dancing waters, a pirate battle, a car chase with police. There was no time to explain it, much less move them. Feidy pointed at Witherspoon and Monck.

"You guys gotta get those people down on the ground," she said. "Everybody down in the sand now."

The detectives looked at Hamill, who nodded at Feidy: *what she says.*

The lights along the drive drew closer; the sound of a straining engine grew louder, and the limousine finally pulled into view, its body scraped and dented, the windshield cracked, one headlight swinging uselessly from its socket. Deets was coming fast, no sign of stopping, until he spotted the police barricade. The limousine skidded to a halt and stalled next to the fountain, smoke pouring from under the hood.

Savella dropped to his knees behind the seawall and peered over the top. The limousine had come to rest facing the lobby doors. Through the windshield he could just make out Deets behind the wheel, a sobbing little boy on his lap. There was no sign of his sister behind the heavily tinted side windows.

In the porte cochere, no one spoke, no one moved. Savella listened to the engine settling, the hiss of air escaping from a punctured tire. From hidden speakers a booming voice announced, "The sultan welcomes you" over and over as a Middle Eastern melody played in the background.

The driver's side window whirred down. A few seconds later, a meaty hand pushed a silver gun through the window and pulled the trigger once. The bullet shattered one of the ornate chandeliers on the ceiling of the portico, sending crystal raining down on the entrance. Several police officers dove to the ground. The television reporter and his cameraman scrambled for cover in the shrubbery. Two ambulance workers hurriedly retreated through the revolving doors into the lobby.

The dented driver's side door creaked open, metal grinding against metal, and a child's wail filtered out of the limousine. Deets slowly emerged, the gun in his right hand, his left arm wrapped around the little boy's waist, using him as a shield. He stood next to the car for a moment, then began to move in languid arcs as he took stock of his situation. Tears glistening on his face, the boy moaned for his mother, and a haunting image flashed through Savella's mind, a picture of another little boy, also surrounded by guns and bombs, standing in the white heat of a still day, begging to be rescued. Always the children, he thought, always the children who get caught in the crossfire.

Feidy approached the car, her arms stretched wide, palms open. "I'm Detective Sylvie Feidy, Mr. Deets."

Deets appeared surprised to hear his name. He tightened his grip on the boy. "That's far enough."

She froze. "OK, here? That better?" Feidy offered a slight smile and held it until he nodded. "Now, can you do something for me? Let the kids go. Let 'em go and then we'll talk. What do you think, Mr. Deets?"

"Nice try." He waved the gun in the direction of the squad cars blocking his way. "How about you tell them to move and we'll get out of here."

Feidy pointed at the boy. "How's his sister?"

"Bawling her eyes out. Just like this one."

"Come on, what do you think? At least let the kids go. Give me the kids. They've got nothing to do with any of this."

"You're wasting your time." Deets rested the barrel of his gun on the top of the boy's head. "And we're not gonna sit here all night, I promise you that. I got two bombs inside, I guess you know. And I got the trigger right here in my pocket."

Feidy raised her hands in a reassuring way. "Look, you don't want that, I don't want that. Let's just take our time and figure this out. But I gotta wait for my boss to get up here. Is that OK? Get the boss up here and we'll figure this out. And I promise *you*—nobody's going to do anything stupid. OK, Elmer? Can I call you Elmer?"

"No." Holding the boy in front of his face, he shuffled backward to the car and lowered himself into the front seat. "Fifteen minutes and those cars are out of here," he shouted. "Fifteen minutes. Or then I don't know what." He pulled the door shut. A moment later, music began to pour out of the open window.

Feidy retreated, her eyes never leaving the car until she reached the seawall. She ducked her head and closed her eyes. "He's a little ragged. Two hysterical children in there with him, 'The Lion King' soundtrack blasting, and I don't think he's a kid person. We can try to talk it out, get hostage negotiations up here. But those kids and that music are gonna get on his nerves a lot sooner than that. We gotta find those two bombs before he gets impatient and goes for that phone. Because at that point, those kids, I hate to say it, they're the least of our worries."

Hamill, eager for something to do, made several calls to arrange for the negotiators. Monck and Witherspoon returned to the beach to move the crowd farther away from the confrontation. Feidy joined a dozen patrolmen behind the seawall and worked the radio, monitoring the search for the bombs. What was taking so long, she wanted to know. The entire audience had passed through police checkpoints on their way out of the building. Now they were assembled in one place, on the beach, surrounded by cops. How tough could it be to ferret out two Cubans in ill-fitting jackets?

Savella lowered himself to the ground and slumped against the wall. Feidy, it seemed to him, hadn't broached the immediate problem: *What did she tell this guy when the fifteen minutes were up?* He had never understood these situations. How did Deets think this would end? Did he really believe the police would suddenly back off, allow him to drive away with two kidnapped children and the trigger to two bombs in his pocket? And if he somehow found a way to break through the police lines, how far did he think he would get? What's done is done, there was no escape, no hiding from it, no matter how far you burrowed into the earth. You couldn't change your history, couldn't outrun it. Either you lived with it and moved on, or else you died. And Deets wasn't anywhere ready to live with it. So what did Feidy do when her fifteen minutes were up? Find the bombs, that was her answer. Find the bombs, take away the threat, and then we'll deal with the kids.

But the radio blurted out only bad news. Nine minutes to go, and only half the men in the audience had been patted down. Seven minutes remaining, and the bomb dogs came up empty in the theater. Four minutes left, a hundred men still to search, and the thinking is the bombers may have hidden in the hotel. "Not looking good," Hamill said, and from the glares the remark drew, Savella was certain he wasn't the only one who thought the captain sounded almost relieved.

At the two-minute mark, the radio squawked one more time.

"Got them," a flat voice said.

Two Cubans, just like the priest said: Guillermo and Tomas, not a lick of English, but all smiles and handshakes, didn't have a clue what was under their coats.

The bomb squad was working on it, but they needed a bit more time. Feidy would have to stall.

The music in the limousine suddenly stopped in the middle of "Hakuna Matata." Feidy lifted her head. Savella scrambled up next to her. Deets was still behind the wheel, his body twisted toward the rear. The gun was in his right hand. He pointed it toward the back and fired once, the muzzle flash lighting up the car's interior.

"Oh shit," said Feidy.

"Did he shoot them?" Hamill yelled.

"He shot *something.*"

The gun still in his right hand, Deets got out of the limousine holding the little boy, who was sobbing uncontrollably. Feidy climbed over the wall.

"What happened in there?" she said, struggling to stay calm. "Is everyone all right? What was that?"

"You think I'm kidding here?" Deets shouted. "You want to play games?"

"I thought we were waiting for my boss."

"I told you fifteen minutes."

"Is the girl all right? Let me see the girl."

Deets pressed the gun barrel into the boy's cheek.

"I need to see the girl," Feidy said.

"And I need to get out of here." Deets raised the gun and gestured at the seawall. "And they better stop pointing those things."

Up and down the seawall the officers had drawn their weapons and trained them on the car. "Down, put them down," Feidy called out, and moved along the line until the weapons disappeared. "OK, now, is she all right, Mr. Deets?"

"Where's your boss?"

"On his way."

"Get him here."

A radio squawked. A moment later Hamill's head warily rose above the wall. "Sylvie."

Feidy looked over her shoulder at the captain and raised an eyebrow. He nodded. She took a deep breath and turned back to Deets.

"OK, here's where we are," she said. "We got the bombs, both of them. That's over."

Deets flinched. "You're lying."

"Why would I want to do that? We got them. Two Cubans, right? Am I right? Guillermo and Tomas. The bombs were under their coats, right? Guillermo and Tomas."

Deets tightened his grip on the boy and glanced around the porte cochere, his gaze lingering on the police cars blocking both ways out. He moved the gun to his left hand. With his right hand he drew a black Nokia cell phone from his pants pocket and shook it in Feidy's direction.

"You just killed a lot of people."

"No, I—"

He lifted the phone and pressed a thumb against the keyboard.

For several seconds, there was silence. Then, very faintly, a cell phone began to ring. Feidy turned quickly to Hamill, who offered a bewildered look and shook his head. The ringing continued: a harsh, insistent *brrng brrng, brrng brrng*. The detective ran along the seawall, desperate for the source. Suddenly she stopped and listened. *Brrng brrng, brrng brrng*. Feidy dipped her hand into the pocket of her blazer and extracted a gray Samsung, the red-white-and-blue of the Cuban flag filling the screen. She held it up for Deets to see.

"It's over, Elmer. Somebody screwed you. Let's end this before anyone else gets hurt."

Rage engulfed Deets. His sweaty face turned a dark red, and the gun in his left hand began to shake slightly. He ended the call on the Nokia, then pressed Redial again. After a few seconds, the phone in Feidy's hand began to ring once more. Deets threw his phone to the ground. He moved the gun to his right hand and hoisted the boy even higher. "You watching now?" he yelled at Feidy and jammed the gun barrel into his hostage's temple.

A dull crack.

Deets's body jumped, then stiffened, and a red splotch appeared in the middle of his forehead. The gun fell from his hand and skittered under the limousine. He sank slowly to the ground, his legs bent awkwardly under his massive torso, his left arm still wrapped around the boy. As he finally collapsed, the child rolled off his chest and began to crawl back toward the open car door.

"Oh man, oh Jesus, Tony, did you get that?" the television reporter shouted, slapping his cameraman on the back. "Oh man, please tell me you fucking got that. Oh Jesus."

Feidy drew her service revolver and ran toward the car. She leaned down and felt Deets's neck for a pulse, then quickly searched him, gingerly passing her hand over his body. Satisfied that he was dead, she holstered her gun and reached for the sobbing boy, shielding him from the sight of the dead man as she wiped a wisp of Deets's blood from his cheek. She handed the boy to an ambulance attendant who had sprinted forward, then moved to the limousine and opened the rear door. Inside, still strapped in her car seat, sat the little girl, shocked into silence and clutching a doll, but very much alive. Deets's bullet had torn a large hole in the upholstery a few feet from her head. Feidy lifted the girl and her doll out of the car, and another ambulance worker raced over to hustle her away.

The driveway quickly filled with policemen. Feidy raised a hand and shouted for quiet.

"Who shot him?" she called out. The milling officers exchanged blank looks, then turned back to the detective and waited, as if she had been conducting a test and would be supplying the answer at any moment.

But Feidy wasn't paying attention to them anymore. She was focused on the edge of the crowd, on a tall patrolman with a chiseled body and hair the color of straw.

"Malinowski!" she yelled. "Where the hell is my priest?"

# 49

Room 617 smelled of furniture polish and air freshener. Unused hangers lined the closet, pristine white towels were stacked in the bathroom, and the soap on the sink hadn't been unwrapped. The brown suitcase still lay atop the luggage rack.

On the third floor of the garage, the Chevy pickup was still parked crookedly in a space half a row from the elevators, Big Mac boxes cluttering the floor. No one had come near it, said the cop in the car at the end of the aisle, who looked as if he might pass out from the fumes.

Savella and Feidy spent an hour watching the lobby, but they both knew it was useless. Remsen was gone in the night. Too many questions, and he didn't want to answer them.

Savella wanted to go home. Feidy wasn't sure, but he insisted. It was safe now. The threat to his life had ended with the bullet that took down Deets; it was time to get on with things. In the end the detective wasn't in the mood to argue. A night's work still lay ahead: a dozen phone calls to put out an alert for Remsen, a stack of paperwork. If Savella didn't think there was a danger, she wouldn't try to talk him into it.

"But at least I'm going to get you home in one piece," she said, pointing to her car. "Then you're on your own."

It didn't hurt that the pageant went on as scheduled. Deets's body still lay on the pavement when Bottach came rushing up to Hamill. "Can we get this thing wrapped up? No reason we gotta lose a whole Saturday night." Feidy looked at him as if he were crazy, but Hamill, beaming, in command again, quickly agreed. Deets was dead, the Cubans were in custody, the bombs were on their way to the police range to be destroyed. The dogs had been through the theater twice and found nothing. No reason to lose a whole Saturday night.

"I don't know what this was all about tonight," Hamill said when Feidy objected, "but how about we don't let the bastards win?"

And why would there be any question, Sylvie thought as she listened to Hamill work out the details. Of course it was a night for a show. Go shopping, someone famously declared after the country was attacked, and what was this compared to that? It was the new bravado, the way we lived now. *Don't let the bastards win.* Especially if there was money to be made.

OK, the pageant contestants might be a little unhinged. But you need to put life on hold if you want to be a star. So you sing a little off-key, stumble through the tap. The important thing is, the show goes on. The hallways are crawling with cops, but the show goes on. A few more empty seats than you might have expected—some people have less bravado than others, it turns out—but the show goes on.

"Wouldn't have made any difference, even if we hadn't found him," Feidy told Savella on the drive home. "The bomb guys say the devices weren't set up to explode."

"What do you mean?"

"Someone had gone to a lot of trouble to put them together. Expert work, sophisticated. But then for some reason, they forgot to wire up the trigger. They left the crucial connection undone. And they programmed in the wrong phone number."

"Maybe amateurs after all," Savella said, staring out the window.

"Maybe," Feidy said, "or maybe somebody just didn't want to kill tonight."

They were pulling up in front of Savella's house when her phone rang: the dogs sniffed out a body in an out-of-service bathroom. Paperwork, a multistate alert for a missing priest, and now another victim. Feidy sighed. The night had just gotten longer.

"You take care of yourself, Michael," she said. "But you'll understand if I say I hope I never see your face again."

He let himself in from the driveway and walked into the kitchen. Dirty coffee cups lay on the counter. Was it only that morning that he'd been awakened by a phone call and heard the police in the other room? He washed up quickly and moved to the living room. The house felt close, as if it had been shuttered for a long while. He cracked a window and stood for a moment, letting the night breeze cool him. It felt good and he threw open the front door.

A small manila envelope fell into the room. He picked it up: his name in block letters, no postage, no postmark. He ripped open the flap and held the envelope over the sofa; a white tape cassette tumbled out.

Savella walked out on the porch. The lights next door were blazing.

---

Mrs. DiLorenzo answered before the doorbell chime died away, dressed in a sweat suit with ruby-red bands running the length of the arms and legs. Evening wear, Savella decided.

"Oh no." She tried to shut the door in his face. "No, no, no, no."

He blocked the door with his knee. "Just one more time, Mrs. DiLorenzo. It's important."

"I saw the paper this morning. I don't want you anywhere near me."

"They got the guy, Mrs. DiLorenzo. No one's after me. They got him. The police did."

She dragged on her Kent and frowned. "When?"

"A little while ago. It's all over now." He held up the cassette with a half smile. "Like I said, it's kind of important."

Mrs. DiLorenzo had been reading. Her glasses lay on a TV tray table next to an overturned paperback and a plate with a piece of well-done steak and a small pile of string beans. A musty smell hung in the air, familiar: wet cardboard. Savella looked around the room. Two flattened shoe boxes had been taped in the window to replace a missing pane.

"The rain the other night," Mrs. DiLorenzo said. "My nephew's supposed to get to it this weekend."

He waggled the cassette. "I'll just take a quick listen here and get out of your way."

The boom box hadn't been moved. Savella inserted the tape and pulled a notebook and pen from his pocket.

Mrs. DiLorenzo sat in a wooden chair and waited for the curtain to rise. Savella pressed Play and bowed his head.

The tape ran about five minutes. When it clicked off, his mouth was dry and his heart was pounding. He quickly rewound it and pulled it from the machine. Mrs. DiLorenzo stood.

"More friends playing jokes?"

"Yeah. I guess so," Savella said, but even he realized how hollow that sounded now.

"I don't like that. The stuff they were talking about."

"Join the club, Mrs. DiLorenzo."

She squinted at him. "You mocking me?"

"No, no."

"Because if you're mocking me…"

"Just some friends. That's all. A stupid game."

"I don't think so. Not even a little bit." Her voice was hard, the way it had been the first time he heard her shouting at the Hispanic kids. "All that swearing. People talking about guns. Don't sound like any joke I ever heard."

She stomped to the door and yanked it open. "I knew I shouldna let you in here. You don't come around no more. You come over here again, I'm calling the cops."

Savella nodded and walked out.

"You hear me? I'll call the cops."

The door slammed shut. He stood for a moment, then slipped down the front steps.

*I'll call the cops.*

Too late, Mrs. DiLorenzo. A long time too late.

# 50

Six hours now and the man had not moved. Five beers and not a single trip to piss. Never touched the bowl of nuts inches from his left hand. Just sat there, the muscles in his jaw clenching and relaxing, clenching and relaxing. What was it with these army guys?

Neil looked around the room. The evening ferry rush had come and gone, the ten o'clock invasion by the after-dinner crowd was starting to thin out. An unpleasant night, not least because of the shit he'd taken from too many people about his strange taste in television. *A beauty pageant.* Neil had considered turning it off more than once, even walked down to the end of the bar to broach the subject, but always the eyes turned him around. Wasn't just him either. At the height of the evening, barely room to stand, forget sitting, and the stools on either side of the colonel had remained empty. Almost like the guy had a force field working.

Anyway, it was over. Miss Something-or-the-other wore the rhinestone crown, had the tear thing going as she waved. That was it, right? Couldn't be some goddamn postgame show, not for this shit. A few more minutes and he could switch it off.

He squinted down the bar. The colonel's beer was almost empty. Neil finished pouring three vodka tonics for the girls in the window table, a little heavy on the

Gray Goose, you never know, and left them on the service bar for the waitress. He watched one of the frat boys stagger toward the bathroom in the rear, then pulled a Budweiser from the cooler.

"OK if I turn this TV off now, Colonel?" he shouted over his shoulder. He cracked open the beer and turned to deliver it.

The man was gone. Neil peered out the front window. The street outside the Iguana was empty. He scanned the bar. The frat boy was weaving his way back to his table. "Anybody else in there?" Neil asked. The frat boy shook his head.

The colonel had disappeared. The only hints of his evening-long siege were a pack of Camels, an empty silver money clip, and a Bud bottle sitting in a puddle of beer. Three damp singles and a handful of change were shoved into the bar gutter.

Neil scooped up the money, tucked one dollar in the tip jar, and pocketed the other two bills. He lifted the money clip and studied it. An etching of an American flag on one side, the colors faded; an eagle on the other. Sterling silver—must be worth something. The colonel would be back for that. But who used a money clip anymore?

Ex-army, he thought as he dropped it in the tip jar. What was it with these guys?

# 51

The ferry left the dock in Red Hook at sunset. Savella stood at the rail on the upper deck and watched the first red and orange streaks wash the western sky. The U.S. Virgin Islands—a long way to run, but still America. A strange choice for a career military man. Or maybe not.

The trip was a gamble. Remsen could have headed south. On the other hand, Savella might find only a bitter old man with no interest in writing an ending to a family tragedy. He felt in his pocket for the last tape. He knew the way the story ended, or thought so. Someone here could tell him if he was right. And he wasn't sure which way he wanted it to come out.

Forty minutes later the ferry docked at Cruz Bay. Savella grabbed his overnight bag and dashed across the grass to a safari cab parked at the curb, the driver perched behind the wheel reading a paperback.

"Can you get me here?" Savella said, showing him the address Feidy had scribbled down on the back of an envelope.

The driver examined the scrawl. "Sure, Bordeaux Mountain. I can take you. Took someone else to that address just this morning."

Savella tossed his bag on the passenger bench. "A priest?"

"No, nothing like that. Just some beat-up guy looked like he hadn't slept in a while."

So it wouldn't be just a bitter old man after all.

---

The driver headed out of Cruz Bay and wound slowly into the hills along Centerline Road. Thick green tropical foliage shielded both sides of the road. As they climbed higher, the natural canopy broke open to stunning views of the Sir Francis Drake Channel, the running lights of the sailboats hurrying to port twinkling in the dusk. Near the peak the driver slowed and turned off the paved road and headed carefully along a rutted dirt trail. Just past a sign for a hike trailhead, he stopped at an open gate.

"This is it, through here," he said. "You'll be all right."

Savella paid the fare and got out. The cab bumped off toward the main road. When the taillights had disappeared, Savella walked cautiously through the gate, ignoring the Keep Out sign on the chain-link fence, and headed up the drive, crushed stone crunching underfoot.

A Jeep Cherokee was parked in a small oval fifty yards on, its windows rolled down. A terraced stone path lined with overgrown ferns and red hibiscus led from the parking area to a lily pond, overwhelmed by water lettuce, which lay amid a circle of long-neglected fruit trees. Beyond that lay Colonel Edward Remsen's hideaway, a large cottage tucked into the hillside, surrounded by walls.

Savella approached the front door and listened. The drone of a television; he could just make out the sounds of a football game. He rapped on the door and waited in vain for a response. After a few minutes, he tried the handle and the door swung open.

"Hello?" he called out, and when there was no answer, he headed inside.

The house was decorated impersonally, as if someone had ordered several rooms of furniture without bothering to select any of the pieces. The wall art—seascapes, a tropical market, a star-studded sky—brought to mind a bargain-rate motel or a doctor's office. Ceiling fans whirred in every room; the stone floors were bare. The white cupboards in the kitchen were closed tightly, and the glazed tile countertops were clear save for a single empty beer bottle. The coffeemaker was at the sink, the remains of the morning's brew still filling the glass urn.

At one end of the great room, a large television hung on the gray lavender walls, Dolphins and Jets playing on the flat screen. A set of French doors lay open at the other end, sheer white curtains billowing in the evening breeze. The doors gave onto a large veranda, tiled with limestone and illuminated by outdoor lanterns that cast a soft glow over a teak rocker, two oversized armchairs, and a hammock, all positioned to offer views of the channel and, far on the horizon, the beguiling lights of Tortola, Norman Island, and Virgin Gorda.

At the edge of the veranda, a body lay on its back. Savella walked over and knelt down by the corpse: an old man, his crew cut flecked with gray, two icy blue eyes wide open to the night sky. Savella carefully pushed the man's chin to one side. A gaping hole, sticky with blood, had been blasted in the side of his skull.

A chair scraped against the tile. Savella jumped to his feet and whirled around. Father Remsen sat in the weak light, a black Colt .45-caliber automatic with a worn brown stock lying in his lap. A half-empty bottle of Crown Royal sat on the table next to him. The priest had not changed his clothes since the day before. His blue windbreaker was unzipped to reveal the buttonless shirt; the laces of his sneakers were undone. Savella eyed the .45 and moved a few steps from the body.

"I knew you'd come," Remsen said. "I wish you hadn't. The tape should have been enough. But I guess I knew it wouldn't be."

"And it's not," Savella said cautiously. He pointed down at the body. "This is your father?"

"Yes."

"I'm sorry," said Savella.

Remsen shrugged and lifted the bottle to his lips and drank.

"Have you called anybody?"

"Whatever would be the point?" Remsen asked, placing the bottle back on the table.

"They're looking for you in New Jersey."

Remsen said nothing.

"Where'd you learn to shoot like that?"

Remsen looked at his father's body. "You grow up around it. You don't have any choice." His voice was flat, not a hint of emotion.

"A *priest*, though," Savella said.

"It was the right thing to do. Like putting down a mad dog. Deets would have killed the boy. Among many other people. He had already killed my friend."

"The man they found in the bathroom?"

"His name was Abel Garcia. I found the body. Took the gun from Abel's belt." He lifted the Colt. "A gun just like this one. One of the many ways they bonded, Abel and my father. Abel Garcia. A good man who wound up with some bad people."

"Like your kids."

Remsen's lips parted in a slight sad smile. "Like my kids, he was a prisoner of his history. And there is always someone around to take advantage of that." He drank from the bottle again. "When you get back, go see a man named Enrique Pena. Ask him what he knows about Abel."

Savella pulled a small voice recorder from his overnight bag.

"No." Remsen waved the gun at him. "No tapes. Too many tapes already."

"All right." Savella dropped the recorder back in the bag. "Can I make a few notes?"

Remsen's face hardened. "Just *listen* to me."

It was several minutes before he spoke again. "Enrique Pena. A casino owner in Nevada. Before Castro, his family ruled Cuba. And they want to go home. Go see Pena. Ask him what he's done with Abel Garcia. Pena and Deets. Pure evil. No matter the motives."

"Still," said Savella. "A priest."

Remsen looked up. "He was about to take more lives. What would you have done?"

"And your father?"

"I came down to finish it. Couldn't let him loose anymore. But he beat me to it."

His eyes on the gun, Savella walked slowly to Remsen, drew the tape from his pocket, and placed it on the end table. He reached into his bag and withdrew the Night Out photograph and laid it next to the cassette. Remsen picked up the picture and examined it closely for several minutes.

"So young," he said finally. "We were so very young."

He handed the photograph back to Savella and got to his feet, the automatic still in his hand. He picked up a blanket from the hammock and gently placed it on his father's corpse, stretching it to reach from head to toe, then tucking in the edges.

"Sometimes, especially when you're young, you think you can deal with anything," he said, his voice barely audible. "And then comes the day you find out there are things you can't deal with, you cannot handle. And right there, at that moment, everything changes."

Remsen turned and motioned toward the chair next to his. This would take a little while.

# 52

Irish twins, born eleven months apart, Dad not very interested in waiting one minute longer after Mom made the mistake of giving him a daughter. Always close, Joey and Mary clung together even tighter those last few months, when their world started spinning off its axis.

The family fell apart the moment the steel-gray staff car pulled up outside their bungalow in Phnom Penh to hustle them out of the country. The sudden departure—one bag, no pets, no good-byes—shocked Mimi and the kids, and by the time they arrived in Texas, exhausted and bewildered, she and the colonel were at war. The small-town girl had thought the gallant young soldier would show her the world; he confined her instead to a string of dreary army bases and the company of fawning young men. Now she wanted her turn. Her future brimmed with possibilities, his was uncertain at best, and they fought constantly about which course to follow. Joey could tell when a storm was approaching. His mother would turn sarcastic; his father's thick eyebrows would contract, hooding his cold blue eyes; and Joey knew it was time to get out of the water. He and his sister would flee to their bedroom, where they would cower through the night, recoiling at the sound of shattering china.

Searching for gas money one morning, Mom discovered condoms in her husband's wallet. She was gone a few days—pizza every night while Dad worked the Crown Royal—and when she returned with a new hairstyle and a jade ring, he threw her out, told her to take the girl too.

*The girl.* And Mary wept.

But for Joey those months in Texas really were the best. In Cambodia he had seen his father only when the colonel called him out to the jungle on "temporary assignment." Now he had him all day, every day. Dad would drop him at school each morning, turn up at baseball practice every afternoon. He taught him to box, they talked about girls. On weekends Joey buzzed around his father's army friends, and met an enigmatic young Cuban named Abel, only a few years Joey's senior but so much more worldly. Abel, he was sure, had killed men.

And quickly it was his turn to draw blood. Dad took him hunting every Saturday, and he would never forget the approving smile and the touch of his father's hand after he dropped his first whitetail buck at seventy-five yards one frosty dawn.

"You got a knack for this," the old man purred, and in the glow young Joey forgot all about the rest.

Not Mary, though, never Mary. She was always in the back of his mind. And always the same image, soft and shimmering, a movie scene shot through gauze: the evening she danced in candlelight for the little prince in Phnom Penh—the *robaim choun por*, the blessing dance—swathed in sequined lamé, more beautiful than anything Joey had ever seen, before or since.

The idyll ended with the summer. Dad woke him early one morning. "Your mother has died," he said, as if he were ordering a sandwich. "We're going to get your sister."

The son in silent mourning, the father grumbling about the inconvenience, they pushed north in the mud-caked Dodge, arriving at dawn at the house of a family who had taken Mary in. She appeared on the second-floor landing, half-asleep, and descended slowly, wary of what awaited her at the bottom. At the foot of the staircase, she kissed her brother's cheek, and he glanced toward his father for a nod before hugging her. With muttered thanks, they were gone.

They returned to Texas in a hurry, driving all day and all night, their father in a frenzy, trying to outrace the past. In the backseat, Mary slumped against the door, staring impassively at the passing landscape. Joey sneaked peeks at her, marveling at how much older she seemed after their brief separation. Two days later Joey and Mary said good-bye to their mother in an overheated funeral parlor just down the road from Fort Hood. The crematory workers were sidling toward the wooden casket even before the base chaplain had finished his words of comfort, but no one tried to stop them. Mary cried quietly throughout the service. Joey and his father stood off to the side, dry-eyed. It wasn't that he didn't love his mother, Joey told himself; of course he did. It was just that the woman lying in the coffin, by his father's telling, was not the same person who had given him the gift of life.

The Remsens squeezed together in a small bungalow in a long row of small bungalows, government-issue furnished down to the toilet paper. The urn containing Mimi Remsen's ashes sat on the kitchen windowsill until one day it didn't, and Dad never explained where it had gone. He was hardly there, working all day, returning home long enough to see to the opening of the proper cans for dinner, then slipping out the back door for an evening with Mrs. Gregoire, the redhead next door whose husband was stationed overseas.

Joey scooted along in his father's shadow, ear cocked for an order, ready to act on a raised eyebrow. Mary ridiculed him—*you're like a little puppy.* She and her father were oil and water. He kept her on a tight leash, with surprise room inspections and punishment for the slightest disorder. She could leave the house only for school, or visits to the library, or to do the household shopping. She hated the man, and made little attempt to conceal it. And Joey could understand her feelings: forbidden to wear jewelry, forced to pull back her hair in a frumpy clip, lights out at ten, no television, the stacks of 45s she lugged south stashed in the closet.

Three times that fall their father went out of town, leaving them under the reluctantly watchful eye of Mrs. Gregoire, whose idea of dinner was bourbon. Each time he came back, inspected his children, then returned to the Gregoire bungalow, where, through the open window, they could hear her moaning as he thanked her in bed. Each time Mary sat silently in an armchair, her body twisted in anger, until they heard his footsteps on the sidewalk.

The breaking point came when he used the insurance money to buy an airplane, a Piper Apache. Mary hated the plane, its ghoulish provenance. Their father christened it *American Patriot,* paid the gas attendant three dollars to emblazon the name on the fuselage. But Mary called it "*Mama,*" as if they needed reminding that Daddy's toy had come at a price. When she wouldn't stop one blustery morning, her father turned to her, his face boiling.

"I should have left you in the cornfields," he whispered.

In late October he disappeared for almost two weeks, "too goddamn long," Mrs. Gregoire reminded them every evening through a cloud of cigarette smoke. When he returned, there was a tension about him that took them by surprise. Every little thing seemed to set him off, until Joey and Mary took to hiding in their bedrooms as soon as they arrived home from school, emerging only to rush through evening meals eaten in silence. When he came home one Tuesday and announced they were flying to Dallas the next day, neither child asked a single question.

That night they heard him again through the open window, trying to entice Mrs. Gregoire to keep Mary while he and Joey were gone, but she was having none of it.

"I got a family already, Eddie," she said. "I don't need your leftovers."

In the morning Joey was packed and ready to go even before his father came to his room to get him. Mary was a problem. Her bag lay empty on the chair where her father had dropped it the night before. She was curled up on her bed, staring out the window, still in her pajamas.

"Mary, let's go," he snapped. "And pack a dress."

She moved closer to the glass until her breath fogged the pane.

"Mary. *Now.*"

"What about Thanksgiving?" she asked, as if she were conducting a negotiation.

"What about it? We'll be back." His biting tone ended the discussion.

The flight was uneventful, Dad at the controls of the Piper, Joey at his side, Mary crammed in the tight quarters behind them, another reason she hated it.

"Good old Mama," she said loudly enough as she squeezed in, and to Joey's amazement, this time she got away with it.

The plane touched down at midafternoon. While Joey and Mary sealed up the Piper, their father walked to a hangar and a few minutes later reemerged behind the wheel of a white Buick for the trip into town.

He had reserved a room at the Fremont, a dump on a sketchy street downtown. Nightclubs lined the avenue, the lights of their marquees extinguished in the cold daylight. A few delivery trucks were parked along the curb, but the only sign of life was a group of women in tight skirts clustered on one corner. The lobby of the Fremont was just as dead—a clerk huddled behind iron bars, an old man snoring in an armchair, the receiver of the pay phone off the hook, swinging from side to side.

The clerk appeared surprised by the new arrivals.

"You sure you want to stay here?" he asked, juggling the room key from hand to hand.

"That's right," Dad said.

"With them?"

"They're *my* kids." That tone again, and the key slid across the desk.

The room on the third floor was a dingy hole: Joey would bunk with his father, Mary got her own bed. Loud, raucous music poured through the thin walls. The kids lay awake all night; Dad slept like a baby. In the morning he told them he'd be back for dinner, gave them five dollars, and disappeared again. At a diner on the corner, they ate greasy eggs under the eye of a gruff counterman who asked them where they were staying and told them he would walk them back when they were finished.

"Not really a place for a young lady," he said, glancing around at the haggard women in last night's make-up, the men nursing hangovers and scratching through the ashtrays for a salvageable butt. Returning to the room, they double-locked the door and hunkered down to wait.

Their father fetched them around seven, told them to dress for dinner. An hour later they were a world away: the opulent Century Club of the Hotel Adolphus, squeezed around a plush red-leather banquette with a shy young woman with a ghostly complexion who didn't seem to speak much English, a bubbly blonde in fur who draped herself over their host, a short man named Jack with slick hair and a gangster's demeanor, and, to Joey's delight, Abel Garcia, his father's protégé, the mysterious young Cuban with the distinctive mustache.

Dinner was slabs of beef, parfait glasses stuffed with cold shrimp, beer for the men, French wine for the ladies. The talk was of betrayal—Diem murdered in Vietnam, freedom fighters abandoned on a Cuban beach—and the devil behind the treachery, the president of the United States. Kennedy and his wife would be in Dallas the very next day, a visit Dad seemed to regard as a personal affront. He dominated the conversation, railing against Communism, attacking Kennedy—and always *Kennedy*, never *President*—for his failure to confront the enemy. When his father paused for breath, Joey picked up the slack, on cue, of course, from the ringmaster. He had learned the lessons by rote, on Saturdays in the woods in search of game, in the car headed home after football, and he recited his lines flawlessly, *always Kennedy, never President*. At the end, the reward: the

oh-so-rare smile of approval that Joey had seen twice before—the afternoon he soloed in the Piper, and the day
he brought down the deer.

But Mary couldn't leave it alone. She dipped a
shrimp in cocktail sauce and took a delicate bite.

"Well, I don't care what any of you think," she said.
"President Kennedy's doing just fine. Maybe it's time
we looked at things a little differently. Maybe"—and she
fixed her father with a defiant glare—"maybe it's time
for young people to run things. And I love his wife."

Joey heard his mother. So, apparently, did his father.

"You shut up now," he snapped. "You keep that crap
to yourself."

Jack coughed, once. The blonde in fur poked a fork
at her baked potato. The shy woman with no English
chewed on an ice cube. Abel picked a piece of gristle
from between his teeth.

It was the house photographer who changed the
subject, popping up at the table and asking, "Anyone
for a picture?" Grateful for the distraction, they moved
glasses, shoved ashtrays aside, peeked at faces in compact mirrors, straightened tie knots. Just before the
shutter snapped, Dad got up and stood off to the side
of the banquette and motioned to Joey to do the same.
As the bulbs flashed, the two Remsen men stood like
sentries, just out of camera range.

"What are you worried about, Eddie?" their host
said. "A picture for the girls. That's all."

Later, as the party broke up, the camera girl came
over with the photographs in cardboard folders. "On
the house," their host said, and when her father turned
away, Mary grabbed her copy and stuffed it in her purse.

Dad, Abel, and Joey returned Mary to the hotel, then
headed down the street to a door between a parking

garage and a diner. Up a narrow flight of stairs was the Carousel Club: a five-piece band playing show tunes in a corner of a wooden stage; women in heavy makeup gyrating along three runways as they stripped down to pasties and G-strings; men chatting up B-girls hustling cheap champagne; a giant painting of a gold stallion hanging from the ceiling.

Jack, their dinner host, greeted them at the door, a yipping dachshund at his heels. "Got a table for you up front," he said. "What are you drinkin'?"

"Crown Royal for me and Abel. And bring my son a beer."

*A beer.* In a daze Joey slid into his ringside seat. The busty blonde on the runway plucked the elastic band of her panties between her thumb and forefinger and, with a wink at Joey, tugged slowly as the crowd whooped. Jack leaped to his feet.

"That's enough of that, Jade," he screamed. "You trying to close me down? Fucking girls. All's I need is the morals squad in here again." His dog barked. "Shut up, Sheba," he muttered, and the dachshund fell silent.

The shy woman from dinner appeared at the table, out of her evening clothes now, wearing tight black slacks and a low-cut white blouse that offered Joey a glimpse of something he'd never seen before. "Ed-die," she said haltingly, with a pout.

"Not now, Lana," his father said, and he glanced quickly at his son. "Jack, let's talk in your office. Joey, you wait here. And leave the girls alone, all right?" He rose, chuckling, and the three men walked away.

Lana drifted to the bar. The strippers soon went on break, followed to the stage by a mediocre magician who rushed through his act to jeers.

Forty-five minutes later his father, Jack, and Abel resurfaced in the back, accompanied by a slender young man who leaned into Abel's ear, talking rapidly. At the bar a woman yelled, one man shoved another, and the room was suddenly a blur of flailing arms and falling bodies. At the sound of broken glass, the magician dropped his handkerchief and dashed backstage. Customers sitting at the tables nearest to the bar spilled their drinks in their haste to avoid the mayhem.

Attempting to steer clear of the melee, Dad was knocked to the floor and got up slowly, holding his right wrist. Jack and two customers waving badges and handcuffs flew into the middle of the fracas, and in a few minutes the battle was over, the instigators dragged to the exit and thrown down the stairs.

"And don't come back, you can't act like gentlemen," Jack screamed after them.

Dad inspected his wrist. "I think it's broken," he said. "Damn it."

"Hey, now." Jack examined the wrist. "A sprain, maybe." He waved to a waitress. "Honey, get us some ice."

Dad laid his arm gingerly on the table. "You see them back there?" he asked Jack. At the bar Abel and the man who had joined them after the meeting in the office were deep in conversation. "This Lee—the guy's got me spooked. You gonna watch him?"

"It'll be fine," Jack said.

Joey soaked it all in. His first beer, strippers, and a bar fight. A night to remember.

---

The mountain had come alive with crickets, nature's jazz, a soothing counterpoint to the hatred and violence that streaked the priest's tale. But so much had already seeped through, thought Savella, and so much more to come. He eyed Remsen through the shadows.

"Jack," he said.

"Yeah."

"Lee."

"Uh-huh."

"And his wife's cousin."

"Svetlana, yes. The star of Jack's amateur nights. My father's out-of-town trips weren't strictly business. Poor Mrs. Gregoire."

Savella leaned forward. "You wanted me to know all this. Why?"

The priest's right hand went to his face, covered his eyes.

"You found Mary. I didn't know what else you might discover. But I wanted you to know she was an innocent." For a moment Savella thought Remsen might cry. "I was her brother. This was the least I could do."

Savella touched his arm. "So let's finish it, Father. Help me understand."

---

It was after nine when Joey and Mary awoke the next morning. Water was running in the bathroom, and a few minutes later, the door opened and their father stepped out of a cloud of steam, his hair damp, a towel wrapped around his waist.

"Ready to go in five, breakfast in fifteen," he said. But Mary took her time, sorting through her suitcase for a half hour before finally choosing a white blouse and a beige jumper.

The morning brought rain, a chilly drizzle from an ugly sky. After checking out of the hotel and stowing their luggage in the trunk of the Buick, the Remsens ran down the block to the diner and crowded into a hard plastic booth, the counterman scowling at the father as he walked his children to the table. The waitress brought coffee and juice, and while they waited for their eggs, Dad opened the *Dallas Morning News*, wincing as he tried to turn the page with the fingers of his right hand. An advertisement paid for by something called the American Fact-Finding Committee covered the second page: a list of a dozen questions for President Kennedy, bordered in black, on the morning of his visit. Their father quickly scanned them, then tapped the paper with his spoon.

"What we were saying just last night," he said. "See what I mean?"

He pushed the paper toward Joey. A corner of the page slipped into his orange juice. "Read the second question. And the sixth."

The waitress returned with their orders, but Joey knew better than to start eating. He picked up the paper and began to read aloud: "'Why do you say we have built a "wall of freedom" around Cuba when there is no freedom in Cuba today? Because of your policy, thousands of Cubans have been imprisoned, are starving and being persecuted—with thousands already murdered and thousands more awaiting execution and, in addition, the entire population of almost seven million Cubans are living in slavery.'"

Joey began to cough and reached for his juice glass, then looked at his father.

"Go on, take a drink, it's OK."

He sipped some juice and cleared his throat and read the sixth question. "'Why did Cambodia kick the US out of its country after we poured nearly four hundred million dollars of aid into its ultra-leftist government?'"

"That one we understand, don't we, son?" Dad rubbed Joey's forearm, a reminder of a bond that had never been broken: human ears on a string, a drunk monkey named Penelope, a business trip to Saigon that turned into time to go—memories shared only by a father and his son. When Joey nodded, when the point had been driven home one more time, his father lifted his fork, and the two of them ate. Mary read the funnies and let her toast grow cold.

---

A few raindrops were still falling when they left the restaurant, and Mary tied a scarf around her hair as they walked back to the car. The radio blared when Dad turned the key: KRLD, live coverage of Kennedy's visit. Crowds at Love Field, warm smiles and applause, people lined up downtown all along the motorcade route waiting for a glimpse of their young president. "Put some music on or something," Dad said irritably, but every station Joey found was devoting the morning to the visitors, and his father finally had enough. "Just turn it off, then."

They drove in silence, in their familiar positions: Dad at the wheel, Joey next to him, Mary in the backseat. After ten minutes they pulled up in front of a two-story brick office building. "I'll be right back," Dad said, and went inside.

Joey switched the radio back on, skimming through the dial, looking for music.

"Did he say what we're doing?" Mary asked.

Joey shook his head.

"Hey."

He turned around and looked at his sister.

"We're never going back, you know."

He scrunched his face. "What are you talking about? Dad said Thanksgiving."

"Uh-uh. We're never going back." Her face brightened and she pushed open the door, held up her gray and silver Brownie. "Come on, take a picture of me." Joey got out of the car, she posed against the car fender, and he snapped the shutter.

Dad returned a few minutes later wearing leather gloves and a uniform with a shiny badge pinned above his right shirt pocket. Under his right arm was a long white flower box decorated with a wine-red bow. He opened the rear door and laid the flower box on the backseat, then examined his right hand, which was now badly swollen.

"Why are you in that uniform?" Joey asked.

"Doing some work for the police. Security for the motorcade."

"The *president?*" Mary asked, her face breaking into a real smile for the first time in weeks.

"Kennedy."

"What's in the box?" Joey asked.

"Never mind." Dad got behind the wheel. "Just leave it alone."

But when he turned his attention to the traffic, Mary quietly lifted a corner and peeked inside, then looked to the front seat in bewilderment.

The sun finally broke through, filling the sky, a few stray clouds drifting east. They drove a few more blocks, then stopped along some railroad tracks. Dad switched off the ignition and pocketed the key. He turned in his seat and stared at Mary.

"You wait here," he told her.

"But I want to see—" she began, but the blackness quickly descended, the dark glower that Mary's voice always seemed to trigger in her father, the storm cloud that Joey had come to associate with the breaking of china.

But again Dad surprised him. He turned away without another word and got out of the car. "Joey, grab the box and come with me."

He walked down a deserted street that ran behind a low hillock. After a few dozen yards, they left the pavement and climbed to a copse of trees behind a stockade fence. Joey glanced through the slats in the fence. The hill sloped down to a broad, curving avenue that wound into an underpass topped by railroad tracks. People, a few of them carrying cameras, lined both sides of the street.

"What are they doing down there?" Joey asked.

"Kennedy," his father said,

Joey looked at him in surprise.

"He's coming right by here?"

"That's right. His motorcade." His father lowered himself to the ground. "Now we wait."

# 53

A luminous night, the lights of the British islands crystal clear across the channel. The palms rustled in a breeze that washed the veranda in the fragrant smell of jasmine. Remsen drank from the whiskey bottle; it was almost empty.

"You know the rest," he said.

Savella shook his head emphatically. "I want to hear it from you."

"It's not necessary."

"It is. I want to hear it. From you."

The priest's hand flew to his mouth. He took several deep breaths to steady himself, then waved toward the house. "I think I'm going to be sick." He rose, tucked the .45 in his belt, and walked unsteadily inside.

Savella sat back and considered his next move. Remsen had plowed through his story as if the slightest interruption would sap his resolve. But if the memories proved too painful, the priest's instinct would be to run for cover, as he had all his life. Don't give him a chance, Savella told himself. Don't let him back out now.

He picked up the tape, walked into the great room, and turned off the football game. A tape player sat on a set of rattan bookshelves. He inserted the cassette and pressed Play, increased the volume until it filled the house. Remsen wouldn't escape it, no matter how long he cowered in the bathroom.

A crackling sound, then a man's voice, muffled:

*"So, maybe we should begin."*

*"OK."*

*"Go ahead, then."*

*"Oh, Christ, I don't remember—"*

*"Bless me, Father..."*

*"Bless me, Father..."*

*"...for I have sinned..."*

*"...for I have sinned..."*

*"You really don't remember?"*

*"No."*

*"How long since your last confession?"*

A hacking cough.

*"That a joke?"*

*"No, I'm curious. In your line of work—"*

*"Hey, don't let's get carried away here. Can we get on with it? You may be a father, but you're sure as hell still my son."*

A snicker, then wheezing.

*"You all right?"*

*"I'm fine."*

*"The doctor said—"*

*"I said I'm fine. Let's get on with—"*

There wasn't time for all of this. Savella pressed Fast Forward, and the tape whirred ahead. Fascinating listening: murder and mayhem around the globe, women in every port. But that wasn't what the priest puking up his guts in the bathroom couldn't bring himself to say aloud. All that came toward the end. He stopped the tape and pressed Play, listened for a moment: still not there. Fast Forward again, another thirty seconds, then Play:

*"I guess the question I have is why. Me, I mean. Mary was Mary. But I was different. I, I, I was, you know, in training, you always called it."*

*"And look how well that turned out."*

*"Well enough, I guess."*

*"Give me a cigarette."*

*"The doctor—"*

*"Fuck the doctor, give me a cigarette."*

The scrape of flint against stone.

*"So what is this all about? Now you regret it? Is that what you want to tell me?"*

*"Of course I do. Of course I do."*

A chair moved.

*"That's bullshit. Someone got in your head. I wonder who the fuck that was. Listen, that book of yours ain't gonna save your ass now."*

*"Sit down. Come on, sit down. We're just talking here."*

Cloth rubbing against metal.

*"So this was your idea from the beginning?"*

Voices instantly clearer.

*"Your plan? Starting way back?"*

*"Let's don't start cleaning this up. You did what you had to do."*

*"I guess I did. Sit down. Come on."*

*"Yes, I guess you did. And you know why?"*

*"Uh-uh."*

*"Upbringing, that's why. Because you love your country. Because you love your country. The way you were raised."*

*"But why me? That's what I can't figure out. Why me?"*

*"We didn't want to miss. Now get me some ice cream. Vanilla."*

Remsen stumbled into the great room, wiping his mouth with a hand towel. Head bowed, he stood in the middle of the floor and listened.

*"But you never missed. You used to tell me that yourself."*

*"I hurt my hand the night before. That fucking fight. Could barely hold the weapon."*

*"So…"*

*"So, nothing. You were a better shot than I was. That day, anyhow."*

Savella switched off the tape, and they walked slowly back to the veranda.

# 54

The crowd had swelled, lining the street, sprawled on the grass. Peeking through the fencing, Joey noticed an older man standing on a concrete step off to his left, filming the scene with a movie camera. He turned in the other direction and slowly scanned the fence line.

*Mary.*

She stood on the knoll, her Brownie to her eye. Then, with a quick shake of her head, she scampered down the slope, crossed the street, and took up a position on the curb. A black woman in a red dress said something to her, and Mary laughed. Still wearing her kerchief, Joey thought, and he squinted at the bright sky. Like it's going to rain now.

"Anything?"

His father had joined him. Joey pointed at his sister.

"Goddamn it." His father looked up at the Hertz Rent-a-Car time-and-weather billboard on the roof of a building a few blocks away: 12:23 p.m. and 52 degrees. "God*damn* her."

In the distance, the sound of engines.

"We don't have time now," his father said, and turned away from the fence. In the shadow of the overhanging elms, he pulled a long rifle from the flower box and held it out with his left hand. "Joey, I got hurt last night. I thought I could do this when I got up this morning, but I can't grip anything. So you're going to have to help me today. If Abel were here, I'd ask him, but he's not. Can I count on you?"

*Beer, strippers, a bar fight. And now he would take Abel's place.*

"Sure, Dad. Whatever you need." Joey carefully cradled the rifle, just as he had been taught every weekend.

"It's loaded and ready to go, son. It'll be just like the woods. Like the deer. You remember, right? Take him in the head. One shot. Clean."

The rumble of motorcycles now, and faint applause and cheers.

"Who, Dad?"

Joey followed his father's gaze down the hill to the boulevard.

"Dad?"

"Remember what we were talking about last night, you and me and Abel? And this morning at breakfast? I need you. We need you."

Tears welled in Joey's eyes. "Dad, I don't want—"

"Stop that now. Stand up and be a man. Like Abel."

*Abel, he was sure, had killed men.*

The boy nodded silently, lifted the rifle to his shoulder, and stared through the scope at the street below. A white Ford drove into view, trailed by three police motorcycles. Behind them came a black Lincoln Continental limousine, American flags fluttering on the bumpers, Kennedy and his wife, resplendent in pink, in the backseat.

The rest of the motorcade spilled into the plaza—four more motorcycles, a second limousine, several cars, and two Continental Trailways buses with "White House Press" signs hanging from the sides.

"On my order," his father said, his voice low, tense. "Line it up, Joey. Just like I taught you."

Down the hill, a motorcycle backfired, and Joey was in the jungle again, Nathan and Steve and a case of franks and beans, and his first shot was whizzing past the frightened mules. *What are you afraid of?* And he fired again and again until the gun barrel sizzled and the magazine was empty. *Not afraid of nothing, sir.*

The limousine passed slowly, heading for the underpass. Joey tracked his prey, the rifle barrel locking onto the unsuspecting buck grazing in the woods. A squeeze of the trigger for the rarest of smiles.

"Do it," his father hissed. "Do it now."

A cherry bomb exploded in Joey's right ear, and the world went silent. A red halo formed around the president's head, a flash of pink swept the backseat, and the motorcade raced into the underpass.

Joey felt a hand rough on his shoulder. His father loomed over him, grabbing at the rifle, pulling at his sleeve, saying something Joey couldn't hear through the ringing in his ears. His father dropped the rifle in the flower box and scrambled down the hill, where he tossed it in a garbage bin. Joey slowly rose to his feet and looked down. People lay in the grass on both sides of the street. At the curb a young father had one arm over his little boy while he hammered the ground with his other fist. The black lady in red bent over and vomited. From somewhere came a solitary high-pitched anguished wail.

"Joey!"

He glanced over his shoulder. His father, waving him down.

"Mary…" he said, pointing behind him.

"She'll find us. Now move!"

Instead, Joey searched the pandemonium until he found his sister, riveted to the curb, her face twisted in horror. Her raincoat was unbelted; a grass stain was streaked across the beige jumper she had chosen with such deliberate care only a few hours earlier. In her hands was her gray-and-silver Brownie.

*We're never going back.*

She had been right after all.

His sister suddenly caught sight of him, and her mouth fell open. He beckoned frantically, but instead she began moving away, walking at first, then a slow trot, and finally running, streaking down the avenue, heading for the underpass and the safety of the dark.

"Mary," he moaned, an animal sound, then he was sliding down the hill.

# 55

The worst was out; the rest came quickly in a whiskey-slurred rush.

Joey and his father flew the Piper Apache to Honduras, the colonel's new posting—he'd known it all along. They were in Tegucigalpa for Act Two, when Jack Ruby silenced Lee Oswald in the basement of the Dallas police headquarters, and deep in the jungle for the denouement, spearing mystery meat from a rusted tin can over an open fire when a little boy saluted his father's coffin on a cold day in Washington.

Every night, the colonel would drunkenly boast about the greatest operation of his career. He and his comrades were killing angry over Cuba, expecting the worst in Southeast Asia, and the opportunity to do something about it fell into their laps. Six days before Kennedy's visit, the papers published details of the motorcade route, and a plan quickly came together. The colonel would do the shooting. Arturo Pena would bankroll the operation. Jack Ruby, whose anti-Castro mob bosses reviled the president, would find someone to take the fall.

The designated patsy was Oswald, the young man Joey had seen in the Carousel Club the night before the assassination. Ruby had met Oswald when he picked up his wife's cousin after her strip shift at the club. He enlisted the ex-marine with a promise to help him escape, and set him up on the sixth floor of the Texas Book Depository with a mail-order 6.5-mm Italian carbine with a four-power scope. Ruby also took it upon himself to make sure Oswald was dead before he got a chance to defend himself. He wasn't worried about the consequences. Once the police had the shooter and his gun, they'd close the books. And Ruby was confident of his hero status; no American jury would ever put him away for killing the president's assassin.

Remsen couldn't stop bragging, but it sickened his son. Joey was numb to the core. Every night in his dreams, he saw John-John saluting his dead father, heard a sobbing world mourning a fallen hero. Every night he watched Mary disappearing into the dark, disbelief on her face as she ran away. One morning it was too much and he flew north. A few months later, the doors to the seminary swung open, and Joey Remsen had at last found shelter from the shattering china.

Remsen lifted the Crown Royal bottle and drained it.

"Men become priests because they're called by God," he said. "I became a priest because I needed a place to hide. So it wasn't fair to stand up in front of a congregation and pretend I was something else. But the kids, they were easier. It was words, that's all. You hope somebody gets something out of it. Then you drink until you pass out and get up in the morning and talk some more."

One corner of the blanket covering the colonel had slipped off, exposing an ankle. Remsen got up and tucked it in.

"Where did the tapes come from?" Savella asked.

Remsen stood over the body, hands clasped in front of him. "He thought he was dying a few years ago. Had to go to Miami for an operation at the VA. So he sent for a priest. That would be me. I came down and talked to him. Put a recorder under my shirt. I suppose I wanted a record of the truth. And I suppose he figured that between blood and God, I'd keep the secret. Not to mention..."

His voice trailed off.

"That you pulled the trigger," Savella said.

Remsen said nothing.

"That first tape," Savella said. "It was postmarked in Philadelphia."

The priest nodded. "A colleague was heading east for a conference." He glanced at Savella. "A *real* conference in Philadelphia. I asked him to drop it in the mail. At that point I was desperate to stay out of it. I just wanted to make sure Mary's name was clean."

"And the second tape?"

"I went by your house on the way out of town last night."

Remsen looked down again at his father's body.

"It was wrong. I was a priest and it was a confession. It went against everything the church stands for," he said. "I never meant to betray him. I thought I'd take this to my grave and let God sort it out. But then you found Mary. And now I'm back in that world again. And my father wants to know if she left something behind, a link to the assassination, because Pena's son and my father were trying to scare up a new war. They needed to make sure there was nothing out there. I decided this time I would say no. Couldn't do it then. But I could do something now."

"So, your father, Pena's father, Abel Garcia, Ruby—that's it?"

Remsen shook his head. "Why does it have to be so complicated? Little people change history too. Especially if they're…"

He searched for a word.

"Crazy," Savella offered.

"Crazy?" The priest thought for a moment, then let it go.

Savella picked up Night Out. "One more question." He pointed to the ring on the finger at the edge of the frame—Eddie Remsen's hand, he knew now—the ring that hung from the priest's neck that afternoon on the Boardwalk.

"Oh," Remsen said. "My sackcloth and ashes. A gift from my father. It belonged to his father, and after… after we were through, he gave it to me. I kept it as a reminder. Of what I did. Of what I didn't do."

Sickening, Savella thought. A father turning his son to murder. And all because Kennedy turned his back on the exiles? Because he wavered on war in Southeast Asia? Different times, certainly: the missile crisis, the Cold War, dominoes falling in the Far East. No escaping the sense of impending catastrophe that engulfed the country. And the colonel had been on the front lines. But there could be no excuse for what he had done, what he had compelled his child to do to his country in the name of hate.

Remsen knelt beside the body, peeled back the blanket, made the sign of the cross on his father's forehead, then covered him again. He leaned back on his haunches and crossed his arms. Savella stood and joined him.

"So what do we do now, Father?"

The priest gazed at the lights on the horizon. "I don't know. I had hoped a lifetime of good would somehow make up for what I did. But it doesn't work that way. I killed a man. And I don't get to decide how to pay for that." He looked up at Savella. "That's what Mary wanted to tell me. That's why she tracked me through the years. She died before she could bring herself to reach out, but she left those two readings behind. Romans— don't take revenge, overcome evil with good. I think she was telling me she approved of the way I led the rest of my life. But Ezekiel—she wanted to say we get points for the good and we pay for the bad. And we don't get to pass it off on someone else. Even our fathers. That was Mary telling me I shouldn't pay for all of it, but I still had a mark on my blotter.

"Probably better readings she could have picked. She didn't know her Bible all that well. But she made her point."

He rose and dug a hand into his hip pocket. "I have my own picture, you know," he said. He pulled out a well-creased page torn from a magazine, the glossy image dulled by time. Even in the lantern light, Savella knew it immediately.

"The babushka lady," he murmured.

"Standing on the curb, waiting to take a picture," Remsen said. "A scarf on her head on a bright sunny day. Maybe she knew in her heart the storm hadn't passed."

He refolded the picture and carefully returned it to his pocket. For a moment he looked down at his father's body. Then he turned away.

"I need to use the bathroom again," he said, and staggered inside.

A broken man, Savella thought, ill-prepared for what came next: the investigations, the media storm, trials, prison or worse. An end to his cloistered life. Or maybe not. Maybe this had been Remsen's moment of truth. He had chosen Savella as his confessor, awaiting if not absolution, at least understanding. What if he never told this tale again? What could Savella do to force the issue? The pictures were intriguing curios, the tapes a jumble of confusion in which Kennedy's name was never uttered. Without Remsen's explanation, none of it meant anything.

*He told me he killed Kennedy.* When the laughter stopped, Savella would end up with cats. And Remsen would bend back into the farm, dish out bromides to street kids, and hope he got through to a few more before he called it a life. But would that be sufficient? After this long evening on the veranda, with his father dead at his feet, did Joseph Remsen still need something more? If not absolution, if not understanding, then at least penance. *I killed a man. And I don't get to decide how to pay for that.* What, then, would it take? The farm? Stopping Deets? Leading Mary, at long last, into the light?

Savella turned and peered into the house.

The priest had been gone awhile.

---

A gunshot. For a moment the hillside went mute, the night birds were quiet. Then one bird trilled, and another, and the symphony began again—life.

---

Savella found the telephone in the kitchen and dialed 911. No need to rush;

JosephRemsen knew his way around a gun

He hung up, walked through the slated vestibule, out the front door, and sat by the lilies, thinking of another pond a couple of thousand miles away. Where was she tonight, he wondered, what was she singing? Savella rubbed his eyes and fought off sleep. Weary, so very tired. But like those boats far below, heading for safe harbor now. He could feel it.

A siren wailed. Savella returned to the great room, pressed Play, and as the tape crackled to life, he leaned against the wall and slid to the floor.

*"Do you want to go back to your room?"*

*"So the fucking nurse can stick me with more needles?"*

A doctor's page, harsh over the public address system.

*"Are we done? Is that it?"*

*"What do you think?"*

*"Where's my penance?"*

*"I don't know. What do you think's appropriate?"*

*"How about some Hail Marys, a few Our Fathers, and don't do it again?"*

*"This isn't like you got caught peeking into the girls' locker room."*

*"Oh no?"*

*"Hasn't it been difficult to live with?"*

*"Nope."*

*"It has for me."*

*"You seem to do all right."*

*"Well, I have the church to fall back on, anyway. But it never goes away. Not for a single day. How about you? Don't you ever wonder? Lose sleep over it?"*

*"Not a wink. It was a war. You do what you need to do. I'd do it again in a minute."*

*"But you didn't do it the first time, did you?"*

The squawking of another PA announcement.

*"Sometimes, when it gets very bad, I sit by myself in a chair in my office, stare out the window at the cornfields, and wonder if I'm responsible for what came after. In obeying you, did I set it off? Was all this violence because of me?"*

*"Don't think so highly of yourself. It was one man. Just a man, that's all."*

*"But still. Did I start this mess?"*

Savella got to his feet and turned off the tape, ejected the cartridge and dropped it in his pocket, then walked back outside. Through the trees he could see flashing red lights on the dirt trail.

*Did I start this mess?*

The names flashed past: King, Bobby, Vietnam, Watergate. Just a man, but what had it meant? The end of innocence, the dawning of a crippling age of cynicism, the reluctant acceptance of limits.

*Did I start this mess?*

Footsteps in the gravel, and the crackle of police radios.

You're goddam right you did.

# 56

The detectives in Cruz Bay plied him with Cokes and mangos while they listened to his story, which they liked very much. A neat fit: a father plotting war and despondent when he failed, a son depressed about a friend's murder, tragedy in the hills high above the azure sea.

Two suicides. Case closed.

A few questions, though: How did the Reverend Joseph Remsen come to learn of the plot in Atlantic City? Who else was involved? How did Michael Savella know the priest would head for St. John? And what did they talk about, with an old man with a hole in his head lying at their feet?

Savella kept it tight:

Abel Garcia, I don't know, gut instinct, a life.

Not a word about assassination.

The detectives wanted to sleep on it. Savella took a suite at the Westin and gorged on room service and CNN. The day's shocker was the announcement that Elmer Deets had been gunned down by a Roman Catholic priest who fled the scene and flew to his father's home in the Virgin Islands. Now both men had been found dead, the bodies discovered by a former reporter—and Savella's face appeared on the screen, his employee ID photo from the *Post-Herald*—who was now in police custody. One hell of a jail, Savella thought as he finished his bacon cheeseburger and drank a beer.

Into the night, the pictures told the story: Deets and the boy crumpling to the pavement in front of the Sultan's Palace; two confused young Cubans being led away in handcuffs; a middle-aged Abel Garcia haranguing a tall redheaded reporter about the evils of Communism; Father Remsen playing basketball with his kids on the farm. Nice package, Savella had to admit, and he switched off the television and went to bed.

The next day Sylvie Feidy called her colleagues in St. John to clear Savella. She was winding up her investigation. Two schoolboys found Abel Garcia's gun in the bushes a few blocks from the casino. The Colt .45 was the weapon Remsen used to kill Elmer Deets, whose own gun fired the shots that killed Marek Ravic and Mary Bloom's neighbor. A knife found on Deets's body also matched Abel Garcia's fatal wounds. The two Cubans identified Garcia and Deets as their recruiters, but what led Deets to kill his accomplice was not known.

Deets, Garcia, and Edward Remsen. The attempted attack at the Sultan's Palace was the work of a fanatic Cuban exile, and a retired army colonel with a long-festering grudge, aided by a homicidal goon. No international conspiracy here. Good news all around, and it was left to the president himself, during an appearance with the prime minister of Denmark, to assure the people that they were safe.

"This time," the president said proudly, "the bad guys didn't win."

The detectives called the Westin; Savella was free to go. And not a mention, not one word, about assassination.

---

A chubby patrolman escorted Savella to Cyril E. King Airport on St. Thomas and sat with him while he awaited his flight to San Juan. Despite the president's assurances, the story continued to dominate the television screens. Fox News had Cubans lurking around the Liberty Bell. CNN said a Cardinals game in St. Louis was in the crosshairs. MSNBC reported authorities were on the trail of Cuban sappers who crossed the Canadian border. Security was tightened from coast to coast. A precaution, authorities called it.

Savella wanted to scream. The bad guys didn't win? Of *course* they did. They won every time you changed your plans because of some vague threat, every time you canceled a trip because a scratchy tape surfaced, every time you wondered what your neighbor was doing in his basement at one o'clock in the morning. The bombs didn't have to explode anymore. In this new age, the threat was all. Life, disrupted. Attention, paid. And they didn't win?

His flight was called. Savella shouldered his bag, shook hands with his escort. One thing was certain, he thought as he boarded the plane. No invasion of Cuba. And if Remsen was telling the truth, that was a colossal defeat for one man.

# 57

Mr. Pena was unavailable, his secretary said, but Savella was having none of that. Go tell him I was with the Remsens, he demanded. Go tell him there are tapes. And tell him I'll wait.

He listened to the Miramar's entertainment schedule twice before Pena picked up.

"Why should I care?" he asked.

Not a man who likes wasting time, Savella thought. Imagine how he felt when the bombs didn't go boom.

"Your name came up."

"My name?"

"That's right."

"I already talked to the police."

Unavoidable. His number in the phones of Garcia and Deets. But an easy explanation: Garcia was an old family friend. Deets occasionally did security work for Miramar. No idea what they were up to, not a blessed clue. And in the absence of anything else, that was good enough.

"The girl mentioned something about tapes," Pena said.

"There are tapes."

"What kind of tapes?"

"A conversation between Joey Remsen and his father. Actually, I guess you'd call it more of a confession. Joey being a priest, and all."

A long pause. On the other end of the line, a dog growled.

"A confession," Pena said finally.

"Something like that, yes."

"Why don't the police know about it?"

"How do you know they don't?"

Pena laughed. "Let's cut the bullshit, all right? You're looking for money."

"Nothing like that."

"Then what?"

"I just want to ask you some questions."

"Hang on."

The entertainment schedule again, but only once this time, and when Pena returned, his attitude had softened. He'd be in New York City in two days. They could get together, go over whatever Savella wanted to discuss. "How about we make it six? My office."

Uh-uh, thought Savella. Too many deaths for closed doors. Maybe that coffee shop on the East Side, where he spent those first drifting months after his return.

"Five o'clock," he said. "Kronos, at Thirty-Eighth and Lex."

"All right."

"You're going to need a description."

"Oh, no." Pena chuckled. "I don't think so."

---

Savella arrived fifteen minutes early, took a booth in the rear, and ordered a coffee. While he waited, he checked his cell phone for messages. Nothing from

Isabella. She had tried to reach him that horrible first day—*Michael, I hope you're all right*—and again when he was in the air between San Juan and New York—*The newspaper says you're in custody?* He was in the shower just that morning when she called a third time—*You still in St. John?* But her own phone wasn't working, so no way to call her back. He slapped the table in frustration.

At seven minutes past five, a black Lincoln Town Car eased to a stop at the curb, and Enrique Pena, tanned and rested, resplendent in a charcoal-gray suit, stepped out. He surveyed the street for a moment, then followed his bodyguard inside.

No hellos. No handshakes. No nice-to-meet-you smiles.

"Check him, Oscar," Enrique Pena said. The bodyguard sat next to Savella and threw a tree-trunk arm around his shoulders, an old friend hugging his pal, then went to work: patted down Savella's arms and chest, squeezed his crotch and thighs, a palm down both legs. Satisfied, he turned to his boss and nodded.

"Wait at the car," Pena said, and the bodyguard got up and left.

Pena looked out at the traffic rushing down the avenue. "New York City in autumn," he said. "I love it here."

"And yet," Savella said, "you live in Las Vegas."

"You don't know much about Vegas, do you?"

"I know it's not New York. Or Havana."

With a barely audible sigh, Pena slid into the booth across from Savella. "Why don't you tell me what else you think you know?"

Savella ran through Remsen's tale of intrigue. Pena reacted only once, a slight frown at the news that Garcia had tipped Remsen to the bomb plot.

The waitress brought over menus. "Can I get you something to drink?" she asked Pena. He ignored her.

She looked at Savella.

"I think what he meant to say was nothing for me, thanks," Savella said, staring at his tablemate. "I think what he meant to say was thank you anyway. Isn't that right, Mr. Pena? Was that what you were trying to tell the lady?"

The waitress frowned and walked away. Pena unfolded a paper napkin and laid it out in front of him.

"So you want to talk about Cuba, let's talk about Cuba," Pena said. "I read in a magazine, I don't remember which one, that the Castros got nine hundred million tucked away, more even than the Queen of England. Nine hundred million dollars, stashed in Switzerland." He refolded his napkin and placed it neatly to one side. "My father's money. But you know what's worse? They were so *bad* at it. They're dictators, they got the whole island for themselves for half a century, and only nine hundred million? With the sugar, the oil, a blank check from the Soviets? With the army, the secret police—only nine hundred million dollars?"

Pena picked up the silver creamer and played with the lid: *up, down, up, down, up, down.* The last time he raised the creamer to his nose and sniffed the contents.

"I'm gonna go down and spend some time with my old man. I want to know what he thinks about that. Not the cripple wasting away in a bed in Miami. Not him. I want to ask Don Arturo, the guy who decided with a flick of his fingers who would lead the nation and who would be dragged out by his heels. Nine hundred million? Don Arturo would spit his contempt."

The creamer again: *up, down, up, down, sniff.*

"OK then, your father." Savella reached into his jacket for Night Out and the photo of the young Colonel Remsen. "Abel Garcia worked for him. Did he know about Garcia's relationship with Remsen? Did he know what they were up to in sixty-three? Was he involved in their plot to kill President Kennedy?"

*Up, down, up, down, sniff.*

"How would I know? My father wasn't home much back then, and when he was, I was having my diapers changed. But please, don't take my word for it. Why don't you go ask him?" He raised a hand and feigned surprise. "Oh, that's right. Of course. He's sitting in a wheelchair in Miami, dribbling Jell-O in his lap. The green's his favorite. Know how they can tell? When they shove it in his mouth, he gurgles the loudest."

Savella tried again. "Your father bankrolled anti-Castro groups for years. We know this."

"So? That was my dad's thing, *la vuelta*—the return. I'm an American, remember?" Pena smiled. "What can I tell you? About a Cuban bomb plot, nothing. About Kennedy, I was a child back then. This is ancient history to me. That's what I can tell you. And if this is all you got, old pictures, some bullshit tapes, I mean, you're wasting my time."

*Up, down, sniff.* "This milk is bad," he said, and set the creamer on the side of the table. "So you solved the Kennedy assassination. Terrific. You know what the Kennedy assassination is today? A computer game. A fucking computer game. Forty-five bucks to some guy in Scotland, and you get to shoot the president yourself. See if you can do it better than Oswald. Or Remsen. Or whoever was up in that window or behind that hill. You hear what I'm saying? And what have you really got?

Three old men, two dead, and the other so out of it, he thinks he's still drinking daiquiris at the Floridita."

Pena reached across the table and grabbed Savella's right hand, squeezed until it hurt. "Everybody's got a story, Mr. Savella, and everybody gets to tell it. And after a while, it's all just so much background music. So call the FBI. Call the TV news. A few weeks of craziness, and then they lose your name."

He released Savella's hand and stood. "Cuban agents running around the country with dirty bombs. Now *that's* a story," he said. "The rest of this is history lessons."

Pena reached into his pocket, pulled out a wad of cash, and peeled off a hundred-dollar bill. "That's for your coffee," he said as the note fluttered to the table. "The rest is for the girl."

---

They put up the money, Savella thought as he watched Pena walk outside and slide into the Town Car. They put up the money and wait for blood to flow. They send boys with guns to fight their wars, boys with guns and not a clue in the world, no idea at all, about the chaos they will cause.

# 58

Isabella, finally, from the bottom of the well again, but better than nothing.

"Michael? Can you hear me?"

"Barely."

He was on the train back to Atlantic City, the gamblers' express.

"I've been calling and calling. All I get is your voice mail."

"I got your messages." A burst of static. "Can you hear me?"

"Yes. Are you OK? Where are you?"

"On the train."

"Where?"

"On the train. I was in New York."

More static, an impenetrable wall.

"Isabella, you there?"

Then they were in a tunnel and the connection was lost.

Savella nursed a scotch as New Jersey flashed by in the dark. Pena was probably right. But no easy way out this time. He would write the story.

He could already imagine the reaction. An FBI agent, more salt than pepper around the temples and talking about retirement, asks him some questions. A few days later, to no one's surprise, Page One across America, the tapes turn up on Remsen's farm, but nothing to tie Edward Remsen with Dallas. If that even was Edward Remsen on the tapes. The Pentagon confirms he passed through Fort Hood in November 1963, along with maybe ten thousand other soldiers. A yellowed flight log in a warehouse shows his Piper took off the day of the assassination, but just a coincidence: the colonel's orders had finally come through.

Arturo Pena is useless, Enrique pleads infancy. Congress announces hearings, but not until the FBI is finished. And that agent, the one with the questions? Gone fishing.

Now the storyteller becomes the story. Interviews with Brian and Diane and Scott. A press conference in Washington. Then Bill and Joe and Rachel and Lawrence and Reverend Al and Matt and Christiane and Bob and David take their bites, toss the leftovers out back when they're done.

It wouldn't be pretty. But Savella would write the story.

As he waited at the Westin, Savella had furiously scribbled down everything he could remember. Notes for a novel, for all it proved.

But Sylvie Feidy needed motive. Randall Emmons needed justice. Mary Bloom needed peace. So he would write the story.

Kennedy was dead, and so were the men who killed him. The world still turned. But not the same way it might have if none of this had happened.

So he would write the story.

## 59

Harold, good old Harold, gave her up without a struggle.

Tomorrow afternoon, car service from Philly. Home by five, the latest.

"Make sure you're waiting for her," Harold demanded. "Months now, been watching you two dance. Hell of a thing to waste, let me tell you."

"I don't plan to," Savella said. "I hope not, anyway."

"Hope," Harold said. "Well, we can always hope. Hey, remember now—she was gonna surprise *you*. I put up a fight, OK?"

Surprise *me?* Savella felt himself relax an inch.

---

The weather had finally turned, a mellow autumn reluctantly giving way to the first chill of fall. Savella walked slowly up the Boardwalk toward Isabella's house. Aside from an occasional biker and the crying gulls, he had the beach to himself.

So much had changed since the last time he was up here, with Sylvie Feidy, trying to wrest the truth out of Joseph Remsen. Not just the bomb plot, the deaths of the priest and his father, the discovery of the nightmare that was their past. Something inside *him*. Savella wasn't quite sure what, but he had a feeling there might be a place for him after all.

Doing what, exactly, he didn't know. Janice had called the day he returned to town. "So you were right. I was wrong," she said cheerfully, wiping away all the bad bits with a brusque apology. "Never should have pushed you into the pageant. I get it. Wanna come back? Swear to God, no more duck decoys." They sparred cordially for a few more minutes, and he promised to think about it. But the *Post-Herald* was out. He'd gone to ground there once. It wasn't going to happen again.

"But I think I owe you one last column," he told Janice. "About a woman named Mary Bloom."

Savella stopped for a moment and leaned against the railing. The dunes were shrinking, pounded by the relentless tide that washed away the sand and brought the world tumbling in behind it. He wondered what Mary Bloom had seen out the window of her tiny redoubt, the waves crashing closer and closer each day. Did she despair of ever being free to roam the world that Mimi had promised her that precious summer? Did she relive, over and over, the nightmare that ended with her desperate dash through the dark tunnel? Did she awaken each morning to pure terror, cold and unrelenting, knowing that the man who had brought her into this world wouldn't hesitate to kill her if he could?

No way out, not in her mind. So she started life over, in the shadows.

One night in the Rendezvous, Bobby had asked him why he had taken such an interest in a woman he had never met. Don't like mysteries, Savella had said, but the truth was deeper than that. The wraith with the cut finger in the front seat of the Honda wasn't a stranger at all.

Michael Savella had known Mary Bloom all his life.

He checked his watch, pushed off the railing, and started up the Boardwalk.

Isabella would be home soon.

---

He was sitting on the steps when the car pulled up at the entrance to the alley. Isabella, a bronzed vision in blue blazer and blinding white blouse, espadrilles with a splash of red on her feet, stepped out of the backseat, carrying a grocery bag, a head of Romaine lettuce protruding over the top. The driver retrieved her suitcase from the trunk. Isabella paid him and waved good-bye, then started down the alley, dragging the suitcase behind her in the dying afternoon light.

She was halfway home when she spotted Savella. The grocery bag slipped for a moment. Her brow furrowed, then relaxed.

"*Har*-old."

Savella smiled. "I had to beat it out of him."

"Not a chance. The man can't help it. He just likes to fix things."

She crossed quickly to Savella, placed the groceries on the ground, then embraced him. "I couldn't reach you," she said, her words muffled in his chest. "Thought I was going to have to sail over there and break you out myself."

"How could you be sure I wasn't involved?"

She lifted her head and kissed him lightly on the mouth.

"You're not a killer," she said. "Not in a million years. You don't even like *writing* about dead people."

She took a seat on the steps and pulled him down to join her. "I'm really sorry about Bobby."

"Yeah. Hard to believe he's gone, you know? He was always just...there. With all the bullshit, the errands. But he was there. And I missed the funeral. Not that Bobby would care. But still…" Savella was quiet for a moment, then exhaled slowly. "So how was the cruise?"

"A lot of sun. Too much to eat." Isabella yawned and stretched. "But at least nobody got sick."

"You make it sound quite inviting."

"It's a living."

She stood and walked to the koi pond. With her toe she pushed a small rock into the water, watched the ripples spread across the surface. "They got the guy that killed my fish?"

Savella hesitated. So much more to the story, but there would be time for that later.

"Yeah," he said finally. "They got him."

Isabella nodded, then turned and made her way back to the stairs. "I'm thinking of getting a dog."

"A dog is good. Of course, you've got to be around to walk it."

"Or a cat."

"Same problem, though. Someone's got to feed it, change the litter box."

"That's true." She sighed deeply, then leaned down and lifted the groceries, toyed with the top of the paper bag.

"Are you hungry? I'm hungry. You want an omelet?" She glanced up the staircase, then back at Savella, a lock of hair falling in her face. "I could send an advance scout if you'd like. Make sure the coast is clear."

Frozen in amber from the very first night: head slightly tilted, a flirtatious smile that screamed I dare you not to. Savella felt his body unclench. There was work ahead; homecoming wasn't simple, not after so long at sea. But this would do for now.

He stood and took the bag of groceries from Isabella.

"An omelet," he said. "An omelet sounds good."

# 60

A boy with a kite, a barking dog prancing at his feet, the kite soaring high in the sky, straining against its tether, a red dot in the blue, threatening to disappear.

Isabella, hanging back, leaning low on the railing, chin resting on her folded hands. Isabella, who makes everything possible. Isabella, who knew you deserved better than a funeral home closet.

Are you ready, then? Is it finally time?

The lid, twisted off.

Dig down deep.

One handful, swept away.

A second, and a third, and a fourth, whipped into swirling funnels and carried up, up, up, past the kite-dot, into the wisps of white cloud so far above, and then who knows.

Does it matter? As long as you go. Nothing to fear, not anymore.

At home in the world. You've waited a lifetime for that.

One last handful. Toss it high, let it catch the wind, not a trace left here. Off to see the world, there's such a lot of world to see.

The urn, tumbling to the sand.

Isabella, applauding wildly.

Mary, in the breeze.

# *Acknowledgments*

Thanks to Philip Tama, Ellyn Toscano, Vincent Rizzo, Jamie Gangel, Daniel Silva, Linda Abrams Reimer, Norman Reimer, Robert Bruce, Virginia McDowell, Maryanne Wilkins, Joe Wilkins, Valerie Strauss, Bill Cramer, Paul Keller, Cecilia Drakopoulos, Joanne Graham, Nicki Byers DeBiaso, Tom DeBiaso, Christine DiNizo, and Tony DiNizo. Thanks to my children, Katie and Darrell Catanio.

Most of all, much love and many thanks to my wife, Jeanne-Marie, who makes everything possible.

Made in the USA
Monee, IL
03 September 2020

41109476R00292